Palagummi Sainath is a freelance journalist based in Mumbai. After taking an MA in History from Jawaharlal Nehru University, he joined the United News of India in 1980. Later he became foreign editor of *The Daily* and deputy chief editor of the weekly *Blitz* in Mumbai. In early 1993, he left *Blitz* to work full-time on rural poverty, after winning a *Times of India* Fellowship to pursue this subject. His work in that area won him a further thirteen awards and fellowships over the next two years including the prestigious European Commission's Journalism Award, the Lorenzo Natali Prize, and the PUCL Human Rights Journalism Award. In 1998 he was awarded the Nehru Fellowship for the research upon which this book is based.

Everybody Loves A Good Drought

Stories from India's Poorest Districts

P. Sainath

review

First published in 1996
by Penguin Books India (P) Ltd.

First published in Great Britain in 1998
by REVIEW

An imprint of Headline Book Publishing

First published in paperback in 1999

10 9 8 7 6 5 4 3 2 1

ISBN 0 7472 6032 X

Typeset by
Letterpart Limited, Reigate, Surrey

Printed and bound in Great Britain by
Clays Ltd, St Ives plc.

Headline Book Publishing
A division of Hodder Headline PLC
338 Euston Road
London NW1 3BH

This one's for Appan

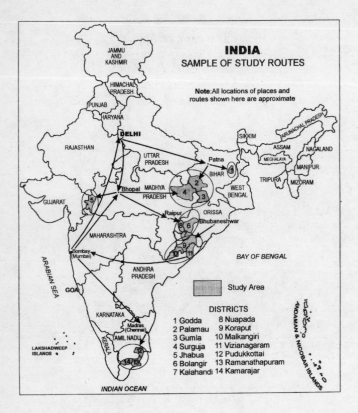

INDIA
SAMPLE OF STUDY ROUTES

Note: All locations of places and
routes shown here are approximate

JAMMU
AND
KASHMIR

HIMACHAL
PRADESH

PUNJAB

HARYANA

DELHI

RAJASTHAN

UTTAR
PRADESH

SIKKIM

ARUNACHAL PRADESH

Patna

ASSAM

NAGALAND

BIHAR

MEGHALAYA

MANIPUR

Bhopal

MADHYA
PRADESH

WEST
BENGAL

TRIPURA

MIZORAM

GUJARAT

Raipur

ORISSA

Bhubaneshwar

MAHARASHTRA

Bombay
(Mumbai)

BAY OF BENGAL

ARABIAN SEA

ANDHRA
PRADESH

GOA

KARNATAKA

Madras
(Chennai)

TAMIL NADU

LAKSHADWEEP
ISLANDS

KERALA

Study Area

ANDAMAN & NICOBAR ISLANDS

DISTRICTS

1 Godda	8 Nuapada
2 Palamau	9 Koraput
3 Gumla	10 Malkangiri
4 Surguja	11 Vizianagaram
5 Jhabua	12 Pudukkottai
6 Bolangir	13 Ramanathapuram
7 Kalahandi	14 Kamarajar

INDIAN OCEAN

Contents

Introduction
Not What The Readers Want

'We have a great drought going here,' Ramji Lakhan told me in Palamau district of Bihar state. He was a peasant activist who organised agricultural labourers to fight for their rights. 'The big people are making much money out of it. And the Block Development Officer (BDO) has gone to harvest the Third Crop.'

I was mystified. 'I know of the autumn crop that's harvested after the rainy season. And I know of the spring crop. But what is this Third Crop?'

'Drought relief,' Ramji said, smiling. He'd been hoping I would ask. 'The money that comes in as relief makes the powerful richer than they were. It's quite a good business. We like a good drought here.'

That was in 1993.

1998: At least two television channels ran the story in their news bulletins during December 1997. Some newspapers had done it earlier. But it stayed topical. It was about the dangers of slimming pills and the 'weight-loss clinics' springing up all over India. The story run on one of the television channels was particularly effective. It showed the damage done to some people who had taken these 'lose-weight-without-exercise' pills.

Thousands of well-off urban Indians fighting excess weight and obesity were going to such clinics. Countless outfits of this sort, some of them quite shady, had sprung up in India's cities during 1991-96.

There was another story unfolding, at least equally important, that was missed. During the same period, hundreds of millions were eating even less than they did in 1991. These were mainly rural people but included some of the urban poor. An official count places the number of Indians going hungry each night at well over 350 million. The diet of these people considerably worsened during this period when a record number of weight-loss clinics were springing up to serve the elite. The quantity of pulses and cereals available to Indians in 1991 averaged 510 grams daily. By 1995-96, this was down to 461 grams.

So while thousands of Indians flocked to clinics to address the problems of excess weight, millions were hungrier than before. The first problem made the front pages, cover stories and even prime time. The second, that of growing hunger, remained largely invisible. This despite the alarming reappearance of hunger-related deaths in some of the richest parts of the country. The irony of these contrasting situations invited no comment at all.

Don't bother to ask an Indian media proprietor or editor why. The mantra isn't much different in most parts of the world: It's not what our readers (or viewers) want.

For six years now, there's been a deluge of cover stories on the many new brands of automobiles gracing India's roads. In the '80s, there were just about three models of car on offer. Since 1991, the number of brands has quadrupled. The largest magazines have run more than one cover story on this. Often, these read like advertorials. One television channel has a whole programme devoted to automobiles. Many international broadcasters have also faithfully covered the 'rapidly expanding Indian automobile market'.

Post-1991, the rate of growth in manufacture and sale of bicycles has slowed. The bicycle is a more reliable indicator of rural well-being than the automobile. Certainly in India. But no cover stories or television shows.

The capital city of New Delhi, since 1993, has what corresponds to 'gated communities' in the West. The opulent farmhouses around Delhi and Haryana and elsewhere; the huge villa and mansion schemes worth millions of pounds. These make their bow in a country with the worst problem of shelter and housing in the world. At a time when very large numbers of people in rural India are losing their homes and lands to projects. And many urban Indians are seeing their only shelter lost in regular slum demolitions.

Themes like 'The Ten Best Colleges' or 'The Ten Best Schools' are popular as cover story ideas with the editors of magazines. The best possible education in the world – at the price – is available right here in some Indian institutions. The gap between this and the over seventy million Indian children who do not go to school excites little attention.

Rising executive salaries has been another favourite of the media. CEOs with packages undreamed of before 1991. Youngsters in the corporate world with salaries their parents could not match in thirty years of work. Both the Indian and foreign media have revelled in such success stories of post-liberalisation India. The real wages of agricultural labourers fell during the same years. The purchasing power of the poor was badly dented. But it was the mythical 'gigantic' Indian middle class that held the world's attention.

India has close to forty million job seekers registered at the mainly urban employment exchanges. That's more than all the unemployed in all the twenty-five OECD nations put together. Pack these forty million in a single queue giving each person no more than half a metre. You get a line that's

20,000 kilometres long. More than three times India's 6,083-km coastline.

No cover stories. But it's not what the readers want.

It is, at least, not what the proprietors and editors want. So I learned when I first tried to get my project off the ground in the early '90s. The idea was to look at the survival strategies of the poor in conditions where the state was increasingly abandoning its duties towards them. Many editors – with two or three exceptions – advised me it was a dumb thing to attempt.

When it did get off the ground, readers reacted very differently. From the day the first of this series of stories ran in the *Times of India*, their support was overwhelming. I could not cope with a fraction of the mail that came in. And it often came in with cheques and drafts that readers wanted to send to the people they'd seen in the stories. So readers did want to know about these things. Their level of response meant the series ran to eighty-four reports. When other newspapers began to run similar stories, it was clear that their readers, too, wanted to know more.

This book is based on those reports I filed for the *Times of India* from some of India's poorest districts. My visits to those districts began in May 1993 on a *Times* Fellowship. My project went on till June 1995, though I returned to some of the districts again in 1996 and 1997. The reports, then and now, are on the living conditions of the rural poor.

The idea was to look at those conditions in terms of *processes*. Too often, poverty and deprivation get covered as *events*. This is when some disaster strikes, when people die. Yet poverty is about much more than starvation deaths or near-famine conditions.

Poverty is the sum total of a multiplicity of factors. The weightage of some of these varies from region to region, society to society, culture to culture. But a hard core of this represents a fairly compact number of factors. They include not just income and calorie intake. Land, health, education, literacy, infant mortality rates and life expectancy are also some of these. Debt, assets, irrigation, drinking water, sanitation and jobs count, too.

You can have the mandatory 2,400 or 2,100 calories a day and yet be very poor. India's problems differ from those of a Somalia or Ethiopia in crisis. Hunger – again just one aspect of poverty – is far more complex here. It is more low-level, less visible and does not make for the dramatic television footage that a Somalia and Ethiopia do. That makes covering the process more challenging – and perhaps more important. Many who do not starve receive very inadequate nutrition. Children getting less food than they need can look quite normal. Yet poor nutrition can impair both mental and physical growth and they can suffer its debilitating impact all their lives. A person

3

lacking minimal access to health at critical moments can face destruction almost as surely as one in hunger.

What *is* the access of the hundreds of millions of India's rural poor to health and education? Do they enjoy the same rights and entitlements as other Indians? If not, what holds them back? Poverty is also rooted in unjust social and economic structures. It has much to do with an inequitable distribution and control of resources. Yet, the forms of exploitation that breed and sustain poverty rarely get more than a cursory glance.

In 1993, an 'Expert Group' set up by the Planning Commission drew up an 'Estimation of Proportion and Number of Poor'. The group, including some of India's leading economists, called for changes in the Commission's methods of estimating poverty. Their approach found that over 39 per cent of the population lived below the poverty line. But in 1995, the government claimed that this had come down to 19 per cent of the population. To get to this result, the Planning Commission recycled old, discredited methods of calculation. And so did away with the suggestions of its own expert group.

Oddly, the same year, the same government of India under Prime Minister P.V. Narasimha Rao took a different line at the World Summit for Social Development in Copenhagen. And that was less than nine months before it found a fall in poverty at home. At that summit, it said that 39.9 per cent of Indians were below the poverty line. It was, after all, begging for money from donors. The more the poor, the more the money. At home, less than three hundred days later, it produced the 19 per cent estimate. (Those intrigued by the mysteries of the official poverty line can look at Appendix 1 at the back of the book.)

By late 1996, the new deputy chairman of the Planning Commission, Madhu Dandavate, ended that phase of the controversy by rubbishing the 19 per cent claim. By 1997 we were back to the 39.9 per cent estimate.

While conceding the importance of that debate, I have largely ducked it in this book. The idea here was to focus on people and not on numbers. Of course, both are related. The people in this book are much like millions of other Indians in many other districts. Of the poor in India, around 40 per cent are landless agricultural labourers. Another 45 per cent are small or marginal farmers. Of the remaining, 7.5 per cent are rural artisans. 'Others' make up the rest. Most of those in the districts I visited belonged to the first two groups. But I did want to escape what Swami Vivekananda once described as the propensity of the Indian elite to discuss for hours whether a glass of water ought to be taken with the left hand or the right hand. So the focus remains on people and their problems.

I mostly visited the districts in the off-agricultural seasons. My questions were: What do the poor do in some 200-240 days during which there is no agriculture in their areas? How do they survive? What are their coping mechanisms? What kind of jobs do they find?

The answers led me to far more than the ten districts I had set out to cover. In most of these areas, huge sections of the population simply upped and migrated after the harvest. Often, they took their families with them. So I ended up travelling and living with the migrants in districts other than those of the study. At the end of it, I had covered close to 80,000 km in seven states across the country. The reports in this book, though, are mostly from eight districts that I concentrated on. These were Ramnad and Pudukkottai in Tamil Nadu. Godda and Palamau in Bihar. Malkangiri and Nuapada in Orissa and Surguja and Jhabua in Madhya Pradesh. There are also a few from old Koraput and Kalahandi, both in Orissa. (I was unable to complete work on two districts I had chosen in Uttar Pradesh.) I spent around a month in the villages of each of the districts during my first year and a quarter on the project. In some cases, I returned to the same district more than once. At the back of the book is an appendix with some basic data on the places I went to and the periods during which I visited them.

I chose the districts on this basis: The state-wise break up of the percentage of people below the official poverty line in 1992 was a *starting point* – no more. The five states doing worst on that list were – from the bottom – Orissa, Bihar, Madhya Pradesh, Uttar Pradesh and Tamil Nadu. Finding two of the worst districts within each state was simple. Mostly, governments and independent experts agreed on which those were. To be sure, I checked these districts on over twenty indicators from infant mortality to irrigation.

The bulk of the reports were mainly around 800 words each when they first appeared in the *Times of India*. Here, I have added to them from my notebooks and tapes and from the second round of visits I made to the same places. In some cases, I have added a postscript on subsequent developments.

I first tried to divide the book into sections on conventional themes: land, water, forests, tribes, dalits, women, developments and the like. It didn't work. Some of these elements appeared too often. How do you have a section on land issues when they come up in forty stories? So, instead, there are separate sections on health and education, for example. On survival strategies. On usury and rural credit and crime. On drought. On displacement. On the characters I met in the countryside. And on how the poor in these places fight against poverty and oppression. Even this way, some degree of overlap was hard to avoid.

The reports are village or district specific. Yet, the issues dealt with in the stories and sections are national. So some sections begin with an essay attempting a brief national overview. For instance, the section on health has three reports from different villages. But, if you feel you need the context, you can look at the essay that precedes them. It has a few of the important numbers on public health in India.

The few footnotes in this book mostly explain commonly used Indian terms. (There is a detailed glossary at the back of the book.) The stories need no footnotes. All sources for the stories appear in the text of the reports themselves. As for the section essays, all sources for the statistics they carry appear in detail at the back of the book. Anyone wanting to follow up on them can do so without difficulty.

The people who figure in this book represent a huge section of Indian society. One that is much larger than the 10 per cent of the population who run their lives. But a section that is beyond the margin of elite vision. And beyond the margins of a press and media that fail to connect with them.

1

Still Crazy
After
All These
Years

A brief introduction to the Indian absurd

Very few specimens – but a lot of bull

Nuapada, (Orissa): Mangal Sunani was thrilled. The government was giving him a miracle cow which would greatly reduce his poverty. The cow would be impregnated with Jersey semen – brought all the way from Pune and elsewhere. So it could, over the years, make him the proud owner of several bulls or high-yielding milch cows.

A little later, Sunani, a dalit* of Ulva village, was even more grateful. The government had given him an acre of land free. On this, he was to grow *subabul* trees (*leucaena leucocephala*) to provide fodder for the cattle he would soon possess. There were thirty-eight such beneficiaries in his village. And a thousand in other villages of Komna block†. The government had targeted them for a major dairy development scheme aimed at reducing poverty.

The beneficiaries were ecstatic when they learned they would also be paid the minimum wage to work on the free land, growing those trees. The project, called 'Samanwita' (integrated programme), evolved around 1978. By the early '80s, it was in full swing. 'Everybody pitched in enthusiastically,' says Jagdish Pradhan of the Western Orissa Farmers Association.

'Five agencies got involved,' he says. Among them the Bharatiya Agro Industries Foundation (BAIF), a body set up by the leading corporate house, Mafatlal. With it, the Satguru Seva Trust, a non-governmental organisation (NGO) linked to the same group. Also in on the show was the State Bank of India. Completing the cast were the veterinary and revenue departments of the state. The theatre of action was mainly Nuapada, now a separate district in the Kalahandi region of Orissa state in eastern India.

The authorities, like everybody else pushing the scheme, were committed to their purpose. The idea was to create a new, improved breed of cattle. Impurities, in any degree, were not welcome. How then to ensure that all the cows given to the beneficiaries received only Jersey semen and none other?

---

* The term 'dalit' simply means oppressed or ground down. Communities formerly considered 'untouchable' under the caste system increasingly describe themselves thus. Gandhi called them 'harijans' (God's people). But many have discarded this term, preferring 'dalit' which indicates their opposition to the dehumanising caste system – and the existence of an oppressor. Legally, they are termed 'scheduled castes'.

† Block – districts in India are divided into blocks. The block is the unit of development.

This dilemma weighed heavily on the minds of those involved. What if those cows mated with local studs? They decided to prevent the cows from crossing with local bulls. That would ensure the purity of the future race. So, says Bishwamber Joshi, principal of the high school at Komna, local bulls were subjected to a massive castration drive. 'The livestock inspector relentlessly castrated all bulls in Komna, Khariar and Khariar Road,' he says. 'Then, they resorted to artificial insemination of the cows with Jersey semen.'

Two years and 20 million rupees* later (£312,500), says Pradhan, 'just eight crossbred calves were born in the entire region. Not one extra litre of milk was produced. And *subabul* trees had vanished from the area, though they were planted in thousands.'

A decade later, the results are even more stark: many villages across Komna are without a single stud bull. The castration drive had rendered the local 'Khariar bull' extinct – in this region at least.

There is not a single bull in this village now, Fudku Tandi told me in Ulva. He was another 'beneficiary' of Samanwita. 'Eight calves were born,' he says, 'very small useless ones. Some died, the others were sold. Their yield of milk was nil.'

Shyamal Kuldeep, also a Samanwita beneficiary, says: 'My wife and I managed to breed six calves, four of which died in a single day. Finally, none survived.'

'When we told them of the problems,' says Chamru Niyal, 'they said they would give more injections and someday the calves would come.' The initial eagerness of the villagers arose from the wage employment the project provided. 'Whoever gives us work that feeds us is god,' says Fudku Tandi.

As Tandi recalls, 'a government officer came from Bhubaneswar [the capital city of Orissa]. He said we would get employment, wheat and rice if we planted *subabul* on the land given to us. At first the *subabul* grew splendidly. Then they told us to cut the trees down for use as fodder. We did this. But they did not grow again.' (Experts like Pradhan say this tree is most unsuited to the soil of the region.)

What upsets the villagers most is that the employment is over. 'The land is back with the government,' says Mangal Sunani. 'A revenue official came and told us to vacate it. So the thirty-eight acres now lie fallow.' This happened in the villages of other 'beneficiaries' too.

The disaster has been enormous. Throughout Kalahandi region, people traditionally keep large numbers of cattle. The cattle population here is among

---

* The Indian rupee is valued at approximately Rs.64 for one pound sterling.

the highest in Orissa and India. During lean years, peasants compensate the loss from agriculture by selling two or three head of cattle. This is about the only insurance they have. Consequently, the decline of the species has battered their fragile economy.

The mass castrations destroyed the Khariar bull. In 1980 – before the scheme had fully blossomed – the *Kalahandi District Gazetteer* had noted the calibre of this species. It recorded that: 'if properly maintained, a cow of this breed is capable of yielding four to five litres of milk per day. This breed was selected for research by the Indian Council of Agricultural Research (ICAR).'

Locals wonder why the Khariar bull has vanished. The fact that the cows and bullocks these days are very small also puzzles them. The number of cattle is not increasing the way it used to. Quality has suffered badly.

'I have five cows and I buy milk daily from the market,' laughs Bishwamber Joshi. 'And I doubt if there is a single decent ox in the whole block now. Several one-time surplus milk producers suffered enormously and are now milk buyers.' In 1977-78, pure *ghee* (clarified butter) was actually cheaper than *Dalda* (processed vegetable oil) in Komna and Khariar. *Ghee* cost just Rs.7 a kg against Rs.9 a kg for *Dalda*.

'The Khariar bull is almost extinct,' confirms Dr Maheshwar Satpathy, the veterinary surgeon at Khariar Road. Dr Satpathy says specimens of the old type may still exist outside Kalahandi. But there is 'definitely a decline in the quality of Khariar cattle as a whole'. For years prior to this, cattle-breeders from other parts of Orissa used to come here to buy Khariar bulls. They were popular as studs and helped improve breeds elsewhere. Now they do not exist.

The Western Orissa Farmers Association here has tried to assess the damage. Their estimate: in Komna block alone, the loss of cattle during the last ten to twelve years has been to the tune of Rs.3 million a year. Bishwamber Joshi believes the decline of cattle wealth has spurred further migrations from the region.

There is much irony in that. Curbing migrations is one of the ideas behind such schemes. When large sections of people move out in the non-agricultural season, development of any sort is difficult. As their children go with them, the schools are empty. There are no takers for jobs on local schemes. Hence the need to give people a buffer against drought. And an income during the non-agricultural seasons. Then they would not need to migrate. Samanwita achieved just the opposite.

Why then did so many peasants line up so quickly to take part in the project even before it began? Many were getting an acre of land for the first time. Earlier, jobs were hard to come by in Nuapada. Now, work opportunities seemed to be on offer. And for the first time ever, the minimum wage was actually being paid in the region. That, too, for working on your own land. So, in the early days, peasants queued up in haste to get into the scheme. In this, the officials running it saw clinching proof of its success. It told them they had got their concept right.

'The project is one of many that brought disaster locally,' says Jagdish Pradhan. 'The people marked out as "targets" are never consulted. There was no demand for a dairy project here. The authorities never realised that people were interested in employment and not in the *subabul* tree. Yet, such mistakes are repeated time and again.'

As he points out, no one in power ever took a critical look at the claims of the sponsoring agencies. Nobody asked: Why do we need a dairy project in a milk-surplus district? Much less did anyone in authority wonder or worry about where the Khariar bull had disappeared to.

Nor did another question come up. The state had given the peasants land to grow fodder for cattle. Why not give them land on which to grow food for themselves? In the early days, some of the 'beneficiaries' did that anyway. They grew vegetables. This annoyed the experts, who pulled them up. Such activity endangered a serious experiment aimed at reducing poverty. The authorities warned them that the minimum wage was there only if they grew fodder, not food. At the end, they had neither fodder nor food. Neither cattle not land.

Pradhan and Ghanshyam Bhitria of the NGO *Jagrut Shramik Sanghatan* (Organisation of Conscious Labourers) are planning a project to revive the Khariar bull. That is, if they can obtain Khariar studs elsewhere and locate them in strategic villages. They also aim to educate people on the subject. Educating the authorities will be no less important. Why? Because, as Fudku Tandi told me: 'The officer came from Bhubaneswar and announced the closure of Samanwita after three years. He said, "Now we have to go and do the same somewhere else".'

Postscript

Even as the Samanwita project was on, some of those involved were strenuously pursuing their vision in other parts of the country as well. On a large scale, too. Take, for instance, the Bharatiya Agro Industries Foundation (BAIF) which finds a special mention in a 1983-84 'test audit' of the Comptroller & Auditor General (CAG) of India.

The CAG 'test audit' was on the Integrated Rural Development Programme (IRDP). Its report listed cases of 'diversion of funds for other purposes' (i.e.

One of the last remaining Khariar bulls, photographed in the Sunabeda plateau, outside the zone of disaster. A species rendered virtually extinct – with the best of intentions.

schemes not connected with the IRDP) in excess of Rs.160 million. Of this, Rs.30 million had gone to BAIF. That money, the CAG noted, went in 'opening 250 artificial insemination centres that did not work for weaker sections of the community'. This was for the period between 1978-79 and 1980-81.

Quite a few projects of this sort are still on in the country today. In some cases, the same agencies involved in the Khariar tragedy are major participants.

I last went to Nuapada in December 1996. Pradhan and his friends had managed to find a couple of young Khariar studs from outside the zone of disaster. People in the villages where they are kept, feed and look after the bulls. It's a great start, but much work and many expenses lie ahead.

Ramdas Korwa's road to nowhere

Wadroffnagar, Surguja (Madhya Pradesh): Somehow, Ramdas Korwa was not overjoyed to learn that he was worth Rs.1.74 million to the government. 'I had no idea at all that they were building a road worth that much in my name,' he says to me at his house in Rachketha village.

A road built in the name of a single adivasi* and his family? This is Wadroffnagar, widely considered Surguja district's most backward block. Late in 1993, the authorities decided to construct a three-kilometre road leading to Rachketha village here.

They did this in the name of tribal development. '*Korwa Development Project – road construction: Length 3 km; approx. cost Rs.1.74 million,*' read the board proudly put up at the edge of the Rachketha woods in January 1994.

Tribals constitute a 55 per cent majority in Surguja, one of India's poorest districts located in the state of Madhya Pradesh in central India. And the Korwa tribe, particularly the Pahadi or Hill Korwas, fall in the bottom five per cent. The Korwas (also found in much smaller numbers across the border in Bihar state) have been listed as a 'primitive' tribe by the government. The special efforts underway for their development often involve large sums of money. Just one centrally funded scheme, the Pahadi Korwa project, is worth Rs.420 million over a five-year period.

There are around 15,000 Pahadi Korwas in India, the largest number of these in Surguja. However, for political reasons, the main base of the project is in neighbouring Raigarh district. It was under the Pahadi Korwa project that Ramdas's road came up.

There was just one small problem about building the Pahadi Korwa road in Rachketha. The village is almost completely devoid of Pahadi Korwas. Ramdas's family is the only real exception.

'Since substantial funding is allocated for tribal development,' says a local NGO activist, 'a lot of projects have to be justified as being beneficial to tribals. That's the way to get the funds released. It doesn't matter if these don't

---

* Adivasi – first dweller or original inhabitant. Tribal peoples. Legally referred to as 'scheduled tribes'. In some countries adivasis would be termed indigenous peoples. The words 'adivasi' and 'tribal' have been used interchangeably throughout this book.

benefit them in the least and are completely useless. Out here, even if you put up a swimming pool and a bungalow, you do it in the name of tribal development.'

Carried away by their zeal to get those funds released, nobody bothered to check whether there were really any Pahadi Korwas living in Rachketha village. Apart from Ramdas's family, only two other Korwa families live anywhere in the vicinity. But they are at least twenty kilometres away from the road.

Secondly, 'there was already a *kutcha* [crude or unmetalled] road here,' says Ramavatar Korwa, son of Ramdas. 'They just added *lal mitti* [red earth] to it.' Even today, after spending Rs.1.74 million, it is not a *pukka* [genuine or metalled] road. 'They succeeded in reducing a six-metre wide track to 4.5 metres,' says the NGO activist. 'And at what cost?'

'Nobody ever spoke to us, no officer even visited us once. They would come down from Ambikapur [the district headquarters] and go away,' says Ramdas. 'But one day I heard in the village about the board. And people jokingly told me – it's your road!'

Ramdas is illiterate and could not read the board himself. The crowning irony was that 'they built the road in our names. But it stops two kilometres short of my house,' says Ramdas. 'Everybody in the village started talking about it. So two months ago, they removed the board announcing the scheme.'

'A week later, another board which said "Pahadi Korwa Road" was also removed by them,' says Ramavatar. But not before a local photographer captured the first board for posterity. 'They were embarrassed,' says the NGO activist, 'because they hadn't checked. Had they done so, they would have found that Rachketha is a village of Gond tribals, not Korwas. These projects are just started for the money they bring, not for the Korwas or anyone else.'

He has a point: a late-1991 survey shows that barring Ramdas's family, all the 249 households in the village are those of Gond tribals. Roads and development are sensitive issues in Surguja. Even the district collector*, R.K. Goyal, lists roads and communications as 'our number one problem'. This district is bigger in physical terms than the states of Delhi, Goa and Nagaland combined. Yet it has just a fraction of those states' road networks.

'Ramdas Korwa's Road' cost over Rs.1.74 million. Official sources confirm, though, that the forest department has laid much longer stretches of roads at far lower cost. So, while there is an emphasis in theory on roads and

---

* District collector – seniormost administrator of a district. A member of the elite Indian Administrative Service (IAS).

development, the reality is different. The more immediate problems of the district's poor go unattended.

Ramdas's own demands are touchingly simple. 'All I want is a little water,' he says. 'How can we have agriculture without water?' When repeatedly pressed, he adds: 'Instead of spending Rs.1.74 million on that road, if they had spent a few thousand on improving that damaged well on my land, wouldn't that have been better? Some improvement in the land is also necessary, but let them start by giving us a little water.'

His fellow villagers would largely concur. Rachketha has 4,998.11 acres of cultivable land on revenue record. Of these just 13 acres, or a mere 0.26 per cent, come under irrigation.

Almost as an afterthought, Ramdas mentions that his neighbour, Panditji Madhav Mishra, seized the best nine acres of land his family had. 'These were the acres on which we grew rice.' With some 400 acres in his control prior to this, Mishra was already in violation of land ceiling laws.

Ramdas has almost given up hope of ever getting back the land. He does not know that Mishra's seizure of his land is in complete violation of the law. (The latter's excuse was that he had helped the family when Ramdas's father was ill and that the tribal owes him money.)

Section 170-B of the Madhya Pradesh land revenue code forbids the transfer or alienation of adivasi land. But the local officials are with Mishra. 'I gave the *patwari** Rs.500 to get back the land, but he wants Rs.5,000 more. Where can I find that money?' asks Ramdas.

Now, the nine-member family ekes out an existence on 5.8 acres. That, too, on a much lower grade of land. Ramdas's experience, says one official in Bhopal, shows the distance between planners and beneficiaries. Ramdas's problems were land-grab and his broken well. The government's problem was 'fulfilling a target'. For the officials and the contractors who come into such deals, it was a straight loot and grab sortie.

'This becomes easier because of the so-called "area development approach" which has failed miserably in relation to these tribal groups. It has largely amounted to handing over the area and its allocated funds to private contractors. They, in turn, are often front men for officials and other vested interests. The process excludes the villagers themselves from any decision-making. Serious auditing of expenditures in these way-out areas is rare.'

The official mockingly calculates the possible uses of all the funds now spent in the name of the Pahadi Korwas. 'If the money were simply put into

---

* *Patwari* – keeper of the village records.

bank fixed deposits, none of these families would ever have to work again. The interest alone would make them very well-off by Surguja's standards.'

Meanwhile, the rip-offs continue. While we are in Rachketha, a local advocate tells the NGO activist: 'In this year's drought, all I did was sub-contract one small dam. I bought a scooter. If there's a drought next year, I shall buy a new jeep.'

Nobody thought of asking Ramdas what he really needed, what his problems were, or involving him in their solution. Instead, in his name, they built a road he does not use, at a cost of Rs.1.74 million. 'Please do something about my water problem, sir,' says Ramdas Korwa as we set off across the plain, journeying two kilometres to reach his road to nowhere.

What's in a name? Ask the Dhuruas

Malkangiri (Orissa): Majhi Dhurua had just learned a strange bureaucratic truth. 'Yes,' said the petty official he was meeting. 'The record does show you are an adivasi [tribal]. But your brother is not one.'

That was a hard one to figure out for Majhi, a member of the Dhurua tribe in Malkangiri. He insisted that if he was a tribal, so was his own brother. 'How can I explain anything to you? You can barely read or write,' said the official, fed up with the argument.

The Dhurua, an adivasi community here, have lost benefits due to them as a tribal group* because of what seems a spelling mistake in the official list of scheduled tribes. Either that, or because of a dispute over how the tribe's name ought to be spelt.

When Majhi Dhurua first told me this, it seemed impossible. But it wasn't. We looked at two documents. The first was the official list of scheduled tribes published from Delhi. And the second, *Basic Data on Scheduled Castes and Scheduled Tribes of Orissa*. Both record the adivasi group as Dharua. The tribals, however, call themselves Dhurua. (The local records, too, call them Dhurua.) That single bureaucratic error at the top, the substitution of a 'u' by an 'a', robbed the tribe of its benefits.

'We cannot recognise your brother as an adivasi,' said the petty official to Majhi. 'His papers say that he is a Dhurua. We have no tribe like that on our records. We only have Dharua.' Majhi pointed out that his own certificate said Dhurua – but he was accepted as a tribal. Then why not his younger brother? 'I don't know about all that,' said the official. 'Now the rule has changed.'

There are fewer than 9,000 Dhuruas in all. Most live in Malkangiri and Koraput districts of Orissa state. The census, too, seems to have spelt the word as 'Dharua'. So there were different spellings at the top and local levels. Yet, this did not pose a problem for years and the two spellings seem to have coexisted.

At least they did until some minor officials made an issue of it over a year

---

* In India a percentage of both central and state government jobs are reserved for members of the scheduled castes and scheduled tribes as a form of affirmative action.

ago. Caste certificates are very important for members of scheduled caste (SC) and scheduled tribe (ST) groups. They need them to avail themselves of reservations in employment, or for admissions to educational institutions. Suddenly, Dhuruas seeking such documents found they were 'not listed' as a scheduled tribe.

Many older Dhuruas, such as Majhi, had already obtained caste certificates that are still valid. So this created a crazy situation. 'Officially, my father and I are tribals, but my younger brother is not. How can that be?' asks Majhi. He gave us a copy of his certificate. It checked out as genuine.

I met Majhi and his brother at the main town of Malkangiri. Some younger Dhuruas from the Mathili block were trying to convince prospective employers that they were indeed tribals. But that little difference between an 'a' and a 'u' posed major hurdles. 'I have shown my own certificate as proof,' says a distraught Majhi. 'But even that has not been accepted.'

The most authentic source we had access to confirmed the claim of the tribals. The Record of Rights for Malkangiri listed the tribe in entry after entry as Dhurua. Besides, there were no applications for caste certificates at the local revenue authority's office under the category of Dharua. That is not surprising, says an official, since there is really no such tribe here.

'The bureaucrats have created a new tribe!' says a local lodge owner, laughing. Those who can see what has happened marvel at the havoc caused by one spelling error. This season the problem became acute, with vacancies announced for some clerical posts in the district. Malkangiri suffers high levels of joblessness, even by the standards of Orissa. (Orissa has a population of only about thirty-two million, but has nearly 1.5 million registered unemployed.)

A handful of matriculates among the Dhuruas, says Majhi, were set to try their luck. Only they didn't have any. So Chanda, Mangalu, and Gopal Dhurua, among many others, returned frustrated. 'We were not even considered as candidates for the vacancies,' says Gopal. That is a pity. The literacy rate for the tribe is less than 7 per cent. So denying the few educated Dhuruas a chance of employment does not help.

However, this is a problem that can be sorted out. They are in luck on one count at least: the new *tehsildar** of Malkangiri, R.K. Patro, is a sensitive and sympathetic official. Rare traits in his line of work.

---

* *Tehsildar* – first original authority on revenue matters within a *tehsil*, which is a unit of a district for revenue administration. Also keeper of land records in his area. The first person a villager approaches on revenue matters.

Patro has only been around a few months. He took swift steps when we brought the issue to his notice. After consulting the Record of Rights and other sources, he shot off a letter to the concerned authorities. In this, he clarified that there was no Dharua tribe in Malkangiri, only Dhurua.

'What is absurd, however,' an official in Bhubaneswar told me later, 'is that it needed outside intervention. We have built a system where adivasis can't get anything set right by themselves. Not through due legal process, at least. When problems like these come up, they are helpless. They are unable to access the bureaucracy, unable to assert their rights.'

Majhi's brother and his friends could not get their job done despite being literate youngsters. This, in a district where the general literacy level is around 16 per cent and that among tribals is 4 per cent.

Malkangiri is a mini tribal India. A large number of Orissa's sixty-two tribal groups find representation here. There is also a spillover from a few tribes from neighbouring Andhra and Madhya Pradesh states. Most groups have their own dialects. And, says one official, 'the scripts of mainline languages suffer many deficiencies in recording the peculiar pronunciation of tribal speech. That leads to mix-ups like the present one'.

Curiously, some non-tribals obtain certificates declaring them as tribals. And they seem to do that without much difficulty. Such cases often involve Bengali Hindu settlers from erstwhile East Pakistan. Resettled in Malkangiri after the 1965 war with Pakistan, they got plots of land from the state. To these, they hold proper ownership deeds.

It works this way: domicile papers are one requirement for the issue of caste certificates. Anyone producing a *patta* (title deed) proving that he owns land in the area can get a domicile document quite easily. This helps a resettled Bengali Hindu or any other landowner getting his land registered. He simply tells the deed writer that he belongs to a particular scheduled caste or tribe.

The deed writer's job is to check the ownership documents. And those could be quite authentic in these cases. Checking the caste of the applicant is not part of the deed writer's job. So he issues the deed – with the false caste declaration written into it. After that, the applicant obtains domicile and caste certificates, using this as the basis.

Many tribals either hold non-*patta* land (without a title deed) or are landless. So it is much more difficult for them to obtain these papers. Meanwhile, forward caste people getting hold of such certificates gain heavily. The educational edge they already have over the real tribals ensures this.

In the present case, the problem of Majhi Dhurua and his kin could be solved. Thanks, mainly, to a decent official in Malkangiri. But as the Bhu-baneswar official says: 'It was taken up so swiftly when a newspaper inter-vened. Surely then, it could also have been taken up over a year ago, when the tribals themselves raised the issue? But our system is not responsive to the poor. Least of all to the adivasis and dalits.'

Malkangiri is a microcosm of tribal India, with many of Orissa's sixty-two adivasi groups finding representation in the district. Here a group of adivasis have come down from the hills to sell their pots at a village haat.

2

The
Trickle Up
&
Down
Theory

Or, health for the millions

The problem with the plague of 1994, really, was that unlike so many other diseases, it refused to occur and remain 'out there' in the rural areas. Nor would it confine itself to urban slums. Plague germs are notorious for their non-observance of class distinctions. Methods are yet to be devised to prevent their entry into the elite areas of South Mumbai (Bombay) or South Delhi. Worse still, they can board aircraft and fly Club Class to New York. Too many of the beautiful people felt threatened.

That, more than a concern for the many at risk, propelled the hysterical media coverage of the 'scourge'. Which, in turn, gave the world an apocalyptic vision of the Black Death mowing down millions in India. Actually, the plague, or anything else you want to call it (to each his own bacilli) took fifty-four lives. Tuberculosis claims over 450,000 Indian lives each year, nearly eight thousand times as many. It would be lucky to get a couple of columns in the newspapers yearly. If it does, it's when the country's distinguished chest physicians, some of whom treat newspaper proprietors, hold their annual Congress.

Diarrhoea claims close to 1.5 million infants each year in this country – one every three minutes. That is thirty thousand times the number of lives lost in the plague. The best *it* can get by way of space is when UNICEF's annual 'State of the World's Children Report' is released. Then it makes an occasional bow on the centre page. Or, in one of those anguished editorials (hastily written because the one on the Stock Exchange didn't turn up) asking: 'Where Have We Gone Wrong?' After which, it can be packed away to be used in identical format the following year. If no Indian has won a beauty contest that season, it could even make the front page. This establishes that the newspaper has a caring editor, who will soon address the Rotary Club on What Can Be Done For Our Children.

Every fourteen days, over 7.5 million children below the age of five in India suffer from diarrhoea. Close to nineteen million contract acute respiratory infections, including pneumonia, in the same 336 hours. Quite a lot can be done for them, but isn't. Plague makes for better copy, anyway.

In the West, the plague helped reinforce old stereotypes (What Can You Do With These People?). One London newspaper said the plague was marching ahead as it was occurring in a region where millions worship an elephant-headed God (Ganesh) who rides a rat. This rendered locals reluctant to kill rats. Besides, there was that supposed risk and courage in covering the disease. One that had swept across Europe in the thirteenth century but could now be found only in primitive places like the Third World. There are cases of plague each year in North America and Europe. Usually, where hikers and campers have come into contact with the fleas of wild rodents. This was pointed out by officials of the World Health Organisation. But it didn't sit too well with the story and so was buried on the inside pages. In any case, looking too closely at India's real health problems has this catch. It raises troubling questions about the West's own role in promoting certain models and enforcing these on developing countries via pressure from funding institutions.

In 1992, USAID gave India Rs.12.6 billion to be spent solely on population control in the northern state of Uttar Pradesh. This programme has serious implications. One is that hazardous contraceptives like Norplant will be pushed onto very poor rural women who have little or no access to proper health care. The same contraceptives are not in general use in any Western country.

Funds are much harder to come by for, say, water-borne diseases which account for nearly 80 per cent of India's public health problems and claim millions of lives each year. These include diarrhoea, dysentery, typhoid, cholera and infectious hepatitis. Water-related diseases, including malaria, take their toll in tens of thousands of human lives annually.

Yet every third human being in the world without safe and adequate water supply is an Indian. Every fourth child in the globe who dies of diarrhoea is an Indian. Every third person in the world with leprosy is an Indian. Every fourth being in the planet dying of water-borne or water-related diseases is an Indian. Of the over sixteen million tuberculosis cases that exist at any time worldwide, 12.7 million are in India. Tens of millions of Indians suffer from malnutrition. It lays their systems open to an array of fatal ailments. Yet, official expenditure on nutrition is less than one per cent of GNP.

But what are the lives of millions compared to the threat posed to 'foreign investments' by news of the plague? And besides – a constant obsession of the Indian elite – What Will *They* (white foreigners) Think of Us? Yet the only surprising thing about the plague was that it took so long to happen. Few nations have addressed the health needs of their peoples with such callousness and contempt.

Never in history have Indian governments spent more than 1.8 per cent of GDP on health. The current figure of public spending is 1.3 per cent of GDP. Nicaragua spends 6.7, Brazil 2.8 and China 2.1 per cent. Among the advanced industrial nations, Sweden spends 7.9 and the United States 5.6 per cent. When newly independent, India committed 5 per cent of the outlay of her first Five-Year Plan to health. In a nation emerging from over a century of colonial rule, exploitation, famines and mass deaths from disease, that was and is a vital step. But this has come down to 1.7 per cent by the eighth Five-Year Plan, falling with each successive plan. In terms of health infrastructures, countries like China and Sri Lanka are way ahead of India.

As much as 80 per cent of people's health costs are personally, individually borne. Only 20 per cent of hospital beds are in rural areas where 80 per cent of Indians live. Across the country are thousands of Primary Health Centres (PHCs) and dispensaries that function largely on paper. Many of these have not seen a doctor for months, even years in some cases.

Yet India produces more doctors than nurses. It also exports thousands of doctors. There were 381,978 registered (allopathic) doctors in India in 1990, but only 111,235 nurses. The then Prime Minister, Narasimha Rao, said in September 1995 that 'the country produces 14,000 doctors but only 8,000 nurses a year'. More than a few doctors, having been trained at the expense of the poorest people in the world, settle abroad to address the ailments of affluent Americans. So some of the most deprived, disease-ridden people subsidise the health of the richest.

With the coming of Manmohanomics (economic liberalisation policies associated with former finance minister Manmohan Singh) and savage cuts in health spending, even the paltry amounts tossed at health have shrunk. So the pressure on the poor has grown. Lack of resources has little to do with it. The western states of Maharashtra and Gujarat are the two states praised for having been at the front line of the economic 'reforms'. Between August 1991 and August 1994, the two attracted investments worth Rs.1,140 billion. Yet, these were the states where the plague broke out. Even before the reforms began,

27

Gujarat was spending only around Rs.49 per capita every year on health. (The reform period brought more cuts.) The figure for the southern state of Kerala, a much poorer state than Gujarat in economic terms, was Rs.71.

How the funds for health are used is also important. Again, Kerala scores high. Kerala's rural infant mortality rate (IMR) is just 17. The figure for Gujarat is 73 and for Maharashtra 69. The average Keralite can expect to live 72 years. For Gujaratis that figure is 61 years and for Maharashtrians 63. Commitment to people's health seems at least as important as availability of resources. Kerala's IMR and life expectancy rates are comparable with those of the USA. Kerala is also the only state in the country with more nurses than doctors.

But Kerala is not India. And as the government further cuts health spending, public services are collapsing even in urban areas. Meanwhile, the burgeoning private sector gets ever more expensive, ever less accountable. Growing dependence on that sector means bankruptcy for some poor families, and the severity of government cuts has hastened the process. In the 1992-93 budget, the Union government slashed the National Malaria Eradication Programme's funds by nearly 43 per cent. In the same budget, the top 10 per cent of the population got tax concessions worth Rs.48 billion. Other health programmes suffered too. This was of a piece with the 'trickle down theory'. (Take it away from the poor, give it to the rich, then watch with bated breath to see how much of it trickles down to the poor.) What trickled up was money, what trickled down was malaria. Still surprised by the plague?

Meanwhile, a big metro like Mumbai (Bombay) has seen the birth of its fifth 'Five Star' hospital. These are extremely expensive institutions which only a handful of Indians can afford. In rural India, a family of five members whose *annual household income* crosses the pathetic sum of Rs.11,000 is considered to have risen above the poverty line. But a week's occupancy of a room in one of Bombay's Five Star hospitals could cost several times as much. How do ordinary Indians then afford health care? How do they cope with their situation? The PHCs handle only nine out of every hundred patients treated in rural areas. So how does the public health system serve them? How, above all, does it serve the poorest – the scheduled tribes and scheduled castes, those with least access in every sphere?

These were some questions I tried looking at during months spent in the poorest districts. The story from Bihar and the two stories from

Orissa that follow represent a flavour of that experience. It included visiting the PHCs – some with a skeletal level of functioning, some being used as cowsheds, others as private residences. It meant talking to patients. And trying to understand what it meant to be a poor person, in one of these areas, falling sick.

Dr Biswas gets a taste of Palamau's medicine

Barhamani, Palamau (Bihar): When the residents of Pochra stripped and beat up Dr Biswas and chased him out of their village, they had reason to be angry. Biswas, a quack without any right to the label 'doctor', had given three bottles of glucose saline drip to Chottan Parhaiya's pregnant wife. The woman, close to delivery time and desperately in need of medical attention, died. So did the child. Biswas, however, runs a fairly healthy practice just a few villages away.

Meet Iqbal Qasim, 'doctor and surgeon'. He is proprietor of the 'Qasimi clinic' in Balumath. This surgeon had practised for some years on the basis of his extensive studies in Deoband. There, he acquired a degree combining 'botany, biology, zoology, gynaecology and *unani* – with a special course in modern allopathic medicine'. Just now, that degree is lying in his home town, far away. Qasim gives his patients ampicillin and tetracycline injections at seemingly the slightest provocation. He also does house calls.

Biswas's brother is also a 'doctor'. Taking a diploma in homeopathy at an institute the name of which he has regrettably forgotten, he now practises allopathy in the same village as his sibling. He says he is an 'R.M.P.' – but that doesn't mean Registered Medical Practitioner. It stands for 'Rural Medical Practitioner'. It's a line in which you can become a doctor, even in Patna, for just Rs.765. All it takes is the signature of your village *mukhiya* (headman) and that of a practising doctor. These can be had for a modest fee.

The vast majority of the countless quacks in Palamau district – and the thousands across the state of Bihar in the east of India – don't bother with such pretences. A little experience as a compounder helps. But mostly, a board saying 'doctor' will do. Conversations with nearly fifteen quacks revealed an engaging array of qualifications. Biswas gave me at least three versions of his own. The last was that he had obtained his doctor's degree by correspondence from a university in Orissa, the name of which had momentarily slipped his mind. His letterhead reads 'B.A.M.S.' (Bachelor of Ayurvedic Medical Science). But out here, he's an allopath.

He has little choice. Allopathy is all the rage in Palamau and much of rural Bihar. Urban India may have rediscovered yoga and indigenous medical

systems. But here, *hakims, unanis, ayurveds**, homeopaths – all ha
the allopathic school. 'Some of them,' says a police official,
compounders or doctor's assistants for two or three years. All giv
which they have no right to do.' Besides, says a senior official,   ...re
accountable to no one, can prescribe anything, and get away with it'.

Tuberculosis, malaria, diarrhoea, and dysentery affect many in Palamau.
But the cure for almost all ills here is the saline drip. In remote areas, quacks
mesmerise people with the drip. Even malaria patients are subjected to it.
Many villagers believe that *paani chadaana* (infusion of water – i.e., the drip) is a
mighty cure. So they borrow money to pay the doctor for the miracle. And
then there are the tetracycline injections.

A bottle of glucose saline costs Rs.28. That's the retail price. Wholesale, the
bottles can be had for Rs.12 a piece. The kit (tube and needle) costs another
Rs.12, retail. But quacks use the same kit for very long periods of time, inviting
more risks. The quack charges patients Rs.100 to Rs.150 per bottle. 'The literate
ones give less. The illiterate ones give more,' says Biswas with disarming candour.

A 30 ml vial of tetracycline costs Rs.8 to Rs.10 retail. From this, the quack
obtains 15 injections of 2 ml each, charging between Rs.10 and Rs.15 per shot
and netting from Rs.150 to Rs.225 on his tiny investment. The needles are
dirty, reused often, and invite disaster. Of course, there are also whole sections
of villagers who cannot afford this game. Their access to health depends on
giving the local witch-doctor a couple of eggs.

Why are the quacks such a force? Why do people go to them in large
numbers? 'Well, look at the state of the public health system,' says Dr N.C.
Aggarwal, a highly respected doctor of Daltonganj, the district headquarters
of Palamau. At least a few quacks do the minimal service of handing out
anti-malaria medicines.

The public health system is a mess. There is a major primary health centre
(PHC) at Latehar itself and eighteen sub-centres across the sub-division. Not
one of the four sub-centres I went to was functional. Three have had every
door, frame and fitting looted by villagers who have gained nothing medically
from them. One, near Ichak, was home to an alcoholic headmaster eager to
sing love songs from the '60s for visitors.

At the main PHC – which does work – a doctor took money, which he is not
supposed to, from a patient for the mandatory malaria test. This, in front of me,
after I had introduced myself as a journalist. None of the sub-centres had any
medicines worth the name left with them. All useful medicines are pilfered.

---

* *Hakims, unanis, ayurveds* – practitioners of traditional systems of medicine.

The Latehar sub-divisional hospital, the biggest in the area, has eighteen employees, five doctors, twenty-six beds – and just one patient. The vacant beds look filthy and disease-ridden. Barring the female health worker, not a single staffer was present during several visits I made to the hospital. The chief doctor was on leave. All the others were running their private practice – next door to the hospital – during office hours.

The female worker called a doctor for me to meet. The doctor came a bit reluctantly – she was losing precious time at private practice. But she did stay long enough to confirm that the hospital's stocks of antibiotics and life-saving drugs were mostly non-existent. Also, that anti-snake bite medicines and anti-rabies vaccine (in an area where they are sorely needed) were not available. The interview over, the doctor went back not to her office, but to her private practice. 'But they do come here once a day – to recruit patients for their own practice,' a local NGO activist told me.

In the nearby dalit colony, Dilbasiya Devi and her friends said they had never once got a medicine from this hospital. They had to buy everything outside, often at shops owned by or linked to the doctors. A senior district official confirmed this was the general state of affairs. 'Doctors and school teachers are two lobbies even the chief minister can do nothing about,' he said.

Successive chief ministers have failed to end private practice by doctors in the public health system. And the doctors can play rough. When senior officials raided the houses of some government doctors and found large quantities of pilfered medicines, a few struck back. They filed fake charges of rape against the officials.

'The public is trapped between these doctors and the quacks,' says a senior official. 'The only hope is for the government to be firm and ban private practice by its doctors. How can anyone call this a *public* health system? The whole thing is a private industry. So what is its relevance? Even in legitimate terms, Bihar, like most of the country, has more doctors than nurses (25,689 doctors to 8,883 nurses!). Add to this the thousands of quacks and see the results. Meanwhile, we continue to build primary health care centres (over 15,000 in Bihar, state-wide). That would be good if there was the slightest attempt to see that they functioned. But we have built a health system for doctors, not patients. For contractors and pharmacists, not for the public. So, we still have some of the lowest health standards in the country, despite innumerable complaints and campaigns.'

The quacks have little reason to complain, though. Business has seldom been better.

A dissari *comes calling*

Malkangiri (Orissa): We had waited nearly three hours for the chickens to be slaughtered. They hung upside down from the hand of the medicine man's assistant. And, in the philosophical manner of their kind, still pecked around for any available food. Meanwhile the two *dissaris* – hereditary practitioners of traditional systems of medicine in this region – went on with their ancient rituals. There was one major departure, though. At the end of their session, the main *dissari*, Gobardhan Poojari, could be giving the patient something quite modern. Like chloroquine or Flagyl, depending on his diagnosis.

Gobardhan's real name is Hanthal, but he wears the 'Poojari' (priest) label quite proudly. When he said we could join him on his rounds in the remote Bonda hills, we were happy. We knew that we were to be witness to something unusual. Just how unusual, we did not quite realise.

Gobardhan's techniques combine indigenous and allopathic medicine. His work here is part of a strategy aimed at ancient tribes in Malkangiri. The idea is to persuade them to blend life-saving modern drugs into their traditional health systems. *Dissaris* often serve as village priests, too, and enjoy high respect here, says Surendra Khemendu of the NGO, Anwesha. Thus, 'they greatly influence health beliefs and practices where modern medicine has not yet made big inroads'. *Dissaris* render health services at their own homes and at those of their patients.

Khemendu himself is studying plant-based medicines. He says: 'The traditional *dissaris* tend to combine the use of herbs and roots with medico-religious practices. They are a mine of knowledge that has real cures for some ailments.' But there are diseases against which tribes like the Bondas have no protection. So the need to reach effective cures through an acceptable medium arises. That medium is the *dissari*.

Malkangiri's energetic Collector, G.K. Dhal, is all for the experiment. His officials are training some *dissaris*. They are being taught to handle drugs for malaria and diarrhoea, both major killers here. 'The *dissaris* continue their traditional rituals,' says Dhal. 'But we encourage them to deliver life-saving drugs at the end of those.'

And so we were in the Bonda hills with Gobardhan. He is a Dom dalit, but is known here as the 'Bonda Doctor' on account of his patients. His first aid box has 'Only For Bondas' boldly inscribed on it in English. That is a language neither he nor any member of his clientele follows in the slightest degree. But he is proud of the box. At the river's edge sits the young patient, rather forlorn. A second *dissari* stands ankle deep in flowing water, chanting mantras. An assistant holds the unfortunate chickens as Gobardhan prepares for the sacrifice. The bright sun isn't doing anyone much good, especially the patient.

There can be little doubt about the value of the experiment. It does make the hours of trekking through the Bonda hills worthwhile. Yet, it can run into problems – if the trainers have not been thorough, or if some rituals backfire. Gobardhan is an intelligent man and, on the whole, a useful doctor. But his ritual involves guzzling large amounts of *mahua* wine. (The ancients wisely made this part of the ritual rather than part of the payment, tying business with pleasure at no cost to the *dissari*.) Four hours into the show, Gobardhan is consuming more evil spirits than he is battling.

Meanwhile the second *dissari* reads his verses and mantras from a palmyra leaf. '*Aam rishi, jaam rishi, naam rishi, kaam rishi . . .*' he intones, breaking off only to inform Gobardhan that he, too, is entitled to the *mahua* wine. Gobardhan mixes in a few secular oaths along with his religious ones to tell the second *dissari* what he thinks of him. But he grudgingly parts with some. The latter then resumes: '*Yam dhoot, brahm dhoot, karm dhoot . . .*' We are later to learn that the palmyra leaves are a formality – he isn't literate. He just knows every word by heart. The patient shifts uneasily as Gobardhan blunders about with a knife, preparing for the sacrifice. Rather him than us, think Khemendu and I.

Gobardhan then holds the menacing blade between the toes of his left foot. As *dissari* Two reads the verses, he beheads one bird by drawing its neck across the blade and throws it into the river. Moments later, the second follows. The third has its wings sliced off and is then allowed to peck at seed – whereupon it stops screaming and proceeds to eat as if nothing has happened. But soon, Gobardhan, having had yet another swig, finds he has left the job unfinished. The bird joins its companions in the river. The second *dissari* thoughtfully picks up all three birds from the water a little further downstream. Plans are made for dinner, Gobardhan gives no medicine to the patient and the session ends. As we move off, we learn that the patient is Gobardhan's own son.

Next comes a house call. A tough, if aging, Bonda warrior says his son is down with dysentery. As Gobardhan staggers around waving a strip of tablets, the old man lets flow rich oaths: 'You drunken pig. Stick to your pooja and I'll

'Bonda Doctor' Gobardhan's first aid box with 'Only For Bondas' boldy inscribed on it in English. Neither he nor any member of his clientele follows that language in the slightest degree. But he is proud of the box. Here, Gobardhan is attending to the young son of a Bonda warrior.

trust you. Don't mess with things you can't handle.' He seems to sense that Khemendu and I are from another world. The one where people are presumed to be able to 'handle' such things. He gives us the tablets to check if Gobardhan is treating his son properly.

Gobardhan has got it right this time. But the old warrior has a point. Words like 'chloroquine' and 'paracetamol' are not easy to handle even for English speakers. For a tipsy *dissari*, mixing mantras with *mahua*, they can be tricky and harmful if interchanged. Clearly, the trainers in this project have to be very careful. Between what they think they are imparting, and what Gobardhan absorbs, is a complex chemistry.

In the interior, we find the traditional *dissaris* to be an intelligent lot. Hadi Mandra of Dantipada village has never seen the world outside of the Bonda hills. Yet, whether for snake bite or fractures or fever, he has an answer. Hadi shows us many local remedies. These include the root of the mango tree, *handa, tulsi, amla, chandau, neem, papaya, donger, biguna* and many other herbs and roots. He also works as a vet when needed. His fee is modest: some rice or chicken, *mahua* or *solabh* liquor.

He plans to train his grandson Mangla soon, in what to collect from the forest, what to use, how to use it and when. He has heard of *dissaris* like Gobardhan but won't accept them. Not until he has seen them prove their worth. 'Who has trained them and how well?' he wants to know. A legitimate question, decide Khemendu and I, recalling the day spent with Gobardhan. For some ailments, the services of Hadi's fraternity are invaluable in an area where doctors and hospitals are few or ill-equipped. One doctor brought here by a foreign-funded NGO ran away after seven days, terrified by the Bondas. He resurfaced months later as a 'water-management' adviser to another foreign-funded NGO.

Attitudes here are complex. On the one hand are those who over-romanticise tribal health systems. These are mostly people who do not subject their own kin to it. On the other hand are those who dismiss indigenous medicine as absurd. Their mantra is the unthinking peddling of some forms of allopathic treatment. Both stands lack balance.

The romanticists can't say why adivasi children should not get the same medical facilities that children elsewhere do. Nor why, if tribal medical systems are so complete, must adivasis suffer such high rates of death from disease and the worst infant mortality levels. The pushy allopathic camp cares little about preserving traditional knowledge of real value.

Perhaps commerce intrudes. 'Traditional medicine' – as redefined by urban elites – is now a huge industry. The global herbal remedy market alone was worth close to Rs.200 *billion* in 1993. Oddly, the reverse is unfolding in much of rural India. There, no villager seems to feel cured unless put on drip, or given an injection. This craze for allopathy has given rise to massive quackery. In the context of these extremes, the 'Bonda doctor' idea has great potential. But, working under grave limitations, the risks it runs are many.

Malaria for all by 2000?

Nuapada & Malkangiri (Orissa): When people began dying of malaria in Birighat village of Nuapada district in 1992-93, Ghanshyam Bithria knew it was time for him and his friends to start recording the deaths. If they did not, no one would. They logged at least seventeen malaria deaths in this Khariar block village. Five others joined the lethal list in January 1994. None of this finds any reflection in the register of deaths at the local primary health centre (PHC).

In nearby Kusmal village, six persons died of malaria in December 1993 and January 1994. The previous year's list was as long as that of Birighat. In Khalna, Bihari Lal Sunani, who had done a survey, told me: 'More than 40 per cent of this village had malaria in January–February. It was worse after the monsoon last year.' In the desolate Bhoden block, Ghasiram Majhi, *sarpanch** of Bhaisadani, echoed this. 'At one point, just after the monsoon,' he said, 'there were four to five people with malaria in each household.'

Malkangiri plays host to *all* the four known malaria parasites in the world. That includes *Plasmodium Falciparum* which causes cerebral malaria. Earlier, it had been assumed that India was home to only three of the parasites. Both Malkangiri and Nuapada are in western Orissa, where malaria has staged a major comeback. They are the worst off districts of that state and are home to some of the poorest people in this country. Those people, though, have some ideas about why it's happening.

'Our villages have not been sprayed for three to four years in some cases,' says Ghanshyam Bithria, who heads the Western Orissa Farmers Association here. 'Medicines, when they are there at all, are not fully effective. The doctors are only active when it comes to family planning programmes. Right now, there are more than thirty malaria patients in Birighat. But no money is being spent on fighting it.' In some places, village health guides (VHGs) had not been paid the Rs.50 due to them each month – for many months.

'The malaria worker for our panchayat was transferred twenty months ago,' said the *sarpanch* of Bhaisadani. 'No one has replaced him. Generally, there seems to be no money.' Some PHC officials in both districts felt there

---

* *Sarpanch* – head of the 'panchayat' or village council.

had been major spending cuts in the battle against malaria the previous year. 'There have been awful shortages of chloroquine at crucial moments,' said one doctor.

They were not too far off the mark. The 'austerity' imposed by the new economic policies saw a crushing 43 per cent cut in the National Malaria Eradication Programme (NMEP) in the 1992-93 budget. The results were dramatic.

Dr Sujatha Rao summed it up in a paper for the Foundation for Research in Community Health, Mumbai (Bombay). As she puts it: 'Several states have reported a setback in the programme for lack of central funds. In fact, the malaria eradication programme is the source of funding for the multi-purpose worker who is responsible for many vertical disease-control programmes at the village level. Thus, a cut in the NMEP funds is bound to have repercussions on other programmes as well.' It has. At least eight persons died of dysentery in 1993 in Sialoti village. There were no multi-purpose workers around to help. Both in Orissa and nationally, the incidence of malaria, particularly of cerebral malaria, is highest in the tribal areas.

Few expect any help from the public health system. Ghanshyam Bithria had his own son admitted to the government hospital at Khariar in October 1993 with high fever. 'For four days, his temperature would not come down,' says Ghanshyam. 'When I asked the doctor why he was not giving him any treatment, he shouted at me, "You are a father and you know nothing. What can I do?" Then other patients explained to me that I had to pay something. So I gave the doctor twenty rupees and he gave my son an injection. The temperature came down and he was discharged a day later.'

In different villages, people said that those visiting the PHCs would be told to go to the doctor's house (also in the PHC compound). 'There,' said one *sarpanch*, 'the doctor runs a private practice and extracts money. This happens in the working hours of the PHC.' Orissa state has not banned private practice by government doctors. The government, instead, gives them an incentive to be honest – a 'non-practising allowance' for sticking strictly to their assigned PHC cover. 'But they have it both ways,' says Jagdish Pradhan of the Western Orissa Farmers Association. 'They take this allowance and practise privately as well, using the PHC premises itself.'

Even in the mid-'80s, 13.6 per cent of Orissa's population was affected by malaria – double that of the state of Maharashtra's. Yet, Orissa's per capita expenditure on disease programmes was Rs.3.41 – less than half that of Maharashtra's. In other words, Orissa's problem was twice that of the other state. But its spending on the problem was less than half that of

Maharashtra's. In 1991-92 came the era of 'austerity'. With cutbacks and a decline in quality of services, those figures went out of hand the next year.

Besides, in Nuapada district, newly carved out from old Kalahandi and the poorest part of that infamous region, there are other troubles. Official data show that twenty-six of fifty-four posts of doctors are lying vacant. There are also ten posts of nurses and pharmacists yet to be filled.

In 1993-94, some spending levels were restored, but the damage was done. Meanwhile, the World Bank, having first pushed for austerity, now took credit for restoring spending levels. In real terms, though, the stagnation continues. But the extent of damage may never be fully gauged.

Why? Because official data tell us very little. Figures at the PHCs and those of the Mission Hospital in Khariar vary sharply. At the latter, Dr Ajit Singh showed us over twenty mosquito-related deaths on his register in 1993. 'We had as many as fifty-two cases of *cerebral* malaria in 1993,' he said. 'There would be at least ten ordinary malaria cases for each cerebral malaria case. This means we treated a minimum of 570 malaria cases last year.' Yet, Nuapada's five PHCs and forty-two subsidiary health centres do not reflect these figures or anything like them.

In the register at the Khariar PHC there were just three deaths attributed to cerebral malaria in six months. However, there were 216 deaths listed as 'Cause Not Known' and eighty-seven listed as having died of 'old age'. Over 95 per cent of deaths had not been medically certified. Over 90 per cent had received no medical attention. Some who died of 'old age' appear to have been in their fifties and 'old age' deaths were concentrated in particular months. In June 1993, before the rains, there was not a single death from old age. In December, there were twenty-one. Some of the deaths were in Kusmal and Birighat villages, the very ones where locals complained of alarming levels of malaria. The very fact that the 'old age' deaths occurred mostly after the rains suggests that several of these may have been caused by malaria.

A disgusted local doctor explains why people will go on dying of 'old age' and 'causes not known' in Nuapada and Malkangiri: 'Say a person falls ill on Day One. On Day Five, the local health worker may visit his or her village. There are often huge distances involved. On Day Six, a test is taken and the slides sent to the PHC by Day Seven, if lucky. The overburdened lab technician will take a week to study the slides. On Day Fifteen, if the case tests positive, it goes back to the health worker and a further delay of two or three days occurs. Then the health worker collects the medicines and may take three days to touch that village. That means a gap of around twenty-one days before the affected person gets treatment. This not only devastates the individual, it also means a mosquito can meanwhile take the parasite from the affected person and spread it to others.'

The steep cuts in the anti-malaria budget saw many malaria workers or village health guides drop out. Even the petty sum of Rs.50 was not paid to them. Their numbers have fallen even as the disease is on the rise. So each malaria worker may now have to cover far more villages than the usual five allotted to him. This increases the duration of suffering of the patients. As the frustrated local doctor put it: 'If this sort of medicine shortage, funding cuts and logistical system keeps up, we could have not Health but Malaria For All by 2000.'

Postscript

Reactions to the story after it came out in *The Times of India* ran true to the official pattern. After questions came up in parliament, two teams visited the Khariar region, focusing on the Birighat area. One of these was a medical team from Delhi. The other was from Bhubaneswar, capital city of Orissa. And one of the first things to happen was this: the people in the PHCs here got hauled up for talking to me and 'leaking' stuff from the records.

On what grounds they could have denied me access to public data, I do not know. But the bosses ticked them off. What the teams that went to Birighat wanted to learn also remains hazy. Locals say that the only persons they spoke to were the health guides – who, for once, showed up. Maybe they thought the Rs.50 owed to them for so many months had come in. The teams ignored the villagers themselves. They, however, took some blood slides. Perhaps they felt the story would fall apart with the results. The reality, says Kapil Narain Tiwari, Kalahandi's most active political figure, was sadly different. They found things far worse than when I had first been there.

On the plus side, the outcry that had followed the story had some results. Lots of medicines landed up at the PHCs in Khariar and nearby areas, I could see this when I went back to Nuapada in May 1995. A few of the vacant posts of doctors had also been filled up.

Yet, as far as I know, neither team put out a report. No word of the original story was challenged. Other journals had picked it up, too. Worse, similar reports soon began to come out of Rajasthan and other places. In tribal areas of the rich state of Maharashtra, the problem has gained awful proportions. Malaria is back in a big way. And back due to the folly and callousness of policies breaking down even the little access that millions of Indians have to health.

3

This Is the Way We Go to School

Getting educated in rural India

'**O**nly three stories in the section on education? That's it?' asked a friend.

There could have been a little bit more on education in this section had there been a little bit more of education in the places I went to.

Actually, over thirty of the reports I filed for the *Times of India* did mention primary schools in the poorest districts. Mostly they referred to schools without teachers. Or schools without teaching. Or schools with no students. Or, simply, to there being no schools at all. Many of those references remain in the reports in this book. But it seemed wise to focus in detail on three that carry a flavour of the education India gives her people.

Of every hundred children of school-going age in India, around seventy enrol into Class I. Half of these drop out even before they complete primary school. Less than ten of the remaining thirty-five may cross Class VIII. Finally, fewer than five finish high school. As Dr Anita Rampal of the Bhopal-based NGO, Eklavaya, puts it, this seems to indicate that 'the average "efficiency" of our massive school system is less than 5 per cent'.

Much less. Drop-out rates render parts of the enrolment figures worthless. Census data tells us that less than half of India's 179 million children in the 6-14 age group attend school. Of over 130 million rural children in this age group, 57 per cent are not in school. Only about a third of girls in the 6-11 age group go to school.

Quite a few rural children have a tough time reaching their schools. Existing data do not capture that reality. Take the Fifth All-India Educational Survey (1989) of the National Council for Educational Research and Training (NCERT). It found that 94 per cent of the rural population was 'served' by a primary school within one kilometre. Better still, 85 per cent had a middle school within three kilometres.

Sounds okay. Until you see the terrain, the schools and the hardship involved in getting to them in many areas. What the experts consider a 'walking distance' ignores these factors.

More than 60 per cent of primary schools in India have only one teacher, or at best two, to take care of all five classes (I–V). Most of these are in rural areas. They lack even the minimal facilities it takes to run a school. The NCERT's Fifth Survey found that of 529,000 primary schools, well over half had no drinking water facilities. Close to 85 per cent had no toilets. As many as 71,000 had no buildings at all, genuine or makeshift. Many others had 'buildings' of abysmal quality.

In many parts of rural Godda and Palamau in Bihar schools are being used to store grain or house cattle. Also schools that have not seen teachers in years. The Fifth Survey found there were *2,628 primary schools in the country with no teachers at all*.

Article 45 of the Indian Constitution calls on the state to provide 'free and compulsory education for all children until they complete the age of fourteen'. It wanted that done within ten years of the adoption of our Constitution. In reality, the state has steadily abdicated its duty towards Indian children.

The share of education in India's Five-Year Plan outlays has been falling. Those who led the country to freedom had a different vision. They wanted that a free India spend no less than 10 per cent of plan outlay on education. Free India honoured that vision only in its breach.

The first Five-Year Plan gave education 7.86 per cent of its total outlay. The second plan lowered this to 5.83 per cent. By the fifth plan, education was making do with 3.27 per cent of the outlay. In the seventh plan, the figure was 3.5 per cent. As the problems of her children's education grew, India spent less and less on them.

Even if you take central and state government spending together, it does not get better. Current spending on education in India is not more than 3.5 per cent of GDP. The central government itself concedes that the minimum should be 6.5 per cent. Tanzania spends 4.3, Kenya 6.7, and Malaysia 7.8 per cent of GDP on education.

Cutting funds and calculated neglect hit the poorest and the weakest. Those at the bottom never get beyond the very early stages of schooling. In one estimate, over 40 per cent of children who drop out cite economic reasons for doing so. Within the less privileged are more divisions.

Far more girls drop out than boys. Boys in school outnumber girls by one and a half times. In rural areas, the disparities are much worse. As Dr Anil Sadgopal, an NGO activist, points out, there are 123 districts in India where rural female literacy is less than 10 per cent. The national female literacy rate is roughly 40 per cent.

The actual gap between literacy levels of the scheduled castes (SC) and scheduled tribes (ST) on the one hand and those of the non-SC/ST population on the other, grew worse between 1961 and 1981. The all-India figure for literacy among dalit women is 10.9 per cent. For tribal women it's 8 per cent. Teachers from SC/ST groups are few. In many districts, such groups make up large chunks of the population. But that seldom reflects in their numbers among schoolteachers.

True, many of the rural poor don't go anywhere near the schools set up for them. In some areas, that is a judgement on the worth of what's being offered to them. Contrary to what the elite would like to believe, the poor do want to send their children to school. Yet, schools aside, even the institutions of higher learning in SC/ST areas are less than a joke.

Denying the poor access to knowledge goes back a long way. The ancient *Smriti* political and legal system[*] drew up vicious punishments for *Sudras* (lowest castes) seeking leaning. (In those days, that meant learning the vedas.) If a *Sudra* listens to the vedas, said one of these laws, 'his ears are to be filled with molten tin or lac. If he dares to recite the vedic texts, his body is to be split.' That was the fate of the 'base-born'. The ancient ruling groups restricted learning on the basis of birth.

In a modern polity, where the 'base-born' have votes, the elite act differently. Say all the right things. But deny access. Sometimes, mass pressures force concessions. Bend a little. After a while, it's back to business as usual. As one writer has put it: when the poor get literate and educated, the rich lose their palanquin bearers.

So dalits and adivasis still have it worst. Fewer SC/ST students are enrolled in the first place. Next, their drop-out rates are higher. Of non-SC/ST students, nearly sixty of every hundred enrolled drop out between classes VI–VIII. For dalits, that figure is seventy and for tribals, eighty. So those most needing an education are largely filtered out by class VIII.

But we can hear all the right things being said. In the recent past, governments have spoken with passion of promoting literacy. We have a National Literacy Mission to show for it. While many of its aims and deeds deserve your support, there's a sleight of hand involved here.

---

[*] *Smritis* – Brahmanical norms of social obligation. There were many *smritis*, composed mostly between 200 BC and AD 1000.

For a government trying to dump its duties towards its children, literacy has another goal. You can, over time, peddle it as a substitute for education.

Making a virtue of literacy is one thing. Making it a tool to further reduce government involvement in education is another. In making people literate, the government is not doing them a favour. Nor is it doing them one in sending children to school. It is merely pursuing a duty – and very badly at that. Literacy is a vital social tool. It is not an education.

The literacy movement *has* scored great successes in parts of the country. Often, it has done this in the face of official barriers. Its best moments have come when people in target areas have shaped it to their own reality, their own needs. That usually frightens governments. Make women literate and they picket alcohol shops. It's nice to have the girls read and write. Having them rock the basis of, say, Tamil Nadu politics, is not the idea.

Where literacy has connected with people's lives, the attendance in schools has actually gone up. Pudukkottai in Tamil Nadu is a good example. So literacy contributes to the educational process. Yet, it cannot replace it. And, no matter how big the successes in some areas, you still have to look at the final balance sheet. It's sobering. Just 52 per cent of Indians are literate.

As Professors Amartya Sen and Jean Dreze point out: 'Literacy rates in India are much lower than in China. They are lower than literacy rates in many east and south-east Asian countries at the time of their rapid economic expansion thirty years or so ago. They are lower than the average literacy rates for low-income countries other than China and India. And also lower than estimated literacy rates in sub-Saharan Africa.'

But the Indian state has had other questions on its mind for some time. Such as how to pass the buck on education. How to jettison that duty. This has spawned one of the great rackets of our time. In polite company, we call it Non-Formal Education (NFE). Always around in some guise, it gained great strength with the 'New Education Policy' (NEP) introduced by the Rajiv Gandhi government in 1985. At that point, the government even said 25 million children would come under NFE schemes.

In this vision, trained, full-time teachers would be done away with – saving 95 per cent of the costs. Untrained 'instructors' would replace them. Schools were not essential, either. Ill-equipped 'centres' would do. In practice, working hours vary from two to zero. There are over 250,000 NFE centres in India. They exist, says Dr Rampal, as 'a distinctly second-rate option. Even more dismal than the rural primary school'.

As she points out, there are 35,000 such centres in Madhya Pradesh. Here, of the 700,000 children enrolled, only 5 per cent of boys and 3 per cent of girls passed the class V exam.

The elite are silent on why things can't be changed by asserting people's rights. If what's in the classroom is not 'relevant' to the lives of millions of Indians, why not make it relevant? Why destroy the classroom? The hidden text to NFE and its variants was and is: universal education is no longer a goal. All children do not have the same rights to a decent education. That is now, clearly, the line of the Indian elite as a whole.

It is possible there have been a couple of 'model' NFE schemes. Everybody seems to know of one. Yet, few show any verifiable results. NFE creates a clear-cut caste system in education. One type of schooling for the children of the poor, another for those of the rich. It's instructive that all those who plug, plan, and get paid to run NFE went through a formal system. Their own children mostly go to very, very formal schools.

It's been a lucrative scam. Whole lobbies have received millions of rupees over the years to take education to the poor: Results: zero. If NFE was such a wonderful, radical concept, why not scrap *all* the schools there are and subject *all* children to it? That would hurt the beautiful people.

What happens to such funds as there are for education in the *formal* school system? Dr K. Seetha Prabhu of the Bombay University's Economics department points to a curious fact: large numbers of schools in India are privately owned. Their funds, though, come from the public. As much as 60 per cent of government expenses on schools goes in grants to privately owned institutions. In fourteen major Indian states, education claims 32 per cent of all subsidies on social services. Much less than half of this is spent on primary education. Paucity of funds does not seem to cripple institutions of higher learning run by and for the elite.

Few areas have suffered so many ridiculous experiments as education. Many of these continue, though almost everyone really knows the truth. The government surely does: there are some basics without which all the tinkering in the world remains a farce. Among these, for a start, is making elementary education universal. Every child, rural or urban, has a right to it.

There's more. If education were not only free but also compulsory, right up to the end of the secondary level, that would strike very hard at child labour. And *that* is a practice that harms India as a whole in many ways. You can't even begin to solve many vital national problems without weeding out child labour. Education, unemployment and the setting up of a national minimum wage for adults are just three of them.

Our present level of funding in education is absurd. There is little chance of doing better without directing *at least* 6 per cent of GDP towards it. Talking about the south-east Asian 'Tigers' as a model has a good deal of hypocrisy built into it anyway. The more so for a nation committed to democracy. In the field of education, it's worse. India is not willing to commit anything like the funds those nations did for schooling.

Mass illiteracy and lack of education hurt in other ways, too. They mean India's most basic capabilities will remain stunted. So economic development will – has to – suffer. No major reforms will last that do not go with basic change in this area.

What is the choice before India? As John Galbraith once said: 'There is no literate population that is poor; no illiterate population that is other than poor.'

There's no place like school

Godda (Bihar): The middle school at Damruhaat here had a unique student-teacher-resources ratio till recently. It had eight classes, seven teachers, four students, two classrooms and one broken chair.

The chair, reserved for the headmaster, is vacant, its occupant having been suspended on charges of embezzlement. Middle school headmasters look after the disbursal of teachers' salaries in a given area. An outraged deputy commissioner, finding this one disbursing them to non-existent teachers, tossed him out.

Two other teachers were transferred. The school now has four teachers and a maximum attendance of about ten to twelve students (of around seventy-five registered). At one point, just two students were attending. 'Even in private tuition,' says Prof. Suman Daradhiyar of Godda College, 'this doesn't happen – two teachers to one student!'

Things are worse in the tribal villages. In Adro, deep in the hilly areas of Boarijor block, the schoolmaster, Shyam Sunder Malto, has not shown up for two years. It took us a fourteen-kilometre walk across awkward terrain to reach the school, now being used to stock *tendu** leaves and corn.

Malto left two years ago, taking the attendance registers with him. 'These he keeps marking at his house in Ratanpur and goes on collecting his salary,' says Madhusingh, a Paharia tribal of Tethrigodda. When angry villagers, led by Madhusingh, went to scold him, Malto had cases of attempted murder, assault and battery filed against them. The cases are still pending.

In Nunmatti village, near Godda town, which has a large colony of Kahars – poorest of the poor – a black goat proves to be the solitary scholar in the primary school building. Two others sit patiently on the windowsills. Not a single Kahar child here goes to school though two of them are 'registered'.

In Seedapada, the foundation of a school laid in 1989 is covered over by dense foliage. In the government's book, says Motilal, a local political activist, this is a working school. Godda, one of India's poorest districts located in the eastern state of Bihar, has 1,063 primary schools with 2,887 teachers. Of course, some of these do function. But the basic reality of the education

---

* *Tendu* – Leaf from which *beedis* (rough native, or country-style, cigarettes) are made.

A black goat proved to be the solitary scholar at the primary school building in Nunmatti village, Godda. Two others were sitting patiently on the windowsills. The basic reality of the education system in the district is that there isn't one.

system in the district is that there isn't one. Certainly not a system that works.

In many Paharia villages, not a single child goes to school. Some, though, are 'registered'. In remote Dorio in the Sunderpahari block, we survey the seventy-nine households of the village – considered relatively advanced. We find that of 303 individuals, eleven can just about sign their names. The village boasts one matriculate, Chandu Paharia – jobless since achieving that status several years ago.

Dorio had just one child enrolled at school and he isn't attending it. The boy's headmaster rushes to the village soon after we showed up. He is anxious, having heard that 'someone looking like a government official' (an unflattering description of me) is camping there.

'I love this boy and want him at school. But these people don't encourage him,' says headmaster Parshuram Singh, passing the buck. Having satisfied himself that I am neither deputy commissioner* nor his agent, he soon leaves. The villagers say this is the first time they have seen their headmaster in many months. It seems the younger generation in this village could end up being less educated than the older one.

'Many teachers here,' says a top district official, 'always keep a casual leave slip ready. And keep it undated. If an inspection takes place, they fill in that date to explain their absence!'

With an estimated female literacy rate of less than five per cent among tribals, the situation here is getting desperate. In many Paharia villages, the few children going to school are all male. And while teachers here deserve much of the criticism levelled at them, that simply doesn't explain the collapse of the system. What does? Acute poverty, certainly. Also, lack of governmental commitment, and the absence of a system of compulsory primary education that gives the children free meals and books. In tribal Godda, the tough terrain adds to the problem.

Further, some primary school teachers, earning over Rs.2,500 a month – a good sum in these parts – have taken to moneylending. But even the well-meaning ones can find themselves defeated. Randhir Kumar Pandey, a man of Gandhian principles, is a teacher at the Goradih primary school. He goes around pleading with parents to send their children to school. 'I tell them, if *this* generation does not get educated, you are finished.' But, he says, 'they simply can't afford it.' Pandey sometimes spends his own money on pencils, notebooks or slates to persuade students to attend.

Teachers, too, says Pandey, can sometimes be at risk in these remote areas. Three died of *kala azar*† in 1991. 'Those with good connections get the transfers they want. Others can get stuck twenty-five, thirty years in such places.' Transfers needed to discipline the teachers and clean out the system don't take place for another reason. State-wide, the teachers' unions are too powerful and have often scuttled the process of genuine transfers. Not a single government in recent years has dared take them on. 'Since teachers count the ballots in the elections, political parties fear them,' says a district official, laughing.

Besides, Pandey admits, attendance in itself doesn't mean too much:

---

* Deputy commissioner – head of the district administration. Also referred to in different parts of the country as the Collector or district magistrate.
† *Kala azar* – visceral leishmaniasis. Disease affecting mainly older children and young adults. Can be endemic, epidemic or sporadic. In India, humans are the only known reservoir. Transmission is done by sandflies. Enlargement of spleen and liver is common. Can be fatal.

'Many students clock in only after 12 noon, after tending cattle, goats or pigs or doing other household chores. Then they have to leave early so they can reach their remote villages before dark.' Is there no way out, especially for the extremely backward Paharia tribals?

Actually, there is. There are seven 'residential schools' run for tribals by the welfare department and these work. In sharp contrast to the regular schools, these give students food, clothes, board and books free of charge. Attendance is far better here and student performance, relatively outstanding.

Pramod Kumar Paharia is a bright, articulate student at the intermediate level in Godda college. As many as nineteen students from the Bhanji residential school he went to reached the same level last year. 'Six others,' he says, 'have made it to various degree courses. One is in his final year in the English (Honours) course at Patna University.'

Pramod is clear that 'the Paharias want education. They just can't afford the present system. The residential schools made a huge difference for those of us lucky to get in.' Why? 'Above all,' says Prof. Suman Daradhiyar, 'it is the economic support system of the residential school. It involves the mid-day meal plus more.' Giridhar Mathur of the NGO Santhal Paharia Seva Mandal (the Santhal Paharia Service Society), who has worked with the tribe for fourteen years, agrees. He says there is a need for 'a residential school for girls in the Sundarpahari block. Now, all three schools here are for boys.'

Randhir Pandey wants every three or four primary schools merged into one residential school where food, clothes and books are free. Even Bimal Kant Ram, the one teacher from the notorious Damruhaat school I was able to trace, holds this view. Most teachers agree that the Paharias, given a fair chance, do quite well as students. 'They show an aptitude for languages,' says Pandey.

Some teachers have heard of Tamil Nadu's mid-day meal scheme*. They believe that model, and much more, is needed. Residential schools combining these features clearly hold the key in the local context. Much still has to be understood about why residential schools, despite serious drawbacks, make a difference. But the fact is that they do.

There are other interesting signs. Laloo Prasad Yadav (chief minister of Bihar at the time this report was written) says he is fed up with an educational system on which the state spends Rs.17 billion each year to get such poor

---

* Under this scheme in Tamil Nadu, hundreds of thousands of poor and vulnerable children are given a daily lunch free of charge. For many, it is the only decent meal they get in the day.

results. So Bihar has begun competitive exams for selecting primary school-teachers. And UNICEF, convinced that Bihar needs more than most other states, has made it 'the thrust area' of its programmes. Let's hope residential schools and mid-day meals are among those programmes.

Then maybe one day there will be more students than teachers at the Damruhaat school.

The Head of Departments

Alirajpur, Jhabua (Madhya Pradesh): S.C. Jain *saab* is the principal of the Government Postgraduate College in Alirajpur. He is also in charge of all University Grants Commission (UGC) programmes in the college. Besides, he is the head of the Botany department, the Physics department and the Law department. In past years, he has headed, at least temporarily, several other departments. He rounds off this portfolio by being the college sports officer. In his spare time – if a person of such onerous responsibilities can have any spare time – he practises ayurveda* and homeopathy. Clearly a man of many parts.

Jain *saab*'s versatility is aided by several factors. There are very few lecturers and students at the postgraduate level. As he admits, it would be hard to find 'more than five students' in many departments. In the MA (Economics) course, a single lecturer teaches all the subjects.

Jhabua, in the central Indian state of Madhya Pradesh, is one of India's poorest districts, economically and educationally. Tribals account for over 85 per cent of the population and the vast majority of them are way below the poverty line. The few adivasis who make it to college struggle to stay there.

'Over here,' one senior staff member tells me, 'some teachers use their salaries to admit students, to pay their fees.' Touching, but not entirely based on altruism. The teachers, drawing UGC scales at the postgraduate (PG) level are relatively very well off in this district. If departments run with less than five students for a while, they are likely to be shut down. That means a loss of jobs or transfers for the lecturers to places they don't want to go.

More than anything, they want the postgraduate departments kept open. In promotions, eight years of teaching at the PG level count as equal to twelve years of teaching at the undergraduate (UG) level. 'So', says one head of department, 'if they were teaching in UG courses only, they would have to wait four years more for promotion.'

With ten years PG-level teaching, one can aim for a professorship. At the UG level that would call for fifteen years. Besides, at the higher level, there are more fringe benefits in terms of evaluation of papers and fees for setting question papers.

---

* Ayurveda – traditional system of medicine.

As a staffer puts it: 'Some have actually gone out and recruited students for their PG departments. They have persuaded their parents that they would pay the fees and even help the youths otherwise. From their point of view, the alternative is closure of the department and transfer.' The generosity ends with keeping the departments open. Students seeking tuition have to go to teachers from higher secondary schools. The college teachers 'find the rates [a maximum of Rs.50 per month] far too low'.

Basic facilities in the college are poor. An ill-equipped library exists. Its records show not a single postgraduate student had been issued five books in the course of an entire year.

Buying books for the library is difficult since the government provides just Rs.200 per subject. A senior lecturer here calls that sum 'ridiculous'. Counting fifty subjects, this would mean a grant of Rs.10,000 for books. The University Grants Commission provides a few thousand rupees more. In any case, says the lecturer, 75 per cent of the books are outdated. What about PG-level books on the open market? 'You have to go to Indore – 220 km away – to buy those,' says one student. 'The average book costs around Rs.100. Often, the cost of going to Indore and back is more than the cost of the book.'

Yet the manoeuvres of a few teachers or the availability of books do not explain the mess that is Jhabua's education. It's more complex than that. This is a district that has even had the odd excellent administrator. But, as an officer in the tribal welfare department points out, 'the rot begins at the primary school level. It starts with the failure to retain adivasi students there.' That problem is typical of the schooling system in many tribal districts.

The alarming drop-out rates, says a senior IAS officer in Bhopal, conceal an irony. In this district, tribals pay for the education of the non-tribals who dominate every sphere of activity. Jhabua being an adivasi majority district, schools here run on tribal welfare department funds. The benefits, however, go mainly to non-adivasis.

At the primary school stage, official data show that 81 per cent of all children enrolled are tribals. By the time they reach middle school, non-tribal children touch 41 per cent while the proportion of adivasis falls to 59 per cent. By the time they reach high school, non-tribals – who account for less than 15 per cent of the population – are now 51 per cent of all those enrolled. By the end of the higher secondary stage, tribals fall to 31 per cent.

In college, their respective proportions are almost the opposite of their share in the population. Now, non-tribals make up 80 per cent of the students or more. The situation of tribal girls – in a district where female literacy is 8.79 per cent – is tragic. Accounting for under 30 per cent of enrolment at the primary school level, they're down to 9.9 per cent by middle school. They fall further to 5.9 per cent in high school and 2.8 per cent at the end of the higher secondary phase. At the level of college education, they're all but eliminated.

A tribal activist in Petlawad put it this way: 'If both adivasi and non-adivasi children are educated on tribal funds, there can be little objection to it. But the tragedy is that adivasi children are not getting educated. Yet, tribals funds run the entire schooling system. In effect, adivasis pay for the education of some of their oppressors.'

By the time Jhabua's children move on to college, the division is stark. A typical picture of a college at the undergraduate level is: there are twenty-two adivasi students in the first year of the B.Com degree. At the beginning of the third year, there are three. In the BA degree, first year, there were fifty-eight tribals. In the third year of the same course, there were just twenty-two.

At the postgraduate level, in Jain *saab*'s college, there is just one adivasi in the PG (Hindi) department in both first and second years. In the Economics department, there is just one tribal in the first year and none in the second. In the Sociology course, there are two adivasis in the first year and none in the second. In the M.Com degree, there are no tribals at all.

'We have a system,' says the tribal welfare department officer, 'with an in-built bias against the tribal child. And that is not just the educational system. With no emphasis on tackling the poverty and backwardness of the tribals, the exercise becomes a sham. You can even blame it on the victims. The schooling system, despite many stupid experiments, is not designed to retain tribal children. And the socio-economic system drives them away totally, though they may be keen on gaining an education. It's not just the funds. It's the lack of commitment.'

Many teachers agree that if primary schooling was both universal and compulsory and more affordable for tribals, things could improve dramatically. All assert that long-term change is inseparable from the task of fighting poverty in Jhabua. They also believe that, given the right breaks, tribal students would do just as well as the rest.

Clemency Dodiyar, a Bhil tribal and trained teacher, gives you an idea of what's possible. Daughter of an illiterate Bhil farmer, Clemency finished her BA in 1979. With that, she became the first adivasi girl in the whole district to get a first class at the degree level. She believes her break came when she went to the Tandla Mission school, among the better ones in Jhabua. The five years she spent there made her look at education with respect.

'After that,' she says, 'I wanted to study. I worked very hard.' Continuing her studies with Mission-related institutions, Clemency went to Ajmer in Rajasthan, Mhow in Madhya Pradesh, Ranchi in Bihar and even Bangalore in Karnataka. She is now back in Jhabua and hopes to help in the education of other tribal children while pursuing her own career. 'Give them a chance,' she says, 'and you will see.'

Ensuring that adivasi children get their 'chance' could be the major challenge facing Jhabua for many years.

Where students want to be masters

Nandapur, Koraput (Orissa): When the fathers and mothers of students at the Nandapur High School here turn up at the campus, it may not be for a Parent-Teacher Association meeting. They could be there to borrow money from the stipend their children receive. The children, mostly from extremely poor tribal or dalit backgrounds, get Rs.150 a month as a stipend from the welfare department.

There are often prolonged delays in the arrival of stipends. So students may sometimes receive payment for six months together at one time. This means they might have Rs.900 in hand on that day. But during the period of waiting, they have been living off their pathetically poor parents. Which means some fathers and mothers might arrive the same day as the stipends to borrow from their children.

This is no ordinary school. It has a fine and committed teaching staff which produces good results. Despite struggling for survival in these educational backwaters, some of its alumni have gone on to take graduate and postgraduate degrees. A few have even moved towards M.Phils and PhDs. All this institution lacks are funds and facilities. Circumstances have combined with governmental neglect to bring the school to its present pass.

The private management exists in name, but is unable to run the school. The welfare department money the school depends on are meagre and often delayed. As a result, what could be a model residential school (residential for poorer students) is facing a crisis on many fronts. There are twenty-two residential students, including Gadaba and Paroja tribals and some dalits. Subash Dantun is one of the tribals.

Subash and his friends don't really like winter. They have no reason to. Only three of the boys have blankets and just eight possess anything approaching a sweater. This is a region where night temperatures drop to six degrees Celsius in winter. All the students sleep on gunny sacks on the floor. Bedrolls and beds are unheard of. The gunny sacks are from their parents' farms.

The twenty-two inmates share two rooms. They have a single 100 watt bulb in the first and use a lower power bulb in the second – when there is electricity. As an official in Koraput tells me later: 'Not many see the link between electricity and education. And I don't mean just in schools. Urbanites take electricity for granted. We are unable to think of students who cannot come home and study because there is no light. Since our own children can, we do not worry about it. Yet, you will seldom find schoolchildren doing well in places with little or no electricity. You have only to look at rural Orissa and Bihar to see this.'

'The cold and the conditions,' says Subash, 'disturb sleep and affects our ability to focus on work the next morning.' But that isn't the only thing that interferes with their studies.

They also do their own cooking.

'Though it should have been a proper hostel for the poorer students,' says one teacher, 'there are no funds to appoint a cook.' So the children, who range in age from ten to fifteen, prepare their own food. 'We collect firewood on Sundays and other holidays,' says Bishwanath Jalla, a tribal student. 'And every day, we need about three hours to do the cooking, since we have to pool our resources and plan on buying the occasional pumpkin or *mooli* [radish] to go with the rice.'

'Besides,' chips in Gobinda Guntu, a dalit student, 'there are other chores related to cooking and these, too, take time.' They can have *dal* (porridge-like preparation using different kinds of pulses) only twice a week. The rice they consume is what they can bring from their villages, which are mostly within a twenty-five km radius. They eat twice a day, a painfully frugal meal on both occasions. Luxuries such as a cup of tea or the occasional tiffin are ruled out.

The boys manage to study between 6 a.m. and 8 a.m. They then spend the next one and a half hours cooking for themselves. Class begins at 10.30 a.m. and gets over around 4 p.m. After that, it's chore time again, until they finish cooking and eating by about 7.30 p.m. In the course of the day, they have spent up to four or five hours on cooking and related tasks.

When they do get the stipend of Rs.150, it goes on uniforms, food and books. A single exercise book costs not less than Rs.5. So the amount is, inevitably, never enough. 'Yet,' says one of their teachers, 'their determination to gain education is impressive. Also, the parents of this region want a real education for their children, even if they can't afford it.' Nandapur is part of Koraput district in the eastern state of Orissa. Koraput is a mineral-rich area that is also home to some of the poorest people in the country. (Two new districts, including Malkangiri, have emerged recently from Koraput.)

'The region is dotted with similar schools,' says Surendra Khemendu who runs an NGO in the vicinity. Khemendu himself was a product of the school before going on to an M.Phil. at the Jawaharlal Nehru University in New Delhi. 'Yet,' adds the teacher, 'there has been a general awakening amongst the poor about the need for an education. It's sad that circumstances prevent them from acting on that realisation.' Koraput's literacy rate is less than 19 per cent overall and, in the case of females, around 8 per cent.

In the face of all these circumstances, do the students wish to continue? Yes, and six of the twenty-two know exactly what they want to be: teachers. But why? 'Many of the children in my village do not go to school,' explains Subash Dantun. 'But everybody wants to go. They just can't afford it. If there were residential schools giving the necessary facilities, all the children in our villages would go. We wish they could.'

4

And the Meek Shall Inherit the Earth

Until a project comes along

Imagine the entire population of the continent of Australia turned out of their homes – eighteen million people losing their lands, evicted from their houses. Deprived of livelihood and income, they face penury. As their families split up and spread out, their community bonds crumble. Cut off from their most vital resources, those uprooted are then robbed of their history, traditions and culture. Maybe even forced to adopt an alien diet. Higher rates of disease and mortality pursue the dispossessed. So do lower rates of earnings and education. Also, growing joblessness, discrimination and inferior social status. Oddly, it all happens in the name of development. And the victims are described as beneficiaries.

Sounds too far-fetched even as fiction?

It's happened in India, where between 1951-1990, over 21.6 million people suffered precisely that fate – displaced by just dams and canals alone. Add mining that has dispossessed 2.1 million people and you have the population of Canada, Further, industries, thermal plants, sanctuaries and defence installations have thrown at least 2.4 million other human beings out of their homes. That's around twenty-six million Indians.

These are bottomline figures. The government accepts a national figure of over fifteen million (up to 1985) arising from 'development-related displacement'. That's the jargon for people losing their homes and lands to projects they may never have asked for. The projects that uprooted these twenty-six million Indians make up a list that is by no means complete. Thousands of less known schemes and the people displaced by them remain uncounted. Also, many projects – big and small – causing forced evictions, came after 1985.

Those being displaced have reason to be wary of official declarations that they will be looked after or properly compensated. The people affected by the massive displacement of villages by a chain of dams being built on the Narmada river in central India know this well. Their active and organised struggle against those projects in the last several years has at least gained international attention. Many relatively smaller but damaging projects escape similar notice. And almost all, big and small, leave in their wake betrayals and broken promises beyond count.

The draft of the government's 'National Policy for Rehabilitation (1993)' admits that almost 75 per cent of those displaced since 1951 'were still awaiting rehabilitation'. (After forty-seven years, 'awaiting' seems a cruel term to use.) It concedes that 'it is not even possible' to arrive at a rough figure of people displaced 'for the country as a whole. Displacement is only taken to indicate direct displacement in terms of land acquired.'

In other words, the estimates leave out many groups who are affected but do not own land. The rehabilitation schemes don't cover landless labourers, fisherfolk and artisans. They ignore millions outside the designated submergence zones or 'project areas' hit by this vision of development. People whose life support systems are crushed by projects. Or families in locations affected by catchment area treatment. Or those losing ground to compensatory afforestation.

So when officialdom concedes that 40,000 families – or 200,000 individuals – will be displaced by the Sardar Sarovar projects along the Narmada river, we're really talking about a much larger number of people. Many of whom remain invisible on the record. People who will never receive any compensation.

No data capture the agony of the 'resource-dispossessed'. These are people who endure displacement without being evicted. The Koya tribe in Orissa and the Bansode in Madhya Pradesh were cut off from bamboo by 'law'. That is a life-sustaining material for both. The Bansode tribe draws its very name from bamboo. Private firms are now in control of the bamboo forests the Koya grew and tended. The firms use them for paper manufacture. Having lost access to this vital resource, both tribes have suffered great misery. Yet, physically, they remain where they are.

Peasants losing their land to moneylenders are not seen as victims of displacement. Still, they face all its effects. No estimates measure displacement on the urban periphery. People tossed out of their homes to make way for new urban colonies do not figure in any calculations.

In official theology, this is 'the price of development'. You want to make progress, you have to sacrifice.

But who sacrifices? And for whom? Why do the least privileged pay such a huge share of the 'price'? What part of this 'price' have the better-off ever borne?

- Tribals make up just 8 per cent of India's population. Yet, as Walter Fernandes of the Indian Social Institute points out, they account for 'more than 40 per cent of the displaced persons of all projects'. And, as the former vice-chancellor of Utkal University, Prof. L.K. Mahapatra, says, there would be an equally big number of dalits and other landless among the displaced.
- Have the marginalised ever been 'beneficiaries' of such schemes? Even in the official sense of that term? Not at all. A large number of hydroelectric projects are located in tribal habitats. Yet, as Jaganath Pathy of the South Gujarat University tells us: 'No more than 5 per cent of tribal lands are assured of irrigation.'
- Roughly one in every ten Indian tribals is a displaced person. Dam projects alone have displaced close to a million adivasis. As Pathy points out: 'Of the 1.7 million oustees from just nineteen public sector projects, a staggering 0.8 million of them belonged to the scheduled tribes. In some projects like Koel Karo, Lalpur, etc., tribals accounted for among 80 to 100 per cent of the displaced.' The last fifteen years have seen a big entry into tribal areas of projects that cause displacement.
- The stories of displaced dalits are, in some ways, even less known. In the early decades, development schemes came up in relatively more accessible areas. Mostly, regions largely populated by dalits and other backward sections. Records in such cases either do not exist or are unreliable. Major stories of displaced dalit groups may thus never be told.
- Within tribal areas, too, dalits tend to be vulnerable. For instance, the Chottanagpur Tenancy Act does not protect dalit land in that part of the country. The barriers to throwing them out are less. There are also fewer hurdles in the way of those – such as contractors – using the period of turmoil that projects bring to grab their lands.

Dr Michael M. Cernea, Senior Adviser to the World Bank, lists some crucial processes affecting the displaced. All of these cause deep impoverishment. They include: landlessness, unemployment and homelessness. Further, apart from being marginalised, displaced groups suffer a loss of food security. Besides, they nearly always record increased levels of illness and disease. Beyond this, they are hit by a loss of access to common property such as water and grazing grounds.

Lastly, points out Dr Cernea, networks and assets that are a great strength of the affected peoples get dismantled. In many tribes, an adivasi building a house can have his whole clan turn out to help him construct it. This free community labour is a big financial saving for him. But it's lost when the clan is split up and dispersed after displacement.

The World Bank is one of the major agents of displacement. Oddly, it is also one of its keenest students. Popular resistance to Bank-funded projects resulting in forced evictions has grown over the years. This has compelled that agency to address the issue. Few studies have the power and sweep of Dr Cernea's work on displacement at a global level.

Speaking at Oxford University in 1995, Cernea made public some of the findings of a World Bank group on the subject. Among these, that '[world-wide] about ten million people annually enter the cycle of forced displacement and relocation in two "sectors" alone: dam construction, and urban/transportation. That means about 90-100 million people have been displaced during the [last] decade.'

As Cernea put it, 'development-caused displacements . . . have turned out to be a *much larger process than all the world's annual new refugee flows.*'

Besides, 'the ten million figure annually, or 100 million people for the decade are still *partial* figures. They do not include the populations displaced within . . . the "new sectors": displacements from forests and reserve parks; mining and thermal power plant displacements; and other similar situations.'

It's unfair to treat the issues of war refugees and development-displaced people as competing problems. But switching on your television set might give you a sense of chaos most major conflicts bring, whether in Afghanistan, Rwanda, Bosnia, Chechenya or Somalia. The lives destroyed, the houses razed, the families split up, people in hunger. These images of conflict touch us. At least they do, where the media telling the story have no stake in the war.

The victims of the other, unseen war, stay largely invisible and rarely touch our consciousness. Their pain unfolds in far less horrendous ways. Still, theirs, too, is a tale of lives shattered, houses in rubble and families split up through no fault of their own. A United Nations resolution of 1993 – to which India was a party – terms forced evictions a 'gross violation of human rights'. Yet, quite obviously, no UN funds are spent on the 'refugees' of development.

On the other hand, those uprooted by conflict and those evicted by development have much in common. Chief among these is the fact that women, children and the aged are more at risk. In India, for instance, displacement and relocation in new surroundings tend to increase the exertion of women on their two main chores: the fetching of water and firewood. Often, host communities in the new areas resent the arrival of the displaced. Women and children tend to be easy targets for their anger.

Compensation for displacement, when given at all, is largely in cash or land. Both these are mostly outside the control of women. They have no real access to either, especially cash. This in turn hurts the children who tend to fare better where the mother is able to make some of the spending decisions. But the existing framework does not recognise the independent rights of women to such resources.

Though governments in India are unlikely to see it this way, forced eviction violates not one but many human rights and citizens' freedoms. It violates the right to liberty and the right to choice. It hits the right to livelihood and promotes discrimination. It also mocks equality before law: the number of tribals and dalits who suffer forced eviction is hugely out of proportion to their share of the total population.

So what is India's rehabilitation policy about? Its title tells the story: *National Policy for Rehabilitation of Persons Displaced as a Consequence of Acquisition of Land.*

It's about land. Yet that does not mean those who give up land for projects get a fair deal. In Palamau and Koraput districts I came across very many people who got a pittance in 'compensation', sums far below the market value of their forcibly attached lands. Quite a few families got nothing at all.

The lands were taken without their consent. Compensation is often based on the *patta* (title deed) showing ownership of the land. In tribal communities with traditions of common ownership, people held large tracts without *pattas* for centuries. That they own those lands is not in dispute. But they get no compensation when the land is attached because validation is based on the *patta*.

Land, as we know, is not the only resource lost when people are forcibly shifted. Grazing grounds, fodder, herbs, forest produce, community labour – these go too. But there is not even the pretence of compensating people for the loss of such assets.

The first line of the draft rehabilitation policy tells its own story. It says: 'With the advent of the New Economic Policy, it is expected that there will be large investments'. These will generate an 'enhanced demand for land'. Further, the 'majority of our mineral resources, including coal, iron ore and manganese reserves are located in the remote and backward regions mostly inhabited by tribals'.

It agrees that taking over these lands for projects 'brings in its wake hardships to the persons whose lands contribute to the process of growth'. However, the document's emphasis is not so much on uprooted persons. It is on how to smooth processes that must necessarily lead to more displacement. In short, displacement is inevitable. It has been so, it will be so. Lands will be acquired as always. But this time, there will be a little first aid for the displaced. They won't be consulted, but band aids will be supplied free.

The laws that govern acquisition are arbitrary and primitive. The Land Acquisition Act of 1894 and the Coal Bearing Act of 1957 are great examples of this. Their philosophy allows no challenge.

Acquisitions of land are made in the 'national interest'. That, at once, places them beyond question. Thousands of terrified tribals are hounded out of their homes and live on the jungle's edge when the army practises firing in Palamau. That too is in the national interest. If residents of Mumbai's elite Malabar Hill were treated the same way when the navy has its exercises, that would not be in the national interest. It would probably bring the government down.

Who constitutes the nation? Only the elite? Or do the hundreds of millions of poor in India also make up the nation? Are their interests never identified with national interest?

Or is there more than one nation?

That is a question you often run up against in some of India's poorest areas. Areas where extremely poor people go into destitution making way for firing ranges, jet fighter plants, coal mines, power projects, dams, sanctuaries, prawn and shrimp farms, even poultry farms. If the costs they bear are the 'price' of development, then the rest of the 'nation' is having one endless free lunch.

In the army's line of fire

Sekuapani, Gumla (Bihar): Badhwa and Birsa Asur lie trembling on the jungle's edge as the sky belches fire and the earth beneath rumbles. The terrified Asur tribals of Sekuapani stay grouped in circles with their children, cattle, goats and pigs. They just hope their village, which they evacuated hours earlier, survives.

Sekuapani in Gumla is in the hot seat of the Indian army's test firing range. This operates from Mahuadanr block in Palamau, one of India's poorest districts located in the eastern state of Bihar. Each time the 23 Artillery Brigade, Ranchi conducts its practice at this temporary range, it affects thousands of tribals. Their families have to evacuate their homes and sleep on the jungle's periphery.

When they go back in the morning, the tribals will receive 'compensation' for the evacuation and for having risked their huts, their possessions and perhaps their lives. The army, in its munificence, will give each one of them Rs.1.50. Sometimes, the exercises can last up to four or five days. This has been going on in different degrees since 1956 at least, and has been stepped up in recent years. Yet the rest of the country knows very little about it.

The army has now decided to make the range a permanent one. Which means acquiring perhaps over 162,000 acres in Palamau and Gumla. That will displace tens of thousands of Munda, Oraon, Asur, Birjia and Kisan tribals. Maybe a few Birhor tribals as well. Their only possession, their lands, will soon be sacrificed to the Pilot Project Netarhat Field Firing Range in Palamau and Gumla.

No one disputes that the proposed firing range will cause massive deforestation. Officials say the devastation of the Betla National Park will follow. Large chunks of the Project Tiger Reserve face damage. But the worst-hit will be the adivasis, including some of the poorest and most ancient tribes.

The International Year of Indigenous Peoples (1993) has not gone well for the impoverished tribals of Palamau and Gumla.

Displacement is the key word across the Chhotanagpur region. Major projects affect millions of people here adversely. This goes with land grab, the fudging of records, dam construction, some types of mining and, of course, 'development'. Most, if not all those uprooted, are adivasis and dalits. Their capacity to resist is the least.

When the Asurs go back to Sekuapani after the fireworks, they count the costs in 'damaged crops and stolen chickens'. Army vehicles and artillery tearing across the fields don't help agriculture much. Crop loss can be as high as Rs.7,000 per acre on occasion. But no one gets any compensation for the crops destroyed. Once, a village elder tells me, 'two bombs fell close to us. Often, trees are uprooted and other trees simply dry out. Sometimes, shells fall close by but don't go off.'

I have seen the casing of one of the shells that had fallen in a village. Empty, it weighed between 12-15 kg. 'Each time they practise,' says Badhwa Asur, 'we get less than twenty-four hours' notice. In that time, we have to collect everything and go some four kilometres away to the jungle.'

Resistance is growing across the affected villages. There are at least twenty-nine in Palamau and over eighty in Gumla. And so, says Pascal Minj, a retired block welfare officer in Mahuadanr, 'they have adopted a phase by phase approach. They will touch only so many villages at one time. The idea is to sow confusion and avoid a big backlash.' An adivasi himself, Minj and his Jan Sangarsh Samiti are organising the tribal protests.

Conflicting reports and some calculated misinformation have caused much bafflement. Many in Palamau now believe the plan is off. It seems the former Gumla MP, Shiv Prasad Sahu, has told them so. Former union minister of state, Sumati Oraon, has also echoed Sahu's claim that the plan is dead. In reality, there is no evidence of this on official record.

Sahu queried the defence ministry about a proposal to build a *sena chhavni* (army cantonment or base) in two blocks of Gumla. The ministry simply replied that there was no such proposal. And indeed, 'they are right,' says an official sympathetic to the tribals. 'The proposal is for a *firing range*, not a cantonment.' The press, too, has been making enquiries on the same lines as Sahu. So the 'denial' has not really been questioned.

Pascal Minj and others believe the cantonment will follow in the next phase. They agree, though, that the term has caused confusion. A junior official here put it this way. 'Let us say you ask me if your village will be drowned by a dam. If it is actually going to be destroyed by a railway line, I will say no, it will not be submerged by a dam. But I would remain silent about the railway line.'

'The problem,' a Jan Sangarsh Samiti activist tells me, 'is that no one bothers to visit these remote villages. So how will they learn for themselves what is happening?' He proved right. More than twenty days after Sahu

A Gadaba family in Chikapar. They need to figure out where to go next as their village is being displaced for the third time. Very few among those displaced have found jobs. Almost no one has received any compensation worth the name.

received his 'denial', the army is still mapping the area. Seven of these villages – Netarhat, Naina, Husmu, Navatolly, Chormunda, Hormundatolly and Arrahans – will be acquired outright. It is from 6,300 acres here that the guns will boom. I have visited five of these villages. In all of them, the residents had plenty to say, despite being kept in the dark about details.

Getting to villages like Sekuapani is not easy. This is where the artillery shells from the army's firing practice actually fall. The affected villages are remote and spread out. Some hamlets are very hard to reach. The rich variety of dialects makes interviews more difficult. And the tribals are at first reluctant to show us the metal scrap from the shells. A few of them try to make the best of a bad job by retrieving the metal and selling it to the traditional smiths of Lohardaga next door. They are a bit shy about this activity, fearing they could be deprived of even these few crumbs if the army gets to know of it.

People here tell us that some villagers died when shells they had picked up went off in their hands. With the army moving to make the range a permanent one, many villages in both Gumla and Palamau are affected. Now, two categories have been listed, 'acquisition' and 'notification'.

The first set of villages will be acquired outright. In the second, or 'notified' villages, people will have to leave their homes each time firing takes place. That will be quite often once the range is permanent. Even the block headquarters could fall under the 'notified' area. This conjures visions of senior local officials having to evacuate their offices each time firing practice is underway. But all this, as Pascal Minj insists, and as some officials concede, is the thin end of the wedge. In the final count, the villages affected permanently could number over 120.

Already, the effects are disastrous. In Chormunda, I was told that land prices are falling. So the small strips of land that families sell off at the time of weddings are finding no takers. This has placed some marriages in jeopardy. 'Can anyone tell us where we are to go?' asks Elizabeth Ainda, a Munda tribal.

A few army *jawans* (soldiers) also live in some of these villages. They are torn by conflicting loyalties. But in every village, two things stand out. The first is a determination to resist. The second is the failure of the authorities to visit a single dwelling and take people into confidence.

'No officer has met us. We have received no notice, though they have done their mapping. Yet we know they plan to throw us out. But we will fight to the last to preserve our lands,' says Manuel Minj, headman of Pakriphat village. In Hormunda, Tethru Munda and others told me: '*Hum jaan denge, lekin zamin nahin denge.*' ('We will give our lives, but not our lands.')

Why not talk to your legislator, I ask Birjiya tribals in Arrahans. 'We don't even know where he lives,' replies Lakhan Birjiya. Neither the MLA (member of the state legislative assembly) nor the member of parliament from here – both belonging to the Bharatiya Janata Party (BJP) – has been sighted in ages. Their party supports the firing range idea.

The army says there will be no 'army cantonment in Gumla'. It is silent on the firing range. The Palamau Students Union has got a letter from the union minister of state for home, Rajesh Pilot. It simply states that he is looking into the matter. Prime Minister Narasimha Rao's note to former union minister of state, Sumati Oraon, merely says he has received her letter. There is no denial in either. And both came long after the army's 'denial'.

If the plan goes through, the army will acquire the main water source at Netarhat. The project will wind up the prospering tourism business in Betla and Netarhat hill resort. Hotel properties worth millions will go down. Forest bungalows, including fine examples of old British architecture, will be lost. It will also deprive Mahuadanr of its main access road. The distance to Ranchi will go up from 180 to 250 km and that to Banari from 60 to 280 km. Many irrigation structures would go. The army project could cover up to 60 km or more. The process would be irreversible. For this time, the firing range will be permanent and not temporary as earlier.

As many as twelve school buildings would go. So would many revenue bungalows and village council offices. But the military seems to have exempted the public school at Netarhat. 'For army children,' says one retired official. 'That's why they've spared the school. Anyway, the army excels at grabbing hill station areas.'

The affected area also has some of the finest *sal** forests anywhere. The Betla National Park, the Project Tiger Reserve and adjoining forests are also home, by one count, to 85,000 wild animals. These include 57 tigers, 60 leopards, 300 bison and 115 wild elephants. A part of the Project Tiger reserved area seems certain to be affected.

The plan, says one Jan Sangarsh Samiti activist, is for a much larger base in the long run. One that 'could be the second biggest in India'. This could not be independently confirmed. But people at the Roman Catholic Mission in Mahuadanr tell me that officers have suggested they develop a poultry farm that could supply the army up to 100,000 eggs each day.

Counter-pressures are at work on different fronts. Anything that affects Project Tiger could gain global attention. Sections of the Bihar government are also opposed to the range. Local officials, too, do not seem to favour the range. Some have filed objections to the proposed land acquisition. I was able to confirm this, though the officials themselves flatly decline to comment.

Protest marches in Daltonganj and Gumla have been impressive. The unity of the affected people has withstood much pressure. That unity has been their main strength and it has a simple basis. As Phulmani Devi Birjiya of Arrahans puts it: 'Better they kill us. Without our lands, we are dead anyway. They will give us some little money. Who will give us land?' Pascal Minj says, 'These adivasis of the hills will be helpless in the plains, dependent as they are

---

* *Sal* – tree (*shorea robusta*) yielding valuable timber.

on forests. Already, some of them are vanishing tribes.' And many more will be affected by the 'Pilot Project Netarhat Field Firing Range'. The very use of the words 'Pilot Project', points out one official, 'suggests that more is to follow'.

Ironically, if the project is scrapped it will be 'due to environmental considerations'. That and the army's financial constraints. They have Rs.800 million but need well over twice that sum to carry out their plans. The laws demand that the army undertake massive compensatory afforestation. Which could mean covering an area twice the size of that suffering deforestation. This the army cannot afford.

'Animals and trees,' says one official sarcastically. 'Their being affected will draw more global attention than displaced tribals.'

'Even if the firing range is scrapped,' Kundra Kisan, an elderly Kisan tribal, tells me, 'people should know how adivasis are treated in their own lands. Our story must be told.'

Postscript

The publication of the firing range story in different editions of the *Times of India* threw a spanner in the works. Sections of the government of Bihar were already reluctant to go ahead with the scheme. Now they tried to get out of it altogether.

Angry army brass called a press conference in Ranchi on December 9, 1993 to denounce the report. They even posted me an invitation to it – on December 18. In a press release, the army singled out this story for attack. It named the *Times of India* in a diatribe against 'absolutely baseless, motivated and false' reports. These, it said, appeared to be 'the handiwork of some parties having a vested interest in the area'. It added that 'the actual facts are entirely different'. In true bureaucratic style, the officer writing the press release got the date of the story wrong.

The army's release invited journalists to attend the press conference. There, they could learn how the project would, in fact, 'affect the locals in a very positive manner'. Nothing very much came of it. A proper press conference would have meant allowing a *Times of India* reporter to be present and ask questions. And denials would have been pointless. I still have a copy of a letter from the army to civilian authorities pushing the latter to move on the 'acquisition of the Netarhat field firing range'. The letter angrily points out that while the army is 'pressing hard for the details' to be worked out, local officials in the district of Palamau had been dragging their feet on the issue. It calls upon a senior government officer in Patna to get the district authorities to fall in line.

Later, however, the army took a press party from Patna on a guided tour of Netarhat. A couple of reporters who never met the affected people wrote a few paragraphs. These stressed the importance of the firing range and how the army was doing a great job. But it won little public credibility. The 'locals' did not for a moment believe the project would affect them, as the army promised, 'in a very positive manner'. Anti-range tribals staged huge demonstrations in Ranchi and even, later, in Delhi. The protesters, from different tribes, stayed largely united throughout, despite the odds.

With local resistance mounting, the Bihar administration found it would be a great folly to push ahead with mass evictions. The more so for a government claiming to speak for the poor and the oppressed. The project for a permanent range went into cold storage. When last heard of, it remained there. The peace is only occasionally broken by the army's tentative attempts to resume temporary firing practice as in the past.

Chikapar: Chased by development

Chikapar, Koraput (Orissa): Mukta Kadam wept as she herded her five children in front of her, luggage on their heads, guiding them through a jungle in darkness and rain. Her village, Chikapar, had been acquired for the MiG jet fighter project of the public sector Hindustan Aeronautics Ltd. (HAL) and her family was evicted on an angry monsoon night.

'We didn't know where to go. We just went because the authorities and officials ordered us to go. It was terrifying. I was so frightened for the children on that night,' she recalls. That was in 1968. Mukta, a Gadaba tribal, didn't know then that she, along with her entire village of 400-500 large joint families, would have to go through the same experience twice more.

Chikapar is almost like any other village on the Koraput map. Almost. Perhaps no other village in the world has faced displacement three times, on each occasion in the name of development. In the late '60s, it was the MiG project. Evicted to make way for the fighter planes, the villagers resettled on other lands which too they owned. And which too they nostalgically named Chikapar.

In 1987, Chikapar residents were tossed out *en masse* from their second location – or what might be called Chikapar-2. Many had not even received the compensation due from the first eviction.

This time, Mukta wended her way down the road to nowhere with a grandchild. 'Once again, it was raining. We took shelter under a bridge and stayed there for some days,' says she. Arjan Pamja, also from the same tribe – the Gadabas are one of the most ancient peoples here – recalls the reason. 'We had to make way for the Upper Kolab multipurpose (irrigation and power) project and the naval ammunition depot.' Incidentally, the lands housing the second Chikapar, too, belonged to the same villagers.

With great effort, the villagers reorganised Chikapar. It came to life again in several little pockets in yet another location after the second uprooting. They have now received eviction notices for the third time. They must leave this place as well.

Chikapar is being chased by development.

Jagannath Kadam, one of the village's few educated members, is a schoolteacher. He works in another village, as there has been no school in

Chikapar for years. Many of its children have never seen the inside of one. Kadam says, 'The reasons being given for the third eviction vary. Minister Harish Chandra Bakshi Patra said at a public meeting here that we had to make way for a poultry farm. Another version is that the present set-up of the village poses problems for the Military Engineering Service (MES) in the area. We don't know. We only know that the villagers are getting eviction notices.'

If the last reason is true, says one official, 'little Chikapar will have, in succession, taken on the air force, the navy and the army. If it were not so tragic, it would be almost comical. Mind you, the lands being confiscated on this third occasion also belong originally to the same villagers. They have simply been grabbed by the state, making these people homeless, three-time land losers. And all in the name of development.'

Kadam, a Gadaba, had stayed on in Chikapar-2. That was the village's location after it was evicted the first time to make way for the MiG project. He did not take the second eviction – for the Kolab project – seriously. The waters of the Kolab did not quite reach his house, so he defied orders and stayed put. 'Since my family has been alone here, we've had to face dacoities, but I'm not leaving again,' he says firmly.

Chikapar was not a village of very poor people. It comprised Gadaba and Paroja tribals, some *doms* (dalits) and a few OBC* families. Originally located in Sunabeda (literally, 'the golden lands'), its villagers owned big tracts of land. 'My joint family of seven owned 129 acres in 1963,' says Balram Patro. 'Of these, we were compensated for ninety-five acres only and got a total of Rs.28,000. And that, many, many, many years later. But there was no help with house sites or materials. Nor was there any kind of rehabilitation,' he says.

'My family owned 60 acres of land,' says Jyotirmoy Khora, a dalit and a HAL employee who has done much to focus attention on the plight of the dispossessed. 'We got Rs.15,000 – Rs.150 per acre of hilly land and Rs.450 per acre of Class I land. Again, the money came much later. And that was it. Not a single paisa towards rehabilitation, not even a home site.'

'They promised us one job per house and one home for each displaced family,' says Narendra Patro. He is speaking to us at what can be called Chikapar-3. 'People did not even resist on either occasion. Yet the authorities went back on every assurance.'

Less than fifteen persons found jobs, at very menial levels, in HAL, which has a total workforce of around 4,500. Another thirty also got into HAL, with some difficulty, as casual labourers. They had no security of tenure. Those

---

* Families from what, in officialese, are known as 'Other Backward Classes'.

who 'made it' as casual workers were offered an alternative home – 120 km away from the HAL township.

Despite being the village's first matriculate in 1970, and taking a diploma from a technical training school, Khora remained unemployed for eight years. Only then did he find a job with HAL. Even for casual labour, says Madan Khasla, a dalit, 'the contractors always bring people from outside. And the recruiting agents want payments from us for other jobs. But what money do we have?' Years after the displacement, a few more of the villagers got permanent jobs in HAL – on a competitive basis, and not as compensation for displacement.

As Chikapar fell apart, another problem emerged. Caste certificates are related to or based on domicile certificates. These, in turn, are linked to land holdings. Without their lands, the residents of Chikapar found domicile certificates hard to come by. That meant it was also harder to obtain caste certificates proving their adivasi or dalit identities. This, in turn, further damaged their chances of finding jobs.

'On the one hand,' said Samara Khilo in Chikapar-3, 'we could not get jobs here as the authorities had betrayed us. On the other, we can't get reserved jobs outside this area because we cannot prove our caste.'

Four years ago, the Naval Ammunition Depot promised Class IV (unskilled) employment to some of the displaced. However, the venue for all these job interviews was Vizag city, says Khora. That made it difficult for the dispossessed villagers to be present as Vizag is in the state of Andhra Pradesh and over 200 km away. 'The few interviews they had right here, those jobs too went mostly to outsiders. The posts available at all are those like sweeper, gardener, porter, peon, helper. Outsiders pay Rs.8,000 to Rs.12,000 to get even these jobs. In their present state, many of our people cannot afford this.'

The same projects displaced many other villages, too. But only Chikapar suffered the fate three times. Curiously, the mood of its inhabitants is more than reasonable. Many tell me that even now, they only want a fair deal. In employment terms, they see this as jobs for each family. In parts of Orissa and Bihar, the jobs offered in compensation have been linked to lands surrendered for the projects. But this hurts artisans and other landless people.

Mukta has had enough of being shifted around: 'As it was we had to cover such distances to get water and firewood. Now, we have to spend twice as much time doing that. My body can't take it any more.' Her neighbour Mantha said: 'At least in the old place we knew everybody. After shifting, it's different. We came to a place where we were strangers and local people

An Asur tribal with one of the army's shells. Enormous damage is caused when the army practises with its guns at the test firing range. The villagers try to make the best of a bad deal by selling some of the shells as scrap metal to the traditional smiths of Lohardaga next door.

behaved badly with us. The men got by. But when we went with our pots for water, some of the men from the area behaved very badly with us. What could we do?'

The revenue inspector of Sunabeda, Purnachandra Parida, confirmed that eviction notices had been sent out a third time. 'They are encroachers and must go,' he tells me.

Khora laughs when told of the inspector's assertion: 'Each time this village has been shifted we have moved, mostly, to our own lands. Remember, we owned a lot of acres in this region. They have made us encroachers on our own land by declaring it the property of the state. If the government declared your house as its property tomorrow, you, too, would be an encroacher in your own home.'

This twice-evicted village may get no compensation at all when uprooted for a third time. That the present site of the village has no water supply and no electricity, and no Primary Health Centre (PHC) seems to be a deliberate punishment.

'Even in our second location,' says Pakalu Kadam, a Gadaba tribal, 'we have been told we are on this land illegally. This is our land. But they want us to vacate it. Our ownership was never recognised on record. So we have no rights, no domicile certificates. Not even caste certificates.' Without these, they cannot avail of loans that are theoretically, at least, within their reach.

After getting the notice of eviction at their third location, about one hundred villagers went to the revenue department in June 1993. The department used the meeting to collect fines from all of them – for 'encroachment on government land'.

Jyotirmoy Khora thinks there are issues more vital than the fines. 'Most crucial,' he says, 'is what happened to the over 400 hectares taken from Chikapar. What did they do with the thousands of acres from seventeen other villages attached by the government in the '60s?' Then, too, Biju Patnaik was chief minister of Orissa. 'And he had this grand idea that all the units of HAL would come to Koraput.' So huge tracts of land were acquired in pursuit of that vision.

Nothing of the sort happened, though. The other units of the HAL came up in Bangalore and elsewhere. As a result, thousands of acres forcibly taken over from the eighteen villages remain unused to this day. 'They are neither returning the land, nor leasing it for cultivation. We are prepared to repay such "compensation" as they gave us if we get back our land,' says Khora, laughing. That seems unlikely to happen.

When the National Aluminium Company Ltd. (NALCO) came up in 1981 in Koraput, says Prof. L.K. Mahapatra, more than 47.7 per cent of the 2,500 displaced families were tribals. And 9.3 per cent were dalits. Dr Mahapatra, a former vice-chancellor of Utkal and Sambalpur Universities, points out that over 55 per cent of the 3,067 families displaced by the upper Kolab project were also from scheduled caste or scheduled tribe groups.

The Machkund hydroelectric project in Koraput district had displaced almost 3,000 families by 1960. Of these, 51.1 per cent were tribals and 10.2

per cent were dalits. 'It is a pity,' notes Prof. Mahapatra in a major study on the subject, that 'out of 2,938 families displaced, only 600 were rehabilitated. Of which, 450 were tribal families. Not a single scheduled caste family was rehabilitated.' The number of those affected was, in the first place, grossly underassessed.

At the national level, less than 25 per cent of those displaced by development have been rehabilitated in the past four decades. The situation in Orissa is worse. Within this dismal picture, Koraput plumbs the depths. A 1993 study funded by the union ministry of welfare is revealing. In it, Walter Fernandes and Anthony S. Raj, of the Indian Social Institute, New Delhi, have looked at 'Development, Displacement and Rehabilitation in the Tribal Areas of Orissa.'

They note that in Koraput district alone 'around 100,000 tribals have been deprived of their land, including 160,000 hectares of forests on which they had till then depended for their livelihood. More than 6 per cent of the district population, a majority of them tribals, have been displaced [by projects]. This trend seems to continue even today.'

Take just the Sunabeda region. Since the break up of Chikapar began, 'nearly 5,000 families or 40,000 people have been displaced by different projects,' says Jyotirmoy Khora. 'And all promises of rehabilitation have proved false.' His own family held land in the original Chikapar.

The process of displacement has brought other results. Many families have simply disintegrated. It has also left thousands destitute. 'After waiting a long time for the compensation many just went away elsewhere to survive,' says Kanum Gadaba.

'When the refugees from erstwhile East Pakistan came into Orissa in the '60s and again in 1971,' says Khora, 'nearly 100,000 rupees was spent on each one of them. Less than Rs.15,000 was given to whole joint families who belonged here and were losing land, not gaining it like the refugees. Better to be a refugee.'

Meanwhile, the various fragments of Chikapar await their third uprooting. Some people have already been evicted. For a poultry farm, or the depot, or yet another project? No one seems to know for sure.

'Basically,' says Khora, 'they don't want us to be around like an eyesore, sticking out here. That way, we would be telling our tales of woe to others – especially the minister, if he ever comes.

'They have got their development and the land. We have got no development, not even a proper school, and have lost our land,' he adds.

'I can't move again, let them do what they like,' says Mukta Kadam, the

81

oldest woman in the village. 'Why does this always have to happen to us?' she asks.

Possibly because they are adivasis and dalits and this is Koraput, home to some of the poorest people in India.

Postscript

The problems of the people of Chikapar and other villages here continue. Actions led by people like Khora seem to have kept up in the past year. And some non-governmental bodies, such as the Institute for Socio-Economic Development (ISED), Bhubaneswar, have stepped in. They have given time and effort to studying the problems of the displaced in the area. They hope to reconstruct facts, details and data lost or destroyed by twenty-five years of neglect and apathy.

Banning the bees from honey

Malkangiri (Orissa): The first thing that strikes you is that the houses are made almost entirely of bamboo. Only their roofs – which have bamboo joints – are of thatch. There are close to 150 dwellings in Sangel village and almost all are suffused with bamboo. The boundary walls around the houses here are also made of bamboo. So is the village Khabutar Khana.

As an irritated sow grunted a warning, we look around at her. At least two of her new litter were encased in tiny bamboo baskets, custom-made. In and around the house of Mhadi Bheema, the village *pedda* or elder in Sangel, there are at least fifty-two objects made, predictably, of bamboo.

From the fishing 'net' or trap Mhadi Bheema brings home with him, to the baby cradles, the baskets for brooding hens, and the rainproof hat an old woman wears, almost everything of significance in the village seems to be made of bamboo. People here even make fire by rubbing together two pointed bamboo sticks.

This is no isolated freak of a village. The villages of Suplur, Kambheda and Pitaghata look very much like Sangel. So do many others spread across several blocks.

Welcome to Koya world.

The brilliant use of bamboo by the Koya tribe makes even parts of Podiya block seem beautiful. (The word Podiya literally means 'barren'.) There are about 87,000 Koyas in the Malkangiri-Koraput region. Almost all their villages have this distinctive flavour. The Koya practise shifting as well as stable cultivation. Now increasingly the latter, if they have any land. But it is with bamboo that their creativity really emerges.

Few humans have interacted so imaginatively, so intensely, and yet so gently with a single creation of nature as have the Koya tribals with bamboo. The Koya in Orissa are mainly in Malkangiri – one of India's poorest districts. Some live next door in Andhra Pradesh. 'From childhood, members of this unique tribal', says Irma Kawasi, *sarpanch* of Pitaghata, 'learn the Koya ethic. We teach them to cut the bamboo in such a way that it grows again. We never destroy the forests because our lives depend on them.'

From regeneration to phased and planned felling, it is all there in the Koya

Few humans have interacted so imaginatively, so intensely, and yet, so gently with a single creation of nature as have the Koya tribals with bamboo. Almost everything of significance in a Koya village is made from it.

ethic. Their relationship with bamboo, far from being a conquest of nature, is a romance with it.

Yet bamboo is also the social and economic oxygen of the Koya. In recent years, forest laws removing their access to that material have denied them this oxygen. Big corporates, however, (via the Orissa Forest Development Corporation) have gained mostly unchecked access. They seek large quantities of bamboo for paper. Their imprint is now all over the place in huge patches of barren land where dense forests once stood. Ironically, the companies and their middlemen often hire the Koya on a casual basis – to fell their own forests.

An Indian Administrative Service (IAS) officer who has had much to do with forestry in Orissa points to the paradox. 'On the one hand, you have the Koyas cutting strictly for their personal needs with sickles. They mostly want the young bamboo. On the other, you have the companies bulldozing everything in sight, on a mass scale. Young or old bamboos, whatever the size, variety or age, it's all the same to them. If there are huge bamboo forests at all, it is in part because the Koya have nursed these with such care. Yet it is the traditional and controlled activity of the tribe that becomes illegal.'

But why cut off the Koyas from bamboo while allowing private companies to access it? Sadhashiv Hanthal, a dalit living in the mainly Koya village of Pitaghata, has an answer. 'From the companies, the government gets tax. From the Koya, what do they get?'

It isn't the first time the Koyas have lost a home. The district gazetteer says: 'The Koya tradition is that they were driven from the plateau in Bastar country [now in the state of Madhya Pradesh] by famine and disputes' about 200 years ago. Now, it's a new form of displacement. One in which, says Kawasi Bheema in Suplur village, 'we have our houses but no home. What are the Koya without bamboo?'

In Kambheda village, Era Padiyami proudly shows us many things he has made from bamboo. These were not for sale in the market, but for use by his family. They include: *eram* (umbrella), *guta* (basket for vegetables), *jaugula* (a mini-basket used as a measuring unit for rice), *osod* (flute), *tekrom* (big fish trap) and *kike kadog* (a bag to carry the fish in). There were also eighteen types and sizes of baskets. Besides, the Koyas use bamboo shoots in their food and medicinal preparations.

'We have used bamboo products in barter,' says Padiyami. 'Now we have to buy the things we could get by exchanging our bamboo items. We also have to buy things we could make for ourselves.' This has hit the living standards of the already poor Koyas. 'The laws also mean,' says Anda Madakami, 'that forest guards harass us. They do not allow us to take minimal forest produce for our personal needs – though we were told we are allowed that by law.'

In theory the Orissa Forest Development Corporation (OFDC) is in full control of bamboo areas in these forests. It sells the bamboo to the companies. In reality, says Kamraj Kawasi, an emerging Koya leader, it works differently. 'Private parties and the Forest Corporation agree on the area to be harvested. The companies employ casual workers after the government has fixed the rate.

'This is where the middleman comes in. And he often brings in labour from Andhra. Those Koyas who get taken on as casual labourers – whoever the employer may be – seldom get the government rate of Rs.25 a day. In practice, they often get as little as a rupee for several bamboos. Even that requires that they go two to four kilometres into the forest, cut and carry the heavy bamboos back to their village. Then they have to walk a further similar distance to the depot.'

Forest Corporation officials deny Kawasi's charges. But the process is so blatantly visible that the denials carry no weight. Simply put, it seems the OFDC is leasing the forests to private parties. This is unlawful since it does not have the Indian government's permission.

The Koya, says Sukdev Kawasi of Suplur, use bamboo 'in our construction materials, in the charpoy you are sitting on, in making beds'. He points to a flagon made of a dried-out vegetable gourd and encased in bamboo. 'See this cask? It keeps the water cool. The Koya can never harm the bamboos. They are so central to our lives. It is a great injustice on the government's part to curb our access. Can you ban the bees from the honey?'

Apparently, governments can. They have already done so. And the denial of access is hurting in more ways too. Indebtedness – unlike the bamboo forests – seems to be growing among the Koyas.

The consequences of being denied access to bamboo have been disastrous for the Koya. They show that physical displacement is not the only action leading to destruction of a people's livelihood and culture. Cutting them off from their most vital resources can produce those results just as well.

The government did not physically shift the Koya villages. They were displaced only in the sense of being barred from a crucial resource. Yet they have taken a beating they are unable to cope with. They are the bees banned from honey.

Only, these bees have no sting.

Postscript

Others, too, viewed OFDC's bamboo forest deals with dismay. One of the country's seniormost bureaucrats warned that officers ran a 'grave risk of prosecution' in being party to such deals. Writing in the bulletin, *Wastelands News* in late 1995, he observed that, among other things, the leasing of the bamboo forests to industry did not have the Indian government's sanction.

The 'entire arrangement is unlawful,' wrote N.C. Saksena, then director of the Lal Bahadur Shastri National Academy of Administration, Mussoorie. He, too, found that the poor were being actively discriminated against by the OFDC. The figures of one depot showed that while bamboo was being sold to local cultivators at Rs.4.30

per piece, it was being sold to industry at roughly 15 paise (roughly 64 paise = 1 p) a piece. But the number of pieces sold to cultivators was negligible, just 350. Industry, however, got over three million pieces – at 15 paise each! The same pieces were fetching Rs.10 to Rs.13 each, in open auction. But a mere 27,000 were sold that way. The depot had sold no pieces at all to local artisans.

Saksena's warning on the legal risks of such deals proved prophetic. In early 1996, the new government of Orissa filed two charge sheets against Biju Patnaik who had been chief minister when the deals went through. One of these was on the subject of special concessions on bamboo royalty to a private business house during his tenure. The state, it charged, rather obviously, had lost out as a result. Will this help alter things for the Koya in any way? I don't know. I just hope it does.

The house that Luaria built

Jalsindhi, Jhabua (Madhya Pradesh): Luaria and his fellow Bhilala tribals still live in this area, probably the lowest slope and point in Madhya Pradesh, geographically speaking. And this is the lowest structure and field on that slope. Which means that as the waters of the Narmada keep rising in this submergence area – already well past the eighty-three-metre mark – this could be the first field and house to go down.

This is the house that Luaria built.

Like many in this part of Jhabua – one of India's poorest districts – Luaria's is a spacious house, built of teak and bamboo, with three lofts. His *falia* or hamlet lies in Jalsindhi village, where the Narmada river demarcates Madhya Pradesh from Maharashtra. He and nine other families in this *falia* are refusing to leave their homes. They want no part of the 'rehabilitation' package offered them in Gujarat. They have, instead, collectively built a second structure alongside his house, as a symbol of their defiance. And to shelter those who come to join them in their risky protest. In other villages, too, some who will lose their homes this year with the continued construction of the Sardar Sarovar Project are holding out. Almost all are adivasis, very backward and mostly illiterate.

Down the slope, Luaria's wife, Boghi, prepares their fields for the rains. It's touching forty-five degrees Celsius, and she often looks up at the sky in exasperation. The first shower has made the heat worse. Preparing the stony slopes for cultivation can't be easy, but Boghi and Revaki, a relative of Luaria's, stick to it gamely. The men, led by Bhava, the seniormost member of the clan in the *falia*, are building the new structure. The determination to stay put is transparent.

The attitude of the villagers here is not entirely shaped by sentimentality. Few would fault them for that even if it were so. By one estimate, of nearly twenty-six million Indians displaced by projects since 1951, more than 40 per cent are adivasis, though tribals account for just 8 per cent of India's population. In Orissa and Madhya Pradesh, that ratio has been even higher. That and the fact of being summarily uprooted from their traditional homes is dismal enough. But there are also sound economic reasons for their not wanting to move.

Down the slope, Luaria's wife, Boghi, prepares their fields for the rains. It's touching forty-five degrees Celsius and she often looks up at the sky in exasperation.

'There are innumerable things that we get from the forests here which we would have to pay for in Gujarat,' points out Luaria. 'Who will compensate us for that?' He has a point. It is not even remotely possible to translate into cash terms some of the many items the Bhil and Bhilala tribals obtain from the forest. 'Our firewood comes from the forest. Our *chara* [fodder] comes from there, our herbs and medicines come from there, the *mahua* flowers* we collect

---

* The flowers from the trees, *Madhuca Indica* and *longifolia,* are distilled to produce an intoxicating liquor.

[for wine] come from there. Our fish come from the river down here. Which rehabilitation scheme of theirs will even look at all these as our earnings, as items to be recompensed?'

So what does Luaria want from the government? 'Nothing. We just want them to leave us alone. We will never be able to live anywhere else the way we live now. Can you deny that?' I cannot. Not after spending three days at Luaria's house and more time in other villages in the region. In one instance, a family demonstrated how they obtained nearly twelve items of consumption from a single tree.

In another (non-submergence) village in Wakner, a family totted up nearly thirty items of consumption. They had drawn all these from the forest in the past week. These included *Mahua, imli, chironji, sitaphal, amla* and *mukha ki sabzi.* Also in the list were *heguan ki sabzi, jatamada ki bajhi, kuliar ki sabzi, goindhi bajhi* and many more greens, vegetables, fruit and other forms of produce.

The people of the river bank have an economy that is close to being self-sufficient. Even their trips to the *haat* (rural market) are to fetch a few essentials like salt. 'We of the river bank never go to work as wage labourers,' says Bhava. 'The forest is our moneylender and banker. From its teak and bamboo, we build our houses. From its riches we are able to make our baskets and cots, ploughs and hoes. From its trees, leaves, herbs and roots, we get our medicines. Our cattle and goats, which are our wealth, graze here freely as they have always done. For all these, we would have to pay money in Gujarat. Stay here for eight days and see how much money you have to spend. Then stay eight days in Kavant or any town in Gujarat and see how much you have to spend.'

It proved impossible to make an accurate calculation. But a few of these items were on sale at the *haat* and we checked their prices there. We also made detailed enquiries about the other items. The results suggested that those moving to Gujarat would have to spend upwards of Rs.800 a month to sustain their present lifestyles even partially. Include fodder costs and the amount climbs further. This among households whose *annual* cash earnings would seldom exceed three to four thousand rupees a year and are often much less.

The point about fodder is crucial, since livestock is a very major form of wealth here. 'People are coming from Gujarat to our lands to graze cattle and cut firewood,' says Luaria's sister-in-law, Janki. 'What will we get if we go there?' Bhava alone owns '60 to 70 goats, 14 cows and 10 buffaloes. All of us also keep poultry. The goats are our insurance. We may not have all that many dealings in cash, but in crisis we can always sell a goat for 500 to 600 rupees.

That's how we manage here. If we go to Gujarat, the *banias* and the *patidars**
will crush us.'

The other crucial factor ignored in the resettlement plans is a calculation of the role that community labour plays in the economies of adivasi
societies. 'Look at this house we are building,' says Luaria. 'The others in
our *falia* come here to help us build it. They have even brought their own
food. It was the same when Bhava built his house. We do not have to pay
for anything.'

All this gets destroyed when they are uprooted, says Dr Amita Baviskar, a
scholar based at the Delhi School of Economics, with a PhD thesis on
problems related to this area. As she points out, 'It goes when they are shifted
and settled separately in Gujarat, not as one unit, but in groups spread out all
over the place. First, it hurts them financially, thanks to the loss of community
labour. Secondly, it disrupts them culturally, since it breaks ties and bonds that
are central features of their very existence as societies. And thirdly, it leaves
them, individually, or in small groups, at the mercy of vested interests there. If
resettled at all, the village as a whole would have to be put together for it to
make any sense.'

'Even in our weddings and funerals, everyone contributes to the bride
price or the funeral costs,' says Bhava. 'If there is a quarrel then the elders of
other villages sit and resolve the disputes. If uprooted from here and settled
separately, how will we arrange for our weddings and funerals? Who will come
to settle our quarrels? If scattered all over the place, we will never have the
same rights to land as in this village.'

It isn't as if all have turned down the official package. But even where a
majority of families have said 'yes', as in the case of Chilakda village, the
results have often been chaotic. Of twenty-seven families who went from here
to Kaveta village in Gujarat, several have returned. They are angry over
broken promises and sub-standard land. 'Only six of the families wish to
remain there,' says Ranja, an adivasi of Chilakda who came back from
Gujarat. 'But twenty-one want a change. All of us, seven brothers, went
happily at first. Then, things went wrong and we got bad land.' All of them say
conditions at resettlement sites are dismal.

Then there are those like Kev Singh. He wants to move, but officials do
not classify him as a project-affected person (PAP). They say his land is quite
safe, a claim he rejects. 'The government is lying when it says my land won't go
down. Just look at the site. How can it not go down when the entire village will

---

* *Banias* and *patidars* – moneylending, trading and landowning castes.

go under?' And there are those like the *patel** of Jalsindhi, whom Bhava charges with 'bringing relatives from outside to claim compensation and land in Gujarat'.

There is another vital question. Is there, in fact, enough land in Gujarat to go round? The real requirements of land seem to have been downplayed by both Madhya Pradesh and Gujarat governments for some years now. Of 3,100 families to have been resettled in Gujarat from Madhya Pradesh in 1992-93, land was found for only 1,190. In 1993-94, of 5,000 PAP families to be shifted to Gujarat, just 986 were moved.

Popular resistance to the dam in Gujarat and Maharashtra has seen some gains. One has been to focus attention on the, respectively, nineteen and thirty-three villages to be submerged in those states. Nearly 193 villages will go down in Madhya Pradesh. But most of the country knows little about that. Many of these villages were never told of their fate officially. How did they get to know of it? When they saw Central Water Commission surveyors installing stone markers to indicate the reservoir level.

The Madhya Pradesh government wants the proposed height of the dam lowered from 455 to 436 metres. This has positive implications. The fields and homes of some 25,000 families will escape submergence. Yet the lucky ones would be mainly in the upper-caste dominated, mixed villages of the higher reaches, in Dhar and Khargaon districts. 'The fully adivasi villages on the lower slopes would go anyway,' points out Jayshree, an activist with the *Khedut Mazdoor Chetna Sangath* or KMCS (Union for Peasants and Labourers Consciousness).

There is some dispute about how many villages in Jhabua will be submerged this year. The Narmada Valley Development Authority says there will be none. But the collector, Mr Dharmadhikari, holds that nine villages would be 'temporarily' submerged. And two, Sakarja and Kakarsela, will go down for ever.

Several villages are yet to be formally told of the schedule of submergence. And no one seems really certain of precisely how the submergence will unfold. For many, like Luaria, it could be a case of a one-year reprieve at the most. His field this year, his house the next. Some believe that Luaria and many like him would settle for degraded forest land within Madhya Pradesh. That would preserve his access to natural resources. Which means his resistance now could be a desperate gamble for a better deal.

---

* *Patel* – chief of a village. A post born of customs and hereditary, but sanctified by government.

As the waters rise, so do the chances of Luaria and his clan being forcibly moved. And with that, the likelihood of their getting nothing at all while losing face with those who opted to go to Gujarat. 'Multiply Luaria's case by ten thousand', says one official, 'and you have an idea of how people really feel about moving. And it's true of even a great many who have accepted the shift mentally and want to make a fresh start.'

'To begin with there has been virtually no development in these villages since Independence,' says Dr Amita Baviskar. 'On top of that now is the threat of displacement after years of oppression. The sheer injustice of it is extraordinary. They were never consulted, never informed. They don't want to go to Gujarat.'

Dr Baviskar also works with the KMCS. The KMCS has organised adivasis in nearly 95 villages of this region to fight for their rights since 1982. While affiliated to the Narmada Bachao Andolan (NBA), the activities of the KMCS go well beyond the anti-dam agitation. They mobilise the adivasis politically on a number of other issues such as land and rights of access to forest resources.

'Jalsindhi's declaration of choosing drowning in preference to moving may seem quixotic. It could even be seen as a desperate gamble for the future, for a better deal,' says Dr Baviskar. 'But it is also an incredibly sincere and brave fight. A symbol of people's resolve to resist such arbitrary treatment. They know they can lose everything, but they're fighting.'

'This is my house,' says Luaria, 'and I don't want any other. We're staying.' He may be fighting with his back to the walls he has just raised. And his eyes may be on the rising river. But Luaria's heart is set on defending his home. This is the house that Luaria built.

Big dam, little water

Kutku, Palamau (Bihar): It's a dam that's still 'under construction' after twenty-five years. Estimated in 1972 to cost Rs.580 million, the North Koel project, or 'Kutku dam' as they call it here, would today cost over Rs.4.25 billion. That's more than three times the entire irrigation budget of the state of Bihar this year.

If completed, the Kutku dam will bring little water to Palamau district, which has often suffered drought during the past three decades. It will irrigate

The 'Kutku Dam'. After twenty years, it's still 'under construction'. If completed, it will bring little water to Palamau. At its best, the dam will irrigate less than 6,800 hectares and generate a little over 20 MW of hydroelectric power.

less than 6,800 hectares in this district. And, at its best, the dam will generate a little over 20 MW of hydroelectric power.

Those who will lose their homes if the dam comes up, are mainly tribals and dalits. Some have already lost their lands. Officials say the dam will destroy fourteen villages. But the *Chottanagpur Samaj Vikas Sansthan* (Chottanagpur Institute for Social Development), a non-governmental organisation (NGO) and social action group fighting for the villagers, believes that over thirty villages would go.

'Even the official maps of the project show this,' points out Shatrughan Kumar, who heads the NGO in Palamau. In all, nearly 14,000 people would lose their homes. These include Kisan, Kharwar, Oraon, Kurwa, Parhaiya, Birjiya and Cheru tribals. Some Dushad and Bhuiya dalits would also be hit by the dam.

The delays plaguing the construction of the 225-foot dam they are battling against baffles even the would-be oustees. Their leader, Baidyanath Singh, bursts out laughing while talking to me about it: 'Here we are, mobilising people with a sense of urgency. Yet the things we predict and know will happen often don't happen. Or they happen years later. It's crazy.' Baidyanath heads the *Mazdoor Kisan Mukti Morcha* (Workers and Peasants Liberation Front), a group leading the resistance to displacement. He may find day-to-day happenings surprising, but he has a clear idea on why the project goes on at all. 'The building of this dam,' he says, 'continues for the sake of the *thekedars* [contractors]. There isn't a single other beneficiary.'

'Very often,' say villagers in the affected area, 'work stops for months at a stretch. Then the *thekedar* goes to Patna, more money is released and activity begins again. Millions of rupees from public funds have been squandered here.'

The lower sluices of the dam, which the villagers helped me climb to look at, are in bad shape. In one, whole chunks of concrete appear to have fallen out of the roof. And that happened 'after just one monsoon', asserts a villager. The other sluice has been sealed off at one end following substantial damage. No inspections of the standards of safety and construction work seem to have taken place. There's probably a good reason for that. My own inspection ends with my slipping on rubble dislodged from a damaged corner. I slide down twenty-six feet along the area in front of the sluice, landing just inches away from the gutter.

The anxiety of the villagers ends when it becomes clear I am bruised more in ego than in body. 'You have had a unique experience,' laughed Baidyanath. 'How many people fall down dams where there is not a single drop of water in sight?' The only water nearby is the narrow stream behind the dam where people have rigged up fishing nets. 'Not that there's much of a catch now,' says Baidyanath. 'These fish are tourists.'

Not a single senior official of the district favours the project. 'If ever finished, the dam could irrigate 56,000 hectares outside Palamau. It will help Aurangabad and Gaya, though neither of those districts is as desperate as Palamau is for water,' says one official. Then who is pushing for the dam?

'If it ever gets built,' says a senior official, 'Kutku will water the territory of irrigation minister Jagatanand. Funds have been held back for the portion that would go towards Garwha district. The focus will now be on the areas around the Sone barrage. That's where the minister's constituency lies.'

So the scheme for irrigating the minister's constituency goes on in spurts, according to the availability of funds. But villagers in the affected zone face growing hardship. Sangeeta Singh of Mandal village who is active in the resistance here tells me: 'The *thekedar* has threatened us. "I will see how you can stop this dam," he said.'

The delays and the changes in blueprint are not the only aspects of the dam with a slightly crazy flavour. Several villagers have received 'compensation' of one or two rupees per tree on the land they have lost. They have cheques that prove this.

'Just imagine,' exclaims Shatrughan Kumar of the CSVS. 'The land acquisition officer issuing these cheques knows that these *sal* trees have a value of Rs.700 per cubic foot.' He also says the oustees were in many cases paid only Rs.6,000 per acre of land taken over in 1984. The real value of the land at that time was around Rs.30,000 per acre or more.

The villagers do not believe the present district set-up to be hostile to them. They even see the deputy commissioner, Santosh Matthew, as quite sympathetic. They say he once brought along a senior minister to hear out their grievances. 'But here,' says one of the anti-dam villagers, 'the *thekedar* bypasses the administration. He goes to Patna, pulls some strings and is back in business once again.'

In Daltonganj, Vashist Narain Singh scoffs at the claimed benefits of the dam. Singh is a highly respected former works manager of the Bihar State Construction Corporation. He is also probably the foremost expert on irrigation in Palamau. Singh sees the North Koel scheme as wasteful. He believes that what is really needed are small dams. 'These should have linkages to perennial sources of water via a moderately big project or two – like those at Auranga or Kanhar.' Singh is right about the gains that a couple of the medium-big projects could bring. But within the present context, could a fair deal be ensured for those who lose their homes as a result?

Many people in the project area have told me of broken promises. Of jobs, schools and compensation that never came. 'There is not one school that works or any *anganwadi** for the thirty villages in this area. Nor is there one functioning hospital,' says Moorthy, one of the women activists of the resistance movement here.

The record does suggest that the fate of those hit by other projects in the district will not be very different. And such schemes are several. The Kadhavan reservoir plan will uproot over forty villages. The Kanhar project would destroy an equal number. The Auranga scheme would surely bring much needed water to Palamau, but will displace at least fifteen villages. Only the Talhe river project will displace nobody. It can irrigate up to 8,000 hectares within a cost of Rs.200 million – infinitely more rational than the Kutku dam.

'Yet on the Talhe river scheme, there has been no action, no funds for it,' observes Vashist Narain Singh. He says that, in any case, the state no longer takes the whole issue of irrigation as a serious responsibility. 'Why new projects? Even existing works are in a dangerous state of disrepair. Where Bihar used to have Rs.3.5 to Rs.4 billion allotted to the irrigation department annually, it now allots Rs.1.2 billion. Of this, around Rs.800 million goes on establishment costs. Only about Rs.400 million goes on projects. Maintenance has come to a standstill. No officer has received his travel allowance for three years. All the vehicles are idle, so important repair work remains undone.'

Activity at the Kutku dam site won't stop completely. The *thekedar* and minister will see to that. As Moorthy, standing against the backdrop of the huge white irrigation elephant, told me: '*Yahan dam bandh ho sakta hai, lekin thekedari nahin bandh hogi.*' ('Here, the dam might be stopped, but not this business of contractors.')

Postscript

Weeks after he took me around the dam site and the affected areas, Baidyanath Singh, poet, singer and leader, was murdered. He was killed by a squad of men in uniforms normally associated with the Maoist Communist Centre. The MCC is an ultra-left wing group active in the area and has a long record of violence. But Baidyanath's friends do not think they were behind the murder. They think that

---

* *Anganwadi* – a centre for children under six years of age for nutritional and health care.

contractors in league with irrigation department touts were responsible and that the uniforms were fakes. The resistance to the dam continues. And Baidyanath's voice remains among the poor people he led. It also remains in the beautiful songs he sang through the Palamau night, which I recorded on two ninety-minute cassette tapes.

Neema: Portrait of a village doomed

Neema, Godda (Bihar): Neema village has a real problem with dust. There's dust in every eye and nostril and the water is thick with it. Liberal portions of it get cooked with the food. It colours the laundry hung out to dry and creeps inside the clothes people wear. Layers of dirt lie on the normally sparkling-clean houses of the Santhal tribals.

Neema is surrounded on all sides by Asia's largest single-pit opencast mining venture. That is the Rajmahal Coal Mining Project, Lalmatiya (of the Eastern Coalfields Ltd.). To the village's east is the mine, belching up an average of 11,000 tonnes of coal each day. To the west is the plant itself. To Neema's south is the project's main workshop and stores, functioning round the clock. And to its north, the village faces what seems practically an artificial hill range. Here, 120-tonne and 170-tonne dumpers pile up mountains of 'overburden' – the surface crust of earth torn up to reach the seams of coal beneath.

All but merging into the Rajmahal Hills, these mammoth dumps provide an odd backdrop to the biggish village. Attractive houses line the slush-choked lanes. These are typical of Santhal architecture and built of mud and other traditional materials. By one estimate, there are over 4,000 people in Neema. About a third of the inhabitants are Santhal tribals. The rest are from other communities, mainly Muslims.

Some of the mud houses are really beautiful, even through the haze of dust that still settles on their walls. The Santhals know how to build for heat. The mud walls, often thirty inches thick, make the spacious interiors cool and pleasant though the weather outside is intolerably muggy. Urban architects could learn a few things here. My interest in the houses amuses Bambihari Murmu, a tribal resident of Neema. 'Yes, take photographs of them,' he says. 'We will need them, too. Soon, these houses could be gone.'

Neema is a village that knows it is doomed.

The coal project has affected as many as eighteen villages, twelve of them within the mine boundary. Neema, Hijukitha and Ghati Simra are the worst hit. Neema, the biggest of these, is in the hot seat. The approach to these villages becomes a nightmare during the monsoons. Coal dust, waste and slurry mix with endless stretches of mud and muck. The mess floats in huge puddles that are partly the result of mining operations in Godda, one of India's poorest districts, located in the eastern state of Bihar.

But Neema's is not a story of would-be 'oustees' taking their last stand. Some residents are employees of the very project that has taken their lands and which is about to displace them. And most are anxious to leave. 'Do you think we want to breathe this all our lives?' asks Jainarain Singh, a resident and project employee.

Neemaites feel swindled by a scheme drawn up originally to benefit them and other locals. They ceded over a hundred acres of land in return for jobs. However, the central government kept changing the criteria. At first, those giving up an acre or above for the project were given jobs. Then, this changed briefly to a rule of one job per family. Lastly, the government allotted one job for anybody ceding two acres.

Many of Neema's residents were already working with the old underground-incline mines of the Lalmatiya collieries that preceded the open-cast operation of the 1980s. Thus, they had to be absorbed into the workforce anyway. For them, the jobs-for-land rule didn't mean much besides losing their land. And for the village's Mohalis, at the bottom of the scheduled caste heap, it spelt disaster. They were mostly landless or held pathetic fragments well under the two-acre cut-off point.

Some of them will receive 'compensation' of Rs.1,500–Rs.2,000 for their huts. They cannot rebuild similar structures at three times the price. Oddly enough, all this occurs in a district falling within the Santhal Paraganas division. Here land is not only non-transferable, it cannot even be gifted away. But here it did change hands, under the Coal Bearing Act of 1957, as the central government took over the land in the '80s through a notification by the President of India. When the project began, Neema's residents had no clue to its enormity, scope and likely results. Realisation came in as the lands went out. Acquisition was swift and relentless.

'They were efficient in that,' says Babaji, an articulate, angry young Santhal tribal. 'But in what else? We have no water, no electricity and the dust is destroying our lives. They want to drive us out but even they don't know where we ought to go.' We have conducted our interviews across two nights, using a torch and candlelight for hours. Though power lines exist, even the four hours of current normally available has been cut off by the mine's management. That, says one official, is a 'punishment for stealing our electricity'.

The chief general manager of the Eastern Coalfields Ltd., (ECL), Rajmahal, R.C. Sharma, says project authorities would shift Neema and treat it the same way as Bara Simra. That is the one village seeing a serious resettlement effort. But villagers point out why Bara Simra was given that treatment: the village directly obstructs the mine's expansion. Sources within the management too confirmed this.

The ECL management seems set to play up their 'achievement' in Bara Simra. It is even planning a promotional video cassette on it. But this cuts no ice with any of the other villagers who believe that there are also political factors involved in the favours shown to this single village. Bara Simra is home to at least one prominent local leader of a Jharkhand faction*. I met his brother at the huge residence that was coming up for his family.

Engineers and architects assigned by the ECL management have helped in the construction of his house and also that of his brother. His brother, the leader, is at the moment 'underground' since their faction has called for a 'Jharkhand bandh', leading to a crackdown by the government. But the work on their houses does not stop. The links between some union leaders and the ECL management are on explicit display in this village.

'They have no intention of giving us a fair deal,' says one mine employee back in Neema. 'Bara Simra's shifting reflected the priorities of the project, not ours.'

Thousands of lives are being altered forever. Yet the ECL's Rajmahal project does not even have a rehabilitation department. That task is handled part-time by officers already holding heavy duties in other departments. 'It shows ECL's priorities,' says a local trade unionist.

The compensation rate for the land was fixed in the early '80s. It varied from Rs.3,000 per acre for the lowest grade to Rs.17,500 for the best. Much of the land was classified in the lower grade. Taken into account were the prices of the plots ages ago, 'But,' says villager Mistry Marandai, 'with our hard work we transformed this land and made it worth much more. At their rates, we cannot buy even ten per cent of the same area at current prices anywhere.' Land can cost up to Rs.52,000 per acre now.

Even that meagre compensation did not reach all, say the villagers. In Hijukitha, many said they had received only a quarter of the compensation sum. They are demanding interest on the remainder since over a decade has passed. Sharma, however, says some villagers had simply not collected their

---

* Jharkhand – various groups, mainly tribal, identifying with different streams of a 'Jharkhand' movement are fighting for a separate state within the Indian republic. This 'Jharkhand' state would comprise parts of Bihar, West Bengal, Madhya Pradesh and perhaps even Orissa. Some factions have sought only 'autonomous council' status within Bihar state.

cheques and that these had lapsed with time.

My first visit to Hijukitha was eventful. A wall and two doors came crashing down to the reverberations of the blasting in the mine.

Sharma does not deny the hardships faced by the villagers of Neema. Indeed, he describes their state as 'miserable and heart-breaking'. Yet no eviction notice has been issued to them so far. 'They are playing a waiting game,' says one resident. 'They feel we will realise it is impossible to live in these conditions and simply go away.'

But it isn't quite so simple. Unlike in other projects where people have been displaced, those pushed out here won't fade away. Instead, they could report for duty at the factory next morning, making an explosive situation even more complicated.

As Ram Swarup, a prominent trade union leader among the miners puts it: 'Some are getting jobs, but all are being uprooted. Not merely from their homes, but from their culture and history as well.' One taste of that came when the waste dumps swallowed the *Jeharthan*, the sacred tree of the Santhals and one of their burial grounds. 'Yet,' says Swarup, 'none of these villages has ever been served an eviction notice formally.' The idea now seems to be to evade issues of compensation altogether. Ram Swarup's United Coal Workers Union (an affiliate of the All India Trade Union Congress*) is fighting not only for its own members, but for all the displaced and affected. 'Why divide the poor?' he asks.

Neema has other worries. Access to the hospital ten kilometres away has become tough even as health problems mount. The attitude of the Central Industrial Security Force (CISF) outfit stationed in the area does not help much. I spoke to frightened women in Neema terrorised by the CISF just hours earlier while fetching water. And to Abu Talif, kicked and beaten up by them while using the latrine area on the village border. Talif was still stammering with fear when telling us of his ordeal.

S. Upadhyay, manager of the projects & planning department, conceded that rehabilitation was 'a process fraught with difficulties. The social problem must be admitted. But they are not mentally prepared to shift though they talk of it and though we are promising better facilities and sites.' But the project's track record on such promises over the years has not been inspiring.

As Bambihari Murmu puts it: 'We were told some years ago, of the great achievements ahead, that it was all for us, that we were making progress.

---

* AITUC – a mass organisation and the trade union front of the Communist Party of India (CPI).

Today, many of us have no jobs and all of us have lost our lands. We have only the dust. Look at our houses. Will we be given something like these when Neema is rubble?'

From dust unto dust seems a frighteningly prophetic cliché for Neema.

Postscript

When I last heard from them, the villagers of Neema had won one part of their battle. They had won the right to be recognised and compensated after being shifted with dignity. The strategy of making life so hard that they would just abandon their homes – thereby sparing the ECL rehabilitation costs – failed.

And silent trees speak

Cut-off area, Malkangiri (Orissa): Acre upon acre of dead forest. Trees without a single leaf that still seem to speak – sticking out above the silent waters, decades after they were submerged. A reminder of the ninety-one villages swept away by the Balimela reservoir and other Machkund river projects. The ferry, noisy till this point, falls silent. It moves slowly because it has to. Built to transport sixty-six people, it is carrying close to 370 just now.

The passengers' minds seem to speak: here people lived. Here, once, children played. For some on the ferry, that was a personal experience before their villages made way for a progress in which they never shared. And as the launch traverses the dead forest, we approach one of the loneliest parts of the Indian mainland: the 152 villages isolated by the Balimela and accompanying projects. A land so remote that even the official name for it is the 'Cut-Off Area'.

Perhaps no other river of comparable size produces so much hydroelectric power as the humble Machkund. It churns up 720 megawatts annually – shared by Orissa and Andhra Pradesh states – through different projects. The 152 villages, completely isolated, afford the two states huge amounts of electricity by their sacrifice. Yet it is virtually impossible to find a single household with electricity in any of these villages. Even the semi-pukka structure in Dharlabeda village where we spend the night has never seen a single bulb. Never mind that it is the office of the village council.

For those who live here are among the poorest of Indians. A woman in some of the cut-off villages can earn as little as Rs.4 for hours of weeding work in the fields. Isolation goes with deprivation here, ensuring that people have no voice. So the services extended to them are minimal. If you leave for the Cut-Off Area for the smallest of chores from Chitrakonda, you can only return on the third day, really speaking. The single launch operating today is old, overloaded, dilapidated and dangerous. It sets out late in the morning and will take many hours to cover its sixty-two kilometre route, stopping at several points between Janbai and Jantri. We board at Chitrakonda and head for Palaspadar.

Along the way, people from the cut-off villages approach the launch in small boats. The launch becomes a moving market-place – and their only contact with the outside world. Boarding it are Gadabas, Parojas (both ancient

One of the loneliest parts of the Indian mainland, the 152 villages isolated by the Balimela and accompanying projects constitute a zone so remote that even the official name for it is the 'Cut-Off Area'. Acre upon acre of dead forest, trees without a single leaf, still stick out of the silent water.

tribes) and even Bengali refugees from erstwhile East Pakistan settled in this region after the 1965 Indo-Pak war. They buy things they need from the launch staff and sell fish and other produce to them.

A Bengali couple, having rowed a good distance to reach the craft, are now bargaining with passengers and staff. After a while, the man returns to his boat and rows off, leaving his wife behind to conclude the transactions. That will take time. So she will get off a few stops further down the Cut-Off Area – and walk back many kilometres to her home through the woods along the river bank in the gathering darkness.

People pay bribes to get jobs on this ferry. You can hawk wares at outrageous prices to a captive clientele in this seller's market. And the launch staff are a smart bunch of entrepreneurs. *Beedis* (rough, country-style cigarettes) are probably cheaper in Mumbai (Bombay), but those living in the Cut-Off Area have no choice. Sometimes, the exchange is on a barter basis on this launch in Malkangiri, one of India's poorest districts.

Down the Machkund valley, you might run into the Didayis, a small tribe of less than 5,000 people not found anywhere else. The river itself goes on to take the name 'Sileru' further down. It also becomes the boundary at some points between Orissa and Andhra Pradesh.

Things looked quite different before the Machkund hydroelectric project – one of the earliest. The old gazetteers wrote of what they believed was one of the greatest sights in all India: the Machkund flinging itself over 300-foot walls of rock into a boiling pool hidden by dense clouds of spray that painted a permanent rainbow where they met sunlight. The Balimela power project, which began in 1962-63, ended that.

Landing at Palaspadar, we walk ten kilometres to reach Dharlabeda, passing through lonely, beautiful woods. The thick, whispering forests give you a sense of what even the submerged area must have once looked like. In Dharlabeda, the Village Level Worker (VLW) from Chitrakonda is distributing free sacks of groundnut. He takes everyone's signature in advance, but leaves blank the column stating the quantity given to each family. The VLW's judgement is arbitrary and he does not use a weighing balance though one is available here.

All the sacks of groundnut have this painted on them: *Do Not Accept Unless Sack Is Closed And Sealed*. All the sacks arrived open, with no trace of a seal: 'The groundnut,' says village headman Saduram, one of the area's few educated individuals, 'is given out to encourage people to grow it. But mostly it gets eaten, people here are too poor.' People like Arjun Pangi, for instance, a Paroja tribal in whose hut we spend part of the evening. Pangi and family are so poor that 'even the moneylender will not lend us anything. He feels we can never repay him even partially,' says Pangi.

The moneylender's reading seems right. There is not a single possession of any value in the hut.

The *coolie* (labouring) work he does – when there is work to do – fetches Pangi perhaps two kilograms of rice for a day's labour. Pangi and his family also go out and collect roots, berries, leaves and bamboo shoots. These make up the bulk of their diet on some days. 'Our time has gone,' says his friend Anandram Khilo. 'But perhaps one day our children, if they get an education, will lead a better life than this.'

Throughout the Cut-Off Area are villages with schools but children too poor to go to them. Also, people who get steady work for no more than four months in the year. There is a thirst for land among the worst off. 'If I had just two to three acres,' says Pangi, 'life would be fine.' But what about the officials who are supposed to come here and make such things possible?

Saduram laughs: 'The collector has come here more than once. He means well. But many other officials just sit in Chitrakonda and send in their reports.

Or they come up to the landing areas and send runners to call people from different villages to go there and meet them. When an official summons you, there is no choice. Once, a party of journalists came and sat with the officials on the river bank. Some villagers had to walk over twenty kilometres taking food for them. After that they went back and wrote, I think, about how we live here – without ever being to our villages.'

'Do the people who live here have any reason to feel they are Indians?' asks Kawasi Kamraj, an emerging tribal leader. Kawasi being with us made our stay in the Cut-Off Area possible. 'In what way do they share in the national life? Governments may change, their lives don't. These people are invisible, though there are some 30,000 of them. They are untouched by any of the gains of the projects they sacrificed for.'

There are some signs of development, though. The *sarpanchas* (heads of the village councils) are building new, pukka houses – for themselves.

In official reckoning, 1,200 families, mostly adivasi, were evicted to make way for the Balimela project in 1962-63. This figure appears flawed. For one thing, it does not seem to have recorded correctly the numbers really evicted. Next, the figures ignore many thousands outside the designated submergence zone who were devastated when their life-support systems were literally drowned. They also disregard those in the Cut-Off Area who suffered all the adverse effects of displacement without being 'evicted'.

Even those evicted were hardly compensated. The old official record shows that the state spent Rs.3.5 million on 'resettlement'. That's Rs.500 per individual if we accept the figure of 1,200 families. The amount spent on the 'staff vehicle', on 'salary to be paid to revenue department' and on 'shifting charges' was Rs.820,000. That is well over double the amount spent on 'building(s)' and on 'land for building(s)' for the thousands evicted.

As we sit in the semi-darkness of Pangi's hut, offered food by people who go hungry half the year, Angra Hanthal tells us: 'Many who lost land in the submerged area were never looked after. In the early years, they told us our names would come in the record a little later on. In our innocence, we believed these things. Some of us, after coming here, occupied some land, half an acre to an acre, maybe. We even got title deeds, but the land quality is poor. Only the forest is the great provider here.'

'After coming here,' says his wife, 'there were so many things the children needed we couldn't provide them. We had no money and even if we had money, we had no place to buy them – medicines, clothes, foodstuffs, so many things. You see them grown up now, but coming here hurt us. It hurt our children worse.'

On the return journey, the same silence falls. The trees, their branches like so many shrivelled fingers, seem to point at us accusingly. Thousands of acres of forest with prime teak and other rich produce were destroyed here forever. Their total worth was several times the Rs.570 million spent on the Balimela power project. The combined investment in all development projects in Orissa since Independence is eclipsed by the commercial value of renewable timber and forest produce lost in making way for them. The gung-ho attitude of the early decades is captured in the ugly concrete slab at the Chitrakonda pier. This announces, almost proudly, that the number of villages submerged by the project was ninety-one. All around, the hills show signs of electric installations. But in the Cut-Off Area there is only darkness.

5

Beyond the Margin

Survival strategies of the poor

What do people do during the 200-240 days when there is no agriculture in their regions? What do those do who haven't the option of agriculture anyway? Is there a way out for those ignored by development schemes – or, in fact, devastated by them? What are the survival strategies of the poor? What are their coping mechanisms?

They are many. Some of them quite ingenious, all of them back-breaking. Yet the resilience of millions of rural Indians is truly astonishing. So is their will to survive – and support their families honourably. Even where they lose out, they try to run their lives with dignity. And lose out, they often do.

A look at what it is they do – and how poorly they are rewarded for it – can be compelling. The brutalising grind they go through works towards reducing them to beasts of burden.

Yet their hard work, their dignity in the face of such circumstances, and their quest for self-reliance, begs one question: is there anything these people cannot achieve if given the right opportunities? If equipped with what quite a few other societies have given their own citizens? That is, among other things – a genuine land reform, education, health, shelter, work opportunities? At the end of many months of recording their strategies, only one answer stood out: with those basics in place, they can and will change their world. And ours.

The risky climb of Ratnapandi

Ramnad (Tamil Nadu): Ratnapandi Nadar has what must rank as one of the tougher jobs in the world. He climbs fifty palm trees daily, some of them thrice a day, to tap juice for *panaivellam* (palm jaggery*). That could mean 150 trips – up and down – trees that might be twenty feet in height. His work begins at 3 a.m. and lasts up to sixteen hours. He can earn as little as Rs.5-8 a day.

Ratnapandi, aged twenty-seven, is a *panaiyeri* (palm tree-climbing) Nadar, as his sub-group within the Nadar caste is known. But a few thousand like him do not share the prosperity of the better-off sections of that hard-working community. That is reserved for the middlemen, traders and wholesalers in the jaggery business.

In his village of Kavakulam in Ramnad district, Ratnapandi does not own or control a single one of the trees he risks his neck to climb. He has never gained from any anti-poverty schemes and enjoys no risk insurance in a trade where a single slip could spell death. While shinning up, he does not have even the protective hoop running around the tree that his counterparts in the neighbouring state of Kerala use. He cannot tap the trees for toddy† as that is illegal in Tamil Nadu. So he taps them for jaggery.

On a lighter day, Ratnapandi has to attend to at least forty trees. Even if these were shorter ones, between fifteen and twenty feet, it means he could be climbing between up to 5,000 feet a day. This is roughly equivalent to walking up and down a building of 250 floors daily, using the staircase. Only Ratnapandi isn't using a staircase. Nor even a ladder. He shins up using his hands and legs. The risks accompanying him are also, quite obviously, far greater.

Once up a tree, Ratnapandi cuts into it near the base of the branches and pre-empts the fruit, by forcing open its bud. This allows the juice to flow into a pot that the tapper fixes below the incision. He replaces the pot every few hours, when it gets filled. When he goes up, Ratnapandi adds a powder derived from calcium carbonate to the flowing juice.

---

* Jaggery – coarse brown sugar made from palm sap.
† Toddy – fermented liquor derived from certain palms.

The powder is the catalyst that converts the extract into palm jaggery. Without the powder, it would become toddy, since the process is otherwise identical. Rani, aged twenty-five, Ratnapandi's wife, will boil and cook the juice he collects in their huge open vessel. She then pours the paste into empty coconut shells where it solidifies into neatly shaped lumps of palm jaggery. Most people find palm jaggery much sweeter and better quality than cane jaggery.

That huge vessel they use is their only possession of any worth. They own no land and their hut has no belongings of even minimal value. They sell their jaggery to a *tharagar* (commission agent) to whom they are already indebted. This ensures a much lower price for the tappers than what the agent will command on the market. But the *panaiyeri* Nadars are not only very poor, they are also quite backward, and often illiterate.

'Look at the amount he earns for the kind of work he does!' says Rani. 'And look at him!' Ratnapandi does look sickly. Most of the *panaiyeri* Nadars seem prone to severe muscular pains, asthma, skin diseases and stress. Though some continue to labour for decades, the strain of the profession mostly destroys their working capacity earlier.

Karukavel Nadar, aged twenty-two, and his two associates in Porpandipuram village in Kadaladi block are slightly better off. They got a loan of Rs.3,000 and took 150 trees on contract from an absentee landlord. They jointly work the trees for the six-month season that ends in September. Each climbs forty to fifty trees, some thrice a day, like Ratnapandi. Unfortunately, the deal does not work in their favour – and is so structured that it never can.

Karukavel and his friends have taken the loan from their *tharagar* at an interest of 36 per cent per annum. The same man is also their wholesaler. They can't manage such interest rates and soon owe him money. So they have to sell their jaggery to him at prices held artificially low. With the state uninterested in crushing usury, they have little chance of escaping the *tharagar* system so prevalent in this ex-*zamindari* region* – perhaps the poorest and most backward district in the south Indian state of Tamil Nadu.

'If we had a choice, we would quit this job,' says Karukavel. With no other skills or opportunities, they have little choice. In the first two months of the season, each of the three could make up to Rs.600 monthly, or even slightly more, by collecting eight to ten kilograms of juice daily. The flow of juice

---

* *Zamindari* area – A region characterised by feudal relations in agriculture and dominated by *zamindars* or feudal landlords. Holdovers of such relations continue in several parts of the country 50 years after Independence despite the formal abolition of *zamindari*.

Karukavel Nadar at work. That means climbing fifty trees thrice a day in peak season. The palm jaggery tappers of Ramnad use only their hands and legs. They do not have even the protective hoop running round the tree that their counterparts in Kerala use. A single slip could mean death.

begins to drop towards the end of the season and they are able to extract only one or two kilos of juice per day.

Though the middlemen get the benefits, the tappers bear all expenses incurred in making the jaggery. The powder derived from calcium carbonate costs Rs.3 or two litres and they could spend up to Rs.60 or even Rs.90 a month on this. Then there is the firewood for boiling and cooking the juice. The cost of this varies, but they could shell out around Rs.15 on firewood to create 10-15 kilos jaggery. As Karukavel points out: 'It is actually cheaper to produce toddy. We don't have to incur any of these costs on that substance!'

Since they get only Rs.4 to Rs.5 per kg of jaggery, their earnings decline to Rs.5 or Rs.8 a day in August and September. The work remains very heavy, though. The middlemen get roughly Rs.12 per kg of jaggery for which the tappers have risked their lives. Meanwhile, the loan and other expenses erode their modest earnings during the months of April and May.

Yet even these low earnings are of some help to them as they will be out of work after September. Steeped in debt, they have no means of repaying the loan of Rs.3,000. They fear unseasonal rain as it would destroy any earnings they could possibly make. No member of the *panaiyeri* community here has a single set of clothes in good condition.

During the off-season the tappers do what they call '*coolie work*' (physical labour on a casual basis) – for a pittance – in Ramnad's exploitative salt pans. Such development as has touched Ramnathapuram (or Ramnad) seems to have bypassed the community. At the age of sixty, Thangavelu Nadar of Kavakulam still has to climb around twenty to twenty-five trees daily to earn a living. He has been doing this work for over forty years now.

A very large number of the tapper families in Kavakulam appear to have migrated this summer to Thanjavur, another district in Tamil Nadu. It seems illegal toddy tapping is still on over there. Many need some work to be able to pay off their debts. In Ramnad, every one of the *panaiyeri* Nadars I interview is heavily indebted. After a while, it doesn't matter how much jaggery they produce. They are not only repaying loans but are also selling the *panaivellam* at absurdly low prices to the middlemen. They have to. That's the result of other debts incurred to be able to eat daily.

The arduous nature of their work means they cannot reduce food intake beyond a point. 'They must have fish and rice,' says Rani, 'so we are always borrowing money to keep going.' That deepens the debt trap. Yet, even the 'fish and rice' meal we saw Ratnapandi consume seemed absurdly meagre when compared to the rigours of his work.

'They have the toughest job, the lowest pay and the maximum danger,' says a Tamil Nadu Kisan Sabha (Peasants Association) activist. 'But no development schemes – and there aren't any, anyway – will help improve their conditions. Not unless we can break the debt cycle, place them in control of these trees and fight for decent prices.' Until then, the *panaiyeri* Nadars may not be exactly out on a limb, but they are certainly up the right trees for the wrong reasons.

Recycling energy, Godda style

Lalmatiya, Godda (Bihar): Kishan Yadav pays Rs.1,200 for a bicycle with one pedal. This odd transaction concluded, he spends Rs.200 to reinforce its bars. Then, he either removes the chain or hangs it loose and tears the seat upwards, towards the sky.

Yadav is now ready to use his bicycle. Not so much for cycling as yet – that can be difficult without a chain – but as a trolley for carrying up to 250 kilograms of coal across distances of forty to sixty kilometres. For his hazardous labours, he earns up to Rs.10 a day, barely a third of the minimum wage in Bihar state.

Yadav will go from Lalmatiya to Godda town and back, taking fully three days in walking, resting and hawking time. A more strenuous form of self-employment is hard to think up, yet nearly 3,000 families in Godda are dependent on it.

Not all the *koilawallahs* (coal peddlers), or cyclewallahs as they are known, will remove one pedal or the chain, but they will reinforce the bars and tear the seat upwards. 'They will learn,' says Yadav, a trifle contemptuously. 'That right-side pedal will break and the chain, if not loosened, will cause obstruction.'

Only after he sells his coal can Yadav restore the pedal and chain and cycle back to Lalmatiya where he buys his stuff. He cannot do this crushing trip more than twice a week. Sometimes, the *koilawallahs* journey to Baunsi in Banka district, sixty kilometres away, or even up to Rajaun in Banka, eighty kilometres away, all the while pushing their huge loads on foot with muscle-tearing effort. Usually, the *koilawallahs* cart loads between 200 and 250 kg, but some claim they occasionally pull even heavier loads.

Officialdom terms their trade an 'illegal' activity. Why? Because they purchase coal from scavengers who scour the waste dumps of the Rajmahal Coal Mining Project, Lalmatiya. The mountains of waste soil the project creates contain almost three per cent of low-grade coal.

'In fact,' admits a top Rajmahal project official, 'were it not for the scavengers, that coal would remain unutilised in the waste dumps. And, but for the cyclewallahs, would never reach the people of Godda, mostly poor consumers, as an extremely cheap energy source. It is a national saving.'

Issues tend to get confused because there are so many unlawful activities

For all the hazardous labour involved in pushing up to 250 kg of coal across distances over forty kilometres, the Godda cyclewallahs could earn less than Rs.10 a day – barely a third of the minimum wage in Bihar.

relating to coal-mining. However, three main illegal forms stand out in the extraction and sale of coal:

- Theft from the depots of the Rajmahal project and piracy while the coal is in transit. But nobody has ever accused the cyclewallahs of that.
- Illegal mining controlled by a powerful coal mafia aided by corrupt officials. That is certainly not run by cyclewallahs like Yadav or Prahlad Prasad Sah earning less than Rs.12 daily.

- The scavenging of coal from the waste dumps by very poor people. It is from them, or via the *dadas* (neighbourhood gangsters) controlling them, that the cyclewallahs mainly get their coal. These are the people, mostly women, largely responsible for what the official calls a 'national saving'.

As a senior Rajmahal official admits: 'About 1,000 cyclewallahs function on a given day. No one manages more than two trips a week. If we calculate all the coal "illegally" sold by the *koilawallahs* in a whole year, it won't equal two days production at Lalmatiya.'

Starting outside Lalmatiya, I tracked the cyclewallahs along the route to Godda, forty kilometres away. Though the distance is not much, they need an overnight halt. A physically intolerable journey at the best of times, it seemed hellish in the wretchedly sultry weather. They moved slowly along miserable roads where they often had to push their back-breaking loads up unyielding inclines.

The *koilawallahs* move in lines of up to twenty. The 'fellow travellers' are essential because, if one of them stumbles, he can't get started without assistance. Besides, each needs help when fording long puddles or mounting steep inclines. I watched Yadav cross one such stretch aided by his friends. He then 'parked' his cycle by planting a stout stick under the sacks and went back to help the next man across.

The cyclewallahs carry two meals with them. Just a bit of rice with slivers of stale vegetable thrown in – and no pulses. Each will spend a further Rs.15 on food during the three-day period it requires to sell their load and make the journey both ways.

From a group that has stopped on the edge of Godda for a meal, I learn this is a multi-caste activity. Barring Brahmins and Rajputs, almost all Godda castes are into 'recycling' coal. Manto Manjhi is a dalit, travelling alongside Prahlad and Arun Sah who are Banias. There are also Yadavs, Koeris, Santhals and a host of others. Economic necessity seems to have broken down social barriers.

Why stick to this excruciating trade when even work on government development projects pays more? Aren't they aware that the daily minimum wage in Bihar is now Rs.30.50? There is derisive laughter. 'That's for the contractors,' says Manjhi. 'Where will they pay *us* that much for working on government projects? Even for Rs.20, we would do other work.'

The economics of their own trade is startling and a superficial look can be most misleading. When I first ran into Kishen Yadav, he was collecting Rs.105 from a housewife in Godda town. That seemed a handsome enough sum for a one-shot sale. It was only after days of working with them that the costs involved in the exercise became clearer. The *koilawallahs* buy up to 250-300 kg of coal for Rs.30 at Lalmatiya. Then they pay Rs.5 each as *rangdari* (extortion money) to local thugs. Next, Rs.10 goes as *hafta* (regular 'cut' or bribe payment) to the police. That is, Rs.2 per cycle at five police posts between Lalmatiya and Godda. Each spends Rs.15 on food and necessities during the three-day trip.

'Almost Rs.10-15 per trip goes on maintenance of our cycles,' says Arun Sah. 'The ball-bearings wear out rapidly and we also have to change tubes every three months, sometimes even tyres.' Having spent around Rs.75, they get about Rs.100 to Rs.105 for the whole load in Godda (in Patna, it could fetch upwards of Rs.300). That leaves them with Rs.30 – their earnings for three days. Since they can do this only twice a week, their weekly earnings will not exceed Rs.60-70, or eight to ten rupees a day. They could get as much as Rs.150 or more for their load in far-off Rajaun. But that's a hard trip to make more than once a week.

Cyclewallahs are 'prime candidates for tuberculosis, severe chest pain, torn muscles, respiratory ailments and a number of other illnesses,' says Dr P.K. Daradhiyar of Godda. He often counts them among his patients. Prahlad Sah lost a month due to illness, fairly common for the *koilawallahs*. He also lost a bicycle when the police decided to confiscate it.

District officials hope to create a system bringing coal to Godda town by truck. They say the cyclewallahs could then operate within town limits. The *koilawallahs* are sceptical, fearing this will only lead to their unique form of self-employment being scrapped. This is their survival strategy and they intend to stick to it. Even if it means re-inventing the wheel, Godda style.

The leaf that topples governments

Kantaroli, Surguja (Madhya Pradesh): Botanists call it *dyospyros melanoxylon*. Manufacturers call it *beedi*. Traders call it profits, politicians call it power and the poor call it survival.

Everybody else calls it *tendu patta** and it is the leaf that can change governments in Madhya Pradesh.

As an issue, it may not have had the high profile of Ayodhya (mosque-temple dispute) in the 1993 assembly elections in this state. Yet, few within the Bharatiya Janata Party (BJP) harbour illusions about the damage it caused them when the then chief minister, Sunderlal Patwa, sought to undermine the co-operativised collection of *tendu*.

His moves hit the very poor and benefited a handful of private traders to the extent of millions of rupees. Some of the beneficiaries were top function-aries of the BJP at the state level. 'The party received the bill for these actions through the ballot boxes,' says one anti-Patwa BJP member bitterly. 'The undoing of the cooperatives, returning monopoly powers to private interests like the traders, hurt people for whom this is the lifeline.'

Yet, though the links are very real and powerful, it isn't easy to immedi-ately connect these events with the poor adivasi women plucking *tendu* leaves in the forests of Surguja district.

When Pyari in Jajgir or Puthuli in Kantaroli village, both adivasi women, get up at 4.30 on a May morning, they begin walking almost before they've overcome sleep. Though – as always – they bear the brunt of the work, this time they're not alone. Tens of thousands of extremely poor families work as whole units to pick leaves, which goes into the making of *beedis*.

By 5.30 a.m. the edge of the forest near Kantaroli village – reached after a four-kilometre walk – presents a spectacular sight. Dozens of women, children and men are moving swiftly, plucking *tendu* leaves with assembly-line precision, a small army of human bees working a forest hive.

As the season, which won't last more than six weeks, goes by, the walks to the forest get longer, the children tire out faster and the load on the women who have to get back to many other chores gets heavier. Still, they have to stick

---

* *Tendu patta* – leaf from which *beedis* (rough native, or country-style, cigarettes) are made.

to it, since the earnings from this will help tide them over the terribly lean days that follow.

'It is a matter of survival,' Puthuli told me breathlessly. For each *gadda* (bundle) of 50 leaves, the leaf-collector gets 30 paise (less than 1p). If Puthuli manages 100 *gaddas* in a day, she will have earned Rs.30. In the early days of the season, she averages between 80 and 100 *gaddas* daily. Only very rarely can she put together more than 100 *gaddas*.

Her activity does not cease for a moment even while speaking to me. With the ease born of doing something a million times, each smooth flick sees a hand reach to a cluster, detach a leaf with minimal sound and effort and transfer it to the other hand or armpit in one flowing motion. When the bunch under the other arm gets too big it goes into one of two baskets hung on a stick that someone will balance on his or her shoulder.

'I pluck 70 to 80 *gaddas* a day,' says Pyari, the leaves piling up rapidly under her arm. Puthuli's is a six-member family including four children, every one of whom can manage 20 to 30 *gaddas* of 50 leaves each. Since her husband can pack away about 100 *gaddas*, the six of them together can average 300 *gaddas* daily in the early weeks. On such days they could earn up to Rs.90.

This means they earn more in the first two weeks of the season than they might earn in the next two months. The flow, however, tapers off a bit as the days go by.

Still, there is little question that May represents the peak earning period for a lot of extremely poor people, especially for the landless or marginal farmers. A family could earn over Rs.2,000 in a month, a fabulous amount here in Surguja. And this is apart from any other income they derive during this period.

The collection work ends around 11 a.m. But the activity doesn't end with the plucking, nor is the payment immediate. The only 'perks' or fringe benefits I notice come as we trudge home after plucking *patta* from 5:30 a.m. to 11 a.m. A young man throws a small boulder against the base of a tree and the children run around picking up the *tendu* fruit that shower down. Back in the huts, after the women have done all the other chores, including cooking, cleaning and fetching water from considerable distances – the process of sorting out the leaves begins.

Taking the leaves out of the baskets, they neatly organise them in batches of fifty, and tie up each bundle separately. This too, takes some hours. Here again, the family sits down as a unit, but the mother and her daughters do the bulk of the work. Often, though, a man does the tying of the string around the bundles.

*Picking tendu leaves in the Kantaroli forest. For each **gadda** (bundle) of 50 leaves that Puthuli puts together, she will earn all of 30 paise. Yet tendu collection is a major source of income for the poor. By working at backbreaking speed, a family as a whole can put together up to 300 **gaddas** a day during the early weeks of the season.*

By 4.30 p.m. they're marching off to the *phar*, the *tendu* marketplace. There the official in charge, the *phar munshi*, jots down each one's account and decides on the payment they will get. The forest department tries to facilitate the entire process right through the season.

The offerings brought to the *phar* are laid out in long, elaborate rows often covering a whole field. The sight of people walking in from the forest, from a dozen different directions, is quite riveting. The *phar munshi* regularly steals twenty out of every hundred bundles. The peasants seem resigned to this low-level racketeering. 'What choice do we have? Over here, he's the boss,' says Pyari.

Earlier, private contractors used to purchase the leaves directly from people like Pyari, Puthuli and their families, paying them a pittance. The present system, while far from ideal, exposes them less to the rapacious traders.

Under the old system, encroachments on forests by outsiders became so severe that the *tendu* collection trade was nationalised in 1964.

Whole areas were then leased out to individuals, which led to private contractors looting the forests. During upheavals on this front, some Madhya Pradesh governments found that the price of the leaf could be the price of power. As the profits of the traders grew, so did the distress of the poor.

In 1988-89, then chief minister Arjun Singh tried breaking this stranglehold. The whole process was co-operativised in the present three-tier system. At the base are the village-level primary co-operatives in charge of procurement, drying and 'bagging' of the produce.

The second tier consists of a group of such co-operatives forming a union that looks after transportation and storage. At the top is the apex body, the Madhya Pradesh Minor Forest Produce Federation, which is responsible for sale and marketing of nearly five million bags of *tendu* leaves annually.

The apex body arranges financing for procurement by the primary co-operatives – this needs nearly Rs.1.5 billion each year – and also arranges the auction of produce to the *beedi* manufacturers.

Madhya Pradesh accounts for nearly 50 per cent of *tendu* leaves nationally, worth Rs.32.5 billion in its raw form. But most of this goes to the southern states.

During its term, the Patwa government struck back on behalf of the traders, hitting the poor and costing Madhya Pradesh a fortune in revenue. Auditors have proclaimed a Rs.550 million loss to the state, while others push the figure above Rs.2 billion.

Few doubt the BJP government paid dearly for this at the hustings towards the end of 1993. Significantly, one of the first things the new Congress government did was to undo that damage. The '*tendu* scam' has since proved a big weapon in Congress hands against the BJP.

At I left Surguja, minor protests were surfacing over delays in payments, though in a few districts the process seems to have gone off reasonably well. Still, the Congress government would be unwise to take the hitches, where they arise, lightly.

Usually it's just *beedis* that go up in smoke. Where this leaf is concerned sometimes it's governments.

The vanishing world of the Birhors

Jhabhar, Palamau (Bihar): The widow of Akhu Birhor sits silently next to her *kumbha*, or hut made of leaves and twigs. The Birhor colony is just outside Jhabhar village in the Balumath block of Palamau. The people of Jhabhar, some of whom have seen the mansions of the district headquarters at Daltonganj, call the *kumbhas* 'air-conditioned'. We find out why, when the cold winds of Chottanagpur cut through the huts and chill us to the bone.

The Birhors are of the same Austro-Asiatic language group as the Ho, Santhal or Munda tribes. They are the people (*Ho*) of the forest (*Bir*). A nomadic tribe of the Chottanagpur belt, they move mainly around Palamau, Ranchi, Lohardaga, Hazaribagh and Singhbhum districts of Bihar state. The Birhors are in many ways a unique people.

They are also a vanishing people. The 1971 census says there were over 4,000 of them in that year. There are just around 2,000 of them now, maybe less. That includes about 144 in Orissa and 670 in Madhya Pradesh. The main group is, of course, in Bihar. In this state there were 3,464 at the time of the 1971 census. An official study in Bihar in 1987 said their number had declined to 1,590. In Madhya Pradesh, their number fell from 738 in 1971 to 670 in 1991.

Their decimation follows the relentless destruction of the forests on which they depend. A development process that takes no notice of their needs or unique character has not helped. The Birhors were mainly hunter-gatherers. They were also engaged in rope-making and woodwork. When the forests were 'reserved'*, they could not cut wood or get rope fibres. Their finished goods fetched very low prices, not even meeting the cost of production. When deforestation ravaged the few areas they still had access to, hunting failed. In times of natural calamity or crisis, they are the worst hit.

'Look at her,' says Sukhra Birhor, pointing to the silent woman. 'When the drought began last year, we were ruined. Her husband Akhu had died of hunger. Food and Red Cards mostly did not reach us.' The Red Card is an

---

* In 'reserved' forests, state control is total. The rights of traditional dwellers and others there either cease to exist or are transferred elsewhere or are in exceptional cases allowed very limited exercise.

emergency ration card distributed in famine or near-famine situations. A top official in Palamau wisely went in for the cards in late 1992. The famine code had not been officially invoked, but the crisis was bad enough. Yet the Birhors did not get them.

'The one or two cards we got were due to the good people of Jhabhar,' says Sukhra Birhor. 'No one else came.' Being so few in number, illiterate and extremely backward, the Birhors can't make themselves heard in a society with little interest in them.

Ignorance about the tribe leads to much confusion. Census data on the Birhors is also flawed for this reason. Here, they are Birhors. In Sundargarh district of Orissa state, locals call them *Mankidi*. In Sambalpur district of the same state, *Mankirdia*. Both labels spring from their expertise in trapping monkeys. Since monkeys often destroy crops and fruit, locals employ Birhors to trap them. As the forests die, so does that line of work.

In 1971, the nomadic group ended up being counted in Orissa as three separate tribes – Birhor, *Mankidi* and *Mankirdia*. This error was set right in 1981 and they were counted as one tribe. So the number of Birhors in that state 'shot up' by 44 per cent though their group was in fact declining. The government of Orissa congratulated itself on the increase. Thus, data on the Birhors is most unreliable.

As hunters, the Birhors lived in complete harmony with the great jungles around them. Their use of the forests is never wasteful and always rational. Even their settlements, as a rule, normally have only about ten huts or so. They spread their colonies across the forest. This allows the different groups fair and equal access to a share of forest resources. Today, in their main home state of Bihar, they are the victims of unprecedented deforestation and 'development'.

Not a single child in the Birhor colony outside Jhabhar goes to school. Female literacy is almost nil. And Raju Birhor believes this is the case with the tribe in all its areas. 'We would like to send the children to school, but who can afford it?' he asks. 'We can't afford food,' says Rambirich Birhor. 'So why talk of school?' Malnutrition is visible on the faces in the settlement, the more so among children. 'Besides,' says political activist Narendra Chaubey, 'they have very high infant mortality rates. Fewer of their children survive, compared with other communities in the region.'

Alcoholism has further contributed to their downward slide. Yet crime hasn't touched them. 'They are an amazing people,' says a member of the Jhabhar *panchayat* (village council). 'If they hear of a robbery taking place on the road a mile away, they take it as a personal insult. And they rush there with their sticks. I have never known of Birhors turning to crime.' Jhabhar's residents are exceptional in their response to the Birhors. Across Palamau and Hazaribagh, the tribe mainly faces neglect and apathy.

Government programmes mostly fall flat. Or a machinery corrupt down the line hijacks them. Housing schemes have proved a disaster, with buildings planned by architects who have never even seen the Birhors. Nor have they grasped their particular character. Petty officials and other crooks have diverted money meant to control and bring down the alarming health problems the tribe suffers from.

'Even the *teesra fasl* [third crop] doesn't reach them,' laughs a Jhabhar villager. Third crop? I enquire naively. I had only known of two. He was clearly hoping I would ask. 'The third crop in this region is drought relief. The funds involved in it are huge but the harvest is generally reaped by block-level officials and their contractor friends. Only a tiny part reaches the people. The Birhors seldom get even that small share. They live on jungle roots and berries, seasonal fruit, and can go hungry for days at a time.'

The concept of The International Year of the Indigenous Peoples (1993) fascinates Rambirich Birhor when we tell him about it. 'Is it really meant for us?' he asks. Then, after some contemplation, he says, 'It can't be, or we would not be in this state.' He picks up his ancient snare – one of his very few earthly possessions – and moves off. It's time to trap a rabbit and end the hunger of several days of at least one family of indigenous peoples. Just at that moment, all the global declarations, resolutions, and seminars on the subject seem a trifle overdone. 'As far as I know,' chips in Chaubey, 'no Birhor has ever been on a voters' list in these parts. This tribe lives in the bottom one per cent of Indian society.'

Trapping rabbits, weaving ropes, selling a few baskets when they can, the Birhors seem to live in a different age. They are a non-acquisitive and, for all their living conditions, a dignified people. 'We didn't beg anything from anybody,' says Akhu's widow, speaking at last. 'But they said when the drought came that everybody would be helped. Instead, we had no money, no food, we starved and he died. We cannot even manage from the great forests where we find less and less of our needs. When the forests vanish, so will the Birhors.'

Orissa's bricks of burden

Bolangir (Orissa) & Vizianagaram (Andhra Pradesh): Everything in this kiln area at Vizianagaram is covered with brick dust. Adolescent labourers stagger out of the pit, carrying around 20 kg of bricks towards the stocking area, passing an old man simply unable to cope with the 45 kg of bricks he is lugging. The bodies of all those working here are caked in a film of brick dust that reappears within minutes of wiping it off. Many have developed a rasping cough, apart from less visible but no less dangerous respiratory problems.

Even the Andhra supervisor at the pit head does not speak in Telugu, the language of Andhra Pradesh state. Almost all the labourers are migrants from the Kalahandi-Nuapada and Bolangir areas of neighbouring Orissa. They are trying to escape hunger at home – by slaving at brick kilns in Andhra Pradesh. Rana Nahak is very pleased though, to learn that I visited his native Tarbod village in Nuapada just days earlier. 'Were all in the village well when you went there?' he asks. Nahak speaks a variant of Hindi. Many in the Kalahandi area feel they are part of Chattisgarh rather than of Orissa.

Meanwhile, the old man moves towards the stocking area. Each brick he carries weighs about two and a half kilos and he carries twenty of them. In the course of the day, he could make forty-five trips between pit and yard – a distance of 25 to 50 metres depending on which end of the stocking area he is headed for. And he'd be lugging along 45 kg on every trip. Each carrier does this with a half-running goose step of a gait. They maintain this sort of rhythm to avoid dropping the bricks and to be able to do the required number of trips. When the old man with or without the aid of his family members has lifted nearly two tons of bricks in this manner, they earn around Rs.9.

'But that's not all he earns,' butts in the supervisor. 'They get more for making the bricks.' Which means that when Nahak's five-member family has pushed its limits to make fully 1,000 bricks in a day, they get Rs.40. 'See?' asks the supervisor. 'They can get Rs.50 in a day.' If any bricks get damaged in the yard, or prove worthless, some kiln owners deduct their value from that Rs.40. And it isn't on all days that they shell out the combined payment for both making the bricks and for carting them to the stockyard. Bricks from this area are generally of poor quality, say builders in the more developed port city of Visakhapatnam, or 'Vizag', nearby.

When Amru Majhi and his family heave nearly two tonnes of bricks in the course of a day between the pit and the stocking yard in this fashion they will earn Rs.9. They earn more by actually making the bricks too. But at end of the day, each member of the families working here will be left with no more than Rs.12 individually.

Ultimately, each member of the families working here earns Rs.8 to Rs.12 daily. The variations depend on the number of working hands in a family unit and the kind of deductions they face. The kiln owners, say those familiar with the building industry in nearby Vizag, earn hundreds of thousands of rupees from just the few acres their pits occupy.

Alien to the area, strangers to the language, many are dependent on the contractor for food purchases. The contractor might direct them to a shop in the nearby town with which he generally has a connection. So, in some of the 'homes' here – dismal-looking hovels under five feet in height that you have to get down on your knees to enter – are consumed the worst qualities of rice. Mixed with liberal quantities of dust and even scrap particles, this rice costs Rs.7 a kilogram or more. 'The supervisor was helpful,' said Rana Nahak innocently. 'He showed me a shop to buy from.' The economics of the operation are baffling. But here, says Ghasiram, 'at least there is work. What work is there, back in Bolangir or Nuapada?'

'The complete destruction of wage employment in the Kalahandi-Bolangir area has taken its toll. Along with steady alienation of land, labour and produce, it is the driving factor for such migration,' says Dr S.K. Pattnaik of the NGO, Vikalpa. The NGO surveyed fifty villages in four blocks of Bolangir (all of them along the Nuapada border). 'One out of every five migrants from here,' says Dr Pattnaik, who went with me to several of the villages from where the migrants originate, 'goes to the brick kilns in Andhra. Sometimes they travel up to 400 km to do so.'

'Just look at what official development strategy has done to employment in the Kalahandi region,' says Jagdish Pradhan of the Paschim Orissa Krishijeevi Sangh. 'The average labourer had 268 days of work here in 1954. (For some reason 272 days was considered 'full employment'.) Now he or she can get only 128 days of work in a year – a fall of over 50 per cent – leading to major migrations. The destruction of traditional irrigation systems caused immense damage. On top of this, people here get dismal prices for their products and absurd "development" projects without popular roots.'

Andhra provides only a few weeks of employment. Many of the same migrants then pull rickshaws in Raipur in Madhya Pradesh for some days. 'On a good day in Raipur,' says Ghasiram nostalgically, 'I can be left with Rs.15 in my hand at the end of work.'

Despite the crude and visible exploitation, none of these labourers can seek redress. They do not qualify for it under the Inter-State Migrant Workmen's (Regulation of Employment & Conditions of Service) Act, 1979.

'One who goes of his own volition and not through a labour contractor does not presently qualify as a migrant,' says Orissa chief labour commissioner B.B. Mishra. He has been strongly urging changes in the Act. As Mishra points out, 'the Act places no responsibility on the labour machinery of the *host* state'.

Simply put, the migrants from Orissa have to suffer because they came to Andhra Pradesh on their own. That they are very much in the grip of contractors here does not count. And secondly, the Andhra Labour department cannot be held legally responsible for their plight.

Who are those who leave their homes to travel 400 km for a pittance? According to the Vikalpa survey, over 42 per cent are landless agricultural labourers. Another 31 per cent own an acre or less while a further 16 per cent hold under two acres. 'In short, close to 90 per cent of the migrants are landless or marginal farmers,' says Dr Pattnaik.

The old man, Amru Majhi, who belongs to the remaining 10 per cent, staggers back towards the pit yet again. He says his family once owned over four acres before the moneylenders got after them. His eyes light up at the mention of Badkani village in Bolangir, from where he came. But he can't stop to talk too long. Neither can Rana Nahak. The supervisor is looking our way and there are trips to be made.

Surguja's silent ban on bullock-carts

Batra, Surguja (Madhya Pradesh): Why is Surguja in Madhya Pradesh the only district in the Hindi belt where you can't find a single operational bullock-cart? The roads of prosperous neighbouring Bilaspur district are thick with them. They can also be found across Surguja's borders with eastern Uttar Pradesh and Bihar. In Surguja itself, which is bigger than Bilaspur, there isn't a single functioning bullock-cart visible.

This in a nation where the humble *baylgaadi* (bullock-cart) is the perceived symbol of the countryside. And also a vehicle that saves India over Rs.40 billion yearly in foreign exchange. That would be roughly the extra cost of oil imports if grain moved by bullock-cart were to be lifted by other, more modern forms of transport. The country has an estimated fifteen million carts. And nearly 90 per cent of these animal-drawn vehicles (ADVs) are pulled by a pair of bullocks.

Reviling an opponent for having a 'bullock-cart mentality' is standard fare in urban debate. A Prime Minister once attacked his critics in the Lok Sabha (Lower House of the central Indian Parliament or People's Assembly) in those terms. Is the cart such a useless relic? India has rail and domestic air networks that are amongst the largest in the world. Also, significant marine and road systems. Yet all these forms of transport carry perhaps a third of the foodgrain the humble bullock-cart does. As N.S. Ramaswamy and C.L. Narasimhan of the Indian Institute of Management, Bangalore pointed out over a decade ago, ADVs generate employment for nearly twenty million Indians, part-time or full-time, directly or indirectly, either for a money wage or in kind.

Then why aren't bullock-carts used in huge Surguja, which at 23,000 square km is more than three times the size of the average Madhya Pradesh district (7,000 sq. km). With its bad or non-existent roads, wouldn't it need them even more? More puzzling, you can find a few carts lying within the yards of prosperous farmers – unused. Some are ancient specimens with wooden axles.

I raised these questions in nearly every village I visited in rural interior Surguja across three weeks. The answers they got point to a unique social contract, the existence of an unwritten, silent ban in Surguja on the use of the bullock-cart. A variety of factors were mentioned, though.

'The bullocks here are too weak,' Laltha Prasad told me in Kalipur village. 'They haven't the strength to plough, how will they pull carts with loads on them? How can we feed them well when we can't feed ourselves? The rich use casual labourers for transportation – they don't have to feed humans. It's cheaper than looking after oxen which have to be fed the year round.' Even in the early '80s, surveys estimated that the annual minimum cost of maintaining an animal in rural India was around Rs.1,169. Nearly 60 per cent of that went towards animal feed. Though no current official estimates are available, maintenance costs have clearly spiralled since then.

The bullocks here are clearly a weak, emaciated lot, unlike their healthy neighbours in Bilaspur. 'I once had to hire a bullock-cart to fetch a 5 HP diesel pump across sixteen kilometres,' says advocate Mohan Kumar Giri of Surajpur. 'It proved enormously difficult. Finally, I paid a mere Rs.15 for hiring the cart, but Rs.100 for hiring the bullocks. People were afraid their bullocks would die in the tough, unrelenting terrain here.' So the owners imposed strict conditions on the place of travel, and Giri took roughly seven hours to cover the sixteen-kilometre route.

M.S. Singh Deo, former Raja of Surguja (now vice-chairman of the state planning board) says he has 'no comprehensive explanation for this phenomenon. I think it has something to do with the fact that historically Surguja's great forests had very large numbers of tigers. Our "roads" were in fact forest trails. And cattle attracted the tigers like magnets.' Singh Deo believes that even the few carts that lie unused 'were probably given to the people during some official bullock-cart distribution scheme or something like that'.

But surely, emaciated bullocks and dangerous forest trails exist in some other parts of the country as well which *do* have bullock-carts? In Batra village, however, Balram Prasad Singh gave us another explanation. This one had most of the elements of the others. But, going beyond them, it focused on the dismal employment situation in Surguja and on the social contract thrown up by that.

'True, the trails are bad and the strain more on the bullocks,' says Balram Prasad Singh, 'but the use of bullock-carts means you have a surplus to take to the market. Here the vast majority have very little produce to take to market. Since they transport so little and bring so little, they use their shoulders to carry it and their feet to walk the distance.

'Besides', he pointed out, 'the small farmer here is unable to sustain himself on his land (and many have no land) and produce. He earns a small but vital amount doing menial jobs and errands for bigger farmers, carrying the big man's goods and produce for him. A bullock-cart would hurt that income. So we don't use bullock-carts in Surguja.'

That rings true. As market day approaches, even the remote roads are dotted with human beings carrying loads that are too small for carts but which seem shattering for human shoulders. And carting stuff by shoulder is a major source of employment in this district. The Surguja collector, R.K. Goyal, says that tens of thousands of people here find employment for no more than 125 days in a year. After that, it's a struggle for survival.

This is where those extra earnings from human transport become crucial. So farmers who can use bullock-carts refrain from doing so because of the distress it would cause. A senior official in Bhopal calls this the 'subsistence ethic at work'. An unwritten understanding that the better-off should not ruin the little stability the poor have. It springs not so much from altruism as from sensing the possible consequences of putting further pressures on the poor.

Perhaps, just as the visibility of modern forms of transport tends to obscure the role of the bullock-cart, the animal-drawn vehicle, in a sense, does the same to others. It makes the peasants and marginal farmers who depend on head-load carrying less visible. More than 80 per cent of intra-village traffic in India's major regions is carried by porters as head-loads. Yet, this other, major form of transport gets little recognition.

In Surguja, people carry head-loads (or rather, shoulder-loads) across unusually long distances. They often do this with the goods and produce of others, certainly going beyond the intra-village framework. In this, here and nationally, lies another little-known truth. That for the very poor, *the bullock-cart is a relatively advanced and costly technology*. Only 40 per cent of all cultivators in India own a pair of working animals. Most others borrow the animals from their neighbours in return for payments in labour, kind or, sometimes, even cash. A few landless labourers also possess animals and earn part of their living from hiring out these for ADV work.

Surguja tops in the transplantation of rice in Madhya Pradesh and its productivity is not far below the state's average. Its wealth, though, is concentrated in the hands of a few. Hence many, in acute poverty, 'have nothing to take to the market'.

Surguja's poverty goes back a long way in history. The Delhi Sultanate, the Mughals, the Marathas and the British – all levied their lowest taxes or tributes on this state. The Sultans and Mughals mostly settled for elephants. As late as 1919, the British, who were extracting fortunes from neighbouring

In Surguja, people carry shoulder- or head-loads across unusually long distances. For the very poor, the bullock-cart is a relatively advanced and costly technology. Only 40 per cent of all cultivators in India own a pair of working animals.

states, were settling for a pittance here. Each year, they took just Rs.2,500, Rs. 500 and Rs.387 respectively from the local feudatory states of Surguja, Korea, and Chang Bhakhar.

In the last years of the eighteenth century, the Marathas overran the feudatory state of Korea, then under Surguja's suzerainty. They did not take full possession of the territory – finding it too difficult a terrain to control. Instead, they demanded a mere Rs.2,000 from the Raja of Korea. Discovering that he could not pay, they lowered this charge to Rs.200 a year for five years and grabbed several head of cattle in warning. Soon, according to the district gazetteer, even the ruthless Marathas came round to understanding that the Raja could not pay a single rupee. They settled, therefore, for 'five small horses, three bullocks and one female buffalo'.

They then released and even returned some of the other cattle they had looted, finding them largely worthless. The hostilities came to an end and the Marathas marched back.

People still find the cattle worthless from the bullock-cart point of view. And, as young Mahajan asked me in Kerhaya village: *'Yahan, aadmi aur bayl mein kya farak hain.?'* ('Over here, what's the difference between men and bullocks?') In Surguja, human beings are beasts of burden.

The hills of hardship

Godda (Bihar): Dharmi Paharini is four feet three inches tall and weighs less than the 40 kg of firewood on her head. She has come to the *haat* (rural bazaar), set up once or twice a week at Devdanmod from her village Serkattiya, seven kilometres away. But before that she had to walk twenty-four kilometres to the forest and back to cut and fetch the wood, covering thirty-one kilometres in all. She will get eight or nine rupees for it.

The route runs through the Rajmahal hills and the terrain is rough. But Dharmi has to do this at least once a week to survive. She is from the Paharia tribe, one of the worst off in the country. Spread across the old Santhal Paraganas division, there are about 20,000 Paharias in Godda district. The fragility of their existence stays largely unchanged after decades of promises, plans and 'progress'.

Poverty forces Dharmi and thousands like her – in the grip of *mahajans* (moneylenders/traders) – to fell trees in order to survive. For many Paharias, wood is a vital source of income. Many also have to do this for a few *mahajans* who are into timber smuggling. 'This leads,' says Dr Suman Daradhiyar of the Godda College, 'to massive deforestation, upsetting the ecological balance' in a large part of the hilly areas. Dr Daradhiyar's study, *Ecology of the Paharia Community in Santhal Paraganas*, links this to 'the merciless exploitation of these poor and helpless people by the *mahajans*'.

At the *haat*, I tell Dharmi I find it hard to believe she has come all that way with her load. The small crowd around us scoffs. Many women cover greater distances than Dharmi, say a dozen voices. There is only one way to check this out. Starting the next day, we have to do the distance in different areas and hills by accompanying the Paharia women.

It doesn't seem such a bright idea at 6 a.m. the next day, halfway up the Tethrigodda *pahad* (hill) route. To reach some of the Paharia villages you have to cross two to three hillocks. We cover eight kilometres, a good part of it uphill. After much indecisive wandering, we see groups of Paharia women, sickles in hand, striding in single file towards the wooded areas. It is hard to keep pace with their swift, smooth movement. But we huff and puff behind them. Further down the trail we see more groups either moving towards the forest or towards their villages. Each woman has a huge bundle of firewood on her head, weighing 30 to 40 kg.

Behind the seeming vigour and physical strength of the Paharia women is the reality that only a few survive the age of fifty. In several Paharia villages in Godda, it is hard to find either males or females past that age. And many women don't see forty-five.

Guhy Paharini walks over forty kilometres the day she takes the firewood to the *haat*. But that's only a part of the long march in her short life. She has to walk six to eight kilometres a day for water.

'The water source isn't very far away,' she says cheerfully (by which she means two kilometres). 'But I can only carry so much at one time. So I have to do the same distance three or four times on some days.' This is apart from her bi-weekly walk to the *haat*. That water source may be 'just' two kilometres away. But it's a steep and tough two kilometres that really taxes the body.

Guhy's case is not unique. Most Paharia women have to slog in this fashion. As we slither down tricky slopes made even more dangerous by the monsoon, we learn what it means. Paharia women like Guhy walk a distance equivalent to that between Delhi and Mumbai (1,100 km) – four to five times a year.

The men practise shifting cultivation on the hillsides. This is sustainable, if you allow a cultivated plot ten years to regenerate its previous level of forest growth. That was how the Paharias once functioned. But debt, pressures on the land and survival needs have seen slash and burn agriculture returning to the same areas well before ten years. Robbed of that cycle, the forests go bare. Besides, overcultivation of the same areas brings declining returns.

Some strains of beans cultivated here fetch high prices in Mumbai. Not for the Paharias, though. 'I have to sell my crop to the *mahajan* who gave me a loan,' says Chandrashekhar Paharia. So he parts with it at a rupee a kilogram. The Paharias are almost never able to consume the item themselves. It all gets 'sold' to the *mahajan*. Dr Daradhiyar's study estimates that 46 per cent of a Paharia's earnings go directly to the *mahajan* in repayment of debt. Up to another 39 per cent go to the lender indirectly (through the purchase of necessities, etc.).

The balding hillsides look pathetic as we continue wheezing behind the women, down one hillock, up another. In the villages we pass, schools exist only as empty buildings or merely on paper. It's almost impossible to find Paharia women who are literate.

It isn't easy to move twenty metres ahead of the women, taking photographs. Just when we think that we can no longer take the scorching heat and pace, they stop on the slopes to rest and drink water from a stream. That gives us a break to soothe our bursting lungs and shrinking egos. They have been walking for over three hours now.

Dr Daradhiyar's studies show that the streams here are iodine-deficient and of 'a very poor quality'. This seems to have much to do, he says, with 'the miserable general health' of people here.

No water supply systems worth the name exist here. Years of neglect have ensured that. So the Paharias suffer from a range of water-borne diseases. These include diarrhoea, dysentery and liver enlargement. Many also suffer chronic diseases like tuberculosis, goitre and sickle cell anaemia. Besides, this is malaria territory. Gandhe Paharia, at forty-five, the oldest inhabitant of Dorio village, says, 'If a man falls very ill here, there is no hospital nearby. We have to carry him on a cot tied to bamboos for perhaps fifteen kilometres in this terrain.'

The women have finished drinking water and try to answer our questions. Here, a woman's ability to fetch water is on test when she moves in with her future in-laws. Among Paharias, the marriage ceremony itself can come much after the woman moves in with her in-laws.

Etro Paharia, an elder of the Upar Sidler village in the Sundarpahari block, says water is a vital test. 'Only when a girl is capable of fetching water in our conditions is she accepted.'

Giridhar Mathur of the NGO Santhal Paharia Service Society who has worked amongst the tribe for fourteen years, feels the 'probation' aspect is exaggerated. He agrees that the male's work abilities are not similarly on test. But, points out Mathur, the woman too can reject the male on other grounds after moving into his house.

The descent between Tethrigodda and Bhoda Khota is steep, slippery and strewn with sharp stones. The Paharias don't seem to care. 'Roads here,' says Mathur, 'are a sign of exploitation, not development.' He has a point. Paharias closer to the plains are more in the grip of *mahajans* than those in the villages at the hill tops.

Such 'development schemes' as have come here have never involved the

Paharias themselves in decision-making. One experiment saw many Paharia families being given two cows each. The Paharias do not milk cows – surely the milk belongs to the calf?

The Paharias do not consume milk products either, but no one knew this. What they do consume is beef and quite a few of the 'loans' were thus consumed. Others tried using the cows as draught animals, leading to their death in the difficult terrain. Some of the poorest people in the country then made repayments on loans they had never sought.

Government funds, points out Mathur, have only 'fattened the battalions of contractors'. Bullied by corrupt officials, the Paharias retreat further into the *mahajan's* grip. Madhusingh, a politically aware Paharia, sums it up simply. 'Officers are a transient reality. The *mahajan* is a permanent reality.'

Political movements have had limited impact. An agitation led by the Communist Party of India (CPI) freed Paharia lands from *mahajan* control in the '60s and '70s. But the state failed to follow up and status quo ante was restored. Many NGOs, some of them well meaning, have worked years in this region with no success.

Dr Daradhiyar and his co-investigator, Dr P.K. Verma, believe that the tribe is dwindling. The government denies this but accepts that such a risk exists. To fight this, it has announced more programmes that are unlikely to touch the Paharias but seem promising for the contractors and *mahajans*. 'Meanwhile,' says Madhusingh, 'our forests are disappearing. Our land is less, our agony more.'

When we reach the *haat* way beyond Paharpur, it is twenty-four kilometres from where we first saw the women. Through the day we have hoofed forty kilometres. It isn't amusing to remember that I have to repeat this process during the next eight days. The women sell their bundles of firewood weighing between 30 to 40 kg in front of us – for Rs.5 to Rs.7 per load.

In Godda next morning, still aching in every limb, I see the 'Freedom Pillar' set up in 1947. The first name is that of a Paharia; in fact, most of the martyrs listed on it are Paharias.

The first to die for freedom, the last to benefit from it.

Kahars take the count

Nunmatti, Godda (Bihar): When Shiv Shankar Laiya passed his matriculation exam in 1967, it was a big event for the Kahars of Godda. He was the first matriculate from the community, believed by many to be worse off than even Godda's Paharia tribals.

With the passage of time, that achievement has dimmed. Especially since Laiya remained jobless for the next twenty-six years. Meanwhile, the second matriculate, Joginder Laiya, died of tuberculosis. Today, not a single Kahar child in Nunmatti or at Gorighat village within Godda town – where significant numbers of them reside – goes to school. 'Two are enrolled in school,' says Shiv Shankar Laiya, 'but who can afford to send them? It costs money. At least here they tend the goats and pigs.'

A dwindling group, the Kahars (also spelt as Kadar or Kadhar) are poorer and more backward than many scheduled caste (SC) and scheduled tribe (ST) communities. They do not figure in either category, though. That excludes them from the benefits those groups can claim. Few castes have borne so many forms of oppression as the Kahars, with so few defences against them.

They are almost entirely landless agricultural workers. The one exception I met in Nunmatti owns 1/20th of an acre. Even the sites on which they build their homes do not belong to them, but are classified as grazing land. 'You should have seen how the other villagers protested when we built our houses here,' says Sibu Laiya, whose grandfather was the first Kahar to arrive in Nunmatti.

There are Kahar colonies in about fifty to sixty villages in Godda, Banka and Bhagalpur districts of Bihar. In almost no place are there more than 200 of them and they do not exist outside the Santhal Parganas division. Other castes shun them. 'Even the dalits do not interact with us,' says Baldeb Badai of Nunmatti. 'We are not allowed into the vicinity of the others' houses. And they won't even let us catch fish in the river or the regular ponds.'

So the Kahars get fish the only way they can – by draining ditches and catching them with their hands. The Kahars of Nunmatti never get more than Rs.12 daily as agricultural labourers. Those at Gorighat, working mainly as porters, may get up to Rs.20 a day. Neither group finds work on more than 180, or a maximum of 200 days in a year.

Not a single Kahar in any of the groups I meet is aware that the minimum wage in Bihar is now Rs.30.50. Bonded labourers till a few years ago, when a Communist Party of India (CPI)-led struggle helped free them, the Kahars tasted the worst of landlord terror in the area. The landlords sexually exploited Kahar women and forced the men to perform every kind of menial labour.

The purchasing power of this group is negligible. Puran, a young and outspoken resident of Gorighat, says, 'We are totally outside the public distribution system. Who has the money here to buy things, anyway?' The Kahar diet seems to be free of pulses and sugar consumption is unknown.

Their social exclusion hurts in other ways, too. Almost no member of the community has been able to develop skills that could at all add to income. Since they are landless, this is a major problem. There are no carpenters or masons, though some do assist people in those crafts as unskilled helpers. Recently, however, a few have started performing in music bands. Baldev Badai is now leader of a thirteen-member brass band that sometimes get to play at public functions.

No such functions, however, light up Gorighat itself or the Kahar colony in Nunmatti. Both are always in darkness. No one here can afford kerosene and electricity is non-existent. Again, being outside the SC/ST categories, residents can't get any of the housing programmes at least theoretically available to those groups. The average Kahar home is really a hovel. Human beings share it with the pigs and few head of cattle they rear. Not a single Kahar dwelling has a door. 'What have we got to steal?' asks Surja Devi. 'We can't afford food, so why talk of doors?'

'How can we manage on four to five rupees a day with six family members?' asks Leela Devi. 'Even the old people in this community are not getting any pension. [The Bihar government gives Rs.100 monthly as social security pension to the aged.] Two of my sons ran away to a place called Kalyan near Mumbai. Have you heard of it?'

In Kalyan, too, the sons are casual labourers, unable to send any money home. But Leela Devi is happy they got away. 'Several days, we eat very little and some days we go without food,' she says. Alcoholism is making inroads and the men, says Matangi Laiya, 'are wasting more and more money on liquor.' The oldest Kahar, Jagdev Laiya, estimates that the younger men spend not less than a fourth of their daily wages on liquor.

There are probably fewer than 15,000 Kahars spread across Godda, Banka and Bhagalpur. They scrape out a living in brick kilns, earth works, harvesting – but always in seasonal occupations. No one has ever bothered to

141

make a systematic count of their actual number. Official data relating to them seem to be flawed. 'They don't count us because we don't count,' says Jagdev Laiya. 'We don't have enough votes to make a difference. It is very difficult to organise our people into a movement if they are scraping around for an existence. Worse, we are uneducated and illiterate.'

The main Kahar demand, in the present context, is that they be included in the scheduled caste list. This is a race against time. As political activist S.P. Tiwari puts it: 'They are a vanishing group and don't count in electoral politics. In every one of their settlements, you hear of how there are far fewer households today than ten years ago. This is a group that has tasted oppression in every form and in all respects.'

Yet the Kahars are not quite passive. Resentment runs deep amongst them and with it the realisation, articulated by Surja Devi, that 'we are in fetters because we are uneducated'. Education and land are the two demands they make, beyond being listed as SC. And if those demands are not met, there may be no Kahars to count some years from now.

And his name was Tuesday

Mudulipada, Malkangiri (Orissa): His name, he said smiling, was Tuesday. His wife's name was Saturday. He had two daughters, both named Sunday and a young son – Wednesday. Members of some ancient tribes often name their children after the day on which they were born. But the Upper Bondas of Malkangiri, especially those in the interior villages, follow this practice with ritualistic rigour.

Hence, the Bondas call a man born on Monday, Soma, and a woman Somvari. They name a woman born on Tuesday Mangali, while naming a man born on the same day as Mangala. The Bondas also name their animals in the same fashion.

Malkangiri district in the Koraput region of Orissa state is the only home of the Bondas. They live nowhere else. One group in the foothills is called the Lower Bonda. They have increasingly become culturally different from the others. The second lives at 3,000 feet above sea level in the hostile hills. This group is called, rather predictably, the Upper Bonda. The term now in vogue is Bonda. Some experts used to call them Bondos. Official documents for long referred to them as Bonda-Paroja.

All these, in any case, are the names conferred on them by outside society. Within the tribe they call themselves Remo, meaning, simply, men. Ethnologists regard the Bondas or Bondos as members of a young group of Austro-Asiatic tribes that had, at some point in antiquity, migrated and settled in the Jeypore hills. There were just 4,431 Bondas in 1990. The Malkangiri collector G.K. Dhal says the Bondas appear in a list of the fifteen most 'primitive' tribes in the world. They are dependent on food gathering, hunting and a type of shifting cultivation.

Wet cultivation, too, has come up, alongside shifting cultivation. The official Bonda Development Agency estimates that, on average, a cultivating household owns just under one acre of land. Of this, only a third of an acre is wet land where they might grow rice or wheat. Just over half an acre is land on which they raise millets and pulses. A tiny fraction of an acre allows for the homestead and kitchen garden. These are individually owned. But clan groups collectively own the areas in which shifting cultivation goes on. In every case, women do the bulk of the work.

143

The Bondas are victims of both backwardness and popular prejudice. The collector and officials of the Bonda Development Agency project are trying to fight that, but it hasn't been easy. The government posted ten teachers between 1988 and 1992 to the Upper Bonda area. Not one took up the post, terrified at the thought of living amongst the fearsome Bondas. Even when the teachers had their pay docked in punishment by the government, several still would not take their posting.

Police officers meant to be at the Mudulipada colony in the Bonda hills stay in Khairiput at the foothills. They work from there. Bus drivers, charging the Upper Bondas with violence and ticketless travel, have terminated bus services between Khairiput and Mudulipada. This means a fourteen-kilometre walk to reach the first settlement if you do not have a jeep. Besides, homicide levels are outrageously high, the worst within any single group in the region.

Hardly an inspiring picture, but one much overdone. The high level of homicide is almost entirely *within* the community and seldom touches outsiders. Crimes such as theft and burglary seem unknown. We moved unhindered in the Upper Bonda villages. And we found that the few times they moved downhill and used a bus there, they paid the fare like anyone else.

The children at Andrahal love their unusual school run by the Bonda project. Their young teacher, Mangraj, is not even a matriculate and his helper, Ahilya, is a Class VII dropout. Neither is a Bonda, but both function untroubled. Some of the stereotypes, too, are breaking as people learn more about the tribe.

'Contrary to what many think,' says Ahilya at the curious Andrahal school, 'the children want to learn.' Ahilya gives them two meals a day, which is a big incentive for them to come to school. As we spoke, quite a few underage children forced their way into the classroom in order to be with their older siblings. They were feeling left out. Maybe the teachers who ran away need to come here and see this.

Some officers dealing with such groups are unhappy with the words 'primitive tribe'. They point out that the negative connotations that go with it do not help. That official term draws on criteria like declining or stagnant population and very low levels of technology. Also, dismal educational standards, extreme socio-economic backwardness and other problems of some ancient tribes. No one, however, is happy with the term. 'Maybe we ought to say "pre-agrarian groups" instead,' says one expert. 'Why brand people "primitive"? It's very dicey, this word.' But with a lack of fresh thinking at the policy levels, such jargon remains in use.

Stereotypes breed fears. And those fears have hurt programmes among the Upper Bondas. Their literacy rate was as low as 3.61 per cent in the '80s. That is

way behind even the disturbing 13.96 per cent for Orissa's total tribal population. Among women, the rate is next to negligible. The Upper Bondas have just
one matriculate, Mangala Chalan. A teacher at the Mudulipada High School, he
was away when we reached there. Instead, we met Gusum and Adibari, the first
working women of the community. That is, both were helpers at the school, and
financially independent of their families in the villages.

Gusum and Adibari motivate Bonda children to come to school – not
every school is like the one at Andrahal. 'When the mother does all the work in
the field,' says Adibari, 'and the father goes to the *solap* [sago-palm liquor] tree,
who will look after the little ones? That's why it is hard for some of the older
children to go to school.' Infant mortality rates (IMR) amongst the Bondas
have been dreadful; at times, higher than 150 per thousand. That's worse than
even Orissa's tragic 122 per thousand.

Adibari and Gusum have faced no hostility despite their breaking with
tradition – in clothing, for instance. The traditional Bonda woman wears a
single piece of cloth around her waist. This is around a metre in length, and
about 40 cm in width. The women weave it themselves. The women wear
many bead necklaces, aluminium bands, brass bangles and other ornaments.
Some also shave their heads with rather primitive implements. This often
results in cases of tetanus.

'The shaving of the heads,' said Gusum, 'is tied to a superstition about an
ancient curse. Apparently, thousands of years ago, Sita Devi [wife of the
Hindu deity Ram], offended by the way some of them laughed at her,
condemned all Bonda women to nakedness and to shaving their heads. But the
main thing about the clothing that worries me is that the children often fall ill
in the cold weather.' She does not want things forced on people against their
will. But she would like to see the younger ones suffer less from exposure in the
Bonda hills where it gets nasty during the winter months.

Bonda huts are without ventilation and the tribe's building skills are behind
those of other groups in the region. That these could be vastly improved is
beyond question. However, some of the schemes that come up are not. At one
point during our stay, some officials came up with a plan for tin roofs for all the
Bonda huts. 'This,' pointed out a project officer, 'will fry them in the summer
and also keep them dependent on merchants and officials for repairs.'

The Sita legend and others like it seem to have sprung from early attempts
to assimilate this ancient people within *Puranic** Hinduism. For the greater part,

---

* From *Puranas* – A compendium of legends, mythologies, beliefs and rituals. The major
Puranas were mainly produced between the third and twelfth centuries AD.

Traditional Bonda women wear a single piece of cloth, which they weave themselves, around the waist. Some also tend to shave their heads with rather primitive implements. This can result in cases of tetanus.

the Bondas retain their own religious customs. And their fearsome image has had some positive spin-offs. For instance, the forests around them – which are not reserved – have been free of timber smugglers. Now their exposure to outside society is growing. And a tribe that has largely remained the same for millennia finds its world swiftly changing. Sometimes for the better. Often, sadly, for the worse.

Footloose, not fancy free

Pudukkottai & Tirukkattapalli (Tamil Nadu): There would be no second crop. Mariappan and his eight-member family had no food reserves and had jointly earned less than Rs.200 in April. Early in May, he decided to become an 'unseasonal' migrant. Taking his wife and children with him, Mariappan left Pudukkottai district.

The families of Manickam, fifty-two, and Muthuswami, thirty-seven, took the same decision. Like Mariappan, both owned drought-withered plots, about a third of an acre in size. They had earned almost nothing in April. The state's mid-day meal scheme was all that was keeping the younger children going. The elders were having meals of *Koozh* (a gruel prepared from millet) once, if very lucky, twice daily. With the rise in prices of grain on the controlled public distribution system (PDS), rice is out of reach. Both families were from the denotified Ambalakkarar tribe.

The purchasing power of Pudukkottai's people has been abysmal at the best of times. One partial measure of that is the Thompson rural market index. This is aimed at 'advertisers, marketers, media planners and practitioners'. Its task is to assess 'the market potential' of 383 rural districts. The index comprises twenty-three indicators ranging from pumpsets and tubewells to electrification.

Thanjavur district, also in Tamil Nadu state and immediate neighbour to Pudukkottai, tops the 383 districts. It scores the maximum of 100 on the index. And Pudukkottai? Its score on the index is just 10.97. And even this clubs the whole population together. Within that, the purchasing power of the Mariappans and Manickams would be negligible. With drought capturing their district this May, thousands of agricultural labourers from Pudukkottai left their homes. Over 160 families quit the single hamlet of Tulakampatti alone. Some left the elders behind. All took their children with them.

Where did they go? What work could these migrants find when major agricultural operations in Thanjavur were over for the season? What are the survival strategies of the poor? What happens to the older people left behind? What do they eat? Where does their food come from? Who pays for the little that they do eat?

One way of knowing was to trace the migrants at their new workplace, if

147

they had one. This meant talking to families, middlemen, lorry owners, contractors. In several cases, the families had no clear idea. 'They've gone for *coolie* [physical labour on a casual basis] work,' was the common reply in village after village where whole groups had left. The complication was that these were not 'regular' migrants with a structured schedule. These were 'footloose' migrants going *anywhere* they believed it was possible to scrape out an existence.

Some went towards Kerala, some to neighbouring Pasumpon district. Others went to just about anywhere they could make a few brooms, cut some trees, or labour at desilting tanks. Work that would bring in maybe Rs.12-15 daily, and last perhaps four to five days – after which they would have to move again. Most days in the month, many go jobless. On several days that they worked, it would be just for a meal.

Searching for the footloose migrants brought back the lines of a Simon and Garfunkel song famous over twenty years ago:

Laying low
seeking out the poorer quarters
where the ragged people go
looking for the places
only they would know.

Tracking representative groups took time. The skills of Raj Kumar, an economist who did his M.Phil thesis on poverty from the Bhartidasan University in Trichy, came in most handy. Now, towards the end of May, we traced the very families that had left Tulakampatti.

They had been 'lucky', having found a month's work. Moving across the border, they had first gone to Thanjavur city. From there they went to an isolated point outside Tirukkattapalli in west Thanjavur district. Here, for a maximum of three months (usually less), they can become brickmakers.

'Those who come in as regular agricultural labourers,' says A. Kalidos, a Kisan Sabha (Peasants Association) leader here, 'can be unionised. Their rights can be defended. But these sort of migrants, though desperately poor, are too difficult to keep track of. The very nature of their movements ensures that. We can't unionise them.' Thus, though earning something, they are more vulnerable to exploitation.

Here, they buy food at higher than market prices, pay higher rates for everything because of their dependence on the contractor. Even tea expenses can run to a few rupees every day for a family.

Work began around 3.30-4 a.m. because the bricks have to be ready for the sun. Since the work was on a piece-rate basis, it goes on for long hours. When we found them in the kiln, the sun was scorching bricks and humans alike. It is the contractor's responsibility to look after the kiln. But if the bricks made by a family got damaged due to some calamity like rain, he deducted the entire value from their wages. Even otherwise, the moment a family completed making 1,000 bricks, the contractor deducted the value of fifty as 'damaged' without even looking.

Manickam, whose deserted house we had visited in Tulakampatti, was here. He said that if his five-member family worked very hard 'we can make 2,000 bricks at a payment of Rs.55 per thousand. But after the first week the payment is reduced to Rs.45 per thousand.'

If they produced around 11,000 bricks a week, he said, each one of them would get an average of Rs.90 or Rs.100 per week, or Rs.13 to Rs.14 per day. This placed them way below the poverty line or almost half way below the minimum wage for the area. Their ration cards showed that each of these families has a joint income of around Rs.300 to Rs.350 per month.

Manickam said the one luxury the family could afford in Thanjavur district was rice. They spent about Rs.180 to Rs.200 of their earnings on just this. Dependent on the contractor, they paid inflated prices and spent about Rs.250 on items like fuel, tea and other necessities. In some cases, they made further petty payments to the contractor. With this, their expenses were already running dangerously close to their total weekly earnings.

There was, however, another important expense to come. It applied to those who had left elderly relatives behind in the village. The entire family returned to their home in Tulakampatti every Friday, the weekly holiday. 'On this day we carry food worth Rs.10 to Rs.12 with some chillies and onions for our elders,' said Muthuswami. The elders confirmed this. They looked forward to Fridays. 'On that one day,' said Mariamman in Tulakampatti, 'we don't know loneliness and hunger.'

The average family spent about Rs.40 or 50 a week on bus fares. This came to three times the amount they spent on the food they take for their elders. But they have never failed to keep the date. In the course of their unseasonal jaunts, they could be commuting several thousand kilometres. The children would never see a school.

'It is an extremely fragile survival game,' said Dr K. Nagaraj of the Madras Institute of Development Studies. 'This sort of footloose migrant lives in a permanent zone of very low income and very high insecurity. It just takes one illness in the family, or one wedding, for the whole thing to fall apart.'

149

Yet, in Muthuswami's words, things were 'better than in Pudukkottai where the fields have all dried up'. An agile resourcefulness born of desperation had kept the family alive. One great difference between Thanjavur and Pudukkottai was the fine irrigation and water facilities of the former. Here, affluence and agony were close neighbours.

The ones that didn't get away

Pudukkottai (Tamil Nadu): What would a map of human movement in the districts of Pudukkottai and Ramnad look like? Draw one and you will have something resembling a giant anthill with enormous activity. It would, of course, reflect the long-term, permanent migration this region is famous for. Also crowding it would be the routes of short-term, medium-range migration and footloose, neighbourhood migration. There would, however, be some fixed points.

Some of the poorest don't even have the option of migrating.

Heavy debt has trapped Chinniah, a dalit in the Annavasal block of Pudukkottai district into staying put. The landlord who loaned him money has first call on his labour. When he needs that labour, he will summon him. Chinniah has to be on standby even during the good days of the harvest season.

In Pudukkottai and Ramnad, you can find ration cards issued as recently as March 1993, recording a joint income of Rs.250-300 per month for families with up to eight members. Like Chinniah, most tend to be in eternal debt.

Their tiny holdings (or, in the case of many, no holdings at all), deprived of water, would be difficult to live off at the best of times. Even allowing that there are no big landlords in this district, land reform in Pudukkottai has largely been a fraud. (The same is largely true of the rest of Tamil Nadu.)

As early as 1972, an official report concluded that the state had taken into its possession less than two per cent of 2.1 million acres declared surplus in Tamil Nadu. Worse, successive governments distributed a total of just about two-thirds of that two per cent of land.

In Pudukkottai, an official study done in 1992 speaks of families in villages like Sirumarudhur which own land in six different names. It also records instances of another kind of crime. Even where surplus land was now legally in the possession of the peasants, the old landlord continued to extract rent from them.

In retrospect, says the report, 'many of the assignees were lackeys of the surplus land holders. And (in some cases) land reform remains only on paper.'

Nor does industry hold out a great hope for the poor over here. Fly-by-night operators have milked the incentives offered by the state for setting up industries in backward areas. They set up units that fold up just as the five-year concessions period runs out.

Ziauddin, a local trade union leader, says the pressures on workers are great. 'Even the militant trade unions are reluctant to press the wage issue here. The need for employment is too desperate.'

'Give us three acres and just a little water,' says Govindrajan of Kovilpatti, 'and we will make this district work.' The people of Periakottai agree. Mistaking me for a government officer, they eagerly point to undistributed surplus land in their village. A political bigwig who lives elsewhere, like other absentee landlords, holds these tracts *benami**. Land reform is just not on the agenda in Tamil Nadu. Meanwhile, private control of the region's limited water resources grows by the day.

Under such conditions, drought and footloose migration seem inevitable. Astonishingly, many thousands of migrant families may never be classified as such. National Sample Survey (NSS) data are certainly the best we have. Yet these data draw on a curious definition of the 'last usual place of residence' of a migrant. That is: the village 'where the person has stayed continuously for at least six months immediately prior to moving to the present village/town where the person is enumerated'. (NSS 43rd Round.)

Many of Pudukkottai's migrants have not stayed in any place for six months. Only some of those who have gone to Thanjavur may have done so. Thus, many who are migrants in the real world, and should be dealt with as such, stand excluded by this kind of a definition. As one officer here puts it: 'It makes you wonder. Are we trying to deal with migrants? Or just banish them by definition?'

No one really knows how many footloose migrants there are. 'Nor are we likely to know,' says the officer, 'as long as we pretend they don't exist. Or as long as we don't treat them as migrants.'

The same survey sums up the 'economic factors' behind migration no less curiously. For instance: the search for employment, the search for better employment, and transfer of service/business contract.

Dr K. Nagaraj of the Madras Institute of Development Studies finds this a flawed approach. 'It does not essentially differentiate,' he says, 'between a corporate executive moving from Mumbai to Delhi for a better deal and an agricultural worker pushed by poverty from Pudukkottai to Tirukkattapalli.'

---

* *Benami* – a transaction where a major party, often a buyer or owner, remains anonymous. Land owned by one person but held under the name of another would be a *benami* holding.

The first is exchanging an already high standard of living for an even better one. The other is into a survival game. But that seems unimportant. Such a definition does not treat a top business person like Russi Modi shuttling between Jamshedpur and Calcutta differently from a Muthuswami who has left his home in Gandarvakottai to cope with the drought. Maybe someone should tell Muthuswami about this. He might be pleased.

6

Lenders, Losers,
Crooks
&
Credit

Usury, debt and the rural Indian

Moneylenders binding peasants in eternal debt? Interest exceeding commercial rates and legal limits many times over? That sort of thing on a large scale, I was assured, went out 'with nineteenth century Bengali literature'. On the eve of setting out for the ex-*zamindari* area of Ramnad, I found that confusing. Earlier forays in rural reporting had suggested otherwise. But it seemed my notions flew in the face of evidence.

After all, the Integrated Rural Development Programme (IRDP) had covered millions of households with loan-cum-subsidies worth billions of rupees. Many soft credit schemes had covered the rural poor. Loans from banks and other formal sources had begun to account for the major share of rural debt. From this, it was possible to infer that dependence on private moneylenders was swiftly falling. Better still, the use of physical violence to recover loans had declined.

In this cheerful scenario, usury would not demand much of my time in the poor districts. After all, government policy did target the poorest. And private interest-free loans argued that things could not be all that bad. That was before Ramnad gave me an idea of how a landlord's 'interest-free' loan or 'advance' could bind a family in serfdom for generations. And before eight districts taught me how 'institutional credit' worked; how moneylenders could set the agenda within poor villages; how levers other than physical violence were no less capable of ensuring repayment.

Maybe the authors of nineteenth century fiction were more effective in expressing the reality of their times than some late twentieth century social scientists have been in capturing the reality of ours.

The last published All-India Debt and Investment Survey came in 1981-82. It showed that the average debt per agricultural household had shot up by about 139 per cent in the decade covered by the survey. Further, indebtedness had gone up in every state but Assam. In many states, more than 75 per cent of agricultural labour households were in debt. Dalits and tribals were the worst off. Household consumption was the single largest factor pushing people to take loans.

157

One claim is that the arrival of the IRDP in 1978 changed much of this. After that, the share of bank and institutional lending gets bigger, and formal credit covers many poor families for the first time. But this is misleading in some ways.

There are many strata within the poor, and different levels of poverty. The lower down the ladder you are, the less likely it is that such credit will cover your family. The Reserve Bank of India pointed this out as late as 1987. True, institutional sources accounted for 60 per cent of cash debt in India. But they accounted for as little as 6 per cent of the debt of households owning assets worth less than Rs.1,000.

In some places, in parts of Tamil Nadu for example, agricultural workers may have gained slightly greater access to such credit. But in others, such as in parts of Bihar, they stand excluded. That makes them turn to informal credit sources like the moneylender. Besides, despite the relief the IRDP has brought some poor families, it has also seen enormous misdirection and leakage. The findings of the Project Evaluation Organisation of the Planning Commission show us that.

In one year, the Comptroller & Auditor General (CAG) ran a 'test' audit of the IRDP. The auditors found, even in the limited sample they examined, 'diversion of funds for other purposes' in excess of Rs.160 million. Quite a bit of this had little to do with rural 'beneficiaries'. It had much to do with corporate hucksters, though. Close to a fifth of the sum used for wrong ends went to bodies linked with urban-based corporates.

The auditors also listed some of the items that had cost the country Rs.160 million. These included 'air conditioners, colour televisions and three-wheeler scooters'. Also, 'jeeps and matadors . . . printing of diaries . . . whisky, rum, beer, soda, lunch, tea, biscuits, etc.'

This is not to say that IRDP loans have never helped poor people. Just that, within the existing political and social framework, such help is likely to be marginal. Seepage, however, is likely to be great. That can only hurt those who really need state credit.

In the early years after bank nationalisation in 1969, rural credit through banks did help tens of thousands of families. It did so even for a while later. But waning political commitment at the top meant declining impact below. By the '90s, just a hundred towns – of a total of 3,768 – accounted for 65 per cent of *all* bank credit in India. Within those, Mumbai, Calcutta, Delhi, Chennai (Madras), Ahmedabad,

Bangalore, Hyderabad and Kanpur grabbed the lion's share. Rural India was way behind.

Besides, even rural banking at its best ran into the reality of village power structures. That often meant that while some did benefit, the poorest got the least.

In most states, the *panchayats** were and are a farce. As a result, many of the *gram sabhas*† involved in identifying beneficiaries did much damage. In parts of Bihar, families of the *sarpanchas* (*panchayat* heads) were often 'multiple beneficiaries'. This means the same family was able to get loans from more than one scheme.

People in Bihar know they have to spend money just to enter the race for an IRDP loan. It was in Palamau that I first heard IRDP given a new and creative name: *Isko Rupiya Dena Padega* (we have to pay for this). Besides, the collapse of the old rural credit format after 1989-90 really hit the poor.

Take the case of a small tribal farmer getting 'a loan of Rs.8,000' under the scheme. Before 1989-90, he would have paid interest of 6.5 per cent to 8 per cent. Today, he would pay 12.5 per cent interest. But surely that is much less than the 18 per cent anyone would pay in Mumbai or Delhi? Not really. It could actually work out to more.

In countless instances, petty government officials and the local bank officer slice off Rs.3,000 as their cut. The 'beneficiary' thumbprints a document saying he received Rs.8,000 and pays interest on that amount though he got only Rs.5,000. In effect, he is paying an interest of 20 per cent, way above commercial bank rates. Beyond this, he returns Rs.3,000 that he never borrowed.

Further, people have been given cows or sheep as part of these schemes. No one checks to see if they can cope with the costs of feeding those animals. Very often, poor beneficiaries I met had lost the animals to disease or simply could not afford to feed them, leading to their death. They had even paid insurance premiums on these live-stock.

An incisive study on 'Wage Labour and Unfreedom in Agriculture' by Dr V.K. Ramachandran touches this aspect. In a Tamil Nadu village he surveyed in 1986, he found that 'not a single household . . . that had

---

* *Panchayat* – Earlier, simply village council. Now often comprises more than one village. To be elected by direct voting.

† *Gram Sabha* – Sub-sect of a *panchayat* and coterminous with a revenue village. The smallest unit of Indian electoral democracy.

been a beneficiary of IRDP schemes for the purchase of cattle or sheep still had an animal'. Moreover, insurance claims were not settled though the claimants had paid the premiums. As he put it, this was a 'cruel epitaph to IRDP for many poor households'.

In Godda in Bihar, officials made Paharia tribals 'beneficiaries' of schemes they had not asked for. They gave many families two cows each. The purchase of the animals was usually riddled with corruption anyway. Officials bought pathetic specimens cheap and handed them over to poor households. In Godda, ignorance about that tribe made matters worse.

The Paharias do not consume milk products, but no one knew this. What they do consume is beef and quite a few of the 'loans' were thus consumed. Others tried using the cows as draught animals, leading to their death in the hard terrain. Some of the poorest people in the country then made repayments on loans they had never sought.

Bashing 'profligate populism' and the unpaid debts of small farmers has kept many editorial writers busy a long time. True, millions of small farmers together owe Rs.210 billion to institutions. Yet, a fraction of their number in the form of big and medium businessmen owe the country's banks nearly three times as much. But the dues of big business do not excite editorial writers. They know where their salaries come from.

In village after village, peasants spoke of their experiences in obtaining official loans: of the many visits they had to make to towns across long distances; of bribes they had to pay to petty officials; of the unending certification process and of working days lost; of big expenses incurred in this run-around.

Household consumption is the main factor leading people to seek loans. Then come marriages and other ceremonial occasions. As do house repairs, productive purposes and the rest. State credit is not available for consumption loans. But what could be more pressing for those unable to ensure the next meal?

In the village, the moneylender is a neighbour of sorts. A peasant seeking Rs.3,000 does not have to run around for weeks. He will get precisely that sum (sometimes minus the first instalment of interest). No one asks him to explain why he is borrowing the money. The interest may finally kill him, but in the short run he gets the loan.

And that brings up this point: the issue does not *end* with heaping denunciation on usurers. Vicious as it often is, usury is linked to the collapse of formal rural credit. It fills a gap. In doing so, it devastates the lives of many. That is crucial. And the stories in this section do try and capture how it does that. But don't lose sight of why and how it arises. And whom it invariably hurts.

With formal rural credit crumbling after 1989-90, even loans for productive purposes are harder to come by. Hence, the peasant goes to the moneylender. The desire to break out of such debt is really strong in rural households, but the chances of doing so are very bleak for many.

The range of loans and their terms are bewildering. There are, of course, cash loans everywhere. Then there are also the 'interest-free' loans of Ramnad, the 'grain loans' of Bhoden, the 'cloth loans' of Khariar, besides other, less important forms. In return, usurers extract land, labour, produce, assets, or combinations of these. In parts of western Orissa, bondage and prostitution have arisen from the inability of peasants to repay loans to creditors.

The word 'moneylender' is no less complex. Full-timers are rare. Most often they are landlords and merchants, or both, plying this trade as one among other activities. These are the big ones. Then there are shopkeepers and petty government officials. And there are also lenders within the poor, though theirs are minor transactions. In Kalahandi, for instance, a group of dalits is into moneylending. But this is a layered operation where the small, local lender plays 'collection agent' for the town-based usurer. However, there are commercial lending deals between poor neighbours as well.

Numbers and categories are vital in explaining indebtedness, but reducing the problem to numbers would be self-limiting. Cash figures tell only part of the story. Moneylending is what moneylending does. Beyond a point, the peasant's ability to cope is so thoroughly crushed that it matters very little whether the annual interest is 120 or 380 per cent.

In Mumbai's red-light area of Kamatipura are women bonded into prostitution. Years ago, their grandparents took loans ranging from Rs.12 to Rs.50. Throughout western Orissa are villages where the breadwinners migrate huge distances not only to earn a few rupees, but also to pay off debts incurred in feeding the family. Across the country are people who have lost their land – and with it their livelihood and status – for the same reasons.

Moneylending creates servility and dependence. The sanctity of repayment, no matter how deceitfully the debt was contrived and how cruel the costs, has been drilled into Indian consciousness since the time of the *Manu Smriti**. 'Manu the Law Giver' listed eighteen main categories of law for the kings in court to decide on. 'Of those,' wrote Manu, 'the first is non-payment of debts.'

Manu's view: 'By whatever means a creditor may be able to obtain possession of his property, even by those means may he force the debtor and make him pay.' The elite, of course, were exempt. While the lower castes would pay a debt or discharge a fine in labour, 'a Brahmana shall pay it in instalments'.

Centuries later, the elite are still exempt. As the inaction on their mountainous debt shows, they don't even have to pay instalments. We could probably do with a couple of nineteenth century novelists to write about it.

---

* *Manu Smriti* – one of the most prominent of the *smritis*. The *smritis*, composed mostly between 200 BC and AD 1000, listed Brahmanical norms of social obligation.

The tyranny of the tharagar

Ramnad (Tamil Nadu): The *tharagar* (commission agent) dips his hands into one of two sacks laid before him by a small farmer and extracts a kilogram of chillies. This he carelessly tosses to one side – as *sami vathal* (God's share).

Ramaswamy, the chilli farmer eking out a living on three-quarters of an acre, watches as though hypnotised. For Ramaswamy can sell his chillies to no one but this *tharagar*. Why? By advancing him Rs.2,000 just before the start of the season, the agent bought up Ramaswamy's entire crop even before it was sown.

This is one important form that moneylending has taken in the ex-*zamindari** area of Ramanathapuram (or Ramnad) in the southern state of Tamil Nadu. Yet, the *tharagar* of Ramnad, one of India's poorest districts, is more than a moneylender. He is often a landholder, a wholesaler linked to the transport business and even, in some cases, an exporter. Ramaswamy's *tharagar* is all of these. And his is a tightly knit fraternity. As the president of the Ramnad Chilli Merchants' Association told me, 'Only those who are our members can operate here.'

Just seventy members of the association control the entire chilli crop brought to the Ramanathapuram town market, and with it the lives of thousands of very poor farmers in one of the country's great chilli-producing districts. Chilli is the biggest crop after paddy in Ramnad.

The moment Ramaswamy entered his *tharagar*'s domain, the agent charged him a commission of Rs.20 – or Rs.5 for every Rs.100 of the total value – on his two humble sacks. Each contains 20 kg of chillies. Only if the *tharagar* does not want the lot will Ramaswamy get a chance to sell it elsewhere.

The *tharagar* has already consulted the wholesalers (who belong to the same fraternity). And he now sets the price along with fellow *tharagars*. They do this by means of a secret language of the hand, fingers clasped and 'talking' under a towel. The actual producer stands watching, in unhappy

---

* *Zamindari* area – A region characterised by feudal relations in agriculture and dominated by *zamindars* or feudal landlords. Holdovers of such relations continue in several parts of the country 50 years after Independence despite the formal abolition of *zamindari*.

awe. The thousands of kilos of chillies brought by the farmers can lie for days in the *tharagar*'s yard while negotiations are on. During this period, they get dried out under the electric lights and fans here. Draining the water out of them in this way finally makes the chillies weigh much less, to the detriment of the farmers.

In this instance, the *tharagar* sets a price of Rs.10 per kg for Ramaswamy's offering. Then comes the *sami vathal*, depriving the poor farmer of another Rs.10 worth of chillies. Next, the *tharagar* cuts payment by a further Rs.20, saying each of the two gunny bags holding the chillies weighs a kilogram. (Actually each weighs less than 200 gm.)

Then Ramaswamy finds that both the bags he had so carefully weighed in at 20 kg each in Keelathooval village, now weigh just 18 kg apiece on the scales. Another Rs.40 to the *tharagar*. Ramaswamy knows he is being cheated but is not clear how. Nor does the *tharagar* explain why he charges his commission on 40 kg but pays only for thirty-two.

By the end of the season, Ramaswamy will have made five trips to the *tharagar*'s lair (with the agent claiming 'God's share' on each occasion), depositing ten sacks in all. For his labours, he will earn, at the price set for him, a total of Rs.1,600. But the *tharagar*, if he is into exports, could earn up to Rs.20,000 or more on the same transaction. He has also got around 40 kg of chillies completely free from Ramaswamy. And he is dealing with hundreds of Ramaswamys.

Even if he was selling only to markets in Chennai, he would get Rs.25 per kg at the least, where he gave the farmer Rs.10 per kg. If he has a good network, he could be selling within neighbouring Kerala state at up to Rs.40 per kg even in the currently depressed market.

Multiply Ramaswamy's agent by seventy and the farmer by several thousand and you have Ramnad. You also have what a senior official here calls, 'a uniquely exploitative relationship'. And a market worth millions in the grip 'of a handful whose entire business is based on trapping the peasant in debt'.

Besides, if the *tharagar* owns land close to that of these farmers, you might find him selling them water. The hatred the poor farmers of Ramnad reserve for the *tharagar* has to be understood against this backdrop.

Take Ramaswamy, again. He spent Rs.3,000 growing the chillies he sold to the *tharagar* for Rs.1,600. Around Rs.300 of his expenses were incurred on hiring the *tharagar*'s electric pumpset for a few hours to pump up water. That places him further in the debt of the latter. He also has a debt hangover from similar deals the previous year. This means Ramaswamy's crop for the next

While the actual producer just stands by looking on, two members of the **tharagar**
*(commission agent) fraternity set the price for the chillies. With one of them standing on
top of a pile of chillies, they discuss a price by means of a secret language of the hand,
fingers clasped and 'talking' under a towel.*

two or three seasons, the seeds of which he has not seen, let alone sown, is
already pledged to the *tharagar*.

There are thousands in the same situation as Ramaswamy, mostly small or
marginal farmers owning an acre or less. In such cases, the agent's control over
the farmer is quite complete. The *tharagars*, though, are quick to point out that
there was 'no interest charged' on the original 'advance'. As for the current
depression in the market, 'Just watch,' says Vidyasagar, a researcher at the

Madras Institute of Development Studies. 'This so-called crash has come simply because they're now buying up stock from the peasants. Once they're through, the prices will go up again in two or three months.'

The chilli farmers of Ramnad see the current depression in prices as rigging by the *tharagars*. Past experience seems to bear out this scepticism. At one point in April, the then collector of the district intervened and pushed the merchants into offering a price of over Rs.200 a bag (of 20 kg). 'They did so' says Bose, a young dalit farmer from Etivayal village, 'in that one market for one week. Then it fell to Rs.80 per bag.'

R. Sridharan, the suave and sophisticated president of the Ramnad Chilli Merchants Association, disagrees. 'Prices are falling due to overproduction. It is happening all over the country,' he says. But why, in that case, do the *tharagars* persist in giving advances to peasants to grow even more chillies when the market has been so poor? 'The advances', says Sridharan airily, 'are a continuous process.'

Of exports, he says: 'In a good season, we can get up to $4.40 per kg.' That's about Rs.150 per kg and is a great deal more than what Ramaswamy, for one, collected on his entire sack of 20 kg. Shridharan is also a wholesaler and exporter. He is most articulate as I interview him in his electronics shop, one of the extremely few that stocks items like washing machines and refrigerators in this town.

What about the government's regulated market scheme here? The merchants scoff at it and the farmers know little about it. Sridharan says that to be effective, it ought 'to give storage facilities to the farmers and credit facilities to us'. He does not say why government should not give credit facilities directly to the farmer. But another *tharagar* does: 'What are we there for?' he asks.

The 'credit facilities' offered by the *tharagars*, says a senior official here, were known in the old days 'as naked usury'. The farmers see it that way in the present day as well.

Natarajan, a dalit farmer from Etivayal, was unable to repay the 'interest-free advance' that he had taken from his *tharagar*. So he had to pledge his next crop as well to the latter. Meanwhile, he needed to survive the season, having sold his crop to the *tharagar* at a fraction of its real value. So he pawned his family's only gold ornaments – worth about Rs.4,000 – with the commission agent. Against this, the *tharagar* gave him a loan of Rs.1,200. The interest rate on this was Rs.10 per month on every Rs.100 of that sum. That is, 120 per cent interest annually. Natarajan knows he can never repay the loan, but could be paying the interest all his life.

'They know that this is precisely what it will come to,' says V. Kasinatha-durai, a local activist. 'That is why the *tharagars* can afford to be most generous with their "interest-free" advances.'

Can this incredible system be broken or even tamed? 'Yes,' says R. Gnanavasalam, district secretary of the Tamil Nadu Kisan Sabha (Peasants Association). 'The state should create a proper market line in Guntur and intervene to assure the producer a minimum price of Rs.25 per kg. Besides, the government should have a weighing system that checks and certifies all bags as they enter town. Further, we need a chilli oil factory here to exploit possibilities that are now left to centres outside the district. And, of course, credit facilities for farmers.'

Gnanavasalam is clear that not much progress can be made unless the cycle of debt is broken. He is actively organising chilli farmers to fight for their rights and hopes to get some of their demands conceded. Meanwhile, Ramaswamy and Natarajan will have to keep on taking their sacks to the *tharagar*.

Slaves with 'salaries' and 'perks'

Ramnad (Tamil Nadu): Meesal village lies about forty kilometres from nowhere. Which is probably one reason why its landowners are able to practise a form of bonded labour that is both clever and vicious, but attracts little attention. At the receiving end are the Chakkiliayans, the lowest strata among the dalits, at the bottom of Ramnad's casteist heap.

Even the Pallans and the Parayans, the other dalit groups here, practise untouchability towards them. The Chakkiliayans cannot even get the barbers among the dalit groups to cut their hair. They themselves are traditional leather workers and cobblers and also drum-beaters.

It doesn't end there for the Chakkiliayans of this village in Mudukulluthur taluka. Almost every single one of the eighty-odd families here has a couple of members trapped in bondage.

It works this way: the landowners pay the bonded labourer a 'salary' and allow him or her a few fringe benefits as well. This means a payment of Rs.1,000 for a whole year and permission to take the leftovers of the last meal of the day home. The owners stoutly insist that it is no more than an employer-employee relationship.

The catch is that the 'employee' cannot work anywhere else and is a virtual slave of the landowner. Jayamani and Armugham needed cash for their daughter, Jayarani's wedding. 'The only thing we had to mortgage,' says Jayamani, 'was our labour power.' So they pledged their son's labour against the advance taken from the moneylender.

From the next morning, their son reported for work to the landowner-moneylender at around 8 a.m. and worked till around 9 p.m. He had to tend sheep and cattle, and do every conceivable job of the owner in the fields besides domestic work in his house. At 10 p.m., he returns home with the leftovers of the last meal in the owner's house. This he will do for one year, on an annual 'salary' of Rs.1,000.

At the end of twelve months, he will go into bondage again for the next year, since the interest on the loan of Rs.2,000 is too high to repay. It was *'pathu rupa vatti'* – Rs.10 per month on every Rs.100 of that sum. Or 120 per cent a year. Already, his father himself has become bonded to the same owner as a result of his inability to keep up the interest payments.

Puchchi, in his sixties, in one of the oldest of the Chakkiliayans. That is his name as recorded on his ration card and it literally means insect. Another name you can find is Adimayee, meaning slave. Their overlords have handed down such names to people of these strata across generations. The names have remained, even been internalised.

Their ration cards show joint family incomes of Rs.200 to Rs.250 a month for households with up to eight members.

Even this, insists Puchchi, was an arbitrary figure arrived at by an officer doing the rounds. 'Most of the year, we earn no cash at all, but he just wrote Rs.250 a month.' There is a pathetic irony in the official queries on the card alongside the income figures. Sample: 'Are double (gas) cylinders available?' Two cylinders and a gas stove cost more than what the entire family would earn in the best months of the year.

Some are slightly luckier than others. Armugham gets fed three times a day at the owner's house, apart from his salary. Others aren't. Bonded female children have to do the same work and more with no 'salary' at all, just the food.

Chitravalli, twelve, daughter of Shanmugham, is bonded without pay. But she can eat at the owner's house and take home the leftovers of the last meal. Velu, fifteen, son of Muthu, is in bondage but earns a 'salary' of Rs.1,400 a year. That immediately goes in paying back interest instalments on the original loan. Velu has been working this way, over twelve hours a day, for five years now. During that period, his master is glad to inform us, his 'salary' has gone up from Rs.1,000 a year to its present grand proportions.

When the master advances a loan of Rs.500, as he did for Srinivasan, twenty-two, six months ago, he immediately deducts Rs.50 as the first instalment of interest. Srinivasan has so far repaid Rs.300 – in only interest. He has little chance of repaying the loan. He has run up more debts with others just to be able to repay a couple of instalments on this one.

We fail to locate a family that did not have some member in bondage. Puchchi's two daughters, Maniapushpam, twenty, and Samiadrall, nineteen, are both bonded without pay. The Chakkiliayans are also weak and backward in other respects.

The dalits of Ramnad are, in any case, worse off than their counterparts elsewhere on some counts. Nationally, the literacy rate of the scheduled castes was, in the 1981 census, around 25.3 per cent. It is nearly 7 per cent lower in Ramnad. Literacy among dalit women is close to 11 per cent nationally, but under 7 per cent in Ramnad. And within the dalit groups here, the Chakkiliayans are right at the bottom. Of 210 illiterates enumerated in

Meesal village over 160 are from this community. Just four of them have ever seen the inside of a high school. They, too, are no longer functionally literate.

Tracking the food habits of the Chakkiliayans can be demoralising. Many families are quite dependent on giveaways and leftovers. Sometimes, the leftovers from their masters' houses can form the main meal. And the great gap between income and expenses ensures indebtedness even for people with such a low food intake.

Caste oppression here has been so bad that even in the recent past the mere sight of a clean-shaven, decently dressed Chakkiliayan was cause enough to spark a riot. The upper castes forced dalits to dress according to their status – meaning poorly. That goes back in history. In the 1850s, the British Governor of Madras tried to change this 'dress code'. He ruled that dalit women converts to Christianity could cover their breasts and shoulders. Till then, the rules set by the higher castes did not permit them to do so. In the 1950s and '60s, this led to a number of the Chakkiliayans converting to Christianity. But that has not helped them much.

This is one community with whom the government has actually tried to intervene. Recognising they were amongst the poorest of the poor, the government in 1981 acquired a piece of land in the village to build them houses. The landowners of Meesal immediately opposed this. The issue hung fire till 1986 when they were finally persuaded to hand over the site.

This means that over thirty families now have some house or house site. But an equal number are without one. On the whole, their status has not changed, with the government taking little interest in challenging caste oppression.

Dalits make up close to 18 per cent of Ramnad district's population and over 90 per cent of them are in rural areas like Meesal. Census data shows almost a third of them to be landless agricultural workers. The rest are mainly marginal farmers and sharecroppers. A young IAS probationer studied over eighty villages in Ramnad around two years ago. In an important but depressing report, he recorded in utter dismay: 'I found that more than 50 per cent of dalit households have assets worth less than Rs.100.' That is, barring a few agricultural implements and tools.

For the Chakkiliayans of Meesal, job opportunities are zero and their landholdings are nil. Even their traditional role of beating the drums at funerals and other functions has suffered. A group led by Puchchi and Shanmugham showed us how their drums had rotted for want of servicing and repairs that they cannot afford. 'At least if these were all right, we could earn up to Rs.750 for playing at an important function,' says Shanmugham. 'But now even that source is gone.'

In a note on slavery in 1871, the Madras Census Commissioner mentioned the Chakkiliayans (clubbing the group along with the Parayans). He wrote that 'without exception, they are slaves of the superior castes'. Over 120 years later that still seems to be the fate of the Chakkiliayans. If slaves can have 'salaries' and 'perks'.

Postscript

Bondage exists here and in some other states in many, often disguised forms. Despite the low priority it gets, the issue won't go away. The Tamil Nadu government says that there are only 'stray cases' of bonded labour in the state. The early months of 1996 saw this claim badly dented. A Supreme Court-appointed commission estimated that the number of bonded workers in the state *exceeded one million*. (And, of course, at the bottom of bondage lies that old factor: debt.)

The commission conducted a survey covering twenty occupations in all twenty-three districts of Tamil Nadu. And, at the end of it, was quite blunt in describing the state's attitude. It said: 'Details provided by the state government and the district administrations do not tally in most districts and even appear fabricated.'

The return of the moneylender

Nuapada (Orissa): With his family owning close to twenty-five acres in an area where the average landholding is mostly less than an acre, Biranshi is one of the big landlords of Amlapalli village in Khariar block. He is also one of the poorest people in a region where acute poverty is the norm. 'Most of my land,' he says almost apologetically, 'had to be leased out to the money-lenders. We've had to do this in every bad year. It started in my father's time, when he had to borrow Rs.50 from the moneylenders during the 1965 drought.'

Today, though he remains owner in name, Biranshi controls less than two of those twenty-five acres. The rest of his land has been 'leased' out in a variety of ways to three or four different usurers. Countless families here have tasted a similar reality. Their land will never return to their control.

Bhoden is the most impoverished block, both in Nuapada district and in all of old Kalahandi. Here too, the moneylenders are in complete control. Poor peasants like Bhagawan, Lakhmidhar and scores of their neighbours owe quite a bit to the usurers and will be at their mercy again next season. Yet they seem 'luckier' than their counterparts in Khariar. Many like them, in several parts of this block, have not lost an inch of land despite being so dependent on the lenders. Nor are they in danger of doing so.

If that sounds curious, the case of Sinapali block seems even more odd. Here the lenders are giving out loans to peasants who, unlike those of Khariar or Bhoden, have no land or assets to mortgage. People like Jagat, Bakardhan and Bandhu Harijan have gained from this strange altruism.

Does it make sense? Plenty. In every block, the moneylenders have set the agenda. They have studied the quality of the land, the infrastructure available, and the potential levers of control. Going by this, they vary the terms of their operations.

Bhagawan, a tribal in the Kotgaon village of Bhoden, explains: 'Our land is rough and hard. Who wants to till it? The moneylenders take our produce instead.' Besides, this is a desolate setting and not many would fancy coming here on a daily basis even during the agricultural season. There are few irrigation facilities worth the name that work. That is why the people of Bhoden have not lost much land. The usurers don't want it.

Bhagawan, for instance, first gave quite a bit of rice free to his creditor in part repayment of his debt. Then he sold his remaining eight bags of rice in a hurry to the same moneylender. 'My family needed cash. We had to sell as fast as we could,' he says. This resulted in his parting with the rice at just under Rs.2 per kg.

Gobardhan Chinda told us he had borrowed no more than a bag of seed from the lender. In return for this, he had to hand over fully half of his produce in repayment. That seems hard to believe. It takes hours of interviews with many people in this cluster of villages to confirm this is not an isolated case. Others have done the same.

The loans arise mostly, but not always, from the desperate need to feed their families. 'The lender,' says Dr S.K. Pattnaik of the NGO Vikalpa, 'gives them paddy loans in the lean season. In return for this, they alienate their produce to him at harvest time. Part of it to repay the loan and the rest because they urgently need to sell their produce to get some money and survive.

'Ironically, the lender stocks up their produce – and during the lean season he is giving them "loans" consisting of the very grain he bought from them. Only he took it from them at throwaway rates during harvest time. So they could be selling him rice at under Rs.2 a kg and, when taking the same rice as a "loan" later on, run into interest rates that ensure they can never repay the debt.'

For Bhagawan, though, the problem didn't quite end with this 'normal' cycle. Illness in the family – malaria is rampant in these parts – soon forced the adivasi to take yet another loan from the usurer. The need to buy food is, of course, a well-known and documented route to debt. But several villagers in the region have also landed in the creditors' nets to pay for such medical treatment as can be obtained here. The interest rates for loans to buy medicines may not be as high as those charged for grain loans, but they are not low either. Bagh Singh borrowed Rs.100 for medicines and owed his creditor Rs.220 by the year end.

Hunger, however, remains the basic impulse. In several villages of the two blocks, Dr Pattnaik and I find interest rates ranging from 120 per cent to 380 per cent a year. (Of course, in one sense, some of these rates matter only in theory after an initial period. Beyond a point, the peasant's ability to cope is so thoroughly crushed that it matters little whether the annual interest is 120 or 380 per cent.) It was only in Bhoden, though, that we came across people alienating half their produce for a bag of seed.

Harigun Chinda explained it to us this way: 'Here, you don't need land. If you have five bags of paddy, that's more valuable than owning land in Bhoden. You can make a great profit on it by lending it out and manipulating those in need. Or you can own land and sink deeper into debt. With five bags of paddy, you can get twenty. With twenty acres, you can lose it all. So who wants the land?'

The peasant does not reach the market with that part of the produce which remains after the moneylender has taken his cut. Since Sunday is market day, the usurers set up their own 'procurement centres' along the routes of this remote region. And, as one of them explained, 'We save the adivasis the trouble of travelling long distances to sell their produce.'

Determined to beat this, the district administration set up – perhaps for the first time in the region – a regulated *mandi* (wholesale market). Here they set up an official minimum support price (MSP). This was, for example, Rs.310 and Rs.330 for fine and superfine grain.

The news came too late for Bhagawan: 'After I sold the rice – at less than half the MSP – the *sarpanch* told me about the support price,' he says regretfully. This happened to many. The villagers, however, think the *mandi* – pushed through with great effort by the sub-collector, Saroj Kumar Jha – a worthwhile attempt. Some believe it could succeed next year if persisted with.

If alienation of land explains the situation in Khariar and the loss of produce tells us why creditors give loans without taking land in Bhoden, what explains Sinapali block? Why do usurers there patronise many who have neither land nor assets? Gotti Harpal in Khalna village in that block explains: 'Here, they extract labour services. Since there is no employment here, we have no money to purchase anything. Since we own no land, we can only repay in labour.' For that labour, the moneylenders sometimes give them rice or money at less than one-fourth the Orissa minimum daily wage of Rs.25.

Which means that across Nuapada, the moneylenders have understood the special characteristics of each area and community. They have set up their operations on that basis. They decide what will be the terms of production and extraction from block to block. So in Khariar, moneylenders take the lands of the peasants. In Bhoden, they extract their produce. And, in Sinapali, command their labour virtually free. As a senior official in Bhubaneswar who has worked in several backward districts later told me: 'No government survey can match the information the moneylenders hold on the property, holdings, assets, debts and needs of the peasants. They have it all figured out.'

The peculiar links between land, labour, credit and market have trapped the peasants of Kalahandi region. With formal rural credit shrinking, their plight deepens. So does their dependence on the usurer. The moneylender,

174

once a central character of late nineteenth century literature and indeed of many newspaper reports, is now the forgotten story of the countryside. Existing circumstances have favoured his resurgence in a big way. And the present lot could teach their nineteenth century counterparts a thing or two about exploitation.

Of migrants & mortgages

Nuapada (Orissa): When young Sanat Podh of Kendupatti village got a brand new cycle as dowry, he saw it as opening up new avenues of earning. Like so many others in the Nuapada-Bolangir region of Orissa, he hoped to migrate on a short-term basis to Raipur in Madhya Pradesh where he could earn some 'good money'. That he would do by pulling a rickshaw for some weeks.

However, Sanat couldn't afford the bus ticket to Raipur – till he got this bicycle. It allowed him to develop a fund-raising technique which he explained to me: 'I mortgage my cycle to the moneylender and get Rs.50. That is, Rs.40 for the bus fare and Rs.10 for the food. And in a few weeks in Raipur, I earn several hundred rupees. I come back, pay the lender Rs.150, or whatever the interest has worked out to, and redeem my bicycle.'

This happy transaction took place three times. The fourth time Sanat returned from Raipur, the lender told him his cycle was lost. However, the youngster was not to worry. He would personally help Sanat look for it. A few futile weeks later, Podh asked the lender whether it was not wiser to inform the police. An excellent idea, said the usurer, offering to lodge the complaint himself, on Sanat's behalf. Pointing out that the police would want some documentation, he took the purchase receipt of the bicycle – Sanat's only proof of ownership. It's been a year since.

Sanat is not protected in either of the two states. He is a footloose, short-term worker who does not qualify for protection as a migrant in Madhya Pradesh. In Orissa, the dependence of his whole village on the moneylender will ensure he can't go beyond a point in fighting that gentleman.

Curious linkages exist here between moneylending and migrations, at least in some areas. Some migrants seem to be doing little more than earning money with which to pay off debts. Most laws and regulations work against their interests. So their fragile world is quickly shattered when things go wrong.

When nineteen Odiya migrants died in a factory explosion in Ropar in Punjab five years ago, the labour department of this state sued on behalf of their widows for compensation. The reply was a summons from Punjab directing the widows to come and depose before a court in that state. Most of the women had never stepped out of their own villages.

Pointing out that this made little sense, the labour department here offered to help. It could record the testimony of the widows. Or extend ground support locally to anyone sent by the court to gather evidence in Orissa. Five years have passed without the case moving an inch forward and the victims' families are suffering. The contractors who took the breadwinners of these households to Punjab have not even handed over their dues to the families.

In quite a few places, like Badkani village in Bolangir, or in Khariar in Nuapada, it seems clear that labour contractors have emerged a new class of moneylenders. 'The labour *sardar* (contractor) gave each of us an advance of Rs.350 to come here,' migrants from Kalahandi told me in Andhra Pradesh. The contractor had also given them loans that would keep them coming.

However, he took care to conduct his deals with them in the state of Andhra Pradesh. Why not in Orissa? There he would be subject to the provisions of the deeply flawed Inter-State Migrant Workmen's (Regulation of Employment & Conditions of Service) Act, 1979.

The Orissa labour machinery cannot act in Andhra Pradesh. And there is no law requiring its counterpart in Andhra to intervene on behalf of migrants recruited in Orissa. So the contractor-moneylender has his way in this fashion. He deals with them only in Andhra Pradesh but tells the labour authorities there that he has hired them in Orissa. Contractors using this tactic are pulling migrants from this region all the way to construction sites in Mumbai, perhaps for just eight to ten weeks.

The deals are very often tied up with 'advances' that are simply binding forms of credit. A survey by Vikalpa, a Bolangir-based NGO, is revealing. It shows that short-term migrants leaving this region for periods ranging from just a few months to two years now account for nearly 15 per cent of all migrants.

Debt seems to be a common feature among the migrants. Take the case of Ganga Podh. He suffers whether he has a good harvest or a bad one. When the year is lean, Ganga takes a loan from the usurer at crushing rates of interest (120 to 380 per cent) and ends up a loser. When the next year gives him a bumper harvest, Ganga loses out again as he has already pledged much of his crop to the lender. It is the latter who will encash its real value on the market.

Meanwhile, like many in his position, Ganga scrapes around in off-season migrations, partly to survive, partly to pay off his debts. In the course of this unfair battle, he incurs debts even at those places he migrates to from time to time. 'I owe the lender in Raipur Rs.380,' he says. 'But he knows I will be back, so he gave me some money.' The same is true of the Kalahandi migrants in the brick kilns of Andhra Pradesh. They have incurred fresh debts there, borrowing from their contractor to tide over the occasional crisis. Advances from moneylenders who are also contractors are emerging as a push-factor in migrations.

According to the Vikalpa survey, of the thousands of migrants from the Bolangir-Nuapada region, over 20 per cent go to brick kilns in Andhra. Another 10 per cent go out for farming and agricultural operations, 8 per cent on construction work and 11.25 per cent to pull rickshaws, the last mostly in Madhya Pradesh. The rest go out on a variety of menial jobs. Scheduled caste and scheduled tribe families account for nearly 50 per cent of the total. Almost all are heavily in debt – some at both ends of their journey.

The number of those going out to work on construction sites in Mumbai is small but rising. In villages such as Badkani in Bolangir, I met men like Raghunath and Dulabha Behera who had been to Mumbai. Their experiences – and those of others in Amlapalli in Nuapada and other villages – raise disturbing questions.

They had all enjoyed their visit – usually a single trip – to the great metropolis and thought the Rs.30 a day they had earned there was okay. It didn't always add up to Rs.30, though, when we worked it out. The contractors had given them some money to attract them, but then deducted these amounts from their wages. All conceded that a chunk of anything they earned went to moneylenders back home. What did they like most about Mumbai? 'The traffic,' said Behera. 'That long unending line of cars. It's amazing.'

What happened if you fell ill in Mumbai, I asked? 'The contractor was very nice,' said the Beheras. 'He brought a doctor who gave us a tablet that made us feel very good soon after.'

When at least three others narrated a similar 'positive' experience, I had questions. Could they describe the medicine? They could not. Perhaps they still had some of the tablets with them? 'Oh no. The supervisor stood there while the doctor made us take it in front of him. They left no tablets with us. We are illiterate people.'

I learned that there had been yet others treated the same way. Unfortunately, most had worked at one site in Mumbai for a few weeks or months and could only name big areas like Colaba and Bandra rather than specific locations. Back in Orissa, none seem to be in particularly great health.

Were these people given steroids to boost their work ability? Some NGO activists in Orissa, like Durga Das Patnaik of ASRA, suspect this to be the case. He points out that shady construction bosses have done even worse harm than that to migrant labourers.

Which raises the question: When will government amend the Migrant Workmen's Act to end such exploitation? Or at least to make it very difficult? An equally vital question is: When will government policies deal with the reality that usurers, contractors and their 'advances' are tightening their grip on some of the poorest people in this country?

Take a loan, lose your roof

Ramanujnagar, Surguja (Madhya Pradesh): Almost all the people of the Bamdhabhaisa *falia* (hamlet within a village) are in the yard of Nahakul Pando's house, making tiles for his roof. Everybody is working for free, if you overlook the small quantities of *mahua* wine that Nahakul passes around. If he had to buy the tiles it would cost him a lot of money, by the standards of the Pando tribe. Making them all on his own would be time-consuming and cut into earning hours.

So it is good to see the whole community turn out to help him. This is a feature common to many adivasi cultures. But why had Nahakul been living without a roof for several days? After much embarrassment, he speaks of a loan of Rs.4,800 he had taken a while ago.

The idea of the loan had not really excited Nahakul. Quite a few Pandos are now wary of loans as these have often made them lose their land. But this one was a 'sarkari [government] loan', specially disbursed through the local bank, for the exclusive benefit of the adivasis. So there couldn't be much harm in accepting it.

There was.

'I took the loan of Rs.4,800 to buy two cows (which was the core of the official scheme) but I could not repay it,' says Nahakul. 'There was pressure to pay up the instalments. I sold different things, but I have few objects of value. Finally, I sold the tiles of my roof to raise what little I could,' he explained.

The loan that was to liberate Nahakul from his poverty ended up literally costing him his roof. He doesn't have the cows either. His cash crunch forced him to sell them. Worse, quite a few people in his situation have paid insurance premiums on cattle given to them under such schemes. Often the animals have been of low quality. And often, the villagers have been ill-equipped to feed and look after them. Several cows or buffaloes have died. It is impossible, in most areas, to find anyone who successfully got the insurance money after the death of the cattle.

'The authorities seldom study the likely impact of their programmes on the Pandos. They never even look at their real needs,' says Surajpur civil court advocate, H.N. Shrivastav. 'The officials just have to fulfil targets – so many loans given out, so many "beneficiaries". How has it helped Nahakul?'

180

Sometimes they do more than just fulfil targets. In Wardroffnagar area, a merchant is drawing the disability pension of a crippled Pando tribal. He is also stealing a chunk of his old-age pension. The collusion of petty officials makes this possible. In many villages, non-tribals have taken out loans in the names of adivasis. The tribals mostly cannot read and write. So they are often gypped into putting their thumb impressions on documents they do not understand.

Very often, a Pando granted a loan of Rs.6,000 on paper, gets only around half that amount in hand. The rest is swallowed by bank officials and other go-betweens. The unlucky 'beneficiary', however, pays interest on Rs.6,000. He or she also has to repay the full amount.

There are around 24,000 Pandos in Surguja, concentrated in eleven blocks. They do not fall in the official classification of 'primitive tribe'. Yet they are, in many ways, as badly off as their neighbours, the Korwas, who do. Various unimaginative projects costing tens of millions of rupees have been run for this tribe with predictably dismal results.

The real problems of the tribe receive little attention. In Nahakul's village, there is no tubewell, no electricity, no school, no roads and no employment. On rare occasions a development project brings them some work. Then, government-appointed contractors tend to pay the Pandos half the legal minimum wage of Rs.28 for their labour.

There is not a single child going to school from Nahakul's *falia*, comprising around sixty houses in Parasrampura village of Ramanujnagar block. The nearest school is more than six kilometres away. 'How can the little ones go all the way?' asks Ram Sai. 'There are many snakes in the woods.'

Besides, points out Bir Sai, there isn't much of a school at the end of that walk. 'The teacher is very patriotic. He unfailingly unfurls the national flag on January 26 and August 15 every year,' he says in a mocking tone. Those are the only two days the teacher ever shows up. He has apparently devised a way of drawing his salary without bothering to put in a single appearance on other days.

However, there are sudden bursts of official activity, when the government announces what seems to be giveaways. The loan scheme that cost Nahakul his roof came under one of these. 'Nahakul really thought the government was doing something for him. How could he know that he was merely a target to be fulfilled?' asks Shrivastav. Any project, he points out, is tailored to fit the purse and priorities of governments, not those of the Pandos or of other groups ending up as 'beneficiaries'.

'Nahakul and the others needed money all right,' says advocate Mohan

Kumar Giri, who has accompanied us to the remote village, 'but they couldn't get it for the things they wanted. They had to take it for schemes that had no relevance to their needs. Normally, you take a loan to save the roof over your head. Nahakul took a loan to lose that roof. Now do you understand why so many people still go to moneylenders?'

Postscript

This is, obviously, not a story on usury. But it's important to look at the level to which formal credit in remote rural areas has sunk since the late '80s. In that sense, it is not only about the Pandos but about millions of others across the country. It's just that the forms of absurdity take on a local flavour in different areas. As Mohan Kumar Giri says, the way this system works is at least one factor propelling villagers towards moneylenders.

Knowing your onions in Nuapada

Nuapada (Orissa): This time, Thakurdas Mahanand was sure he had beaten the system. A dalit farmer with a tiny holding of a quarter of an acre, he was sick of selling his onions to middlemen and merchants around his village of Pudapalli. They made profits, he got a pittance. 'So I thought I would take my produce directly to the Tarbod weekly market,' he tells me.

So Thakurdas raised some money and hired a bullock-cart – he had never owned a bullock in his life, let alone a cart – on to which he loaded ten quintals of onions. This time he hoped to sell to the retailers at Tarbod himself or directly on the open market. The bullocks were exhausted by the end of the eighty-kilometre trip to Tarbod.

But Thakurdas's hopes were shattered at Tarbod. 'No one would buy from me. The rates they offered when they spoke to me were grossly unfair and much lower than what they gave to the middlemen who used to bring it to them previously. It was all rigged. They knew I was desperate to sell. Finally, one man picked up four quintals on credit, for which I never got the money even though the rate was so low,' explains Thakurdas.

The traders' monopoly proved effective. 'Even though there were many onion buyers locally, no one could bypass them,' says Thakurdas. 'Onions from that market go on to Khariar Road and from there to outside of Orissa. The bulk goes to Raipur in Madhya Pradesh.'

The wholesaler-retailer-moneylender-merchant linkages are simply too strong for Thakurdas and thousands of other small farmers in the Nuapada-Kalahandi region. Besides, he had an immediate problem. 'If I had reloaded the six quintals onto the cart, I would have killed those bullocks. And they were not mine in the first place.'

So Thakurdas left 60 per cent of his season's produce lying on the streets of Tarbod and went back to his village. 'Onions are perishable. I tried for some days to sell, but then I was needed at home. So I just gave up and left the lot there.' When he next grew onions, which was a long, long time after, he settled for an absurd price offered by his local middleman. All he wanted was payment in cash. By this time, Thakurdas knew his onions.

Cultivation has never been easy in Nuapada. Just 9 per cent of the land here is under irrigation and 91 per cent rain-fed. Yet the rigid cartels in both Nuapada and the entire old Kalahandi region pose far more problems and make things that much more difficult for the cultivator.

Raju Dholakia, a senior member of the local chamber of commerce, says: 'There are about 500 traders including 300 small ones. But only fifteen big families really matter here.' Those fifteen have developed linkages across and between various goods, products and markets.

'There are really just seven big traders in paddy,' says Dholakia. 'And most of the produce from here goes outside the state.'

Its popular image as an area of permanent scarcity does Kalahandi grave injustice. In reality, it produces more food per person than both Orissa and India as a whole do. But its own inhabitants consume only 25 per cent of the food produced here. The rest goes out of the region through the merchant-moneylenders, causing acute local distress.

'The rice mill owner has a monopoly over the trade in paddy. Nobody else can enter it,' says Dholakia. The same families who own the rice mills are also entrenched in pretty much every other business there is. You can walk through the main market in Nuapada and not find any shop there owned by an Oriya local. Marwari traders from Raipur and other parts of Madhya Pradesh own most of them.

There are few spheres of production into which the trader networks have not entered, very few where they are not in control. Raipur is clearly the major base of such networks, whatever the goods or produce. A few hours at the Orissa-Madhya Pradesh border can be instructive. Most of the trucks entering Nuapada-Kalahandi are empty. Most of those headed for Raipur are full.

'The same groups,' says a senior official, 'are into usury through many tiers of intermediaries. They give capital to some merchant-moneylenders, who may in turn give out sums to smaller lenders and so on. Yes, the Kalahandi area has good production figures. Yet the truth is that a huge potential in agriculture even now remains untouched.'

When there is so much money to be made from usurious operations and rigged markets, there is very little incentive for productive investments in agriculture. Even poor Thakurdas, at the bottom rung of this ladder, has drawn his own conclusions about that. 'Now I grow onions for my family and myself. As for my main produce, whatever I grow, I sell to the trader *before the harvest.*'

Organisations of small farmers have begun to emerge, and are trying to change that situation. Bodies like the Banabashi Sangha, Jagruk Shramik Sanghatan (Organisation of Conscious Labourers) and others are coming up with methods, some of them quite creative, to help farmers get a better deal. But it will be a long time before Thakurdas takes his onions to the market.

7

Crime
&
No
Punishment

Targeting the poor

Going to court in some parts of rural India can be quite an experience. Many dalits and adivasis have found it so. Often, their own lawyers treat them very badly. The crimes reported in this section do begin with those tried in the courts. But they go beyond them. There are crimes against the most defenceless. Against those too weak to access the courts. Or even actions defiant of the law itself – where court decisions are flouted or sought to be subverted.

Then there are crimes against whole communities. Like those committed by 'mainstream' society against the Parhaiyas, for example. There are crimes that a stupid political regime and its bureaucracy perpetrate. Like those suffered by the Korwas for instance. There are also crimes that some commit in setting one community against another.

There are the crimes emerging within groups that were earlier free of those particular sort of offences. Like bonded labour within the Bonda tribe. Lastly there are also the follies committed in the name of development. Like the mining of coal by certain methods in Godda. Some of the things that happened there might have been done with the best of intentions. But their effect in destroying the homes and livelihood of many was, nonetheless, a crime.

Bhoodan – *the last believer*

Latehar, Palamau (Bihar): Gopal Singh has fought a curious battle. Decades ago, Vinoba Bhave's *bhoodan* ('Gift of land' – to the poor) movement came to Palamau. At its best, this was a noble attempt to persuade rich landowners to voluntarily give up some acres of their property for redistribution to the poor and landless. At the height of the movement, Gopal's neighbour gifted land to the cause. A very generous gesture. Except that the land belonged not to the neighbour but to Gopal Singh with whom he had a running feud. Gopal then spent close to twenty years fighting to regain possession of the land his neighbour had 'donated' under the *bhoodan* movement.

Shakoor Mia was another who gave generously in *bhoodan*. He gifted eighty-eight acres of land in Vinobanagar. That is an area located at the top of a hill. Over the years, great sums of public money went in developing this remote place and its facilities. That meant a sub-centre, a road, a school. In reality, nothing more than one *kutcha* (crude, unmetalled) road exists. Shakoor Mia's kin have not suffered as a result of his altruism. Their *benami* lands today exceed their pre-*bhoodan* holdings by many acres.

Muneshwar Singh of Rehaldag village was shouting loudly when I met him outside the Latehar court. He had, apparently, reason to be angry. More than twenty-five years ago, Mangra and Ganga Oraon had donated land under *bhoodan*. And Muneshwar's father, Bittu Singh, was the beneficiary. Over a quarter of a century later, the land remains with the two Oraons. But the legal battle for control of it has worn out Muneshwar.

Decades ago, K. Suresh Singh, then deputy commissioner of Palamau, sought to promote the whole area as a *bhoodan* zone. To this day, its people recall his name with respect. The spirit and idealism of the time saw some real achievements. But a good deal of those have come unglued. The voluntarism displayed by the landowning classes was largely driven by opportunism. And the descent from idealism to racketeering in the *bhoodan* movement has been ugly. Palamau has had and still has some of the finest administrative talent at the top levels. Even that has not helped halt this slide.

There are startling exceptions. Bishwamber Dubey of Chandwa, in his late sixties, still gets around on his bicycle, helping the landless. He is all over the place, trying to settle disputes, to retrieve plots grabbed by corrupt landlords. For Dubey, sub-divisional president of the NGO Rachnatmak Karyakartha Samaj (Creative Workers Society), is one of the last true believers. He is also a man of great integrity. Ironically, this makes him the most sincere chronicler of the downfall of a movement to which he has given more than half his life. One thing disgusts him above all else: that the very landlords who were to donate land under *bhoodan* in fact utilised it to acquire more illegal holdings.

'It started idealistically, with a *padyatra** by Vinoba Bhave†, in 1952. And by 1957, redistribution of land actually began,' says Dubey. Bhave's belief was that a direct plea to the hearts of the landlords could work. If it did, they would, on their own, give up some of their surplus lands and these plots would go to landless peasants or marginal farmers. Most of those holdings were illegal, anyway, being in violation of land ceiling laws. One part of the idea was that voluntarism would replace militant, often violent, land struggles. Bhave even founded an ashram in Palamau from where the *bhoodan* drive in the region would work.

Things didn't work out quite the way he thought they would.

'Even Vinobaji's ashram in this district has not been spared,' laments Dubey. 'It has been grabbed. That too, by the very people who were to protect it. Now, only a well survives from the original ashram.' Dubey has every fact on *bhoodan* and land distribution at his fingertips. The figures he rattles off show that 'about 2,734 acres were distributed in 268 villages to 1,032 beneficiaries' in three blocks of Palamau. Those were Maduadanr, Barvadi and Garu.

Hardly impressive figures in this huge district. But even these, says Dubey, can be misleading. 'They include 50 per cent land that is uncultivable and some other very low grade plots. Besides, since 1988, 1,500 acres were distributed in the Balumath block but no formal deed has been given to the new owners. The same happened with 400 acres in Chandwa block. And about 75 per cent of all "beneficiaries" are bogged down in litigation they can ill afford.'

Some of those cases are driving the courts crazy. In Sherakh village of Chandwa block, one man had 'donated' land jointly owned by him with

---

* *Padyatra* – a walk or journey on foot. Undertaken as part of a mission, to further a cause.
† Vinoba Bhave – A leading Gandhian of that era. Also a well-known figure in India's fight for freedom from British rule.

three others. He gave away not only his own share but that belonging to the other two as well. They went to court and the case has stayed there for ages. In the village where the *gram sabha* grabbed Vinoba's ashram, 'it also dissolved the original *bhoodan* committee. Next, it destroyed all the relevant papers. The ruling group then seized even the common property lands of the village.'

In Chandwa, the kin of Lal Kundernath Sahudeo are challenging the *bhoodan* generosity of the late landlord. 'Sahudeo gave the land to Vinobaji and adivasis are now tilling it. They cannot afford costly legal battles. But his kin want the land back.' In the Latehar court, Jaffer Mia fights to regain land donated to him by Rasool Mia thirty years ago. Rasool's son did not stop with grabbing back what his father had donated. He went on to usurp even the little plot of land that Jaffer had always owned. The list of such incidents seems endless. And the tales of the many litigants thronging the courts are bewildering. There are some patterns, though:

- Several landowners who donated land never really parted with it in practice. Some gifted land only to take it back not very much later. Some 'donated' lands that never belonged to them. A few claimed 'compensation' for the trees, fruit and bushes on the lands they were 'giving up'.
- In a few cases, the unhappy 'donor' is a tiny farmer. Such a person would own an acre or less. His land, like Gopal Singh's, is likely to have been gifted away by rivals manipulating records.
- Some landlords seized back the 'donated' plots and threw out their 'beneficiaries'. In some cases, the victims had some tiny plots of their own as well. The landlords grabbed those too. Many land-related legal disputes run well beyond two decades. Often, the 'beneficiaries' have been crushed by the costs.
- In the early years after abolition of *zamindari*, some landlords came up with a smart move. They vested the *same* surplus lands with both *bhoodan* and the government. That led to massive confusion, with both those entities trying to take control of the land. The lengthy litigation that followed while each fought the other, enabled the landlords to keep the land much longer.

'Some gains have been made over time,' says political activist Narendra Chaubey. 'They are the work of people like Suresh Singh, some of those who came after him and individuals like Bishwamber Dubey. People like Dubeyji play a crucial role in monitoring the process and fighting for justice. But in the real world, can we depend on the large-heartedness of the landlords? The impact of people like Dubeyji in ensuring fair play is great, but it would be greater where political forces having the will to do so, simply take control of surplus land and see that it goes to the landless.'

Dubeyji seems to know this too. But his boundless faith remains unshaken. As we depart in our jeep from his office, he sets off on his cycle, moving the wheels of justice towards yet another village.

The sorrows of Subhaso

Kalipur, Surguja (Madhya Pradesh): The auction was being held in near total darkness. There was no shortage of curious onlookers, though. It was 9 p.m. yet almost the whole village was there. But there was only one buyer present for the land being auctioned. The timing had been arranged to make precisely this possible.

The real buyer was Rajendra Pandey, an employee of the forest department. The nominal buyer, his brother-in-law. The adivasi woman losing her land was Subhaso, a Gond tribal. The village was Kalipur. This is Surguja, one of India's poorest districts, with a tribal majority.

Subhaso had failed to repay a loan taken from the Bhumi Vikas (Land Development) bank. And the bank put up her 9.73-acre landholding for auction. In the process, those behind the auction were violating virtually every law relating to such transactions in the state of Madhya Pradesh.

To begin with, Subhaso had taken no loan.

'Jaiswal *saab* [the local *mahajan* or moneylender] asked my husband to put his thumbprint on a document, saying he would fetch us rations from the town,' says Subhaso. On the strength of that thumbprint, Jaiswal *saab* took a loan of Rs.7,700 in her husband's name. That, too, under a scheme meant only for adivasis.

Using their names, he also managed to acquire a pumpset and have a well dug on his land. Or rather, on her land. When Jaiswal first showed up in Kalipur with his family, Subhaso's husband generously gave him a couple of acres free to build a home.

'See how he has repaid us,' wails Subhaso. Both Jaiswal and his son are dead. But the loan, amounting with interest to Rs.13,720 by 1986, crushed the old lady.

The bank, which had not sent out any notice in the preceding years, now woke up. It suddenly sprang the trap on Subhaso – who had no idea that such a loan existed. The bank officials, too, were breaking the law. It is illegal to auction, alienate or transfer adivasi land here.

Indeed, Section 170 B of the Madhya Pradesh Land Revenue Code allows the state to reopen any dubious deal relating to adivasi land all the way back to 1956. 'One of [former chief minister] Arjun Singh's more

194

progressive contributions to politics,' as an official here puts it. Yet Section 170 B did not work for Subhaso. She had never heard of it in any case.

'Every step taken was illegal and the officials knew it,' says advocate Mohan Kumar Giri, of the Surajpur Civil Court. The auctioneer added to the crime. 'He came in the morning and there were many merchants from nearby with their "thailis" [bags] bulging,' says Subhaso's son, Kamesh. 'But Pandey took the auctioneer aside and had a talk with him. Soon, they disappeared till the night, returning only after all the other buyers had left.'

They then sold the land, currently valued at over Rs.200,000 – for Rs.17,500. Pandey smartly took the land in his brother-in-law's name to cover his own tracks as a government employee. Nor did the bank bother to return the Rs.3,780 theoretically due to Subhaso after the deduction of the loan amount. They pocketed that too.

'I begged them,' says Subhaso, 'how I begged them. They knew I had taken no loan. But they auctioned my land.' And at an impossible rate. 'Even at the time,' says Laltha Prasad, a neighbour, 'that land was worth a fortune, more than Rs.15,000 an acre. Yet they disposed of it to Pandey at less than Rs.2,000 an acre. I think they decided to close in on her after her husband died, knowing how helpless she was.' Another estimate by locals places the market value of that land at between Rs.25,000 and Rs.40,000 an acre. Either way, at the end of it, Subhaso had little beyond her homestead land.

The bank had more than recovered its money on this absurd deal, points out advocate Mohan Kumar Giri. So what if they had taken the real value of the land into account? Subhaso should have got a sizeable sum even if they had repaid her only the amount left over after deduction of the 'loan'.

But surely, with every law on her side, redress was possible? 'I went twice to the collector and each time he said, "Subhaso, you go till your land. No one can stop you." But Pandey threw me off forcibly. How could I resist him?' asks Subhaso. Given his job, he could use official machinery or power in the coercion process. Typically, tribals are most fearful of the forest department. It is the most powerful – and often the most heartless – branch of government that they deal with directly on a daily basis.

Besides, Kalipur is a remote, isolated village. It was even more so in 1986 when her crisis began. Each trip Subhaso made to the collectorate was a harassment. It meant walking scores of kilometres.

However, the sub-registrar's court passed strictures against the land-grabbers. The sub-registrar of co-operative societies, R.P. Bhatti, held that all the officials involved had violated a large number of regulations. He also advised Subhaso to seek redress in an appropriate court.

But Subhaso was broke. The collector had changed so she tried the next one. He, too, in theory, upheld her rights. He even gave her a letter for the *tehsildar* (local revenue authority), instructing him to take action. The *tehsildar* pocketed the letter handed over to him by the innocent Subhaso. 'He laughed at me and said: "You will never get this land back, fight all you want," and sent me away.'

After that, Subhaso never went back to a government office. Ranged against a coalition of moneylenders, forest department staffers, bank officials and a corrupt *tehsildar*, she found herself defeated.

'The adivasi woman is the most vulnerable and the least protected of Indians,' says advocate H.N. Shrivastava. He has fought cases like Subhaso's at the Surajpur civil court. 'In some instances, such persons can end up drowning in litigation. Often, they spend more money than their land is worth. Years go by in just sending out notices. The legal system is so tedious.'

Subhaso has no money left for litigation. Nor for anything else. The four-member family is in dire straits, eking out a living from grossly underpaid casual labour. Subhaso can't even speak about it coherently any more, choking on tears that stain the tattered sub-registrar's order of 1988 which she hands across to us.

'Subhaso's is more than a personal case,' says Shrivastava. 'Her plight is typical of that of thousands of adivasis. They simply cannot access their rights or enforce them. It matters little how progressive the law is. In her case, you have a picture of their world. Of the oppression of adivasis, of how the government machinery works. Of the fraudulent local set up, the tediousness of court procedures, the ruthlessness of the moneylender. And how keeping the tribals illiterate makes all this possible in the first place.'

For just a moment, looking at her strange visitors, hope reappears in Subhaso: 'Do you think something will happen if I go to the new collector?' There is a new government as well. How both will answer her question could decide the fate of thousands.

Has anyone seen my land?

Kachan, Palamau (Bihar): Ranbir Korwa has a problem: he can't find his land. A member of the desperately poor Korwa tribe, Ranbir was the beneficiary of a surplus land redistribution programme of the Bihar government in 1991. He became the proud owner of 1.8 acres. Two years later, he is yet to find the land.

'I don't know where the plot is,' he tells me mournfully when I meet him in Kachan village. The *patta* (title deed) in his possession names the village as Sarguha. It gives the *khata** number as 2, and the plot number as 424/26. It also records the land area as 1.8 acres. 'But,' says Ranbir, 'there is no real address on it, sir. The numbers did not help me find the plot.'

Ranbir's case is not unique. Phaguni Devi, also a Korwa, was allotted land in the same village on the same day as Ranbir. Her plot number is 424/27 – making them neighbours – and the land measures 1.92 acres. It's just what she always wanted. All she has to do is find it. The fact that the *patta* lists two borders of the plot as *van* or forest, does not help.

Many similar cases dot the rocky road of land redistribution in Bihar. Here in Palamau, a number of Korwa tribals find themselves in this situation. (The main body of the tribe, particularly the Pahadi or Hill Korwas, live in Surguja district across the border in Madhya Pradesh.)

Lending complexity to their plight is the state's land survey that began in the second half of the '80s. This opened up new avenues for land grab and other forms of corruption. Coming on top of those already in place, it proved fatal for some. And the huge bureaucratic errors built into such exercises made things worse.

Any land distribution scheme rouses hope amongst the poor here. Too often, their actual experiences are not unlike those of Ranbir and Phaguni Devi. But can't that pair, for instance, have their problem sorted out by a visit to the circle office†?

'I have made several trips to the circle office,' says Ranbir, 'but the circle

---

* *Khata* – an individual's account in village land records.
† Circle office – A 'Circle' is mostly a unit of revenue, sometimes coinciding in area with a block. In some states it could be a unit of development below a block, with some revenue functions.

karamchari wouldn't let me see the officer. He wanted a bribe of Rs.50 per acre, so I would have to pay around Rs.80. Where do I have that kind of money?' It is a gigantic sum for a poor Korwa. So, too, for other groups, in a region where families have gone into bondage borrowing half that amount.

The dispensation at the *panchayat* level here hardly matters. The circle officer is the real power on revenue and land matters and in this small world, his powers are immense. For poor adivasis trekking long distances to reach him, it is always an arduous and often a futile pilgrimage. Yet nothing can happen without him.

Ganori Korwa, who is also hunting for his 'allotted' land in another village, says: 'The C.O.'s office is thirty kilometres away. Just going there costs money.' It also takes him away for hours from the crucial business of gathering food enough for that day. He sums up the standard responses at the C.O.'s office: 'The C.O. won't let us in. The C.O. is in a meeting. The C.O. is out of town. The C.O. won't take note of us, or makes us wait all day but won't see us. The *chaprasi* [uniformed office messenger or attendant] wants money to let us meet the C.O.'

The fate of an adivasi or a dalit visiting a government office is not a pleasant one. At more than one such office I visit during over fifty days in Bihar, the adivasis met with contempt and humiliation. Yet, as the upheavals caused by the land survey continue, their need to make such visits becomes greater.

'From big landlords down to small local centres of power like the postmaster, school headmaster or advocate,' says a senior official, 'many have taken part in the land-grab. Earlier, this often involved direct physical violence. But with the coming of the land survey, manipulation has gained importance. It can be more effective. The *karamchari* [worker] doing the survey is bribed. And he records the poor peasant's lands as belonging to those who have bribed him.'

This creates curious situations, as in Khudag village. Here, land belonging to Ganpat Singh and other tribals is clearly listed in their *pattas*. Yet, the *karamchari* doing the survey has recorded these lands in the name of a postmaster from another village, Lavarpur. And he did this after extracting a bribe of Rs.2,000 from Ganpat, who has lost both his land and all his money.

Coming atop decades of subtle and not-so-subtle land-grab, these developments have put more pressure on the poor. The tribals and dalits can hardly cope with lengthy litigation. When the grabber is an advocate, for instance, this becomes impossible. But they do fight back, at great risk, in many ways.

And there are factors in Palamau that help them.

The Chottanagpur Institute for Social Development, an NGO headed here by Shatrughan Kumar, is in the fray. At present this body is handling cases of land-grab totalling 8,000 hectares on behalf of the victims. The focus right now, says Kumar, is on 'four blocks in which we are working – Chainpur, Ranka (Garwha), Bhanderia and Barwadi. In just those blocks, over 5,000 tribal and dalit families have suffered land-grab.'

It also seems common here to allow marginalised groups to settle on 'GM' land. That is, *ghaiyar mazaruwa* or government wasteland. After they make the land cultivable through hard work, they get thrown out physically. The Chottanagpur Tenancy Act offers protection, in theory at least, to tribal land. Even an adivasi wanting to transfer land can only part with it only to other tribals living in the same police station area. That too, needs the permission of the deputy commissioner.

In reality, tribal lands do pass into non-tribal hands. This is most likely in places where the adivasis do not have political bodies to fight for them. The Sarwangin Gram Vikas Kendra (Sarwangin Village Development Centre), an NGO surveying the issue, found hundreds of such cases in just a handful of Palamau villages.

The Act does not afford even theoretical protection to dalit lands. So these are now the main targets of land-grabbers. Almost every member of the Bhuiya dalit community I stayed with in Latehar had lost some land in this way. It also means that most of the litigation now coming up in the courts involves dalit lands grabbed by an array of sharks. (One family I stayed with had their land grabbed by a man who had once been their own lawyer.)

That dalits should be the target of so much land-grab and land-related violence seems, on the face of it, to be odd. After all, they own so little land. Many of the dalit communities here are mostly made up of landless labourers. Yet, a good deal of land-related violence and disputes involve them. Most legal cases here that dalits are party to tend to have a land element to them.

'It's confusing, but not really surprising at all,' says political activist Narendra Chaubey. 'Dalit-held land is very tiny. But since they are weak and relatively defenceless, their holdings are always an attractive target. Secondly, being the poor in the villages, they are most dependent on common property resources, on the village's common lands. So when somebody grabs the commons, they are the worst affected. Where will they graze the few head of cattle or goats they own?'

But a host of organisations, political parties and forces are fighting land-grab. To an extent, even the ultra-left Maoist Communist Centre (MCC) seems to have a sobering impact on landlord terror. With such a wide array of forces and highly sympathetic senior district officials in the battle, it could perhaps be won. But until then, Ranbir Korwa will have to keep searching for his land.

The pain of being a Parhaiya

Balumath, Palamau (Bihar): It took some hours to persuade the men to return from the fields and the forest where they were hiding. Immediately on sighting us, they had fled leaving the women and children behind. Pakri was one of those rare Parhaiya settlements where our vehicle could actually reach within a few kilometres of the village. But that meant a jeep. And a jeep means police. And police mean beatings and bestiality.

Much negotiation followed, with a local leader of the Communist Party of India – Marxist (CPI-M) stepping in. The men then emerged, slowly, fearfully. He had to assure them that I was not from the police or any other branch of authority.

For the Parhaiyas, a declining group that is also one of India's poorest, continue to bear the stigma of a 'criminal' tribe. This was a label pinned on them by the British. Very often, the police respond to any crime in the Balumath block by picking up all the Parhaiyas they can lay their hands on. This happens even if there is not the remotest ground for suspecting their involvement in the offence.

Less than fifteen hours before I reached Pakri, the police had picked up young Gopal Parhaiya. 'They gave us no reason, mentioned no charge, nothing,' said Ganga Parhaiya. Later, at the police station, an officer told me that they had picked up Gopal 'in connection with a petty theft that occurred some time back'. When? 'About two years ago,' he said. What about the large-scale illegal mining going on quite openly within two kilometres of here? 'That isn't our department's problem,' he replied.

'We can't escape even if we work for the police,' said Bhola Parhaiya, laughing. He ought to know. He slaved as a domestic 'helper' in a police officer's house two years ago. So did Ganga Parhaiya. Once, they got a payment of Rs.10 each for their labours of several days at his house. To which a local landlord added another Rs.10 for work they had put in at his place. With this, they purchased two kilos of rice each. But police arrested them on their way home, along with Phaguna Parhaiya, and then beat them up. The fact that they were able to afford rice at all was proof enough of crime. 'Nothing we said mattered,' said Ganga Parhaiya. 'The policemen simply said, "How else can scum like you get money for these purchases except by thieving?" and beat us after taking us into custody.'

Just days after their release, members of the ultra-left Maoist Communist Centre (MCC) paid the villagers a visit. After lecturing the Parhaiyas on the evils of crime, they made an example of Phaguna, whom they accused of 'looting the forests'. Since the MCC earns high revenues from the levy it imposes on local timber smugglers, this seemed a strange charge. It did not stop them, however, from thrashing Phaguna, who fell very ill thereafter and died.

Petty officials of the forest department are another source of constant torment. 'Even if we're found carrying dried out, ant-eaten wood, they come after us,' said Turva Parhaiya. 'During the drought, several trees and other growth dried up completely. The forest ranger had us beaten for using that wood. He said: "You first cut this wood and then dried it out" – then his men punished us.'

Along with the Birhor tribals, the Parhaiyas were among the worst hit at the height of the drought and near-famine conditions affecting Palamau till mid-1993. They could not find work on even the relief projects that came along. And finding jobs in government offices is not easy at the best of times for the Parhaiyas. No one is willing to give them character certificates. At one stage, a kind-hearted official gave some of them certificates on his personal responsibility. 'Because of this, four of our people joined the Home Guards,' said Turva Parhaiya. 'But after that officer left, they are all jobless.'

'When the drought came,' said Ganga Parhaiya, 'we found it almost impossible to get the local *getti* roots and *moulla* leaves [a species of spinach].' The Parhaiyas' tiny plots of land are unable to support them. Even as we spoke, a young woman was cooking the balls of *getti* that are a crucial part of a diet innocent of sugar and short on pulses. When the drought came, the trees and vegetation dried up, *getti* disappeared and a few Parhaiyas died. Luckily, a few top-level district administrators came up with some excellent crisis management. That contained what had all the makings of a catastrophe across the district. Many more would otherwise certainly have died.

The Parhaiyas, though, had to deal with the lower rungs of a machinery deeply imbued with contempt, even hatred, for them. And that was not pleasant. Attempts at rehabilitating the Parhaiyas have not been a great success at the best of times. The 'houses' built for them under the Indira Awas Yojana (Indira Housing Scheme) are not yet five years old. 'Yet,' laughed the NGO activist who had accompanied me, 'their ruins look worse than those of the old Palamau *qila* [fort].'

Turva Parhaiya smiled at me rather apologetically as he stood before the

A Parhaiya woman cooking the balls of getti *that are a crucial part of a diet innocent of sugar and short on pulses. When the drought came, the trees and vegetation dried up,* getti *disappeared and a few Parhaiyas died. Top-level district administrators, however, averted an even worse disaster with some excellent crisis management.*

ruins of his Indira Awas house. '*Bilkul bekar hain* (it is totally useless),' he said. He spoke somewhat sheepishly, as if afraid we would somehow hold him responsible for the disaster. Seeing we weren't doing that, he went on: 'The roof fell down with the first monsoon, less than two months after it was put up. As you can see, all the structures they put up came down this way.'

Not a soul has ever stayed in most of these houses. That seems typical of most Indira Awas colonies in the remote areas. In many places, these curiously misshapen structures stand deserted. Sometimes they house cattle or grain. They are suffocating, dark, damp, dilapidated sheds with no ventilation. And impossible for people to live in who use firewood as their fuel source.

In Pakri, contractors and corrupt officials built these houses that collapsed with the first rains that followed. Of course, not a single official visited the village thereafter. 'Even where the walls have not collapsed,' said the NGO activist, 'you will find a whole colony near the Balumath block HQ, deserted for two reasons. One, because the internal construction is so poor and two, they fear having the police so close by.'

The defensive mechanisms of the Parhaiyas work non-stop. No youngster in Pakri stays in the village at night – the police might come by. They sleep on the edge of the fields bordering the woods. Not a child here presently goes to school. 'Anyway, no teacher is willing to come,' said Turva Parhaiya. Once, Ramachandra Parhaiya started a school. Having studied up to the sixth standard, he was the most highly educated member of this tribe here. 'After some months, the police took him away on some charge and that was the end of it,' said Ganga Parhaiya.

When Martin Tirkey, a well-meaning and educated tribal from the block HQ volunteered to run a school here, the government immediately appointed him. He ran his school honestly for several months, said the NGO activist. However, 'he quit when he received no salary and no help of any kind. But during his time, Tirkey made a useful survey on how many Parhaiyas were in jail, how many in destitution. Yet, I don't think any local official has bothered to see the report. If ever a community can say it was driven to crime, it is this one. The records of those amongst them who have gone to jail reveal the petty nature of their offences. But they are always being punished, crime or no crime. Society has tried and convicted these people without even bringing a charge against them.'

Bondas in bondage

Mudulipada, Malkangiri (Orissa): An adivasi labourer held in bondage by another tribal? Unusual. More so among the ancient tribes. Yet that's exactly how some Bondas like Mangala Kirsani live. They work as bonded labourers on the fields of other Bondas.

Needing to raise the bride price at the time of his marriage, Mangala borrowed two oxen and Rs.1,000 from Budha Kirsani. Later, he was unable to clear the debt. He is now Budha's bonded labourer. Mangala could settle the debt by performing free labour for a set period of time. But Budha will not allow this. Until he repays the sum *in cash*, he remains bonded. So he not only does Budha's work in the field but also serves as a domestic labourer in his house. His pregnant wife continues to work in the fields to keep them both going.

Didn't the Block Development Officer (BDO) settle Mangala's case under the law? 'No one did anything for me,' Mangala says to us at his house in Bandiguda village in the Bonda Hills. 'Please free me,' he pleads. The official with whom I've trudged for hours to reach this place scribbles a note to the BDO and hands it over to Mangala.

The Bondas are an ancient tribe found nowhere except in Malkangiri. In official reckoning, there were just 4,431 Bondas in 1990. Malkangiri collector G.K. Dhal says the Bondas appear in what he calls a list of 'the fifteen most primitive tribes in the world'.

Their interaction with 'mainstream society' has not been a great success. And bonded labour seems to be just one outcome of it. 'They pick up many of these [criminal] habits from us,' says an assistant sub-inspector of police, Anirudha Nayak, candidly. Nayak, posted at the Mudulipada settlement, is something of an authority on crime amongst the Bondas.

The tribe records a stunning homicide rate – sometimes crossing fifty murders a year. This means that of every 1,000 Bondas, nearly twelve die this way. That, points out a police officer in Koraput, would be an outrageous figure anywhere in the world. For such a tiny population, it is truly alarming. The murder ratio for New York city is 13.2 per *hundred thousand* of population, making the Bonda Hills many times more violent. Here, however, the killings are almost entirely within the tribe.

Things are beginning to improve, helped by changing attitudes within the Bondas. Some project officials and sections of the local administration have also put in much effort to make things better. In recent years the ratio of homicides has fallen to around six to eight per thousand. And there were just seven murders in the first half of 1993, the last period for which figures were available. This represents a very sharp drop. Violence against outsiders remains a minor worry.

'Try understanding why even the little violence against non-Bondas occurs at all,' says a local NGO activist. 'A Bonda entering the *haat* (rural market) is accosted at the edge of the village by merchants who grab whatever he has. They shove a few rupees and maybe some liquor into his hands. Thus, they arbitrarily decide the price and value of his produce or goods. Later, the Bonda, believing this is the accepted mode, does the same, especially when drunk. This often results in violence – and the Bonda is a tough warrior.'

Crimes other than homicide, says Nayak, are very few. 'And even those involved in killings mostly turn themselves in at the station. Often, while doing so, they bring with them the first news of the event.' Sometimes, a Bonda warrior who has slain another shows up with the body of the victim and turns himself in. Many of the killings arise from clan rivalries dating back many generations.

'There is no crime-solving expertise or detection required here,' says Nayak. 'These people don't lie. I have seldom come across anyone here who, after committing a criminal act, would not admit to it. Sometimes, from the more remote areas, we might know of a killing a day or two after it happens. The elders of the village may first discuss the issue and then call us in, but there's no lying.'

'Theft and burglary, in the sense we know it in mainstream society, is almost unknown. Yes, one clan may get drunk and eat the cows of another in pursuit of some ancient vendetta. But they would proudly announce their deed.'

The problems really begin, says Nayak, when they get sent to prison in Jeypore. The same Bondas change after a while there. 'There they meet criminals from the mainstream and it has an impact on them. Before going to prison, they might be reluctant to tell you something, but whatever they tell you is the truth. Once they've been to prison, they learn to lie from our mainstream criminals.' However, a crime other than homicide has clearly emerged: bonded labour.

'This bonded labour headache seems to have arisen during the past three to four generations only,' says Raghu Nath Sahu, in Bhubaneswar. Sahu was

206

project leader of the official Bonda Development Agency for eleven years till 1987 and is an expert on the tribe. 'I identified 144 such cases of bondage,' he says. 'We were surprised by its extent. But we freed those workers.' Sahu now works as a senior research officer at the Tribal & Dalit Research-cum-Training Institute in the state capital. But though he has left Malkangiri, he retains his interest in the Bondas. News of the resurgence of bonded labour saddens him.

'Curiously,' says Sahu of crime in the tribe, 'it was the prison aspect that helped me make a breakthrough with the Bondas. In those days we were still working hard to win their confidence. I used to arrange for family visits to the jail and they were all very grateful for that.' Sahu concurs with Nayak's view that the prison experience gave some of them new and unpleasant habits.

They also seem to have picked up a few from some of the pop anthropologists visiting the Bonda hills to 'study' this ancient tribe. Many of the instant experts seem to have been on assignment for some journal or the other in the West. And mostly they seem to have contented themselves with sticking to the 'safe' villages. That is, those immediately next to the Mudulipada settlement.

Their legacy still remains. In these villages, the sight of a camera will bring Bondas around you demanding money. Sadly, they even adopt ridiculous poses to please. Someone had clearly paid them for this in the past, tutoring them to fit pre-conceived stereotypes in the West. We have no such experiences in the really interior villages that we reach on the third and fourth day in the Bonda Hills. There, many have never seen a camera.

Worse has happened in the past. The traditional Bonda woman wears a single small piece of cloth. This is only a metre in length, about 40 cm in width, and worn around the waist. Some Western visitors have misused the photographs they have taken of these women. In this, they were aided by shady tour operators from Bhubaneswar. That has led, understandably, to curbs of a sort on their visits here.

One zealous official even told the Bondas to take into custody any foreigner they saw using a camera. This led, shortly after, to an elderly, bona fide and frightened French anthropologist being marched some twenty kilometres over hostile terrain by the Bondas. Luckily, they did this to turn him over into official custody. So he suffered no more than exhaustion and embarrassment before his release.

Back at Bandiguda, village elder Sama Kirsani speaks to us of Mangala's case. He says: 'It is a practice that who borrows when in need must repay or be punished.' He agrees, though, that this is no ancient custom. The older method was to extract work for a set period of time from the debtor. A council of villagers used to decide on how much work the debtor would do, and for how long.

The 'integration into the mainstream' of adivasis is a staple of government programmes relating to the ancient tribes. Here it seems to be acquiring connotations that perhaps nobody intended it should. 'If this is what "mainstream" means,' says the project official accompanying us to Bandiguda, 'maybe it's better if we all remain unintegrated.'

After the second silence

Jogikhura, Garwha (Bihar): It reads like the script for a film on the essence of evil. Almost thirty years ago, powerful landlords grabbed over 180 acres of land from Kharwar tribals and dalits in the then unknown village of Jogikhura. Led by political activists and aided by a few honest officials, the villagers fought to get back their land. The struggle led to a court order more than a decade later, in 1976, restoring the land to the tribals and dalits.

Jogikhura, then in Garwha division of Palamau, shot to national fame. Documentary maker Sukhdev celebrated that battle in his award-winning *After the Silence*. The film came out shortly after the end of the Emergency in 1977. But fifteen years later, the dispossessed are still to regain control of the land. The landlords have also struck back by laying the basis for what could be the region's first ever communal riot. (Palamau stayed calm even at the height of the Ayodhya mosque-temple dispute frenzy in 1992.)

After managing to get around the land restoration order, the landlords made their next move. They settled a community of poor Muslims on the disputed lands. Today, after the second silence, the tribals and dalits on the one hand and the Muslims on the other are in conflict. The tension is deadly. All the groups are very poor and almost completely illiterate. Some actors in this drama are no longer present, yet dominate the stage. The shadow of one still hangs over Jogikhura. That is Jagnarain Pathak, veteran Congress leader and once president of the party's district committee in Palamau. A local Sahu landowner tells us the story.

'The Pathaks bought around fourteen acres here, perhaps in the early '60s,' says the Sahu. He alleges that they then seized around 160 acres from the Kharwar tribals and the dalits. 'This displaced at least twenty-five Kharwar families and an equal number of dalits.' Meanwhile, the tribals and dalits have rustled up old deeds, court and administrative orders for us to look at. The records, some of them falling apart, are quite revealing.

'Look at the incredible greed involved,' exclaims Shatrughan Kumar of the Chottanagpur Samaj Vikas Sansthan (Chottanagpur Institute for Social Development). The CSVS is a body that has vigorously fought land-grab. The old papers show that those done out of their land included the poorest among the farmers. As Kumar points out: 'Some have lost little plots of 0.12 acre;

some, pieces of land not exceeding 0.35 acre.' One peasant lost all he had – 0.03 acre (or decimals, as people here call them). 'How can you even think of stealing from such a person?' asks Gopal, a tribal.

One court order (No. 51/61 of 1966) observes that 'prima facie irregularities [were] noted'. These included 'opening of demand in the name of other non-adivasi persons even though the recorded adivasi tenants were alive.' Also 'settling [of] government lands in the garb of rent assessment for which the Circle Officer was not competent . . .'

Over the years, some administrators tried to help the victims. They include people like K. Suresh Singh who has a legendary status amongst Palamau's poor. Political activists, mainly those of the Chattra Yuva Sangarsh Vahini (now mostly with the Janata Dal party) joined the fray. There were court battles fought and orders passed. The ruling cancelling the annexation of these plots (Misc. Case 16 of 75-76 and No. 4 of 76-77) came in the High Court in October 30, 1976.

At one point during the Emergency, officials arrested Jagnarain Pathak's nephew after he bullied villagers and confiscated their cattle. Not for long, though. 'I went to Indiraji [then Prime Minister Indira Gandhi] in Delhi and saw to it that he was released by Jagannath Mishra!' exults Pathak. Speaking to me from his sick bed in Daltonganj where I called on him, he relives the battle. Soon after his visit to Delhi came the transfer of officials whom Pathak saw as hostile. Now, at 90, he is frail but still mentally alert.

Yet Pathak constantly contradicts himself on one claim: that he never owned 'a single *naya paisa* of land' in Jogikhura. This, at one level, is technically true. The names on the record are those of Gobind Pathak, Anand Mohan Pathak, Alok Pathak, Avinash Kumar Pathak and others. All are children or relatives of Jagnarain. At the same time, the politician's recollections are replete with expressions like 'I bought the land . . . I sold the land . . . I decided . . .' All of which show he was the real power behind the deal. Even as the fight went on, Garwha became a separate district.

Much of what happened after that stays lost in the mists of time and the must of courtroom records. Obtaining a stay on the manner of the administration's execution of its orders, Pathak got the matter held up at a civil court. 'And while the dispute was on,' says an official at the circle office in the Ranka block of Garwha, 'he sold the land to the Muslims. He was able to entice them with concessional prices.' Yet, these prices entailed no losses for Pathak. He still gained a far greater sum of money than he had originally paid for the land. Pathak recalls his victory with relish: 'I defeated Suresh Singh and the others,' says he. The effect of his victory? It pitted the unsuspecting Muslims against the real owners of the land, the adivasis and dalits.

Back at Jogikhura, a perturbed Ainul Haque explains that his kin had no clue that they were buying into trouble. They did not know the land was under dispute. 'We were thirty poor families living far from here. We knew Jagnarainji was a big leader and believed he was trying to help us. We sold all our earlier possessions to come here. Where can we go now?'

Haque and his friends speak the truth. Yet theirs is a dilemma not easily appreciated by the Kharwars and dalits. 'We want our lands back. They should not have come here,' says Ram Naresh Ram, a dalit who has been led to believe that the Muslims acted deliberately. The tension is at hair-trigger level and could lead to a communal conflagration in Jogikhura.

'It was a Chanakya-like* political masterstroke,' says a CSVS activist. He shakes his head, in disbelief, at the enormity of it. 'Jagnarainji first fixed the adivasis and dalits. He has made it difficult for them to regain the land except with bloodshed. He has fixed those elements [of the latter-day Janata Dal] who led the fight against him by settling Muslims on the disputed lands. [Muslims here are part of the JD's base.] And he is out of the fray himself, having disposed of the land at above its original value. Lastly, he has handed an administration that turned against him a time bomb of devastating potential.'

And so Jogikhura waits a third time, simmering, for the silence to end.

---

* Chanakya-like – a rough equivalent would be 'Machiavellian'. Chanakya is said to have been the pseudonym of Kautilya, to whom is ascribed authorship of the *Arthashastra*, a massive treatise on government, economics and statecraft, believed to have been compiled during the reign of the Mauryan dynasty around the third century BC. Kautilya was the shrewd chief advisor to Chandragupta, founder of the Mauryan empire.

Where projects matter and people don't

Lalmatiya, Godda (Bihar): It seemed a good idea at the time. A super hi-tech public sector venture worth nearly Rs.10 billion to be located in one of the country's poorest regions. When the idea came up in the early '80s, it promised to make Godda, with its 98 per cent rural population, unique among India's most backward districts.

The Rajmahal Coal Mining Project, Lalmatiya (of Eastern Coalfields Ltd.), would create infrastructure in a region not linked by rail. It would set an example for other industries too timid to take such risks and notch up record levels of production. Above all, it would bring jobs to Godda. High levels of unemployment have been a chronic problem in this district.

There was also the mundane geological reality that you have to mine coal where you find it, though you can use different methods. The importance of this experiment went way beyond Godda (carved out as a separate district in the Santhal Parganas division in 1983). It was crucial for the country as a whole. Godda was to be a laboratory where various elements of development strategy would be fused together. If it worked, the miracle was worth replicating in other depressed areas. In a country with more job seekers than all those of the OECD nations put together – without a tenth of their infrastructure – it could have been the start of something spectacular.

However, the technology used was not only relatively advanced, it was also entirely foreign, ushered in by Met-Chem, a Canada-based multi-national (linked to U.S. Steel). Met-Chem has been collaborator-consultant to ECL in creating this, Asia's largest single-pit, opencast coal mine. The Rajmahal venture aimed to produce 10.5 million tonnes annually by the end of 1995.

The project came into being with an agreement between the public sector Coal India Limited (CIL) and the Canadian Commercial Corporation (CCL). Under that, the CCL extended a loan of $166 million (Canadian) for the scheme. And the Canadian International Development Agency made a grant of $4 million for training.

The potential for jobs – a maximum of 2,441 – was not high to begin with. Of these, 700 were already held by employees of the old Lalmatiya Collieries. They had worked in what were underground-incline mines before the World Bank got into the act with a pilot project creating an opencast mine around 1981.

Besides, locals lacked the skills to handle tasks in a hi-tech setting. So the ECL had to transfer in around 400 trained personnel from elsewhere to fill in that gap. This means that since the CIL and the CCL signed their contract in 1989, only some 1,300 new jobs have come up. These, at an average cost of roughly Rs.6.5 million per job! If the proposed Hurra-C mine in this district comes off, together with the Rajmahal project, it would mean the creation of employment for around 1,800 persons at a cost of around Rs.10 million per job.

'If the aim was to create work,' says political activist S.P. Tiwari, 'then the potential was there. Imagine how many people you could employ if you used that sort of money properly. We could have created jobs that could be sustained.'

Top ECL officials say that even Hurra-C may not take off. It has run into serious hurdles on environmental issues. It could also face problems already troubling Rajmahal where the project has affected as many as eighteen villages. With twelve of these within the mine boundary, thousands of people are to be displaced. (See 'Neema: Portrait of a village doomed' in the section: 'And the Meek Shall Inherit the Earth'.)

Ironically, several among those to be uprooted are employees of the Rajmahal project themselves. They exchanged – without too much of a choice – land for jobs. Those surrendering two acres to the project, found work in the Rajmahal opencast mine. But the total life of the project is forty-eight years.

In other words, less than forty-five years from now, Godda will have a lot of people with no agriculture to fall back on and no jobs in Rajmahal. Since the district is something of a national backwater, all this goes largely unnoticed in the mainstream press. It causes much concern in Godda and Bihar, though.

It deserves wider concern. Rajmahal, as one of its own officers points out, is a classic example of 'development strategy' gone berserk, hurting those it meant to help. That the mine is very far from its projected annual output of 10.5 million tonnes is the least of its problems.

Rajmahal began as a captive project for the Kahlgaon and Farakka super thermal power stations of the National Thermal Power Corporation. These, the planners thought, would need 13.5 million tonnes of coal annually by 1997. But with both way behind their own schedules, the idea has misfired. Rajmahal has piled up lakhs of tonnes of coal it cannot sell. This raises the danger of a major, almost inevitable fire, say top officials here.

Rajmahal chief general manager R.C. Sharma declines to reveal the per

A coal scavenger moving through the waste dumps of the Rajmahal project. Less than forty-five years from now, Godda will have a lot of people with no agriculture to fall back on – and no jobs in Rajmahal.

tonne cost of coal production here. That, it seems, is a confidential matter. But senior sources within the management say it is around Rs.450 per tonne and the sale price could be as low as Rs.260 per tonne. I am unable to independently confirm this. What is clear is that the sale price is much lower than the production cost per tonne.

A second paradox comes with the Rajmahal worker. He is most productive in terms of output – and yet has the highest rate of absenteeism. Rajmahal produces an average of around 11,000 tonnes a day. That's many times more than most other ECL mines manage.

The workers handle machines of much heavier capacities. Operators work eight hours a day without the slightest break. And, says a senior official, there are also more physical problems and strains. The rate of absenteeism, according to official sources, is at almost 30 per cent and can go higher than that in certain periods. But here, 'each machine hour is more important than manpower, so the work goes on'.

R.C. Sharma joined the project only in late 1990, inheriting a ten-year overlay of problems he did not create. Still, he stoutly defends the Rajmahal adventure. The problems, though, continue to fester. And about the only thing everyone here agrees on is that these are not the problems of an individual or two, but of an entire 'development' process.

But not everybody is doing too badly at the ECL's Rajmahal coal mining project. The Canadian multinational Met-Chem, for one, has done well for itself.

Project director J.C. Menard says, 'Met-Chem has not lost. We are here as a company doing business, and have been in India since 1975. Our share of the project is interesting. We have signed a contract and we'll deliver on that.'

Menard is right, but perhaps modest, in saying that Met-Chem has not lost. Its share is certainly more than interesting. A document I obtained shows that Met-Chem has charged a consultancy fee of Rs.1.05 billion in a project worth Rs.9.66 billion. That's an astronomical figure and one without a precedent in any comparable deal.

The 1989 deal struck by the CIL with the Canadian Commercial Corporation saw Met-Chem gain a unique status at Rajmahal. It took charge of many functions. For instance, 'procurement of equipment, technology transfer, and technical consultancy in mining'. Also, 'mine planning, maintenance and truck despatch systems'.

In effect, Met-Chem became purchaser, partner, middleman and consultant. That, for the biggest single-pit mining project in Asia. It proved a lethal fusion. 'It is not true just here,' says a senior officer. 'If you concentrate those sort of functions in the same hands anywhere, you are asking for trouble.'

All the machinery of the project is imported – via Met-Chem. The machinery cost Rs.4.74 billion. An inventory of 'spares and floating spares' notched up a further Rs.660 million in twenty-four months. In short, of Rs.9.66 billion, Rs.6.45 billion went to or through a company that was at once consultant, procurer and provider.

There's more. Sceptics point out that each time anything goes wrong with the machinery, the project has to import spares, often at a cost of hundreds of thousands of rupees for a single part. Since this also takes time, big machines can lie idle for months together.

An internal document I obtained shows that as much as Rs.1 billion worth of machinery can be out of action at a given moment. In just the week covered by the document, equipment lying damaged or 'under rehabilitation' was worth Rs.840 million. And, one official told me, 'That wasn't a particularly bad week.' Incidentally, the amount spent on welfare last year was about Rs.1.2 million.

With the project way off its targets, Met-Chem is in danger of being fined US $12.5 million under the terms of the agreement. That does not deter the Canadian company. It is eager to continue, and sees that fine as no big problem. It looks forward to a renewal of its contract less than a hundred days from now. Clearly, as Menard says, 'Met-Chem has not lost.'

Rajmahal chief general manager R.C. Sharma believes there is another side to the story. A noble one. A technology where no worker actually touches the coal with his hands. An advanced idea in a backward area. A production capability no one else can match.

But questions about its value to the people of Godda remain.

Its technology, seen as the project's strong point, has not helped the district. The giant electric rope shovels and the huge 170-tonne dumpers brought in by Met-Chem had two implications. First, fewer jobs. And second, Rajmahal has not created around itself the kind of busy ancillary networks that, say, Bokaro has.

As one management official puts it: 'There's no point in anyone opening a service shop or a garage here, because they can't so much as make a ball-bearing for these machines. So the local spin-offs are nil.'

There have been other spin-offs, though. Dozens of officers, some of them senior executives, have been able to visit Canada for 'training'. This, on a programme meant for operators and supervisors.

Both R.C. Sharma and Menard assured me that the trips to Canada were, by the rules, only for executives. However, Met-Chem's own publicity journal states otherwise. It says that 'a separate contract was awarded for the training of supervisors and operators in Canadian open-pit mines and at the mine site'.

The fact that no operators and very few, if any, supervisors have gone to Canada has caused much heartburn among those categories of workers. Yet one of those who made the trip was the officer in charge of approving Met-Chem's purchases.

Quite a few workers who got here by trading land for jobs are angry. Their villages are being displaced and they don't trust the management's promises of rehabilitation. The project is way behind its schedules and countless other problems plague it daily.

So who has gained from Godda's brave new world experiment?

The district remains as backward as ever. Godda still has no rail link and the nearest railhead is Jasidih, two hours away by bus. Job opportunities remain limited, though a 'coal mafia' has developed. Prostitution has come in a significant way to villages where it was never a major phenomenon. Antisocial elements have grown powerful. Union leaders also allege that officials 'sold' some of the jobs at the plant. A few have got jobs but many more have lost their homes or are about to do so – ironically, to enable the others to get those jobs! No major infrastructure of any consequence has come to Godda. The ECL is making losses, though officers get trips to Canada.

As an officer within the Rajmahal management asks: 'How has India benefited? Or the public sector? Or the people of Godda?'

The only visible beneficiary is the multinational company which, by its own admission, is doing okay. 'If a foreign MNC can make money out of one of our poorest districts, what about the people who live there?' he asks. 'Why can't they get a chance to do the same?'

Seasoned political activist S.P. Tiwari has worked in Godda for many years. Rajmahal, he says, 'is a classic example of development strategy that works in terms of projects, not people'. If the road to hell was paved with good intentions, Godda seems pretty much to belong to that highway.

Postscript

Questions came up in Parliament, soon after publication of the story. Details of the 'consultancy charges' outraged some MPs. Met-Chem's contract was not renewed and it has left Godda. The ECL has put the best possible face on the issue, under the circumstances. It says the MNC has left as its work 'was over'. It has no comment on why Met-Chem looked forward so eagerly to a renewal of contract if its work 'was over'. While I was there, Met-Chem had a board in the main hall counting down the number of days to the expiry of the old contract. The MNC was pretty sure it would stay. At the end of the episode, though, Menard is still right. Met-Chem has not lost. Godda has.

8

Despots,
Distillers,
Poets
&
Artists . . .

Characters of the countryside

He knew an awful lot about moneylenders. He also knew how many exactly there were in town. How many held licences, how many worked freelance. But, he insisted, he was not one himself. Heaven forbid. So how did he know so much about them? Oh, that was easy. You keep your eyes and ears open. You observe, you learn.

We were in Kapil Narain Tiwari's house in Khariar. Tiwari is a leading political figure in Kalahandi. Few have fought so fiercely as he has for the rights of people there. We had wanted to talk to a town-based moneylender with rural clients. He had invited one to meet us. And the man had agreed to speak. Such is the respect Tiwari commands. All of us maintained the polite facade that our guest was not really a moneylender. He just knew a lot about them. He kept his eyes and ears open and observed and learnt.

In a selfish sense, rural India is a journalist's paradise. You'd find it hard to match its rich array of characters, for one thing. 'Characters' here does not mean just individuals, but also groups. There were people like the Manatu *Mhowar* (the Maneater of Manatu). That tyrannical landlord of Palamau began a meeting by politely suggesting that I threw in a lot of abuses about him in my report. Otherwise, he said, 'I hope you know that your editors won't publish your story.'

Then there were the illicit distillers of Ramnad who taught us how to make arrack. Or the writer in same district who felt that 3 a.m. was the ideal time for an interview. There were the two male poets of Pudukkottai who wrote songs of women's liberation. The hordes of small farmers who make the cockfight of Malkangiri such a unique social event. The remote village in Godda where children were trained to sing a song of welcome in English for a visiting minister who could hardly speak the language himself.

Though they are very strong individuals, all the characters here represent more than just themselves. They mirror trends, groups, even movements. Writer Ponnusamy is very individualistic, indeed. Yet few can catch the flavour of Ramnad as he does in his work. Interviewing people like him was fun. But it was, above all, an education. Fire-brigade journalism – the flit-in, flit-out school – really misses out on this. It's re-stating the obvious, but: learning something about the area you are going to, or of the people you want to speak to, helps catch that richness. Patience and the right questions help, too.

After that, as our moneylender so correctly put it: You keep your eyes and ears open. You observe, you learn.

The ex-man-eater of Manatu

Daltonganj, Palamau (Bihar): 'The public promoted my cheetah to a lion – thanks to journalists like you – that's why I got such a bad image. You are interviewing me now. But I hope you know that your editors won't publish your story unless it contains a few *gaalis* [abusive remarks] against me?'

Meet Jagdhishwar Jeet Singh, the Manatu *Mhowar*. Once, the most feared of the tyrannical landlords of Palamau – and perhaps of all Bihar. Also, the subject of documentaries, and of stories by the BBC, among a host of others. A holder of the world record for the number of bonded labour cases brought against a single person (ninety-six at one point). And a Jharkhand Party candidate who lost his deposit in the 1991 assembly polls.

The terror of the Manatu area of Palamau, the *Mhowar* allowed no one outside his family to construct a pukka house in his fiefdom for decades. He levied fines and taxes on villagers and ran an empire of thousands of acres on forced and bonded labour. His reputation – fully earned – was terrible. Villagers dreaded the man who kept a cheetah for a pet.

'Look, some people raise goats and some people, gardens. Now goats devastate gardens, don't they? But I like to raise both gardens and goats, all creatures. I only kept a simple cheetah [it died in 1982]. People say I threw peasants to it. If so, could I have let it run about free in my own house, endangering my own family? But you journalists need a sensation. So my cheetah became a lion, and I a man-eater.

'You charge me with bonded labour, but we live in an era where even a man's son feels no bond to him. So how can anyone remain bonded?

'Are you taking my photograph? Get the angle right. I have to look sufficiently wicked. You'll probably have to touch it up, you know. The last journal did that – apparently I didn't look evil enough for their story.

'And let me stand for a photograph in front of my car.' The car is an ancient, decrepit-looking Dodge that has not seen the road in a long time. 'You see my wealth and splendour? Like car, like owner. Both are in the same condition.'

How does the actual record fit with such seeming simplicity? With the charm and the easy humour? Badly. Across the villages of Manatu lies a trail of bloodshed and pain. A trail of families bonded ages ago for having

223

The Manatu Mhowar in front of his ancient Dodge car. 'You see my wealth and splendour?' he mocked. 'Like car, like owner. Both are in the same condition.'

borrowed Rs.5. Of people subjected to unspeakable terror. And of cases falling flat in court due to witnesses being too afraid to appear against the mighty one of Manatu.

But the *Mhowar's* downfall began in the late '70s and accelerated in the '80s. It came about more from the loss of forced and bonded labour than perhaps any other single factor. Anti-*Mhowar* officials and a vigorous Communist Party of India (CPI) agitation in the '70s made it very difficult for him to retain bonded labour. By the late '80s, Naxalite groups had become active in his area. And today, squads of the extremist Maoist Community Centre (MCC) stalk his domain, forcing him to spend more time in Daltonganj than in Manatu.

The actions of a block development officer, Bumbahadur Singh, put Jagdishwar Jeet Singh under a great deal of pressure in the 1970s. The landlord found himself bogged down. All of a sudden, he was fighting a whole lot of cases brought against him. The charges ranged from large-scale timber smuggling to atrocities against villagers. Bumbahadur Singh also curbed the landlord's habit of trampling on the common property rights of the villagers.

'Bumbahadur? Only the first bit of his name goes well. He was anything but Bahadur [brave]. I defeated all his cases. They were motivated by caste and personal jealousy,' claims the landlord. (The officer was a Rajput and the *Mhowar* is a Bhumihar.) Yet those battles seriously eroded his position.

Why join the Jharkhand Party? 'Because they are for the poor, the oppressed and the tribals. I too am oppressed. I'm an old man [now about seventy] who has lost so much land and who just wants to live in peace. The Jharkhand Party wants a separate state and development for the adivasis. And I am for that.'

But he is hardly an adivasi? 'Don't confuse the Jharkhand Party with other Jharkhandi movements like the Jharkhand Mukti Morcha [Jharkhand Liberation Front]. The Jharkhand Party sees all of us living in this region as adivasis.'

'He joined the Jharkhand Party,' says a leading businessman of Daltonganj, 'because he wanted to save his land. For that, he needed some political clout. The Congress was not strong enough to help him after the '70s. And he had alienated the Janata Party and its successors.'

Jagdishwar Jeet Singh has still managed to hold on, by one estimate, to about 1,200 acres of land. That is over thirty times the legal limit. And the filthy, decaying house where I interviewed him in Daltonganj sits atop property worth Rs.3 million. Yet he has gone to seed. As a peep at the backyard discloses, the 'man-eater of Manatu' is selling buffalo milk – he has a sizeable fleet of bovines there – to earn an extra buck. What explains the combination of wealth and decay?

'He has money,' says the businessman, 'but even he knows his reign is over. This sort of landlord simply cannot make the transition to new situation. Some feudal tyrants have made that transition cleverly. But this sort doesn't want to pay anyone anything. They have been used to terror, forced labour and unpaid services all their lives. When these are curbed, they become pathetic. Only a part of the land with him is cultivated. If he wants to resort to forced labour, he has to contend with the Socialists, the Communists and the MCC. So he just decays. His fangs have been drawn.'

Once in a while, he still does try enforcing his writ. The Chottanagpur Samaj Vikas Sansthan – a local NGO – had successfully overseen the distribution of some of his surplus land last year. This had gone to eighty poor families in the Pathan block who officially received *pattas* (title deeds) to that land. Even as I was interviewing the *Mhowar*, a group close to him attacked those families.

The local police, claim villagers there, are either with the landlord or seeking bribes from them. But as I am leaving Palamau, an angry deputy commissioner and the superintendent of police seemed to have called the

Mhowar's bluff. The poor families retain control of the land.

'Palamau,' says a local political activist, 'will prosper when the curse of people like these is removed. We have to wipe out these feudal vestiges in land and agriculture. Else, there is no future for us.' All the evidence suggests he is right.

'So you are leaving?' asked Jagdishwar Jeet Singh. The man-eater who could be on his way to becoming the toothless tabby of Palamau waved goodbye: 'Don't forget to give me those *gaalis* in your article. Your story won't be complete unless you throw in some abuse against me. And I can't do anything. What's the point of taking on journalists? If I take on one, the rest will start giving me *gaalis*.'

Hey, hey, hey, it's a beautiful day!

Godda (Bihar): There was some cause for jubilation. The minister was not going to be more than two and a half hours late. Pretty decent punctuality by ministerial standards. Not that anybody really minded. I certainly didn't. The two tribal cultural troupes (one Santhal, one Paharia) were holding us spellbound. It made even the oppressive heat a bit more tolerable.

The sheer beauty of their skills made some of us wish minister Birendra Singh wouldn't show up at all. Once he did, they would be restricted to a song each and goodbye. The over-enthusiastic vigour of the drummers had, possibly, something to do with the refreshments plied to them by a couple of stage managers a while before. At least, the stage managers referred to them as refreshments. It seemed the polite thing to do. In any case, the troupes were magnificent.

Scores of people running around and behind a retinue of cars signalled the arrival of the minister. '*Mantri aa gaya*' (the minister has come), went the cry. People swiftly gathered under a shamiana to listen to the minister. '*Mantriji ka samay bahut kam hai!*' (the minister has very little time), said the block development officer* at lease thrice – over the mike. This was a message to the cultural troupes that the minister's performance required more time than their own.

After the ritual garlanding, a group of young girls from the local mission school began singing in angelic voices. In parts, their song sounded vaguely familiar. When they hit the chorus for the second time, I sat up. It couldn't be.

It was.

They were singing: 'Hey, hey, hey, it's a beautiful day! Say, say, say, happy welcome to you . . .'

A strange but entertaining medley of different popular songs, perhaps woven together by some mischievous priest with a sense of humour. But since these lines were sung in English, they didn't make the impact they deserved to, here in Godda, Bihar.

---

* Block development officer – main officer presiding over development in a block. Districts in India are divided into blocks. The block is the unit of development.

'*Mantriji ka samay bahut kam hai*,' intoned the BDO when the girls had packed it in and the boys were just about to begin. The BDO wiped the sweat off his forehead – far from being a beautiful day, it was insufferably sultry. '*Samay bahut kam hai*,' he said again twice, as if afraid of forgetting the line if he didn't repeat it often enough.

Soon he parroted his incantation over the mike and the boys finished their last two verses at a gallop. The cultural troupes stepped forward.

The political-level floor organisers had problems now. The over-excited state of the drummers had deepened. Perhaps they had had more refreshments. The drummers of one troupe mischievously rattled off practice beats as the singers of the second were belting out their welcome. However, with some deadly glares, a few whispered warnings and some deft work on the sidelines, the situation (as the BDO was later to observe) was brought under control.

Quickly, the cultural component of the day's proceedings was brought to a close. All of it, by my count, within twenty-five minutes, perhaps even less. It had to be so. Because, as the BDO reminded us, '*samay bahut kam hai*', (there was very little time) and there was so much work to be done.

After the BDO concluded his signature tune, MLA Hemlal Murmu took the floor to welcome the minister. 'This isn't possible!' I exclaimed to my neighbour as Hemlal mounted the podium. 'The man's a Jharkhand Mukti Morcha MLA and there's an all-Jharkhand bandh [total stoppage of work across an area] and blockade on. He's supposed to be blockading Birendra Singh, not welcoming him. JMM activists are being arrested not ten kilometres from here. How can this be?'

'This is Bihar,' my neighbour said proudly. 'Besides, this is about what the blockade amounts to, anyway.' Perhaps, chipped in another member of the audience, we ought to read more into it. Hemlal had defected once, from the Communist Party of India to the JMM when he thought (correctly) that would help him win an election. Could it be that he was poised to move on again, this time to the Janata Dal?

We pondered the matter while waiting for Hemlal to begin. That took some time. His first five minutes were spent in battling, rather ineffectively, with a defective mike. A replacement mike was found and Hemlal effusively welcomed *mantri mahodhyay* ('respected minister, sir'). That took some time, too. Almost as much time as all the cultural troupes and performers together. When he finished, another official had his say briefly and then it was Birendra Singh's turn.

Now, as we discovered, *bahut samay tha* (there was plenty of time). When I left about half an hour later, he was still speaking. I withdrew, disappointed by

Godda's version of the all-Jharkhand blockade.

A week later, I was treated to some blockading myself. The lodge where I had parked my stuff was raided by the police at night. An energetic, youthful and highly suspicious Deputy Superintendent of Police was in charge. He had just taken into custody my neighbours, a couple of 'suspicious characters' against whom the police had apparently received some tip-off.

Suspicions about their characters were not without basis. They were found with equipment that possibly had some artistic uses, but is associated in the minds of the police with counterfeiters. They even confessed to having been in that trade once. But that was long ago. Now they were honest, upright citizens. They had clung on to the equipment for purely sentimental reasons. For old times' sake, as it were. But policemen, especially DSPs, are notoriously unsentimental. He was not willing to see reason.

There was no electricity during most of this period, as in any other period in Godda. So I stumbled on the raid in darkness. The place was alive with rats and police. The first squeaked at me derisively as I mounted the stairs. The latter strode towards me decisively as I approached my room.

The DSP wanted to know if I was (as I claimed) a journalist and had been (as I claimed) in the district so many days – then why had I not registered myself with 'the authorities'? Had I, for instance, notified his boss, the Superintendent of Police, of my arrival in Godda? Since I wasn't a convicted criminal on parole, nor a habitual offender on the police list, I didn't know the answer to that one.

Mercifully, for once, I had my accreditation card on me. The police left with my neighbours whom I haven't seen since – the enterprising lodge keeper immediately re-letting rooms they had booked for the next several days. He seemed to sense, shrewdly, that the police would be offering them alternative accommodation for a while.

I was tempted to go down to the station myself and have a look. But it was late, a four-day slog in the hills had exhausted me, and better sense finally prevailed. I have new neighbours, but I still occupy the same room and not a cell.

Hey, hey, hey, it's a beautiful day.

A day at the distillers

Mudukulluthur (Ramnad): Melt down eight kilos of palm jaggery in a big pot. Throw in four kilos of kadukai (a dry fruit), a dollop of nutmeg and a dash of poppy seed. Add the ayurvedic preparation, Carburaharasai, a finger of ginger and alum. Top off with banana skin and date fruit. Bury for a week, recover, boil and distil. And what have you got?

Probably, a conviction and a Rs.500 fine. Arrack (a distilled country liquor) is illegal in Tamil Nadu. If you've added optionals like battery cells, chillies and cow dung to the recipe to speed up the fermentation process, your punishment could be stiffer. His worship might wag a finger at you while raising the fine a few hundred.

This is Tamil Nadu's most widely patronised illegal industry. But who are its 'grassroots' operatives?

Finding an answer to that clearly involved talking to the distillers of illicit arrack themselves. Here, this meant looking for them in the woods of Mudukulluthur in Ramnad district. After hours of what seems aimless wandering, we find them.

The meeting doesn't go quite as intended. At the sight of us, the distillers make a strong assault on existing land speed records, leaving all their equipment behind. This, it later turned out, is because I am wearing khaki trousers – symbolising the police. Their flight does allow for calm, unhurried photographing of their abandoned apparatus, but the pictures are clearly not going to speak a thousand words. We still needed to talk to them.

An hour and a couple of kilometres later, we find and pacify them. 'Why did you have to run like that when you saw us?' I ask. 'Why did you have to wear khaki trousers?' they want to know. Swamy and Kannan, our two distillers, are cheerful, courteous and charming – and completely outrageous liars, especially on the economics of their trade. They make very little, they plead, out of it.

But if this line of work is so unrewarding, why choose it? Their spiel for the next half-hour makes arrack distillation seem a virtue. They were only doing this, Swamy explains, to keep the wolf from the door.

In that, they seem to have succeeded admirably. They admit to producing up to fifty litres a day (which makes them small to medium operators). This

230

means they can generate a turnover of around Rs.1,600 daily. And Kannan seems to be wearing an expensive make of sunglasses. They never, they explain piously, use filthy stuff like battery cells, though they know others who do – their rivals in the same woods.

'We also drink what we make here,' said Swamy nobly, reminding me of similar signs about food in some Mumbai restaurants.

I say I thought they had the police well in hand: then why the record-shattering sprint when they first saw me? 'Normally, there is some co-operation,' agrees Swamy coyly. 'But this new Deputy Superintendent of Police, Kannappan who has come here is a terrible fellow, *saar* [sir]. He won't accept bribes.' While there is grudging respect for this strange policeman, they abuse a sub-inspector who 'took bribes and then beat us on orders'.

Both distillers and the look-out they've posted seem ever-ready to bolt deeper into the woods if necessary. But we meet only their wholesaler and a client so tanked up he can't tell whether he's coming or going. The client stops only a few minutes to convince us his father was a *zamindar* (big feudal landlord). Swamy and Kannan speak eloquently of their own humble agri-labour origins. But they were clearly better off and now prey on other agricultural workers.

Yet at another level, both are small links in a chain that reaches to ministerial heights in this state. That is a chain of payoffs, bribes and demands totalling tens of millions of rupees. But these two are, relatively, small-timers. They do not enjoy a great deal of political protection. The big distillers do.

What about the ethical dimensions of their trade? For them, there are none. 'What other employment is open to us?' asks Swamy.

Arrack, both insist, is a necessity for those who do hard labour. But don't women labour more without getting into the same habits? Oh, well, women, after all, are women. There's not much that can be done about that, is there? They now shift to explaining their distribution and sale system.

All this while, the mix is boiling in a big lead pot. On top of this sits a smaller – empty – mud pot with a hole in the bottom and a tube jutting out of its side. The inside end of the tube rests on a suspended plate. Atop the mud container is an even smaller copper pot with plain water.

As the mix in the lead pot boils, the substance begins to vaporise and rise to the top of the mud pot. There it hits the copper bottom of the water container, returns, and gets distilled out through the tube into a waiting bottle. The first three bottles – they will get ten in all – contain a highly concentrated substance. When they mix these ten bottles with about four bottles of water, they will get roughly ten litres of arrack.

The arrack distillation process at a glance. Arrack is Tamil Nadu's most widely patronised illegal industry. The distillers, Swamy and Kannan, generously allowed me to take these pictures. They were a bit shy, though, of appearing in the photographs themselves.

Ramnad, among India's most backward districts, has a big list of convictions of arrack distillers. Nearly one every two hours, according to official data here. That rivals the record of Pudukkottai next door. Fine collections are also substantial: over Rs.1 million in the past 150 days.

Yet, the trade is huge and widespread. As in Pudukkottai, it traps a big part of the earnings of male agricultural workers addicted to arrack. Here, too, most women hate it as a destroyer of family income and peace.

In several villages along the coastline, many fishermen, too, admit to drinking a lot of arrack. Sometimes at a cost of three-quarters of a day's earnings – daily in some seasons. Arrack merchants allow credit to those they know they have hooked.

Swamy and Kannan allow me to take photographs of the distillation process but are shy, though, of appearing in the pictures themselves. I explain as I get up to leave – for they had never imagined anything so foolish could exist – that I am a teetotaller. Ah well, their philosophical looks seem to say as we part, it takes all sorts to make a world.

Fowl play in Malkangiri

Malkangiri (Orissa): Dhanurjoy Hanthal is delighted he could speak to me in Telugu. A poor peasant knowing both that language and his native Oriya, he had run into us at the most popular social event in Malkangiri: the *kukuda ladoi*, or cockfight.

In a region where people can labour fourteen hours to earn less than Rs.10, the cockfight is an event where thousands of rupees can change hands in minutes. Many of the fighter cocks are brought to the battleground by little peasant farmers who immediately face a barrage of bids for their birds from agents and brokers. Some of the birds sell for Rs.600 to Rs.800. The agents, who know a good fighter when they see one, want to buy the bird off the farmer and earn big money. They can do this by matching it against the 'appropriate' opponent. Some agents buy more than one bird.

This means the agents can sometimes select both the fighter and its rival and, to that extent, rig the outcome. They could make money both ways: from the betting the fight attracts and its actual result. No agent, however, could persuade Dhanurjoy on this day.

'He is the champion,' says Dhanurjoy proudly, cradling a cantankerous-looking white cock in his arms. 'He will just destroy his opponent. Lay your money on him.' Dhanurjoy was shouting to make himself heard. *Samosa* vendors, makeshift tea stall-owners, *jalebi* (an Indian sweet) makers and biscuit sellers have shown up at this odd venue a few kilometres from Malkangiri town to hawk their stuff at the top of their voices.

And then there are the birds.

We could hear them from nearly a kilometre away across the plain. Piercing, hair-raising shrieks of aggression hit the air as they worked themselves up into a rage before the fight. The venue is a sea of strange colours. An arena crammed with battling broilers of different hues, each bird tied, comically, by a thin string to a little clump of grass.

Villainous white cocks hurl abuse at rowdy red ones. Huge black birds spit fowl expletives at their spotted challengers. Even from a distance, it sounds as if heated debates have led to violence at an all-India poultry convention. And still more men are coming, many with blindfolded birds in their arms, walking single file down different pathways from the hills. Farmers themselves, they move respectfully in lines along the ridges dividing the plots of cultivated land to avoid trampling on crops. Some have come all the way from neighbouring Andhra Pradesh. We are now standing at the middle of the bowl of land they are converging on. From there, the lines of people from the hills make a spectacular sight.

Already, in Malkangiri, we have seen trainers put birds through their paces very early in the morning. It's a bit disconcerting to step out onto a street in that tiny town and watch a cock being tossed over a wall or other barrier. 'They have to learn to leap with force and anger,' explained Anand, one of the trainers. There was also Krishna Reddy who had turned up just for the coming big fight, his blindfolded bird screeching in rage at unseen enemies around 5 a.m. From them, we had learned of the main event and its venue. When we left, the birds in training were still learning to leap with force and anger.

At the venue, the event takes its time getting started. The matching of the birds and the leech-like persistence of the agents and brokers delays proceedings. Finally, loud cries announce the fixing of a couple of bouts. Now the bets are on. '*Das rupya rengda,*' (Ten on the red), '*bees rupya dabbla,*' (twenty on the white), and so it goes – upwards. Among those accepting bets is a respectable-looking, elderly gentleman of enormous dignity. Dhanurjoy tells me he is the headmaster of a school in the vicinity.

The *kukuda ladoi* has been a Malkangiri tradition for centuries. Gambling has always been a part of it, though many poor peasants enter for the love of the battle. But in the last few decades, commerce has crept in. Now, owners attach frighteningly sharp, narrow knives to the feet of the birds, to speed up the combat and ensure swift results.

This cruel feature has transformed the traditional cockfight. Earlier, a single bout could last an hour or more, with the contestants rambling all over the area. With the knives, it's all over in minutes. Dhanurjoy showed us five pairs of knives, explaining how his champion would change his footwear for each fight, depending on the capability and size of his rival. Clearly, the bird has a long day ahead.

The ring is about twenty-five feet in diameter, creatively constructed from twigs and bamboo sticks. The organiser gets an entry fee from each bird owner. Also, a percentage on everything, from the bets to a liberal share of the blows during any fist-fight. This one allows me the privilege to taking photographs from within the ring.

First come the flyweights. The heavier birds are reserved for later when both crowd and betting are at their highest. The opening bout closes almost immediately. A white cock, pitted against a red, bolts the ring and shoots off across the countryside. Its owner moans in despair. In *kukuda ladoi* the defeated bird's master loses not only his money, but also the bird – which ends up as the rival owner's dinner.

Once the flyweights were out of the way, the middles take possession of the ring for a while. The fights begin with the owners of the two birds holding the contestants in their arms and swinging them thrice towards each other, beak-to-beak. This, apparently, is a way of getting the fighters acquainted with their antagonists. A sort of squaring-off, allowing each a quick opportunity of sizing up its combatant. After the third swing, they seemingly begin a fourth, but this time fling the cocks at each other in mid-air. With that, the bout is on.

Not always so, though. As we learned at the training sessions, cocks are curious of temperament. One moment, their rage is terrible, completely focused on annihilating the rival. The next, it is seemingly spent – and then back again a minute later. We had watched two birds outside the tea stall in the morning. They were pecking at something or the other peacefully, in the usual manner of their kind. Suddenly, they would look up at each other and charge into combat uttering hideous oaths. For a few moments there would be a flurry of feathers while we held our breath. Then, equally suddenly, almost on an invisible, inaudible signal, they would break off and go about pecking for food peaceably. Next, without warning, but perfectly synchronized, came blistering bird blasphemies as they charged one another yet again at tremendous speed. This leisurely war and peace scenario continued for nearly half an hour.

Here, at the event, they are allowed no such luxuries. This is the real thing. Once the birds are thrown at each other, the masters circle around them as they fight, now encouraging, now abusing, hurling them back into the fray if they break off for too long.

Dhanurjoy's big moment comes after a few more bouts when his white champion is matched against a ruffianly red rooster. Even as the owners swing the two birds beak to beak, allowing them to size each other up, the red cock catches Dhanurjoy's bird a deadly if unscrupulous blow on the neck. An impartial referee would stop the bout at this point. But the man who could have been that is busy counting the gate receipts, which are mounting satisfactorily. With the result that Dhanurjoy's champion goes woozily into:

Round one: The birds move their ungainly feet with unsuspected speed, agility and power. But our champion is clearly off colour. The Red Menace comes in, firing on all fronts, his deliberately sharpened beak and the knives on his feet traumatising Dhanurjoy's Great White Hope.

The champ takes at least four ugly nicks on the breast and under the wings. The audience is hysterical. But the knives on the birds' feet are coming loose, so the owners enforce a temporary truce to retie them. This allows the contestants a minor respite before:

Round two: Both birds shoot into the air, ripping away relentlessly. Dhanurjoy's champion, still smarting from the early blow, is just a fraction of a second slower. It is a fatal fraction of a second. His rival rips upwards as he lands, cutting into the neck. The Red Menace then closes in for the kill. Two razor-sharp jerks draw bloody patches on the white one's breast.

At this point, the white cock turns philosophical. Almost as if there is no such thing as a fight on, he strolls off to a corner and sits down to meditate,

The **kukuda ladoi,** *or cockfight, is the most popular social event in Malkangiri. In a region where people can labour fourteen hours to earn less than Rs.10, this is an occasion where thousands of rupees can change hands in minutes.*

oblivious to the jeers of an unsympathetic crowd, unmindful of his master's admonishments. His mind seems occupied by higher matters, such as how to leave the ring alive.

While he takes the count, Dhanurjoy addressed his charge in language that would not be tolerated even in the state legislature. I see him again later, the limp champion in his hand. It is hard to say who looks more crestfallen, farmer or fowl. Most of the subsequent winners, too, are reds and blacks. It is a bad day for White supremacists.

Krishna Reddy, whose red rooster is among the victors, tells us there was a cockfight almost every day of the week in some part of the district. Some of these draw even larger crowds, he says. The season begins around October and ends in February.

The light is now too poor for photography, and my flash is behaving badly. As we leave, the bets have multiplied by several times, the crowd and noise are unbelievable. Many of those we spoke to, such as Madhaba Gonda, Vasant Pinki or Krishna Reddy, have been to cockfights for over a decade.

We pass Dhanurjoy on the way out, his hands empty, knives dangling unused by his side, as he trudges towards his village, beaten but not broken. There will, after all, be another day, another bird, another bout, another bet.

Minstrels with a mission

Pudukkottai (Tamil Nadu): One is a schoolteacher. The other, a Life Insurance Corporation (LIC) officer. Both are thirty-seven years old and male. Sounds very commonplace. Yet Jayachandar and Muthu Bhaskaran are hardly that. They must rank as an unusual pair in any setting, rural or urban.

Each is an independent songwriter. Both write highly popular songs in Tamil. They often aim their lyrics specifically at women – urging them to stand up for their rights, to rebel. The songs call on women to realise their potential and to prove they are every inch as capable as men if not more so. Of course, they have written songs on other subjects, but what's striking is the way women in Tamil Nadu's least urbanised district have responded to their songs.

And it's strong stuff: 'Never get entangled in the words of those who say "it's impossible for women",' go the lines of one Jayachandar song. 'Dispel these illusions . . . throw fire on the atrocities they threaten you with. Like a bird with wings clipped, society has enslaved you within the home. Now come out like a gathering storm.'

Muthu Bhaskaran's song, 'O sister, come learn cycling, move with the wheel of time . . .' has proved a classic. Almost every female neo-literate, neo-cyclist here has sung or knows of this song. A sample line: 'The men are riding the cycles with the women on the carriers? That's an old story, sister. Let's rewrite it now with you in the driver's seat.' In a district where women have taken to cycling in astonishing numbers as part of the literacy drive, the popularity and impact of this song is immeasurable. But it has gone beyond Pudukkottai, too. The song has been translated into Hindi, Telugu, Kannada and Malayalam.

Jayachandar's songs, too, are now sung in more than one language. The fame of both poets has gone beyond this obscure, backward district. Jayachandar revels in the curious pseudonym *Vettri Nilavan*, or 'Moon of Victory'. The last time I met him, he had just returned from Coimbatore where he had gone to record a pro-literacy song aimed at that city's textile workers. And there are other themes. 'Human Once Again' is the title of one of his anti-liquor songs. Its protagonist is a reformed alcoholic.

The pro-literacy songs go beyond advocacy of the ABCs: 'Things won't change simply because we say so . . . we have to fight in many ways . . . and one of these is learning,' goes one of his numbers. 'The mighty hands, that plough the lands, and pluck the weeds, now take the lamp, the light of knowledge . . . and drive away the darkness of illiteracy . . . change your life . . . if we learn to read and write we can't be cheated any more.'

'So what if a female child is born,' goes another popular Jayachandar song, written after the poet was moved by reports of female infanticide, 'keep aside, and take your mourning with you. Is there any world without women? Give me an answer.'

It's much more powerful in Tamil, of course. Between them, the two have written over fifty songs. These are on literacy, against arrack, for advancing women's rights, and promoting science and scientific thinking. And people are listening. In large numbers.

Muthu Bhaskaran, an MA in Tamil from Madurai University, is a teacher at the Government Model Higher Secondary School. Jayachandar, a BSc in maths and from a family of agriculturists, works in the LIC. What was the turning point in their thinking? Both speak of their participation in the 'East Coast *Jatha*'. That was a march from Pondicherry to Kanyakumari in the late 1980s. 'It was my first exposure to a scientific literacy campaign,' says Jayachandar.

Both also gained from their contact with the Tamil Nadu Science Forum and the Progressive Writers Association. And both were deeply moved by their work in and interaction with the literacy movement, *Arivoli Iyakkam* (Light of Knowledge), in their own district. 'I noticed changes within me and as society changed me, I thought I would try to change society,' says Muthu Bhaskaran. Before his *Arivoli* experience, he says, 'I thought of women in the old way, that they can't really come out and do things. But in *Arivoli*, I have learned very different. Given the chance, there is nothing they cannot achieve.'

How do men react to songs asking women to call their bluff? 'Why men?' laughs Muthu Bhaskaran. 'Some mocking from them was inevitable, but a few of the older women, too, were scandalised. However, girls in the 15-25 age group picked up the songs very quickly.'

Has either ever had reason to look back and find that events have overtaken one of his songs? 'Yes,' says Muthu Bhaskaran. 'I felt that way after watching an eight- or nine-year-old dalit girl weave wonderful circles on a cycle late at night in the near-darkness of Ambedkar Nagar village. So I wrote an on-the-spot sequel to my earlier song. This begins: 'Yes, brother, I have learnt cycling. I'm moving with the wheel of time . . .'

Valia the honest chowkidar

Petlawad, Jhabua (Madhya Pradesh): 'My policy is very clear. I am not paid to be a hero. For what we are paid, we need do nothing. Yet I do try and stop group clashes in the village. I try my best. Should we stick our necks out to do what the police are paid for but fail to do? *Raat ka jhagda, subah jayenge* [a clash in the night, we look at it in the morning]. Then we act.'

Valia Deva Katara is the lowest functionary, the last link in the mighty apparatus of state. He is paid by the revenue department, but reports to the police. His immediate boss is the patwari. Valia is a village *chowkidar* or *kotwar**. (Spelt *kotwal* in some states.) Officials describe him as the smallest unit of the police in India. But that is not a description he relishes. He prefers to distance himself from the police. And Valia is a modest soul. This Bhil tribal's record in stopping intra-village clashes is really quite good. That too, in a high crime region where people can resort to violence very fast.

The village *chowkidar* is also the most poorly paid and least looked after minion of the state. He might not be paid in cash at all. The government could just give him a few acres of land to till. This would be only for the duration of his tenure. The land would then revert to the state. He gets no pension, no provident fund, just two sets of uniform, one shirt and a cap. If the government is in a generous mood, he might even get a pair of shoes. Until Valia led his fellow *kotwars* in revolt, those given land received salaries as low as Rs.18 a month. The rest got close to Rs.40.

Fed up with those conditions and constant ill treatment, he formed the 'zilla *kotwar* union' (the district *kotwar* union) around twelve years ago. That was probably the first of its kind in the country. All did not join, but a few score did. Their fight, against huge odds, saw the trend catch on. *Chowkidars* in other districts formed their own unions. Then came joint action. This culminated, five years ago, in the *kotwars* being paid Rs.500 a month if they took no land.

Even that came after many rounds of battle. 'The salary went from Rs.40 to Rs.50 to Rs.100 and finally to Rs.500,' says Valia. 'It took many years to get

---

* Village *chowkidar* or *kotwar* – maintains register of births and deaths in a village. Paid a small sum in cash or given a little land or both. Paid by the revenue department but reports to the police.

that far. Most of the other conditions of work have not changed, really.' Even if given just the daily minimum wage in Madhya Pradesh, the *kotwars* would get at least Rs.900 a month. The most any *kotwar* seems to have studied is up to Class VIII. Valia is a self-educated man.

Organising the *chowkidars* was not easy. It still isn't. 'The nature of our jobs means that each of us gets tied down to his village. And your nearest friend is a village away. So when the *kotwar* goes back to his village, he is isolated and at the mercy of his bosses.' But persistence paid off. The *kotwars* fought official-dom's attempts to browbeat them. They took marches to Indore and twice to Bhopal itself. It was in Indore that they met leaders of the Centre of Indian Trade Unions* (CITU) who first helped organise their unions and actions. 'That's how we got the Rs.500 a month,' says Valia.

I first met Valia in Petlawad block HQ, a little away from his base in Bamnia. I also met *kotwars* from other parts of Jhabua district. 'Valia?' asked one *kotwar* in a village in Jhobat. 'That man is too honest. I think we need far more strong-arm tactics to get a better deal.' But he respects Valia. 'He was the first to tell the government what they could do with their land,' he says.

Valia is amused when I tell him about that. 'You only have to see the kind of land they give us to know why,' he laughs. He and his nine-member family have five acres of their own. Another *chowkidar*, Giridhar Dev, told me in Thandla block: 'Valia at least tries to stop group clashes. Most of us are not stupid enough to do that. Especially when a clash is just exploding. Why go to the village and invite both sides to target you? Don't wave a stick unless you are sure you can use it.' Babulal, *chowkidar* in a Petlawad village, agrees. 'Once I see them (village clans) getting ready for battle – that's when I visit my relatives in a nearby village.'

It may not be Valia's way. But the others have a point, too. Valia himself concedes that. The *kotwar*'s job does not end with maintaining the register of births and deaths. He has other, semi-police functions too. He reports the arrival of 'new' or 'suspicious' characters in a village to the police *thana* (station). 'The *chowkidar* is seen by the villagers as a police agent,' says Valia. 'At the same time, the police suspect his loyalty lies with the clans in his village. So he can get beaten up by either side. Sometimes, by both.'

Valia's policy when a clash seems to be brewing is simple. 'There was a dispute between two groups in my village just this week. I met both groups – together. (After a while that could be impossible.) I tried hard to work out a

---

* CITU – mass organisation and trade union arm of the Communist Party of India – Marxist.

settlement but failed. So I went to the police *thana*. But I took both groups with me. They took up their dispute there. I am out of it. One thing is crucial. *Both* groups must be present during all your efforts.' Valia may not know it, but he is adopting the 'transparency' that so many top functionaries of state preach but seldom practise.

'At our level,' says Valia when I put this to him, 'there is a compelling reason to be honest. The likelihood of violence from those who perceive themselves as being cheated by you is very high. [Jhabua has one of the highest homicide rates in India, say jail officials in Alirajpore town.] Whatever happens, one party is going to get angry with me. So I do my best to curb doubts about my own role.'

There is corruption among the *chowkidars*, he says. Wouldn't there be with the kind of deal they get? Some *kotwars* also seek safety by aligning with the police and bullying the odd villager. 'Yet, remember,' he says, 'this is Bhil territory. If you take money and can't deliver, you are in big trouble. Is a little extra money worth your life?'

Those are not the only problems. Giridhar Dev points to other hassles of the '*sabse chotta jaanwar*' (the smallest animal of all). 'The *patwari* [keeper of village records] ill treats us. The *tehsildar* [revenue authority] and his flunkeys harass us. The sub-divisional officer bullies us. Every small *havaldar* [police-man] pushes us around.'

'Last week,' says Babulal, 'the *tehsildar* came by. I was ordered to go and fetch a chicken and cook it for him. So I did that. I also waited on him hand and foot. There are no working hours for us. We are up at all hours for every small despot who arrives. Later, they threw Rs.15 at me for the chicken. It was worth at least Rs.50 if not more. The man I took that chicken from has a violent temper. How can I explain it to him? Now he hates me and one day will do me more damage.'

Many of the *kotwars* I met echoed this complaint. Much of their time went in catering to the whims of visiting petty dignitaries. What if the slave labour of the *kotwars* fails to please such small officials? 'Then the *patwari* suspends us,' says Giridhar. 'Anyway, they suspend us frequently.' That has happened to Valia, too. And more than once. 'They can't reach any lower than us. We are the final scapegoats for all ills,' says he.

'In bad situations,' says one *kotwar*, 'we are supposed to help the police in night patrolling. They never come, but you have to patrol. If they come at all, it is at safe hours to give us orders. The risks are all ours.'

'I am getting old now,' says Valia. (He is over fifty.) 'A younger man will have to take the reins. We are in a bit of disarray now.' His tiredness and their logistical headaches have posed many problems for the unions in recent years.

Valia has, in fact, put in his resignation from the *kotwar*'s post. The *patwari* had sent him a rude letter demanding that he present himself in a few hours or face the sack. But when Valia resigned, the *patwari* didn't accept it. 'It's a joke,' says Valia. 'They sack me three times a year. But they won't let us go, finally. Where will they find such cheap labour to perform such a high-risk job?'

Postscript

Note: The names of the *kotwars* (other than Valia) in this report are not real. The names of their villages have been held back altogether. As they put it: 'Officials have a way of reaching back to the *sabse chotta jaanwar* and hurting them.

The writer and the village

Melanmarai Nadu, Kamrajar (Tamil Nadu): He dropped out of school in the fifth standard. Some of his short stories are now required reading at the university level. But irony, always a strong point of Melanmai Ponnusamy's writing, dogs him all the way. Those stories are read at the university level in other districts. His beloved Ramnad does not have a single university of its own.

I first saw him when he was addressing a public meeting late one evening at a crowded hall in Pudukkottai. Leaning forward against a table, Ponnusamy told his audience of the dramatic impact of the Gulf War on his little Ramnad village. Some farmers there thought they had figured out their 'modernisation', tractors and all. Then the war began. The steep rise in the prices of petrol, diesel and imported components shattered their plans.

At this point, the electricity in the hall went off. Ponnusamy didn't pause for a moment. He got on to the table and went on with his speech. Nor, after the initial noise, did the audience budge. They remained spellbound in the darkness.

That was a month ago. Now we were likely to hear him in darkness again. We have spent hours searching for his lonely village and it is almost 2 a.m. when we arrive. I have broken a foot en route and the pain is at its peak. While the dogs rouse everybody for miles around, we apologise profusely for waking him up at this hour.

He seems surprised: 'Isn't this the best time to have a discussion?' he asks. Moments later, we are deep in one.

Apart from being a highly regarded writer, Ponnusamy is also, in some ways, one of the great experts on the backwardness of this district. His isolated little village, Melanmarai Nadu, is now in Kamrajar district after the division of Ramnad. From here, he churns out insights into why Ramnad remains the way it does. Every story he has written in the past twenty-one years is about and located in Ramnad.

Though a prize-winning writer and a leading figure in the Progressive Writers Association, Ponnusamy prefers to live in his cut-off village. Why not move to a big city? 'That would harm the integrity of the writing,' says he. So he remains in Melanmarai Nadu. A place so difficult to find that I arrived six hours late for our appointment.

'You're going to interview me as an expert on Ramnad's poverty? Not as a writer?' Ponnusamy clearly finds that entertaining.

'Ramnathapuram district was formed in 1910,' says Ponnusamy. 'To this day it does not have a university of its own. It has now given birth to three districts and two ministers, but not a single medical college.' Nor a government engineering college. And the one private engineering institution here might wind up this year. There are just three colleges of any sort across the new district and only two postgraduate courses offered at these.

'Backwardness breeds its own mindset,' says Ponnusamy. 'There has hardly ever been even a demand for a university in Ramnad. Only in the recent past have political parties begun to speak about it. Accepting basic education is going to take a couple of generations here.

'Making demands and petitions didn't come easy to the people of Ramnad. For eighty-three years, the district headquarters was located in another district, in Madurai! Even our law courts were located in that town till just six months ago. Only with the division of Ramnad into three districts in 1985 did that change.'

This means, says Ponnusamy – who calls himself an unrepentant leftist – 'that the administration has always been distanced from the people. Officials were so far away, they knew little of local issues. The area's complexity was not understood. Now we have the courts, collectorate and other structures. Yet, the old pattern prevails because basic issues have not been touched.'

The district is among the lowest in the state in terms of income and, as a rule, lags behind the rest of Tamil Nadu by about 20 per cent on that score. 'This is an ex-*zamindari* area. It really consisted of many small fiefdoms or principalities, mostly run on a caste basis. The extent to which caste has contributed to backwardness here is enormous.'

The British period unsettled even that way of life. It destroyed the few avenues that existed for employment and income. 'A large number of people took to illegal activities. They were left with few other means of survival.' To this day, Ramnad has a very high level of violence, mainly caste-based, and of crime.

'Land reform here, of course, has been meaningless. Contrary to common belief, this district does have good agricultural potential. But who has ever worked with that view in mind?' More than 80 per cent of landholdings in Ramnad are less than two acres in size and uneconomical for many reasons. At the top of the list is a lack of irrigation.

'Employment and the nature of employment mould such a great part of the human character. If you have a cement factory, you have not just cement, but jobs, of a certain character. But first you need to find the location and the resources to set up such a factory. There has never been a real mapping of Ramnad's resources. And no steps ever taken to create employment of an enduring nature.'

Ponnusamy has a point. Ramnad has perhaps the lowest proportion of 'economically active population around the year', less than 40 per cent. This means a very large number of people are really scraping a living off odd jobs in most months. 'On the one hand, agriculture has failed because of poor harnessing of water resources. On the other there is no industrial development. In short, no 'consciousness-generating employment'. Productivity per worker lags behind the state's average by about 20 per cent.

Ramnad has also always had a predominance of economically weaker sections. Scheduled castes and tribes make up close to 20 per cent of its people. Besides, the district has a very high proportion of backward classes. Unemployment levels, among the worst in the state, are highest among these sections. 'We also have some of the most exploitative relationships in this district.'

Whether it is the unique Ramnad moneylender or the sorrow of the chilli farmer, Melanmai Ponnusamy has chronicled it all. Recurring drought, long-term migration or the effects of joblessness – very little escapes him. And the insights he has gained looking from down-up, just from his little village, can be startling. Often they match the results of the best research.

'New types of seeds are being used by the chilli farmers. I do not know where exactly they have come from; but they are distorting the farmer's economy. These seeds may temporarily yield more. But they also compel farmers to spend more and more on fertilisers and agro-chemicals. They are killing the land. The yield begins to fall after a while. The cost of production is now much higher for those who have begun to use these seeds.'

All his six collections of short stories and his single novel, however, reflect an irrepressible optimism. (One collection is titled *Humanity Will Win*.) 'The people here have a fighting spirit and they will change Ramnad themselves. But we cannot be complacent. We have to work for that.' And will he meanwhile continue to write only on Ramnad?

'I must be true to my writing. Simply by being very honest to the realities of this village, I might be producing something relevant to the reality of a village in Uttar Pradesh. It depends on whose problems you address, doesn't it?'

The art of Pema Fatiah

Bhabra, Jhabua (Madhya Pradesh): 'The *havaldar* (policeman) was sitting there, looking over my shoulder, sir. How can one paint under such conditions? He would keep telling me, "Pema, do a good job or *bada saab* [the big gentleman] will be angry." Can one work under supervision of the police? My hand stops and it shakes in fear. This happened to me many times.'

His paintings have been on display in London, Rome and other parts of the world. People pay the price of admission to see them in Bharat Bhavan cultural centre in Bhopal (capital of Madhya Pradesh). He has twice won state awards for art in Madhya Pradesh. Several of his works decorate the walls of senior government officers. But Pema Fatiah, perhaps the foremost exponent of the Bhil art of 'Pithora', now lives in penury. Recovering from a paralytic stroke at his home in Bhabra village of Bhabra block here, the Bhil tribal is struggling to regain his prowess. The stroke affected his painting arm.

The Pithora painting can vary in size, but is usually large. The artist mostly does his painting directly on walls. Some of Pema's works are grand murals. The 'Pithora' is a tribal world picture. Everything the Bhil sees, senses or experiences is captured here. The horse, central to Bhil mythology, figures prominently. But figures less connected with mythology also appear. The moneylender, for instance. Or often, the police *thanedar* (officer in charge of the police station). Both are very major realities in the lives of the Bhil tribals. You can also suddenly come across a motorbike or an aeroplane in one of these paintings. Pema may be among the best but is by no means a lone representative of the art. Many creative artists across this region produce works that really delight.

But the Pithora is more than just a form of traditional painting, says Dr Amita Baviskar of the Delhi School of Economics. She is a scholar who has worked among communities in this area. 'The Pithora has a ritual context,' she says. And that is a deeply religious one. The painting work usually comes up as part of a religious ceremony or puja. 'The artist while working is said to be possessed. The gods are speaking through him. When the painting is done, the *pujari* [priest] will scrutinise the work to see if the essence of what the gods are saying has been captured. The Pithora draws its authenticity from its sacred character.'

Pema was trained by his father in a line he says is a hereditary occupation. Quite a few of the materials that go into his work he makes himself. Some of the pastes and colours come from oxides, minerals, fruit and other substances locally available. He still has to buy a few materials, though.

Some of Pema's murals are stunning. One that hangs in the Jhabua collectorate (done on cloth), for instance. Even more appealing are the traditional works he has done directly on walls in his area. One was not less than eighty square feet in size. Its colours seemed almost luminous. The work itself captured a mix of myth and daily life. Alongside the horses were wells, a pump, a motorbike surrounded by snakes, a policeman. Green, red, brown and patches of white seemed to change hue as the angle of sunlight changed. Here, the gods of painting, at least, have spoken.

'That one was done when I was well and enjoyed my work,' says Pema. So how did it come about that he ceased to enjoy it?

Pema was first discovered – outside his own societal context – by R. Gopalakrishnan, Collector of Jhabua in the mid-1980s. Astonished by the quality of his work, the officer commissioned Pema to do a painting for the Collectorate. He paid him Rs.5,000 for it, a huge sum in those days and the first time Pema was getting anything like it. (For his work, locally, he got payments in kind, and sometimes a little cash.) It was also perhaps the last time he got paid that way in Jhabua.

Gopalakrishnan had Pema's work displayed in Bhopal. There it won the artist his two state awards. It also caught the attention of many leading artists, including J. Swaminathan. Pema's work was now widely exhibited. The artist remembers that part of his experience with relish. Gopalakrishnan and Swaminathan are the only individuals from that world he remembers fondly. He was really pained to learn from us that Swaminathan was no more. With that painter, perhaps, Pema struck an artist-to-artist connection. Of the officer, he says: 'Gopal *saab* was very good to me.'

Gopal *saab* himself is not so sure. He is now secretary to the chief minister of Madhya Pradesh. 'If I had known what was to happen to him subsequently,' he says ruefully, 'I do not know how I would have gone about it. The man was a genius. I did not expect the events that followed.' All that he had intended was that a great artist get the recognition due to him.

Pema's problems began when Gopalakrishnan left the district. He now had recognition, but no protection. A large number of officials, high and low, began to force paintings out of him. 'The *havaldar* would come and tell me, *saab* is calling you,' he says. 'And I went. It could be one of many *saabs*. The superintendent of police, the deputy superintendent, the sub-divisional magistrate or even the *tehsildar*.' And so, Pema Fatiah worked, sometimes with a *havaldar* or some other flunkey keeping an eye on him. 'Sometimes, they would give me a little money. Sometimes, I paid for that work out of my own pocket,' he says. Pema was now working for a bunch of gods very different from his own.

Soon the pressure of this got too much for Pema to bear. As his fame grew, so did his misery. His visits to Bhopal were a sort of release. At the same time, he ended up doing even more paintings that he never got paid for. For a Gopalakrishnan, to whom he mattered as a person, Pema was a great artist. For many others, he was just a peasant producing something of value. Perhaps a work that could be profitably sold in the future. For the policeman overseeing his work in Jhabua, he was just a contemptible adivasi who produced something his bosses wanted. 'Pema's story is a good example of how an urban elite can appropriate tribal art,' says Gopalakrishnan. His work was torn from its roots, robbed of its context. Under this pressure, Pema became an alcoholic.

Finally, he cracked. He had a bad fall while on tour. This came towards the end of a night where he had drunk quite a bit. That was in November

Perhaps the foremost exponent of the Bhil art of 'Pithora', Pema Fatiah now lives in penury. This is a mural done on the inside wall of a hut by Pema with his right arm which has been affected by a paralytic stroke.

250

1993, around divali time, he recalls. 'The next morning, I woke up and found my right hand paralysed. I was really frightened.' The stroke also affected his speech. He returned home immediately. He soon found he could do no other work, either.

Learning of his tragedy, Gopalakrishnan arranged for the government to bear his medical expenses. That ran to over Rs.20,000. The officer also found a job for him in the Bharat Bhavan. 'But,' says Pema, 'I could not take it up in my condition.'

When I first met Pema Fatiah in Bhabra, Meerza Ismail Beg, a retired teacher from Indore – himself an artist – was with me. The depth of Pema's knowledge and the simple way he explained his craft to us held us spellbound. His wife proudly posed by her husband when we took photographs. But she would not raise her veil until his elder brother was out of the way. She was quite happy about the photographs, though. She clearly knew her husband was a great talent, a great painter whose fame went far beyond Bhabra.

When I last met him, a month later, Pema was exercising his right arm. 'I think it might heal in time,' he says. He held my elbow and directed me to a nearby house to show me the work he had attempted. 'It helps me to try and paint,' he says. It was not Pema at his best, but it was, at least, a fresh start. Perhaps one day the art of Pema Fatiah will work for his own gods again.

9

Everybody
Loves
A Good
Drought

Water problems, real and rigged

Drought is, beyond question, among the more serious problems India faces. Drought relief, almost equally beyond question, is rural India's biggest growth industry. Often there is little relation between the two. Relief can go to regions that get lots of rainfall. Even where it goes to scarcity areas, those most in need seldom benefit from it. The poor in such regions understand this. That's why some of them call drought relief *teesra fasl* (the third crop). Only, they are not the ones who harvest it.

A great deal of drought 'relief' goes into contracts handed over to private parties. These are to lay roads, dig wells, send out water tankers, build bridges, repair tanks – the works. Think that can't total up to much? Think again. The money that goes into this industry in a single year can make the withdrawals from Bihar's animal husbandry department look like so many minor fiddles. And the Bihar scam lasted a decade and a half. The charm of *this* scam is that it is largely 'legal'. And it has soul. It's all in a good cause. The tragedy, of course, is that it rarely addresses the real problems of drought and water scarcity.

In 1994-95 alone, the rich state of Maharashtra spent over Rs.11.7 billion on emergency measures in combating drought and on other water-related problems. This was more than the combined profits the previous year of leading companies all across the country in the organised sector of the tea and coffee, cement and automobiles industries. Their profits after tax came to Rs.11.49 billion, according to a report of the Centre for Monitoring the Indian economy. ('Corporate Finances: Industry Aggregates', CMIE, November 1994, Mumbai.)

In August 1995, Prime Minister Narasimha Rao inaugurated an anti-drought project in Orissa. This one will involve spending Rs.45.57 billion in six years. That is, over Rs.7.5 billion a year on just a few districts including Kalahandi, Bolangir and Koraput. Every paisa of that huge sum would be worth spending if it actually fought scarcity and built better infrastructure. That, however, is most unlikely. In part because the main causes of the problems these areas face do not even begin to get addressed.

In theory, drought-prone blocks come under a central scheme known as the Drought Prone Areas Programme (DPAP). But bringing blocks into the DPAP is now a purely political decision. The central allocation for DPAP may be nominal. But once a block is under DPAP, a phalanx of other schemes follows bringing in huge sums of money. The same blocks then get money coming in under the employment assurance scheme (EAS), anti-desertification projects, drinking water missions and a host of other schemes. Well, *some* people do benefit.

In several states, official data on DPAP show us many interesting things. In Maharashtra, the number of DPAP blocks was around ninety six years ago. As of 1996, 147 blocks are under the DPAP. In Madhya Pradesh in the same period, the number of DPAP blocks more than doubled from roughly sixty to around 135. In Bihar, there were fifty-four DPAP blocks right through the 1980s. This became fifty-five when Rameshwar Thakur became a union minister in the early '90s. His home block in Bihar came under the scheme. Today, there are 122 DPAP blocks in that state.

All this has happened during a period where there have been several successive good monsoons. There has been scarcity, too, for some people. But that's a different story.

Kalahandi's major problem, as the reports in this section show, does not arise from poor rainfall. Water resources experts and administrators would largely agree that, barring problems of erratic timing and spread, most Indian districts could get by on around 800 mm of rainfall annually. The lowest rainfall Kalahandi has had in the past twenty years was 978 mm. That is way above what some districts get in 'normal' years. Otherwise, Kalahandi's annual rainfall has been, on an average, 1,250 mm. That is pretty decent. In 1990-91, the district had 2,247 mm of rainfall. Besides, Kalahandi produces more food per person than either Orissa or India as a whole do. Nuapada, the worst part of old Kalahandi, and now a separate district, got 2,366 mm of rainfall in 1994.

In Palamau, too, average rainfall is not bad. The district gets 1,200-1,230 mm of rain in a normal year. In its worst year in recent history, it received 630 mm. Some districts in India get less without experiencing the same damage.

Surguja's rainfall seldom falls below 1,200 mm. In some years it gets 1,500-1,600 mm. That's roughly four times what California gets. And California grows grapes.

Yet all these districts have problems relating to water that are quite deadly. Very different ones from those the funds address. Simply put, we have several districts in India that have an abundance of rainfall – but where one section, the poor, can suffer acute drought. That happens when available water resources are colonised by the powerful. Further, the poor are never consulted or asked to participate in designing the 'programmes' the anti-drought funds bring.

Once it was clear that drought and DPAP were linked to fund flows in a big way, it followed that every one wanted their block under the scheme. In many cases, the powerful are not only able to bring their blocks under it, but appropriate any 'benefits' that follow.

Take Maharashtra. Around 73 per cent of sugar cane produced in the state is grown in DPAP blocks! And sugar cane is about the most water-intensive crop you can get. Secondly, the area under irrigation in Maharashtra is pathetic: just inching towards 15 per cent of crop land. But in the DPAP blocks, in one estimate, it is 22 per cent – nearly 50 per cent higher than the state average. Annual rainfall in Lonavla near Pune seldom falls below 1,650 mm and can touch 2,000 mm. Lonavla is a DPAP block.

Yet the many billions of rupees spent in Maharashtra on relief and on irrigation over the years have not led to any appreciable rise in land under irrigation. In the DPAP blocks are small farmers who really feel the pressure. The water is cornered by the rich and the strong. Governments kid themselves that by throwing money at such regions, the small fish, who have big votes, can be pacified. In reality, the lion's share of funds going there is again appropriated by the powerful. And irrigation water? About two per cent of farmers in the state use around 70 per cent of it.

Drought is a complex phenomenon. You can have an agricultural drought, for instance, even when there is no meteorological drought. That is, you can have adequate rainfall, yet have crop failure. Or you can have hydrological drought, with marked depletion of rivers, streams, springs and fall in ground water levels. The reasons why and how these can and do occur are well known but seldom addressed. It is so much nicer to just put the whole thing down to nature's vagaries. It also works this way because so many forces, at different levels, are either integrated, or get co-opted, into the drought industry. The spiral from the drought scam touches the global stage before returning.

Here's how: Take any one district. Say Surguja (it could be any other). The peasants face many water-related problems. Block-level forces – contractors and politicians – take up 'the cause'. The complaint, typically, is: Our block got far less funds than the others. The collector is ignoring us. That's why it's happening.'

Well, two things are happening, really. One, the peasants of Surguja face serious problems that are intensifying. Two, specific forces are making a pitch at the district headquarters to bring more funds to the block.

The local stringer of a newspaper (based in, say, Bilaspur), takes up the theme: The collector is neglecting 'our block'. Most newspapers pay their stringers a pittance. Some stringers get as little as Rs.50 a month. So only those with other sources of funds can work in this capacity. In many parts of these districts, you will find that the stringer is often a small shopkeeper, a petty businessman.

If contracts for various 'public works' come to the block or district, the stringer might be among the beneficiaries. This is not true of all, but does apply to quite a few stringers. I met many intelligent, resourceful people amongst them. They are bright, have an ear to the ground, react quickly to situations. Quite a few of them are also small contractors. So are many block-level politicians. (So are many national politicians and newspaper owners, but that's another story.)

Reports of raging drought put pressure on a district administration strapped for resources. (Some of the stories have strong elements of truth, though death counts are often exaggerated.) The collector calls his friends: the district level correspondents. He explains that his district gets far less from the state capital than other, neighbouring ones. This could well be true. The collector is also pitching at the state capital for a better share of the resource cake. Reports of 'step-motherly treatment' of Surguja, or whichever district it is, start appearing in newspapers in the state capital.

That embarrasses the state government. How does it respond? While doing what it can locally, it also pitches at the centre for more funds to deal with the drought. State governments often bring down correspondents from mainline journals to the state capital. These reporters then set off on a guided tour of the 'affected areas'. Governments often have vehicles reserved for the purpose of press tours. And often, a senior official goes with the journalists to the trouble spots.

The sophisticated writers of the urban press are superior to the local press when it comes to the heart-rending stuff. The drought becomes a national issue. Copy full of phrases like 'endless stretches of parched land', accompanied by photographs, reaches urban audiences. (Now parched land is not necessarily a symbol of drought. You can have it in very wet places if you drain a pond. And you can have an acute water shortage in seemingly green areas. But parched land makes better copy and pictures.) This is especially true of the English press. The Indian language press has serious problems, but is closer to the ground.

If it is, say, mid-May when reporters reach the affected region, the searing heat will impress some. With your skin and hair on fire, it is easy to believe there has been drought in the area since the dawn of time. There could be flooding here two months hence, but that doesn't matter now. Unlike the quick-on-the-uptake local stringers, the national press is seldom clued in on ground reality. There are, of course, many reporters who could handle the real stories of the place. They don't often get sent on such trips. Those are not the kind of stories their publications are looking for. Every editor knows that drought means parched land and, hopefully, pictures of emaciated people. That's what 'human interest' is about, isn't it?

The state has made its pitch at the centre. The centre is unfazed. It uses what it considers examples of responsible reporting (that is, reports that do not vilify the centre) to advantage. It makes its own pitch for resources. International funding agencies, foreign donors, get into the act. UNDP, UNICEF, anyone who can throw a little money about. The global aid community is mobilised into fighting drought in a district that gets 1,500 mm of rainfall annually.

The reverse spiral begins.

Donor governments love emergency relief. It forms a negligible part of their spending, but makes for great advertising. (Emergencies of many sorts do this, not just drought. You can run television footage of the Marines kissing babies in Somalia.) There are more serious issues between rich and poor nations – like unequal trade. Settling those would be of greater help to the latter. But for that, the 'donors' would have to part with something for real. No. They prefer emergency relief.

So money comes into Delhi from several sources. The next step in the downward spiral is for central departments to fight over it. Nothing awakens the conscience like a lot of money. One department or ministry remembers it has a mission to save the forests of the suffering district. Another recalls a commitment to manage its water resources.

Then there are all the hungry, Rs.30,000-a-month consultants to be clothed and fed. Projects are drawn up with their assistance for fighting drought in the district. Or for water resource management. Or for anything at all. Studies of water problems are vital. But some of these are thought up simply because there are funds now. (The collector and a lot of peasants in the district could probably tell you a great deal about the real water problems. But they're not 'experts'.)

The money goes to the state capital where the struggle over sharing it continues. At the district level, the blocks pitch for their share. Contracts go out for various emergency works. A little money might even get spent on those affected by the water shortage. But it cannot solve their problems.

The next year the same problems will crop up all over again because the real issues were never touched.

At the end of it, many forces including well-meaning sections of the press have been co-opted into presenting a picture of natural calamity. Too often, into dramatising an event without looking at the processes behind it. The spiral works in different ways in different states. But it works.

And yet so many people do suffer from water-related problems. Several of India's more troublesome conflicts are linked to water. It may have taken a back seat, but the sharing of river waters was a major part of the Punjab problem. The ongoing quarrel between Tamil Nadu and Karnataka is over the Cauvery river waters. (Some of India's tensions with Bangladesh have their basis in water sharing disputes.) The struggle over water resources operates at the micro, village level, too, in many ways. Between villages, between hamlets within a village, between castes and classes. (For more on drought-related issues, also see the sections on displacement, survival, usury and fightback.)

Conflicts arising from man-made drought are on the rise. Deforestation does enormous damage. Villagers are increasingly losing control over common water resources. The destruction of traditional irrigation systems is gaining speed. A process of privatisation of water resources is apparent in most of the real drought areas (take the water lords of Ramnad, for instance). There are now two kinds of drought: the real and the rigged. Both can be under way at the same time, in the same place. As the reports that follow seek to show, they often are.

The sale of a girl

Amlapali, Nuapada (Orissa): In India, it was *the* human interest story of the '80s. A story about the sale of a girl in this village. A story that touched the conscience of a nation and brought Kalahandi into sharp focus. In a sense, the journalism of that period does symbolise some of the better efforts of the press. As it does some of its limitations.

It was in July 1985 that Phanas Punji, in her early thirties, shot to notoriety. She had, so the story went, 'sold' her fourteen-year-old sister-in-law, Banita Punji, to the nearly blind Bidya Podh. He paid Rs.40 to 'buy' Banita and use her as a 'domestic servant'. Phanas's husband had abandoned her two years earlier. And she was widely quoted in the press as saying: 'My own two children are starving. What could I do?'

Everyone observed that she did not deny selling the girl. The story shook the nation. It appalled Rajiv Gandhi, then prime minister. Worse, his office received confirmation of the sale. He decided to go and have a look at Kalahandi himself.

Hordes of officials descended on this part of Kalahandi. (It is now a separate district called Nuapada.) Not so much to set things right, as to prepare for the prime ministerial tour. And scores of reporters reached Nuapada, even today one of India's poorest districts. After all, the Prime Minister himself was going there. You couldn't miss an event like that.

The episode produced some of the most stirring journalism of the '80s. Some brilliant reporting destroyed the efforts at a cover-up by the then Orissa state government headed by J.B. Patnaik. The misery of Kalahandi stood naked. More reports followed as journalists met the myriad faces of poverty in the region. Moving stories on drought and scarcity conditions appeared in profusion. There was an almost missionary zeal to it.

Television did what print could not. It brought the actors in the drama, including J.B. Patnaik, in person before the public eye. Indian journalist M.J. Akbar's TV interview with Patnaik rattled the chief minister. He later denounced it in public as 'concocted'. Patnaik also damaged himself further in the state assembly. There, he implied that the sale of children was a 'tradition' in parts of western Orissa.

The press crusade had an effect. It forced two prime ministers, two chief ministers and countless ministers to visit Nuapada-Kalahandi over the years. That meant better roads, improved communications and some repairs to bridges. These receive attention only when a VIP shows up.

The crusade also brought huge funds for development. Innumerable projects were announced, mostly for Kalahandi – though poverty is hardly exclusive to this region. Voluntary agencies, many of them floating in foreign funds, descended on the district in droves – to promote development.

Those were proud moments for the media.

A decade later, all the principal actors in that drama are in much the same state they were. Perhaps, in some ways, worse off.

Kalahandi and Nuapada remain seemingly untouched by the crores of rupees and hordes of projects thrown at them. J.B. Patnaik, too, is worse off. He is no longer chief minister*.

In February 1994, nine years after those events, I met Phanas Punji for the first time at Amlapalli. (My last visit to this part of Nuapada was in December 1996.) I also spoke to Banita and Bidya Podh at Badtunda. With me was ex-MLA Kapil Narain Tiwari. He was instrumental in breaking the original story. He has also done more than any other politician to highlight Kalahandi's plight.

Now an *anganwadi*† worker, Phanas has lost even more of the meagre land her husband's family once owned. All of it to moneylenders. Her husband, however, is back. But, she says, 'he is unemployed most of the year as before'. Banita, now twenty-two, lives at Badtunda village in Bolangir district. That's just a few kilometres away. She is still with the 'blind old man' and they have three children to whom both seem greatly attached.

- Banita and Bidya Podh are no better off than Phanas. Banita, too, is an *anganwadi* worker ('I do the cooking there'). The effectiveness of the *anganwadi* scheme is apparent in the condition of her own three children. All are malnourished, the youngest one severely so. Both Phanas and Banita were earning Rs.100 a month in their jobs till a short while ago. Now they earn Rs.210 a month. That's about a third of what they would get if paid the official minimum wage of Rs.25 per day in Orissa. Neither is able to feed her family properly. Both look after out-of-work husbands.

- As for Bidya Podh, no one ever spoke to him. Not even when the reports on

---

* He has returned to that post since this report first appeared in print.

† *Anganwadi* – a day care centre for children under six years of age.

the 'sale of a girl' were being done. That might have spoilt the story. Apparently, humanising the story meant demonising some. Podh was a soft target. After all, he wasn't even going to read the stories, anyway. He became, in some reports, the 'blind old man' who had 'bought Banita' and cruelly exploited her. One story cast him as the blind old 'landlord'. Another had him buying the girl for Rs.40 and then 'abandoning' her after satiating his lust.

Far from being the 'landlord' Banita was sold to, Podh is landless. He does not even own homestead land. The roof over their heads belongs to one of his uncles. Podh's sight is very badly impaired indeed. Some might call him blind, yes. But he can see well enough to recognise his visitors. He certainly knew me the second time I went to his hut.

Old? The 'blind old landlord' was a young man in his twenties when the episode first took place in 1985.

- Kapil Tiwari hasn't changed either. It would be a great pity if he had. The man who described himself as 'a below-the-poverty-line ex-MLA', is as

From left: Phanas Punji, ex-MLA Kapil Narain Tiwari, and Banita and Bidya Podh with their three children. Nine years after the drama which shook a nation, all the principal actors are in much the same state as they were. Perhaps, in some ways, worse off.

angry as ever at what is happening in Kalahandi. He still relentlessly fights injustice in his role of independent political maverick.

I met and photographed all of them together: their lives ridiculously untouched by the furious national debate that raged around them.

'Prime Minister Rajiv Gandhi's visit made no difference,' Phanas told me. 'Others may have got loans, I got nothing. Only a lot of people came and took photographs of me.'

The cover stories on Phanas and Banita in 1985 emphasised the issue of the 'sale of the girl'. That touched a nation's conscience and brought some relief to Kalahandi – never mind who cornered the benefits. Yet the 'sale of a girl' issue proved a double-edged sword.

It had one truly positive result: had the press not rammed home that aspect so powerfully, the story would never have gained the same emotional appeal. And it is highly unlikely that Kalahandi would have got the attention, sympathy and relief that it did. At the same time, the focus on the *event*, and the subsequent dispute over whether it was indeed a sale, obscured important processes leading to it.

Sure, the 'sale' story linked up with the coverage of drought and poverty. But the reporting on the latter was not so brilliant. Indeed, it bristled with errors and stereotypes. In any case, whatever the reports aimed at, the focus was on the 'sale'. Politically, that took centre stage.

Now Banita sees the issues beyond the sale. Her family, like that of Phanas, is very poor. 'Phanas sold some of my land,' points out Banita. 'She wanted me out of the way so she could sell it.' When Phanas's husband deserted her for two years, he left the village as well. Who knew if he would come back? Banita was the other owner of the family land. Did Phanas sell her sister-in-law (or force her into wedding the unassertive simpleton Podh) as a means of doing Banita out of that land? Banita was just fourteen at the time and hardly in a position to protest.

This seems Banita's major concern on that score and with good reason. Much of the land is already with moneylenders. 'Amlapali,' as Dr S.K. Pattnaik of the NGO, Vikalpa, points out, 'is a classic example of land alienation via debt.' Phanas and her family remain in that trap.

Bidya Podh did not 'abandon' Banita soon after 'buying' her, as stories in 1986 suggested. Fed up with her mother-in-law's behaviour, Banita returned to Phanas – the very woman said to have sold her. Podh begged her to return, promising his mother would behave and that he would work to support Banita. She returned to him and has remained for years. The second promise has fallen through as Podh remains jobless. The mother-in-law, though, behaved. Podh's entire family, actually, was all in favour of the wedding. They did not look on it as a sale or a purchase. Whether in the rural or the urban world, it is very difficult to find a partner for a physically disabled person. That is why Podh's uncle gave the homeless couple a hut to live in.

Interestingly Banita does not see it in 'sale' or purchase terms either. As for Phanas, if she calmly accepted the 'sale' story, she had reason to. It helped. If this was the story that would get her the help and the attention, it would do. She is extremely media conscious and knows her lines to perfection. She quickly understood that the 'sale' story was what mattered. And she stuck to it. 'Yes, I sold her for Rs.40,' she says. Yet, when Banita walked out on Podh for that period, Phanas did not hesitate to take her back into the house. All of them recognise each other as family. It was Phanas who took me to meet Banita.

Banita was purely a victim. Phanas is a victim, too, of much the same forces as Banita. But she has also been a bit of an operator. She always kept the focus on herself: the miserably poor woman forced to sell her sister-in-law. Everybody but everybody spoke to Phanas. She has told and sold her story many times over. From the Prime Ministers to reporters, everyone making the pilgrimage to Amlapali has left some money with Phanas. And indeed they might. Hers is a story of grinding poverty. So is that of Banita and Podh. But no one sought a single statement or quote from either of them. In the 'relief' that followed, they got nothing.

How come Banita – even allowing for social pressures – remains with Bidya Podh when she could leave? After all, the entire force of the state would be behind her. The sale of children still occurs. But Banita wasn't exactly a child then and certainly isn't one now. Phanas Punji admits land has passed out of the family's hands. Did all of them understand their problems the way the rest of us did?

Banita's is a trap of economic necessity and social pressure. But she displays no resentment towards Podh. 'We had no proper marriage ceremony. After all, who has the money? Looking after my children is the main thing. If Bidya gets a job, it would be better. Can you help him get one?' Her anxieties capture one of Kalahandi-Nuapada's biting problems: unemployment. Phanas's son Jagbandhu is also jobless. One thing repeatedly strikes us in our talk with Banita: how clearly this young woman sees the issues the experts and the press miss out on.

Thousands here migrate each year to survive. 'Things are so bad,' says Duryodhan Sabar, 'that even smaller landowners who once kept bonded labour are migrating.' Sabar, a tribal, is an activist of the Jagrut Shramik Sanghatan (Organisation of Conscious Labourers). As a former bonded labourer, he once led a struggle against bondage in this region.

If Phanas and her kin are still the way they are, one question comes up. If all the development projects worth tens of millions of rupees, all the media exposures, and all the NGOs with their foreign funds could not transform the lives of this one family – after all that publicity – then what, really, has been achieved in Kalahandi? Imagine the state of those who received no such attention.

The achievements of the press in the mid-'80s were very real. At one level, they set a trend, however transient, of more sympathetic coverage of the poor. If a nation was sensitised to the misery of Kalahandi, it was due to the relentless assault of the press on the hypocrisy of the J.B. Patnaik government. Yet Nuapada-Kalahandi's problems are much more than just the result of Patnaik's incompetence. And more than just the result of drought or scarcity.

What got obscured were the linkages between conditions in Kalahandi and policies at the state and national levels. Drought is still mostly viewed as a natural calamity, despite considerable evidence to the contrary in many cases. It is ridiculous to expect the press to transform reality. Yet, it can contribute a great deal by deepening public understanding of problems. Doing that requires some analytical rigour.

Even the best reports on Kalahandi in 1985-86 spoke of 'perpetual drought and scarcity conditions'. Some even talked of 'twenty years of drought'. The truth? As Jagdish Pradhan of the Paschim Orissa Krishijeevi Sangha (Western Orissa Farmers Association) points out, the lowest rainfall Kalahandi has had in the past 20 years is 978 mm. That is way above what some districts in India get in 'normal' years. Otherwise, Kalahandi's annual rainfall has been, on an average, 1,250 mm. That is pretty decent, though the spread is uneven.

In 1990-91, the district recorded rainfall of 2,247 mm. The spread was okay. But it did not greatly reduce suffering. So maybe poor rainfall is not the problem?

Besides, as Pradhan says, 'Kalahandi has remained a food surplus district all this while. And that, despite monumental crop failures.' Kalahandi produces more food per person than both Orissa and India as a whole do. But its own inhabitants consume only 25 per cent of that food. The rest goes out of the region through networks of merchant-moneylenders.

Per capita production of food for all of India was 203 kg per citizen in

1989-90. For Orissa – with the largest percentage of people below the poverty line – it was 253 kg. In Kalahandi the same year, per capita production of food was 331 kg. That beats the state and national averages hollow. Even so, people do suffer acute hunger. And parents do abandon children because there isn't enough to survive on.

But at the best of times, the press has viewed drought and scarcity as *events*. And the belief that only events make news, not *processes*, distorts understanding. Some of the best reports on poverty suffer from trying to dramatise it as an event. The real drama is in the process. In the causes.

Deforestation has much to do with drought. But being a process, it becomes a 'feature'. And then disappears into the newspaper ghetto called 'ecology' – presumed to be of interest only to rabid 'Greens'.

The reality? The combined investment in all development projects in Orissa since Independence is eclipsed by the commercial value of renewable timber and forests lost in making way for them.

So many other factors get nowhere near the attention they need. The destruction of Kalahandi's traditional irrigation systems, for one. And flawed development strategies that hurt thousands, for another. Some of these end up spurring the migrations they seek to curb. Also, vicious usury that sees people in distress selling paddy at less than half the official support price. And a skewed landholding pattern with ever growing alienation. These too need to be viewed in conjunction with the sale of children they result in.

- As I write, migrants from the poverty-stricken border zone of Nuapada-Bolangir are moving, as in 1985. Only, in larger numbers. Their destinations range from Raipur, where they will pull rickshaws, to Mumbai where they will toil at construction sites. The frightening levels of joblessness propelling them are rising.
- The flesh trade sending women to Raipur's brothels is thriving. The inequity of land-holding patterns of old Kalahandi has not improved. The moneylenders to whom the Phanas Punjis of the world alienate their land may be less in numbers. They seem more powerful in scope, though. The public health system is a mess. Worse, malaria is rampant.
- The development projects meant to help Kalahandi have changed. But only in name and number. In effect, they are mostly the same. Lacking popular roots, they tend to fail. Some district administrators have tried the odd positive intervention. Yet distress sales of land, labour and produce are very much there, too. In short, Nuapada, and all of Kalahandi, are largely the same.

267

Postscript

When I last visited Nuapada, it was clear that most of the basic problems remained the same. Incidentally, Phanas's house continues to be a place of journalistic pilgrimage. The other villagers of Amlapali resent this quite a bit. 'Everyone comes here and gives her money,' they say. 'Have the rest of us no problems?' Even on an earlier trip, while I was looking at the pattern of land alienation in the village, people made a point of telling me this. Everyone in Kalahandi has a story.

Was Banita's a case of a child 'sale'? Just as there is such a thing as dowry, there is the practice of bride price. Which framework does Banita's case fall into? Who is to decide? Banita's decision is to stay with Podh.

The stories that appeared in 1985-86 had a strong impact on me, as they did on most others reading the newspapers in the '80s. After the first two trips I made in 1994, I had a more detailed look at the stories of that period. Alongside the achievements were also distressing attitudes. Positive impact does not excuse stereotypes.

One of the most widely read stories of that period began: 'Here is a picture of hell.' It went on to say that all those who were 'unable to get away' from Kalahandi were 'dead or dying'.

Those who remained 'move in groups, licking water, like dogs'. There you have the essence of an upper middle class view of the poor – as animals. Animals to be pitied, perhaps, but animals all the same. Like dogs. But that wasn't all.

'For food they pick up the poisonous roots and leaves – the only thing that will grow there.' It was the first time I got to know that people went out to pick up poisonous roots. I had thought that happened by accident. But, after all, what else can you pick up if this is the 'only thing that will grow there'. The story very correctly spoke of the 1965 drought as a major event. But then went on to speak of a twenty-year drought. (The rainfall data says otherwise.)

There was much to respect in the story's detailing of the crisis and drought of 1985. It deserved great credit for its exposure of official failure. It did speak of some economic factors. But the focus remained on the 'sale' and on natural calamity. And the attitudes and stereotypes keep coming through. 'Nature (had) been cruel.' There had been a 'long famine'. There was 'no longer any hope in the area'. These only help take the focus off *why* people stay poor.

Things haven't changed too much in some ways. Quite a few journals still freely interchange the words 'drought' and 'famine'. Obviously, these two mean very different things. But the word 'famine' is more alarmist and makes better copy. In 1986, one editor argued that the difference between the two was merely 'semantic'. Present-day efforts at covering poverty still insist on the *events* approach. Poverty gets covered in breathless tones of horror and shock that suggest something new has happened, even when it hasn't.

Apparently, crisis merits attention only when it results in catastrophe, not earlier. It takes years for a food surplus district like Kalahandi to arrive at where it has. But that is a process. It does not make news. Maybe it is still worth writing about, though?

The water lords of Ramnad

Ramanathapuram (Tamil Nadu): Ramu doesn't spend too much time on agriculture these days. True, he is one of the bigger landowners in Keelathooval village here. But he is into a business that pays far better. Ramu owns a borewell and an electric pumpset.

That makes the young entrepreneur a 'water lord' (*thaneer adipathy*) in Ramnad (more properly called Ramanathapuram). This is a chronically drought-prone district that has suffered an average rainfall deficiency of around 112 mm per year in the last decade. And rainfall in the first five months of this year makes even those bad days look good. It's less than 10 per cent of what it was during the corresponding period for any year in the awful 1980s.

Close to 90 per cent of irrigated area here depends for water on 1,841 rain-fed tanks. That means the people of Ramnad live at the mercy of the monsoon. This district does not have a single perennial river. Even its share of wells is 20 per cent below the Tamil Nadu average. Farmers who don't have access to water resources and pumpsets have to buy water from those who do. Those in Keelathooval and some other villages of the Mudukulluthur taluka have to hire Ramu's services to draw water from the dismally low levels at which it exists in wells and tanks.

Ramu charges Rs.12 per hour for the use of his three-horse power (HP) electric pumpset during the agricultural season. On that basis, he netted Rs.2,000 in forty-five days from just one small farmer and neighbour of his, Karuppannan. And he has a long list of clients.

Two factors further favour Ramu in such deals. One, he has few overheads. As an agriculturist, he gets electricity free. Two, a terribly low voltage is the norm here. This leads to the pumpset running twice the number of hours it should, increasing Karuppannan's burden and Ramu's profits. Karuppannan owns less than an acre and Rs.2,000 is a huge sum for him. Another farmer, Nagarajan, also paid Ramu Rs.2,000 for water during the season. 'And that,' he points out, 'was for a crop like chilli. Paddy needs much more water.'

Raju in Nallangudi charges Rs.30 per hour. That's because he uses a 5-HP oil pumpset. He operates on a grand scale, servicing farmers in Etivayal, Thiyanoor and five or six other villages. He's also more into drawing water

270

Privateers have grabbed a public tank bed at Sayalgudi, Ramnad, and bring small fleets of bullock-carts to carry away water from there. They even station a few of their people at the site to prevent anyone else from drawing water from the wells dug in the tank bed.

from the public *kanmoi* (the giant irrigation tanks of Ramnad). Is the level in your *kanmoi* low? Ask Raju about it. But be sure that there are enough of you. Unless there are forty to fifty clients from a village, he may not find the job worth his while.

Govindarajan owns two oil pumpsets and an electric one as well. His fee for hire of the electric set is the same as Ramu's. But he charges Rs.30 an hour for the use of an oil pumpset. Unlike electricity, oil does not come free. He is also able to sell water from his own wells. The drought has made him richer by Rs.70,000 this season.

There are other crucial factors common to these three water lords. All own sizeable tracts of land, and have access to a water source. And the extent

271

of development of Ramnad's water markets is astounding.

The drinking water market doesn't lag behind. It couldn't, in this district. On an average, each person gets zero to six litres of water daily in most villages. That's less than half a bucket per villager for all purposes. In Ramnad town itself, the owner of a local bakery runs a lucrative sideline, specialising in selling water to lodges and hotels.

The 'water market' at Sayalgudi is a spectacular sight. At any given moment, ten to twelve ox-carts carrying huge barrels are drawing water from the public *kanmoi* for private sale. Privateers have dug new wells or deepened existing ones in the bed of the public *kanmoi*. They charge 30 paise (less than 1p) a pot for the drinking water they draw from here.

Others have set up bathing ghats in the *kanmoi* area. The going rate is 50 paise for a bath. Locals in Sayalgudi told me that the new collector of Ramnad, L. Krishnan, had come down to the town on their complaints. Fed up with the racketeering, he got the local panchayat union to take over the bathing ghats. This worked.

Then, a week later, the water lords proclaimed they 'owned' wells within the public tank in Sayalgudi. Muthuchellan, Arunachalam and Sivalingam between them 'own' thirteen 'private' wells sunk in the tank bed. 'There is a giant water market here,' says R. Karunanidhi, a Tamil Nadu Kisan Sabha (Peasants Association) leader fighting the racket. At just 30 paise a pot and at a modest rate of 500 pots a day per well, these three clean up around Rs.60,000 a month. The water lords are often people with some political links. But the more important 'market' in the long run is, of course, the invisible one in the villages. The market in which people like Ramu and Govindrajan operate.

In the dalit hamlet of Etivayal, there is not one tap, no piped sources, and only salt water in the well. To top it all, a minor official of the water board sells residents drinking water at 20 paise per pot. How does he get that water? By diverting some of the supply bound for Ramnad town. When I reached Etivayal, the official was away, offering prayers at a distant temple. The villagers went without water for the day.

'We go to Saveriarpattinam and Mahidi for drinking water,' says V. Nagarajan of Keelathooval. 'And across that distance, you can't carry more than one pot at a time.' A woman here spends up to four hours each day, maybe more, just looking for water during the summer months. And the implications of the water crisis do not end there.

Kalahandi district in Orissa is often held up as a sort of symbol of drought. Kalahandi's annual rainfall has been, on an average, 1,250 mm. The lowest rainfall Kalahandi has had in the past 20 years in 978 mm. In Ramnad, that would be considered a rare bounty. 'Normal' rainfall here would be around 827 mm. Right through the '80s, the district actually averaged less than 720 mm of rainfall annually. In some years, it can fall to around 650 mm or less.

Ramnad has always had one of the highest levels of long-term migration. As in Pudukkottai, the sex ratio is favourable to women – contrary to the state and national trends. This is not because women here enjoy a higher status, but due to drought-driven migration. The failure of agriculture sees large numbers of adult males seeking work outside the district.

Then there is the landlord-cum-water lord selling water to neighbouring small farmers. He may and often does decide to hold it back at crucial moments, crippling those who have based their season's calculations on getting that water. This can mire them in debt and, over time, result in their losing land to the landlord.

The creeping privatisation of water resources is going to end up dispossessing the peasantry in more ways than one.

One answer, as the collector well knows, is going in for community borewells rather than private ones. But Krishnan also knows that the problem doesn't end there. 'Every administration tries to reach assets like community borewells to the weakest sections,' he says. 'And the moment we sink one in, say, a scheduled caste hamlet, what happens? There are half-a-dozen vested interests in the village out to damage that well. It affects their profits and dominance. We really have to educate people on the value of this asset so that they defend and maintain it properly and well.'

There's irony in Ramnad's historical sobriquet: the 'Land of Tanks'. The ancients clearly knew that if the region was to survive, then proper management of its water resources was essential.

In the old Ramnad, which includes the present-day districts of Pasumpon and Kamrajar, there were over 6,000 ancient tanks. There are 1,841 in present-day Ramnad, some over a millennium old.

The giant 'Ramnad big tank' has a capacity of over 618 million cubic feet with a free catchment area of over 8.24 square miles. No one seems to know exactly how old it is, not even the gazetteer. The Vaigai river empties itself into this tank.

The Rajasinghamangalam tank in Tiruvadanai taluk is huge. It has a 13-mile-long bund and irrigates 4,500 acres.

The great tanks of Ramnad were, interestingly, constructed in series. This means the surplus water escaping from one tank went via channels to feed other tanks lower down the line, and so on. So, within limits, deficient tanks were fed by surplus ones.

It isn't as if the ancient Tamil kings were filled with altruism. As David Ludden, a scholar who studied irrigation methods spanning two millennia in Tamil Nadu, puts it: 'Rich peasants dug wells, chiefs built tanks and kings built dams.' But there was at least a concept of rational use of water, a clear idea of water harvesting.

To this day, close to 90 per cent of the irrigated area here depends for water on the 1,841 ancient tanks. For the rest of Tamil Nadu, the area dependent on rain-fed irrigation averages only 38 per cent. Ramnad's traditional irrigation system is its lifeline. But it is a lifeline in crisis.

Most of the tanks desperately need repairs. But as one senior official here put it, 'The funds allotted for the upkeep of tanks are less than 40 per cent of what is needed. So only very important repairs are carried out in specific cases. With the available funds, it is not possible to carry out repairs on the supply channels feeding the tanks.' Though strapped for funds, the public works department (PWD) has tried hard to keep the tanks going.

So far as drinking water goes, desalination of sea water has proved technologically feasible. The collector, L. Krishnan, is justifiably optimistic about this option. The cost factor is not yet right, though. Besides, this needs large investments in an era where governments are spending less. And it could run into problems if the costs are passed on to a public already fed up with having to buy water from privateers at absurd prices.

Plain political neglect and a failure to see the outcome for Ramnad of projects like the Vaigai dam have worsened the agony of this district. The coming of the Vaigai dam (from the '50s) in the Madurai area actually reduced the inflow of that river into Ramnad.

'We have our own internal Cauvery-type dispute right here within Tamil Nadu,' says one political activist. 'The lack of will at the top is to blame for Ramnad's water problems.'

Meanwhile, with its extensive 265 km coastline, Ramnad does have a large groundwater potential. But wells are already being sunk in the range of 150 metres and deeper. Officials say that, unlike the rest of Tamil Nadu, Ramnad has not grossly over-exploited its groundwater resources.

In fact, it has made use of less than a third of its supposed reserves. But the wells are going deeper, costs are going higher and villagers increasingly complain of *upu thaneer* (salt water).

One study in Ramnad compared the levels of forty-nine wells in June 1992, with those obtaining in the same wells in June 1990. It showed that water levels had improved by a pathetic 0.23 per cent in just ten of the wells. In the remaining thirty-nine, they had stagnated or declined.

At the Tamil Nadu level, of 1,793 wells surveyed only 1.65 per cent showed minor increases. The implications for groundwater in the long run are not encouraging.

It is in agriculture that the problem hits hardest, thanks to governmental neglect spanning decades. A techno-economic survey of Ramnad in 1973 concluded that its ancient tanks were essential to the district. It advised that 'repairs to them should be taken up immediately'. Twenty years later, with shrinking funds, many of those repairs are yet to begin.

A visit to the 'Ramnad big tank' brings home the last aspect of the 'water markets'. A private merchant has acquired rights through an official tender – at a cost of less than Rs.200,000 – to catch fish in the great tank. This he does for a season of just thirty days, during which he earns anything from Rs.1.2 to Rs.2 million. On the whole, the Pandyas and Cholas had better uses for tanks and water.

Searching for water in Pudukkottai

Pudukkottai (Tamil Nadu): it was a swift, silent raid, launched under cover of darkness as the train crept into Pudukkottai railway station at 2.30 a.m. The passengers remained asleep. I was pinned back in the corridor with my knapsack. A befuddled security guard who had been dozing, leaning against his rifle, looked on helplessly as the men swarmed on board. They were armed with pots, buckets and jerry cans.

And all they wanted was water.

This they obtained by emptying the toilet tanks with practised ease. A couple of minutes later, I was alone on the platform. They were gone. So was most of the train's water.

Scarcity has promoted a thriving water market in this district of 1.3 million people. This operates in terms of both irrigation and drinking water. Right here, in Pudukkottai town, you can witness all-night searches for water at many points. In the villages, no one gets more than ten litres of water daily. That's the average on the good days – and ten litres won't fill one standard-sized bucket. Often it falls to six litres and on some days to nil. Compare that with the daily average of 220 litres each resident of Delhi gets. That figure is 190 in Calcutta, 155 in Mumbai and 70 in Chennai.

A few days after that curious welcome at the Pudukkottai town railway station, I arrive in Gandarvakkottai. The police has just moved in on the drought-stricken block. They are herding hundreds of angry villagers into the panchayat union office for talks. The villagers have been picketing all bus and lorry traffic in their area. 'How else can we get them to pay any attention to the water crisis?' ask the protesters.

Drought here means much more than a lack of drinking water. It shatters income and livelihood in a region where irrigation is heavily dependent on thousands of rain-fed tanks, some of them centuries old. The area irrigated by canals and wells together (approx. 22,000 hectares) is about one-fourth of that irrigated by the rain-fed tanks (over 82,000 hectares). 'Rain-fed' means being at the mercy of a monsoon that has failed all but once during the past ten years.

Lack of water spurs the huge migrations of human beings that occur each year in this least urbanised of Tamil Nadu's districts. I find whole colonies of deserted houses in rural Gandarvakkottai. In the Tulakampatti hamlet, for instance, over 160 of 200 families have left their homes. Most have gone to neighbouring Thanjavur district, one of the richest in the state. Many will return only months later.

It is eerie walking past rows of houses without a single occupant. The only human being I do spot in the lifeless lanes is Vijaya, twenty-four, an agricultural worker. She has just come down for a day from Thanjavur to see if the family hut is still in one piece. One of many poor Kuravurs (a denotified tribe) in this colony, Vijaya feels they have 'no choice but to live this way'. Many Muthurajas (a most backward caste) have also left Tulakampatti.

'It's seasonal,' shrugs one official at the block level, making it sound as simple as tourism. But Kaliamurthy, forty-six, a Kuravur who has stayed behind in the hamlet, describes the crisis in one word: 'Water.'

In three other villages of the same block that I visit – Periakkottai, Ulavaigal and Kovilpatti – people in the 18-45 age group are invisible. In many cases, their families did not really know where they have gone. They only know they had gone out looking for work because, 'here there is no water. What agriculture can we have?' No member of the state legislative assembly or of the Central Parliament seems to have been to any of these places.

Pudukkottai has had a fine total literacy campaign (TLC). It has seen the most successful drive in the 9 to 45 age group in any district of the south outside of Kerala. Leading that drive was the remarkable *Arivoli Iyakkam* (Light of Knowledge Movement). This is a government sponsored body of which the Collector is the president. Yet *Arivoli* draws huge numbers of dedicated volunteers from diverse sections of society.

At an *Arivoli* meeting in one block, we get to know of the damage water scarcity can inflict on even the literacy drive. Many activists report that the survey for the post-literacy campaign (PLC) in their villages is a mess. Mass migrations have hurt it badly. Worst hit are places like Sangamvidudhi and Palaya Gandarvakkottai. This will cause long delays in the PLC. Worse still, the time lag could hurt the neo-literates, causing many of them to slide back into illiteracy.

The trend in Tulakampatti is causing *Arivoli* activists a good deal of worry. There, migrant workers are taking their children along with them to Thanjavur. Earlier, they would leave them with elders in the village. 'This means,' says one activist, 'that a whole section of these young ones will not only miss the net of the literacy drive, but may never see the inside of a school.' If it keeps up, Tulakampatti could have a next generation of hard-core non-starters and illiterates.

There is another long-term effect that persistent water scarcity has had here. And that is its role in the loss of land by the peasants. In many parts, the development process has hurt poor people. For instance, the coming of borewells some years ago meant that the small farmers of the Muthuraja colony of Kovilpatti lost most of their lands. The borewell owners were richer and higher-caste farmers of the next hamlet. And they used their new weapon to deadly effect.

As Dr K. Nagaraj of the Madras Institute of Development Studies puts it: 'The man controlling groundwater becomes extremely important. He sinks the borewells. He has the resources and the bank contacts.'

In Kovilpatti, many things happened once the borewells appeared. The first effect was the drying of the traditional dug-wells of the small farmers. The next step was for the borewell owners to sell water to these farmers, or to deny it to them at crucial moments, ravaging their crop and often entrapping them in debt as a consequence. The third step was to demand a part of their produce. The fourth was to dictate what they would produce. The fifth was to move from exploiting their dependence on water to acquiring their lands.

Govindarajan, fifty-six, of Kovilpatti, recalls the time when many of the Muthuraja families owned up to three acres of land each, even more. Now, those who hold any land at all own a third of an acre or less. The villagers lost more than forty acres to the bigger farmers, says Govindarajan. 'Now, we have no borewells and no water. It made all the difference.'

This is a bit of an oversimplification. A farcical land reform and unviable land units are also big factors. Yet, water or the lack of it deeply influences the lives of hundreds of thousands of people in this district. If you're looking for a link between control of water resources and poverty, Pudukkottai and Ramnad next door provide stark examples.

Water is also a major element in caste and other disputes. The plight of the dalit colonies deepens in this season. The upper castes, who restrict their access to water at the best of times, shut it off completely when there is a drought. So quite a few of the Gandarvakkottai protesters are dalits.

'We are migrating to West Thanjavur for now,' says Mahamayee, fifty, a dalit from Saveriapatti village. 'We have no water, no roads and the upper castes don't allow us even drinking water. They say go get it from the officials. Sometimes we spend the whole day searching for water, being chased away from one tap or well or another. The pumps are under repair for ever.'

Even where the block development officer is well meaning, as in Gandarvakottai, he is often helpless. He has few resources at his command. For even minor repairs, he has to go through an 'approved list of contractors'. Some of the 'approved' ones can take months to fulfil a trivial task.

Lack of water touches every aspect of life in Pudukkottai. From health and education to industry, the literacy drive, debt repayment and land – all feel its effects. Now, under drought, it spurs mass migrations.

A visit to some of the district's villages brings home this reality: on the day we visit Thachankurichi, we find a car mysteriously circling the little community.

We do not know whose it is, but the villagers do. They are telling us of how the drought has wrecked their fragile economy, when the car draws up close. In it is an agent of the Pudukkottai Central Co-operative Bank. We are standing outside one of the more affluent dwellings of the place, and that interests him. He drives past us three or four times, eyeing the jeep a friend has brought me in. He is wondering if it is an asset he can seize as part of his dues recovery crusade.

It is the middle of May and the drought is biting hard. In block after block people are unable to pay their dues to a variety of creditors.

Intriguingly, Pudukkottai district as a whole is not under the drought-prone areas programme (DPAP) run by the central government. This is a district that often gets less than 800 mm of rainfall annually. It could end a bad year like this one with less than 600 mm. Some districts in the north and east get much heavier rainfall, but have every block under DPAP. The logic is baffling. Unless, of course, the placing of blocks under DPAP is purely a political decision.

The centre has brought only four of Pudukkottai's thirteen blocks under the DPAP. It seems wary of the costs involved in such schemes. The more so in a district where well over 40 per cent of the people live way below the official poverty line. As one senior official puts it, 'The idea that the drought will respect administrative maps and confine itself to four blocks is laughable.'

The Tamil Nadu government, too, has not declared the district drought-affected. That could mean waiving land revenues and other dues. It feels this would be a 'bad example', one that could prove expensive for the state. Demands from a wide spectrum of political forces have left both Centre and state unmoved.

Apparently, it costs too much.

There is no spate of deaths or raging disease here. And perhaps because so much of Pudukkottai's pain is silent and hidden it has drawn no attention from both government and press. A minister represents this sparsely endowed district in the legislature. But it wields little clout in the state capital. And invisible agony doesn't make headlines. 'Does the crisis here have to descend into a catastrophe to merit attention?' asks one official. 'Would that not be a great tragedy?'

'They are worried about losses to the state government,' says Chokka Radhakrishna, who heads the primary school teachers' association here. 'But they just do not worry about the losses to the people of Pudukkottai.' Those losses are very real and the drought has left thousands of peasants unable to repay their debts. It has also pushed them further into the grip of private moneylenders. This is at its worst in the dalit colonies.

The water crisis also sparks off peculiar disputes within the poor. In Mannavellanpatti of Annavasal block, quarry workers are in conflict with the villagers. Quarries tend to retain water very well. Last December's rains filled the Annavasal quarry – which now resembles a medium-sized lake. The quarry workers need to drain it to get back to work. The villagers feel that would rob them of drinking water. Both are from the same poor class backgrounds.

Top officials warned the state government as early as February of the crisis that was looming. The district has an active and energetic collector, Anuradha Khati Rajivan. And she is doing her best under bad conditions. In that sense, this district has been lucky. The poor here still speak with awe of their last collector, Sheela Rani Chunkath.

But as one senior official with many years in the district put it: 'The problems lie with the development process as a whole and with the politics spurring that process. These go back decades, keeping Pudukkottai poor and backward.'

Khati Rajivan does not believe the water problem is beyond solution. She is confident of tapping 'a groundwater belt that we are sitting on. We've done some groundwater mapping and we believe there is good potential.' She has seen the negative effects that private borewells had early on and says that the government will now promote 'community borewells'. To be effective, though, these would have to be at least 150 feet deep. They might even have to reach 300 feet in depth. That costs money. But there is little doubt that the development of 'community water resources' is essential.

Khati Rajivan also pins her hopes on a World Bank-assisted project that would bring Cauvery waters to this district. That might solve at least the drinking water problem of Pudukkottai town. She is quite sincere about it. But governments in this region have an awful record in implementing such schemes.

The Veeranam project of 1969 is best remembered by the unused water pipes that still provide shelter for the destitute in Chennai. The Telugu Ganga project of 1983 is nowhere in sight. The first proposal to bring Cauvery waters to Pudukkottai, according to the district's gazetteer, 'was made in 1837'. Now, 156 years later, it remains a proposal. The drought, however, remains a reality.

Surguja's politics of drought and death

Rameshwarnagar, Surguja (Madhya Pradesh): Did more than sixty people really die here in Surguja between February and April of 1994? That too, of starvation, cholera and poverty-related diseases? Did this have a good deal to do with the 'drought'? If true, what's being done about it? If not true, how do such stories build up and why?

The press is full of it. Cholera seems the chosen villain. It conjures just that right vision of horror. More mundane causes won't do. Yet is the drama running in the press the same as the one on the ground?

Most of the press reports come out of Bilaspur and Raipur. Some have appeared in Bhopal. To the extent that reporters have visited this district, they appear mostly to have gone to the headquarters at Ambikapur and perhaps a couple of villages nearby. (There have been, however, one or two major exceptions in the Hindi press. They have at least given the developments a context.)

Briefly, the reports say that thirteen people in Kantaroli and ten in Rameshwarnagar villages of the Premnagar block starved to death in this period. They were mainly poor Binjhwar tribals. The newspapers also report that in Matringa village of Udaipur block, thirteen Majhwar tribals have died of cholera.

Press reports have named as many as twenty-five Pahadi Korwa tribals who starved to death in Bansajaal village of Batauli block in the same period. The *sarpanch* there confirmed this list. Earlier, a study by a Sagar University researcher revealed very low haemoglobin levels (8 gm per cent) in the tribals of Bansajaal. On the whole, though, the favoured cause for most of the deaths in Surguja is cholera. The press in Bhopal, over twenty-four hours away by rail and road, is full of that theory. Yet, if it were not for these events, Surguja would not get written about at all. It remains invisible in the press for long periods of time. So maybe 'cholera' helps, after all.

Curiously for all their lashing out at faceless bureaucrats and their negligence, most of the reports seem shy of a debate on the public health system. There is no picture of that system as it functions in Surguja. Why is it the way it is? Why did it fail here? What kind of funds does it need? Why are there so many primary health centres (PHCs) with no doctors? Why do these things happen to Surguja each year? What is the water 'crisis' here about?

In Bijakura village of Wadroffnagar, notorious for the starvation deaths of 1992, crisis is just around the corner. Rameshwarnagar village seems set for disaster. As the summer sets in, Surguja, known for drought-related deaths, braces itself for more of the same. Some of these deaths have been the subject of heated debate in the state assembly.

Over twenty days in the affected area, meeting the families of victims and their neighbours, officials and medical staff, proved useful. Here's what came out of it:

First of all, in every one of these villages, malnutrition is the norm. Conditions here are appalling and there is great distress. Many of the deaths were due to poverty-related causes and a lack of infrastructure. *However, both the number of deaths and their causes have been exaggerated – by almost a factor of three to one.* Facts have been liberally spiced with political fiction. While this has ensured some relief of a temporary sort, it sadly takes the focus off the real problems.

For example, in the village of Bansajaal (pop: 1,441), the total number of deaths from all, including natural causes, during the February-April period, turned out to be eight. This, against the reported figure of twenty-five. On joint examination of the village *kotwar*'s records, the *sarpanch* admitted this was the case. He modified his figure of twenty-five deaths to eighteen. This, he now clarified, was over a fifteen-month period beginning February 1993. Finally, eighteen turned out to be the total number of deaths in that period – *from all causes* – in the village.

Some villagers challenged the *sarpanch*'s version of their relatives' deaths in front of him. The *sarpanch*, unsurprisingly, is up for re-election in Madhya Pradesh's panchayat polls starting on May 22. That list of deaths came up just in time for the early phase of his campaign.

Yet deaths did really occur in these villages. There were six in Kantaroli, six in Rameshwarnagar, seven in Matringa and eight in Bansajaal. They seem to have followed an outbreak of measles and gastroenteritis. Dr Akhand of Surajpur came down to the Udaipur PHC following the Matringa deaths. He says: 'The gastroenteritis need not have proved fatal. But these people suffered from malnourishment. They lacked body resistance. Hence they were much more vulnerable to disease.'

'Besides, they had to drink water from the filthiest *nullah* [watercourse] since the village did not have a hand pump or well at the time. You can't solve this without tackling malnourishment and the water problem.' He finds any talk of cholera absurd.

Health services in all these villages are mostly non-existent. Officials suspended some village health workers for not functioning – after the deaths. The ill-equipped PHCs are in charge of huge areas. And some of these go for months at a stretch with no doctors. The Premnagar PHC alone covers forty-seven villages of which thirty-seven are out of reach during the monsoon. At other times, you have to walk five kilometres in very difficult terrain to reach them. Lack of irrigation water has crippled the peasants economically. The quality of drinking water has hurt them physically.

However, the spotlight is off these basic issues. The trend is to favour more spectacular causes like cholera. Or even, in one case, arsenic in the water. And then there is the recurring and genuine fear of drought.

Drinking water sources here are stagnating badly. So cholera can surely resurface in Surguja. But there is not a shred of evidence proving it to be the cause of death at Matringa. There was no bacteriological test done. The facilities for that simply do not exist in the area. Many of the symptoms were not consistent with those of cholera. And the reports citing cholera quote no medical source, official or independent, explaining how they arrived at this conclusion.

The last time Madhya Pradesh saw a notification of cholera was in 1992. And that was in the capital city of Bhopal! But in Matringa, the story was quite different. Most children in this region have not been inoculated against measles. The health services directorate feels that measles, coming on top of malnourishment and dysentery, proved fatal.

Most of those who died at Matringa had fever for five to ten days. 'Cholera would have proved fatal much faster,' says Dr Mangeshwar of the Udaipur PHC. And relatives said that none of the victims had the projectile vomiting linked with the disease. Almost all the victims at Matringa were under six. 'It seems unlikely,' says Dr Akhand, 'that cholera could restrict itself to the children without touching adults.' The measles factor would explain the high number of child deaths.

But why exaggerate what is anyway a frightening problem? One *sarpanch* gave me a frank reply. 'Unless we have news of people dying like flies, we won't get a single handpump.' A shiny new handpump in his village offers proof of his point. A top official from Bhopal put it this way: 'These are the weapons of the weak.' That seems true. But at the district level, other political factors also intrude.

In 1992, when the BJP ruled Madhya Pradesh, events in Wadroffnagar block shook the state. Some members of the family of Rewai Pando, a pathetically poor tribal, died of starvation in Bijakura village there. The Congress (I) launched a crusade on the issue. Three former chief ministers visited the place. The present chief minister, Digvijay Singh – who then headed the state committee of the Congress (I) – went on a protest fast close to Bijakura.

Prime Minister Narasimha Rao, too, went to the area, though not to the actual village. His visit, with many ministers in tow, still draws adverse comment. 'The suicide or starvation deaths of eighty weavers of Pochampally in his home state of Andhra Pradesh produced no such sympathetic visit,' points out one official. 'His trip here meant that millions of rupees were spent and roads were laid. Not for the villagers but for the VIPs.' Nothing changed, though.

The next year, when a miserable Rewai Pando himself died, the state was under President's rule. This allowed the BJP to 'retaliate'. An embarrassed Congress remained silent. Now, in 1994, the deaths have occurred under Congress rule and the BJP is pushing the issue. This has produced some ministerial visits. To Matringa, for instance. Declarations have been issued, some officials suspended and enquiries ordered. But there is to be no prime ministerial visit, though the deaths outnumber those of 1992.

The situation in the villages remains largely the same. A couple of handpumps installed to mark the ministerial visits are the only real difference. Why the villagers exaggerate the number of deaths and their causes now seems quite clear. They seem to sense that controversy is the best bet for relief.

Hence the willingness to go along with raising twenty-odd deaths to over sixty, citing cholera and other dramatic causes. This brings some gains but has bad effects too. It shifts the focus from infrastructures and policies to relief. Many *sarpanchas*, *patwaris* and *patels* prefer the relief mode. It means money for them. Some of the 'roads' laid for the ministers lie incomplete or abandoned. The water problem remains acute.

In reality, for all the talk of drought, Surguja has no great rainfall problem. It has a major *water* problem. That is because water harvesting systems are non-existent. Only around four per cent of the district is under irrigation. Over the decades, Surguja has had an annual average rainfall of close to 1,500 mm, which is excellent.

Yet tens of millions of rupees have been spent on fighting 'drought' in this district. That means drought relief. And *that* means racketeering. For years, the PWD, forest and other departments have wreaked havoc in the name of drought – arguably the biggest 'industry' in Surguja. 'Drought' has made the district a contractor's dream. Projects spawning tens of millions of rupees have come and gone leaving little impact.

The last five years were 'the worst ones' for rain. Yet, even with massive deforestation and a falling water table, rainfall has not been less than 1,200 mm in any year. That places Surguja far above other drought-prone districts in the country. In 1991-92, it got 1,500 mm. Pudukkottai or Ramnad in Tamil Nadu in many years get as little as half of that. The difference is, both harness their poor resources better. Oddly, with all its drawbacks, Surguja's food production per person is not below the national average. Which means that if managed properly, this district could really be turned around.

While being home to many of India's poorest citizens, Surguja enriches the revenue kitty. It coughs up more than Rs.2.4 billion. About Rs.1 billion of that comes in coal royalty alone. But state investment in Surguja is far less. Both state and central expenditure together barely equal Surguja's revenue contribution. The district has had little presence in successive ministries. Its few representatives have been unable to articulate its real needs. There is no rail link between the district and the state capital. And owing to its distance – it is more than 1,000 km away from Bhopal – Surguja has mostly been forgotten.

Though crucial, these issues get sidelined. For instance, silent or invisible hunger that lowers people's resistance to disease. Or low investment in the social sector. So low that Premnagar block has the lowest literacy rate for any block in Madhya Pradesh – just 4 per cent. Its female literacy rate is 1.04 per cent. This is the block in which the Kantaroli and Rameshwarnagar deaths occurred.

'Illiteracy is the biggest killer disease,' says one doctor. 'Even if medicines do reach these villagers, the dosages are a mystery to them. The village health workers themselves can barely read or write. Sometimes, people have swallowed chlorine tablets given for their *matkas* [earthenware pots]. In many cases, relatives of patients have not pressed them to take vital tablets.'

But that is not all. It is possible to die without a chance of being treated. The Khenda sub-PHC is responsible for Matringa, where some of the deaths took place. Khenda has no permanent doctor. It also has no compounder, no female health worker and no auxiliary nurse midwife – even after the deaths. For three months preceding the deaths there was no doctor at all. The emergency appointee has just twenty days more to serve. Some doctors make rounds and some are into private practice, neglecting their work.

In no case did the victims see a doctor before they died. Often this was because the village health worker never showed up and it was impossible in this terrain for the ill to reach the PHC. For the whole Batauli block, with 80,000 people, there are just 1,250 Septran (antibiotic) tablets though the PHC feels a great need for them.

With its enormous spread of 23,000 square km, Surguja is larger than the

This young resident of Rameshwarnagar village had walked several kilometres to fetch drinking water. Oddly enough, at one level, there is no shortage of that substance in the area. The fields of the villagers have been submerged by operations relating to the Bango dam.

states of Delhi, Goa and Nagaland combined. Besides, the spread of the households in this huge district is extraordinary. A single village can lie across twenty to thirty square kilometres. And sometimes, each household rests atop a separate hillock. This not only makes the logistics a nightmare, it means the per unit cost of development in Madhya Pradesh is higher than that of any other state in the country.

'Where does one install the handpump?' asks a block official. 'To service the same number of people with handpumps,' says a senior government official, 'we have to spend four times the amount that Maharashtra does, since we need four pumps.'

In Rameshwarnagar, the Bango dam has destroyed the farming land of poor peasants. It serves landlords of the rich district of Bilaspur next door. For four years, people in Rameshwarnagar have been living off the meagre compensation they received for what the dam has done to them. They face disaster after the next monsoon when the submergence is complete.

No moves towards solving the district's irrigation and drinking water problems are visible. Many water sources have gone bad and could cause more deaths. And the deaths that did occur owed much to malnourishment causing a lack of resistance in the victims.

But the focus is on the spectacular. The long-term trends that spell chaos don't make good copy. 'The spectacular offers better mileage. And it doesn't really require you to address basic problems,' says one official. 'Welcome to Surguja's politics of drought, death and development.'

Postscript

When this story (in two reports) appeared in the *Times of India*, I was in Jhabua district. Suddenly, the police were looking for me. At first, I believed the authorities were tossing out all journalists in the Narmada submergence zone. Phone calls to Bhopal proved me wrong. The Madhya Pradesh chief minister, Digvijay Singh, had seen the reports. He was going to Surguja and wanted to visit the very places described in the stories. As author of those reports, would I go too? I tagged along.

We went to Matringa where the deaths had taken place. But we also made a couple of unscheduled stops at points where the local administration had no idea he would visit. What he saw there had Singh truly appalled. In Barkela village an elderly woman told him: 'We have not seen rice on the public distribution system [PDS] here for three years now.' To his credit, Singh checked out and verified the reports for himself.

The same evening, a very angry Digvijay Singh acted.

He shunted out twenty-four top and senior officials from Surguja. Heading the list was the collector. That was the largest ever transfer of its kind in Madhya Pradesh made at one time. The state government then appointed a young IAS officer as the new collector. This was Prabir Krishna, highly thought of in administrative circles. He was part of a team of three IAS officers set up to handle this huge district.

The government also suspended a few medical and forest personnel. It blacklisted some contractors too. Digvijay Singh set up a committee headed by the state's chief technical examiner. This was to study the quality of infrastructural work undertaken in Surguja during the past four years and submit a report in a hundred days. These swift developments galvanised the press in Bhopal. Surguja captured more space in the newspapers in the next ten days than it had in the past two years.

Palamau – after the drought

Daltonganj, Palamau (Bihar): Does Palamau have any right to experience drought? That seems an odd question to ask about a district that has seen some of the country's worst droughts. But it is one that makes sense to many, including top officials running the district.

Palamau gets as much as 1,200-1,230 mm of rain in a normal year, which is pretty decent. In its worst year in recent history, it received 630 mm. That's more than what a district like Ramnad in Tamil Nadu gets in some 'normal' years. Yet drought causes far more devastation in Palamau than in Ramnad.

As a senior official here points out: 'There are many places across the globe getting around 200 mm yearly – without erupting into unmanageable crisis.' Anantpur district in Andhra Pradesh has worse rainfall figures than Palamau's. There have been years when Anantpur has got well below 500 mm of rain. However, Anantpur seldom captures the headlines with drought-disaster stories the way Palamau often has over the past three decades. The way Palamau did, for instance, from late 1992 to the middle of 1993.

Many areas of India face droughts that do not turn into famines or near-famine conditions. By one estimate, an eighth of India's land surface suffers aridity at any given moment. But in Palamau, the distance between drought and famine or near-famine conditions seems to be much shorter. This means wrong decisions can produce very high costs. A mistake that could cause minor problems in another place could lead to disaster here.

Besides getting more rainfall than many other districts, Palamau has been lucky in other ways as well. It has had a string of committed senior administrators over the years. From the time of K.S. Singh in the '60s, to the present dynamic young deputy commissioner, Santosh Matthew.

A third, relatively positive aspect is that, despite the ravages of deforestation, the district still enjoys decent forest cover. Officially, 40 per cent and, unofficially, around 25 per cent. Compare that with Ramnad's 1.06 per cent forest cover. Then what is it that goes wrong with Palamau when crisis strikes?

Some of Palamau's problems are extremely complex and vast. So administrators, however talented, often find themselves working more as crisis managers. 'We are so busy coping with problems,' a block-level official told me, 'that we seldom have time to approach them with a long-term perspective or any real planning. When we succeed in doing that – who in Patna listens?'

Yet, Palamau is a region of enormous potential. And not just for its minerals, as many seem to think.

Deputy commissioner Matthew is optimistic about the district's future. For him, the area of hope is agriculture. 'We did a check out. At any one time, only 48 per cent of our cultivable land is really under cultivation. The rest is fallow.' Matthew is clear that, given the resources, his priority would be 'water harvesting'. Palamau is presently not equipped to conserve the water it receives.

Matthew wants much more done in that direction. Besides, 'we need forestry to restore the sponge effect to the land. That will help keep the streams live. We also need a number of surface water-harvesting structures. In addition to the right kind of forestry, we need horticulture to help fill the gaps. *Guava, ber amla, papaya* [all edible fruit] – cultivating these would help.'

Many of his assessments ring true. But other realities intrude. Bihar's irrigation budget has been shrinking and, at Rs.1.2 billion, is less than a third of what it was just five years ago. Of this, Rs.800 million goes in establishment costs. This means that a state of eighty million has to make do with Rs.400 million or Rs.5 per capita on irrigation. So there's not going to be much money coming.

Land-grab over the decades has removed the one cushion of many poor people – their land. For the landless, it's worse. There is a large seasonal migration of agricultural labourers from Palamau each year, towards destinations ranging from eastern Uttar Pradesh to Punjab. But the poorest do not seem to have even that option. Bondage, semi-bondage or debt holds them back.

For the 'primitive tribes', the effects of deforestation have been disastrous. And those displaced by mining or 'development' projects have neither land nor employment. Corruption at many levels punches holes in the relief efforts that follow a crisis. 'Often,' says a senior official, 'there is more money for relief than for development. That suits a lot of people.' It's one reason why people here call drought relief '*teesra fasl*' – the 'third crop'. It reaps a rich harvest for the local elites.

Pudukkottai district of Tamil Nadu is also a zone of aridity. Migrant peasants or odd-job seekers here do not earn much more than those in Palamau. But when crisis strikes, their chances of survival are higher. Tamil Nadu has decent infrastructure, communication and transport networks. It also has superior levels of literacy and schooling, more safety nets and better governance. When crisis strikes in Palamau, the very poor, especially the tribals with their unique problems, take a battering.

This year, a great effort on the part of the district administration has seen the success of the maize crop – crucial to the survival of the poor. But the following rice crop hasn't been all that good. In village after village across the district, where everyone acknowledged the success of the maize crop, they also told me: 'It [the crisis of late 1992] could happen again.'

'The whole thing is tremendously fragile,' a senior official told me. 'The maize crop keeps them going for three months and the rice crop for two. Lac, *mahua* and *tendu* leaves see them through another two months at the most. Then for five months they have to really struggle. They migrate, live off roots, berries, anything they can gather. So if crisis strikes in that period, we reach the famine stage quite swiftly.'

Drought and famine in Palamau grab the headlines because they are spectacular. But they are, still, *events* that flow from a number of less spectacular *processes*, as political activist Narendra Chaubey points out. Among those are deforestation, land-grab and poor water harvesting. Eroding infrastructure, shrinking funds and stagnating agriculture have made things worse. Growing unemployment, decaying relief and distribution systems, and rising corruption have not helped. A lack of land reform seems to be the large canvas on which the other factors fit in.

'For real change,' says Chaubey, 'there has to be a major land reform. That would include the distribution of surplus holdings, and securing of the title to the land of the poor. We need to root out feudalism in agriculture. Besides, serious planning for both irrigation and drinking water and for employment is needed. Given that, Palamau can really prosper.'

10

With Their Own Weapons

When the poor fight back

Given a chance, people hit back at the forces that hold them down. They may have different ways of doing this. Some less effective than others. But fight back, they do. Wherever the literacy movement has taken root among women, they have gone on to picket liquor shops. Yet too often covering the poor, for the media, gets reduced to romanticising the role of saintly individuals working among them. Often these heroes are from the same class and urban backgrounds as the journalists covering them. A latter-day version of the noble missionary working among the heathen savages. Far more sophisticated, perhaps, but not too different at some levels.

True, the linkages between local protests, outside intervention, and mass consciousness are quite complex. For instance, the actions of a good district collector can have great impact. So can the mechanistic actions of a government. In conventional terms, the story then becomes one about the individual hero, or the government, preferably the former. If the hero or heroine belongs to an NGO, that makes for an even better story. It helps establish the journalist's 'independent' credentials, too.

In all this, however, the role of the people themselves tends to get obscured. As do the political trends shaping within them. For their battles are most effective where they are organised. One of the reasons the poorest districts are the way they are is the pathetic shape of organised political movements within them. Were they better organised, they would have faced a lot of problems more firmly. The poor would have wrested a better deal much earlier.

Even allowing for limitations, the role of the poor themselves is worth looking at. So is the role of political trends and activists who have sprung up within them. The literacy movement has been most successful where such activists were either directly from the people in a region or shaped by their movements. People politically, culturally and classwise, close to the poor and, importantly, who learned from them. Or even village-based NGOs run on local will and not on the whims of external funding agencies.

The movements to save forests in some districts have often come directly from the poor. Again, the politically-minded among them have often taken the lead. So have the anti-liquor agitations come up within them. In the quarries of Pudukkottai, women from the poorest sections have fought heroic battles. Again, organised action with a degree of political vision allowed them to capitalise on a situation where others have failed. Sometimes the 'external' factor can be one as modest as a Bishwamber Dubey, strongly critical of his own *bhoodan* movement. (See: 'Bhoodan – the last believer' in the section 'Crime & No Punishment'.) But Dubeyji is no urban middle-class hero. He belongs to the people of Palamau.

Of the battles these stories record, some might end in failure. Mainly because of the lack of sustained and organised democratic politics in those areas. Yet they also argue hope. People are not passive. They revolt in many ways. And as long as that is the case, there is hope.

A success carved in stone

Pudukkottai (Tamil Nadu): It's forty-three degrees Celsius in the shade. Only there's no shade. It's around forty degrees in Pudukkottai district. But down here, in the stone quarries of Kudimianmalai, it's at least three degrees hotter. Heat spews out of the stone surface and blinding light reflects off the surrounding rocks, while the sun blazes down to vaporise any remaining resistance your body may hold out.

And then you notice that most of the women in the quarry still stride around barefoot. And that they work with an attitude suggesting that here they are the bosses.

And, for once, they actually are.

Pudukkottai has 350 operational stone quarries. In a radical move in 1991, about 170 of these were leased out at nominal rates to extremely poor women from the scheduled castes and the most backward castes. Leasing them the quarries meant throwing out the old contractors. The then district collector, Sheela Rani Chunkath – virtually a legend among the poor here – pulled this off under the Development of Women and Children in Rural Areas (DWCRA) scheme. That's a government-sponsored anti-poverty programme.

The groups of women holding leases to the quarries usually have twenty members. A few have more. (Almost all registered themselves as *societies* and not as co-operatives.) So over 4,000 very poor women now control the quarries they toiled in as bonded or ill-paid labourers before. Their husbands are in the same quarries – as daily wage workers. Wages depend on productivity, but all members of a society share its profits equally.

The results have been startling. The living standards of the women and their families have improved very quickly. Earlier, more than half of them were from the poorest sections of dalits here. I visited five of the DWCRA women-led quarries in Pudukkottai.

At Kudimianmalai, there are three women's groups led by Palaniamma, Chintamani and Vasantha. They keep their own accounts and do their banking themselves. All have learned to read and write, thanks to Pudukkottai's creative literacy movement, *Arivoli Iyakkam* (Light of Knowledge movement). The *Arivoli* has even held leadership training sessions for the women. Both Palaniamma and Chintamani are proud of their new skills and read

297

The women in the quarries work with an attitude suggesting that here, they are the bosses. And, for once, they actually are. Their husbands too are in the same quarries – as daily wage workers.

aloud news items on issues ranging from arrack to Somalia. All the reports they read are from *Thenral* (Cool Air), a handwritten newspaper for neo-literates put out by the *Arivoli*.

The women insist on hovering around their visitor with umbrellas. They are anxious, doubtful of this urbanite's ability to survive the next few hours in the heat of the quarry. I have to plead that this is upsetting the light reading on the cameras.

'The work here is always hard,' says Palaniamma. (With my skin already

298

on fire, it was not difficult to believe that.) 'Earlier,' says she, 'we were slaves of the contractor. We made only Rs.6 for working from 6 a.m. to 2 p.m.' At present, they can earn up to Rs.35-Rs.40 per day if the going is good.

'Now,' says Chintamani, 'our children eat more. They go to school and we clothe them better. If they fall ill we can afford some medicines.' Chintamani is about to buy a house. Palaniamma and Vasantha have already bought theirs.

With the women and not the men in control, points out N. Kannammal, a leading *Arivoli* activist, family spending patterns change. 'Most of the money is spent on the families, not on arrack. The women have proved much better at fighting poverty.' Their husbands seem quite content with the situation.

Revenues from quarrying are booming. All quarrying is subject to a 'seigniorage' fee – the sum paid to the government on the amount of material quarried. It's now about Rs.110 for a truckload of jelly. Under the old contractor regime, the state got very little. Most of the quarrying was illegal but went on thanks to the connivance of many officials. The state once collected a seigniorage fee of Rs.525 *in a whole year* during the 1980s!

In 1992, within a year of the women's groups settling in, things changed. The fee raked in by the government was Rs.2.5 million. For 1993, the assistant director of mines, N. Shanmugavel, anticipates 'a collection of Rs.4.8 million of which Rs.3.8 million will be from the DWCRA women's groups'. This means that 106 other quarries, run by contractors, will contribute merely Rs.1 million. The women's groups, Shanmugavel says, are 'infinitely more productive, law-abiding and always regular in their payments'.

I ask the women why they have registered their groups as societies. Why not as co-operatives? 'If we did that,' says one of them, 'we would then have to accept representatives from the co-operative department. Worse, we'd have to pay their salaries.' One group that did form a co-operative had seven department employees foisted on it. The group is now forking out about half its turnover to pay their salaries.

Despite their record of success, the women's groups are fighting for survival. A powerful coalition stands arrayed against them. Contractors done out of leases, their political patrons, and corrupt officials done out of kickbacks have hit back at the women. When the groups were first formed, the contractors refused to allow trucks entry to the areas. They even damaged the approach roads to the quarries.

The women also need an independent marketing system. Their survival could depend on breaking the grip of the contractors over the sale and distribution of their stone. Dr Nitya Rao of the National Institute for Adult Education, New Delhi, drew up an excellent proposal for that last year. It is yet to be implemented. When and if it is, making sure the women control the system will be crucial. The arbitrariness of petty officials here is alarming. Some go along with the DWCRA scheme only because two successive collectors have wanted it. They have lost the 'cuts' they used to get under the old regime. Under a new dispensation, many of these officials could turn hostile.

A while ago, some contractors discovered a passion for the environment and for their architectural heritage. They alleged that quarrying in the Kudimianmalai belt was damaging an old temple in the area. The Geological Survey of India was called in. At one stage, experts placed thin-walled glass tumblers filled with water inside the temple. Next, they simultaneously set off twenty blasts in the quarries, each with 150 gm of explosives. They then studied the effects of the blasts. There were no signs of damage or stress anywhere in the temple. Nor did any dust settle on the water. Soon after, a court threw out a private complaint on the same issue.

Now the Archaeological Survey of India (ASI) has filed its own complaint! No one here denies it is the ASI's duty to look after old monuments. But it does seem odd that the same ASI stayed silent for years while private contractors illegally worked the same quarries. The old contractors used a lot more explosives. The women can't even afford them on that scale.

The contractors have come up with another, more dangerous ploy. They are forming fake DWCRA outfits as a way of sabotaging the women's groups. In a district with a large number of very poor people, this is not as difficult as it might seem. In these groups, the women appear to be owners but are simply a front for the old contractor. In Sandhanavidudhi, a genuine group had been pushed out of its quarry by a fake outfit acting at the contractor's behest. The women are not pressing their case too hard, though. Too many of the contractor's toughs live in the same villages as they do.

The old regime has also moved through its political friends. There is tremendous pressure on the government to scrap the whole scheme when the leases come up for renewal. But the balance sheets suggest that, if anything, the experiment here is worth emulating across the country. State revenues from the quarries have gone up many times over. At the same time, the quality of life of the women's families has improved. 'What happens,' I ask Palaniamma, 'if the leases are not renewed?'

'We are doing well and can do better with our own marketing system,' she says. 'In future, the state should bypass middlemen and come to us for stone for government construction projects. After having tasted freedom these years, how can we ever go back to the contractors? We will fight for renewal of the leases.'

Postscript

I returned to Pudukkottai in April 1995, nearly two years after my first visit. The women-led quarries had come under great pressure, but had held out. They had even scored major victories in their battle for survival. They had taken major blows as well on four fronts. First, the old contractors continued to form fake DWCRA women's groups. In the long run, this cannot but discredit the whole show. *Arivoli* once again came to the aid of the women. Along with officials, it began a sort of 'census' to find out which were the fake groups. Also, to know which of the genuine groups had been subverted by contractor pressure.

This was done with much sensitivity. The idea was not to punish the women in the fake groups. As one *Arivoli* activist put it: 'Why set poor against poor?' Rather, the point was to get them to assert themselves within their group and make it a genuine one. By using the same scheme as the others, they could become independent of the contractor.

On the second front, petty officials were causing havoc. The best of government schemes are vulnerable in this way: when good officials at the top move out, good projects often suffer. At the village level, this means the women have faced threats and even coercion. The coalition against the quarry women is very much alive.

Thirdly, some of the fallout from the literacy drive had provoked the powerful. The anti-arrack stir of Pudukkottai's women, for instance. (See the two stories on arrack in this section.) Layers of officialdom are now bitterly hostile to *Arivoli* in this and other districts.

The fourth battle is really complex. An official marketing scheme called the District Supply & Marketing Society (DSMS) did come up. It also caused great damage. The original idea was that such a body would facilitate the work of the women. Over time, it tried instead to take over their rights and curb their independence. Instead of working for the women, it seemed to be working on behalf of the middlemen.

The tyranny of petty officials here could not quell the quarry women. But it did seriously affect other DWCRA outfits. For example, the women's gem-cutting units. A working venture was made insolvent by the DSMS. When some women workers of the DSMS itself protested, they were sacked. In one instance, units producing masala for ICDS centres were told they had to buy chillies from only one particular retailer. The chillies were sub-standard and the units had their produce rejected. They then lost many clients.

Through all this, the women of the quarries held out on their own. Only *Arivoli* was with them. Finally, their day came. The then chief minister, J.

Jayalalitha, announced a five-year renewal of their leases a little after my second visit. They have many large battles ahead, though. Their opponents have taken the matter to court. But the women have lit the candle of a fight back. And what a candle it is.

Women versus arrack

Pudukkottai (Tamil Nadu): Pursuing a story on the links between arrack*
and poverty wasn't easy. It took a couple of days to catch up with the
appropriate anti-arrack officials in Pudukkottai – they were busy auctioning
brandy shops. Oddly, this is perfectly legal in a state that has banned the
distillation of arrack.

The Tamil Nadu government's concern over the sale of illicit arrack is not
totally selfless. Arrack affects excise revenues collected on the sale of legal
alcohol. For instance, it hurts earnings from Indian manufactured foreign
liquor (IMFL) – sold to private outlets through state marketing agencies.
(People here call the IMFL outlets 'brandy shops'.)

So the same officials entrusted with cracking down on arrack and
preaching its evils to the public may also be duty bound to enhance the sale of
other varieties of liquor. They certainly have to fulfil higher targets of excise
revenues each year.

These ironies don't go unnoticed. At one public meeting held to promote
prohibition here, a Dravida Munnetra Kazhagam† (DMK) activist embarrassed everybody. He got onto the dais and presented a leading revenue official
with Rs.5. This, he said, was 'a tribute to your fight against the evils of
drinking while promoting brandy shops'.

Arrack seems a close companion of poverty across this state, and not just
in Pudukkottai. Each year, the poor in Tamil Nadu part with billions of rupees
to the makers of illicit arrack. Countless numbers of male agricultural
labourers spend much of their daily earnings on hooch. Consequently, the size
and scope of this industry are astonishing.

In Pudukkottai, Tamil Nadu's least urbanised district, official data show
that one arrack distiller is arrested every forty-five minutes. One is *convicted*
every two hours.

In a 150-day period for which figures were available, there were on an
average thirty-one raids and nineteen cases booked each day. About 420 litres
of arrack were seized – and half that destroyed – every twenty-four hours.

---

* Arrack – a distilled country liquor.
† DMK – a political party that presently rules Tamil Nadu state.

Fines alone in the 150-day period amounted to Rs.1.3 million. The amount of arrack seized in these raids was close to 65,000 litres.

'And if you believe all these figures even begin to measure the reality,' an experienced local advocate told me, 'you need to have your head examined. The high rate of convictions occurs because the distillers rarely contest the charge. Why waste days in court when the same time can be used to make more money from arrack? Since the convictions only lead to fines and not imprisonment, they gladly pay the fines.'

The moment a case is brought to court, said the advocate, the defence counsel says, 'Yes, yes, my client admits to everything.' The fine is paid. 'Every rupee you invest in arrack can bring you up to Rs.9 in return. So fines of a couple of thousand rupees don't even scratch you mildly.'

Though it is illegal, village panchayats have been auctioning the 'right to distil' arrack locally, since it is so profitable. Their excuses for this can be interesting. In more than one village, the ruling group assured me that the money made from breaking the law would go towards building a temple.

Is it possible to make even a sketchy estimate of the industry's turnover? That too, in a poor district like this one? Take Neduvasal village, for instance. Officials confirmed that the panchayat here had auctioned the 'right to distil' for about Rs.300,000.

There are close to 500 village panchayats in Pudukkottai. Even if only half of these were into such auctions, the lease amounts alone would total Rs.75 million annually. Not bad for a small district with a population of 1.3 million.

Experts here believe the number of panchayats into this racket is really far higher. They also make another point. Even if we take the auction amount to be as much as a third of the turnover (though it is probably much less), we have Rs.225 million for the villages alone. Throw in the towns and it is, at the very least, a Rs.300 million business annually. And this, points out the local advocate, does not take into account the cuts that the police and officialdom get.

There is some heat just now on the distillers since the collector of Pudukkottai has been tough in implementing the anti-arrack drive. That might even account for the spectacular figures of seizures and convictions. Still, the problem is not merely an administrative one and its scale is massive.

I spoke to male agricultural workers on this subject in many villages across several blocks. (Women consume very little arrack by contrast.) Almost every single one admitted to drinking arrack. If he could get it, he would have it.

'If I had to spend four hours looking for work,' said one, 'and if I find it, I have to work for 10-12 hours to earn Rs.12-15. After that I may have two glasses, no?' There is some embarrassment if you ask them why women, who work even longer hours, don't feel the same need.

The price of arrack varies from village to village. In Tulakampatti hamlet, it was Rs.2 per glass. In Kilakuruchi village, Rs.5 a glass. You can, however, buy just a rupee's worth – which in Kilakuruchi means one-fifth of a glass. Many of the agricultural labourers did not see two to three glasses as heavy drinking. I clearly surprised them by suggesting as much.

'A heavy drinker,' said a senior excise official, 'is not necessarily one who has two glasses in the evening. He might have much less at one time, but will keep having shots throughout the day. In the course of the day, he might have up to five or six glasses in this manner.'

The impact of arrack on the economy of the peasant households is devastating. In some cases, the male agricultural labourers I spoke to were spending *more* than their day's earnings (especially during a lean work period) on arrack. That links arrack to debt. Quite a few said they were getting hooch on credit from the man running the local arrack business. Most of them were earning daily wages of Rs.12-15, or, at best, Rs.20.

'Besides, if my husband spends so much on arrack,' said Veliamma in Tiruvarankalam, 'then we have to borrow to buy rice, no?' A drinker in Kilakuruchi having three glasses a day would be consuming more than he earned, Adiappan, an ex-alcoholic there, says. 'But you can't beat this racket,' he felt. 'There's money in it for everyone at all levels.'

There are also health problems. Swami Sivagnanam, the articulate assistant commissioner of excise, spoke with disgust of how distillers throw all kinds of muck into the 'product', including 'sulphate jelly from battery cells, chillies, and even cow dung'. These help to 'speed up the fermentation process. These fellows can't wait, sir. They can't wait even for one week. They must make money.'

A doctor at the government hospital in Pudukkottai town, with much experience of arrack-related problems, said: 'This stuff is full of chemicals. I see countless cases of cirrhosis of the liver. Also ulcers, cardiac problems and neuritis, which I know are related to this habit. Arrack is a silent killer.'

So what can be done about this silent killer? The women of rural Pudukkottai seem to be getting ready to answer that one, as the following story indicates:

She had only the children with her at home when they broke open the door and dragged her out. The women sent along by the 'elders' of the Neduvasal village in Pudukkottai district beat her up, snatched her *mangalsutra** and

---

* *Mangalsutra* – a marriage ornament worn by a Hindu woman whose husband is living.

dragged her to the panchayat. There she stood for several hours, till well past midnight, while the 'elders' poured abuse and scorn on her. That, they hoped, would teach her not to preach against arrack.

Meet Malarmani. The twenty-six-year-old could well be the pioneer of an infant but potentially powerful anti-arrack movement in the district. One with implications for other parts of the state as well. The highly successful total literacy drive here seems to have set in motion forces that many may not have bargained for. Leading the campaign is the remarkable *Arivoli Iyakkam* (Light of Knowledge Movement), of which Malarmani is a staunch volunteer.

In Thachankuruchi village of the barren Gandarvakkottai block, local women, many of them active in the *Arivoli Iyakkam*, decided they had had enough. The village had become unsafe due to high levels of alcoholism. Worse still, the illicit arrack brewed locally drew devotees all the way from Trichy, forty kilometres away.

That was before twenty-one-year-old Matilda sparked off a move against arrack. Her drive, joined by other women, resulted in Thachankuruchi banning the making of arrack within its limits. 'Now,' she says, 'the village is clean.' It may be hard to sustain, but the victory is significant.

Malarmani and Matilda see arrack as a symbol of backwardness. For both, it reeks of poverty and degeneracy. Most rural women here agree with them. With many male agricultural workers spending much of their daily earnings on hooch, this is an explosive issue. The more so when it affects what is, in this small district alone, a multimillion rupee industry.

Malarmani is paying a price for her stand. As the district Collector had stood by her after the beating up incident, the panchayat could not harm her directly. So the arrack mafia in her village, helped by some policemen, enforced a social boycott of her family.

The day I meet Malarmani, the barber in Neduvasal has turned away her two little sons. One son, who had managed to buy his mother a cup of tea from a shop, had it knocked out of his hand by a villager. The 'charges' brought against Malarmani are many. One is about her conduct during a 'prohibition week' public meeting in February. There, say her critics, she 'knowingly' let dalits speak from the podium, using the same mike.

That was a state-run prohibition week. So Malarmani is being punished for implementing a government programme. To buy provisions, she has to go to Avanam village four kilometres away by bus. For water she has to walk to the Kuruvadi village two kilometres away. Her husband, who was also beaten up, is now away, working in Nagapattinam.

'I have seen for years what arrack does,' says Malarmani. 'The beatings it brings women, how it keeps people poor and ignorant, how it kills them.' Then why did she only act on it this year? 'Because *Arivoli* gave me confidence. Before, I would not have dared stand up like this.'

Matilda in Thachankuruchi agrees. Anti-arrack feeling predates the literacy drive. But the movement has given firm expression to that anger. Above all, it has given rural women the confidence to stand up and protest. (In the literacy movement here, every block and panchayat has a woman convenor, apart from a male one.) During the prohibition week, the *Arivoli* ran a campaign on the dangers of arrack among its neo-literate audience. With that, the issue gained momentum.

Soon, other villages began to ban alcohol distillation. It's tempting to draw a parallel here with the anti-arrack movement in Andhra Pradesh, but there is one big difference. The protesters in Andhra wanted a government ban on arrack. In Tamil Nadu there is already a ban in place. But it is so feeble that village communities are now enforcing their own bans. Matilda's Thachankuruchi was the first to impose one. That was on Christmas Day last year. The village gave the distillers a week to pack up. 'After that,' she says, 'all equipment relating to arrack distillation was confiscated and destroyed.' The Andhra parallel, however, holds good on literacy being a catalytic factor.

Will local bans at the village level work? A top *Arivoli* activist, Vivekanandan, says yes. 'Distance and availability are major factors. If it can't be got locally, it makes a big difference.' Vivekanandan ought to know. He is from the same village as Malarmani. And he, too, is being victimised for his stand on the issue.

Besides, claims Lourdaswamy, headman of Matilda's village, 'if you have to go far off and drink, the 'kick' wears off by the time you are back. Then such people even tend to beat their wives less and cause less nuisance.' For all the zest the villagers show, the stand the government finally takes will be very important.

In village after village in rural Pudukkottai, one thing is clear. Where the male labourer drinks heavily, the family is mostly dependent on the earnings of the woman of the house. Separate interviews with the women give you even more alarming figures of spending on arrack. Their figures tend to be more accurate, too.

There is much hatred of the police, who, the women say, are the driving force behind the business. 'Once, one distiller in our village agreed to give up,' some women tell me. 'But the police started harassing him to resume business because they were losing their cut.'

The women say they won't suffer in silence any more. But the arrack lobby is hitting back at them as hard as it can. In some villages, it will be very tough for the women to sustain their offensive. The boycott of Malarmani has become a major issue. The problem is larger than an administrative or a law-and-order one. The political-bureaucratic network that arrack has nourished is vast and all-pervasive. 'Can you introduce me to a big distiller?' I ask one self-confessed arrack consumer. 'Certainly,' he says, only half in jest. 'Let's go call on the MLA and minister immediately!'

Still, *Arivoli* has changed things. The confidence it has given the women promises big battles on the issue. Malarmani and Matilda have set an example. People in villages far off from their own have heard of and welcomed their actions. They are even emulating them. The arrack lobby has survived many governments. But in the poor, neo-literate women of Pudukkottai, the lobby is finding tougher opponents. And the battle's only just begun.

Postscript

The anti-liquor movement has had its ebbs and flows. While the women's ban on arrack spread to some villages, it also collapsed in some of the original ones. Though it has proved hard to sustain the momentum, two things have changed. First, the women have changed. They might be on the defensive in periods where the lobby hits back or when faced with less sympathetic officials. But the drive against arrack is never off their mental agenda. And it periodically re-emerges in physical terms. Secondly, they know and have proved that where a serious ban is in place, consumption levels are affected and that earning levels do improve. So while the government of Tamil Nadu can disrupt their movement, it simply won't go away and is likely to keep bouncing back. That this has begun to sink in is evident from the hostility sections of the state government have since shown towards the literacy movement and its activists.

Van samitis and vanishing trees

Latehar, Palamau (Bihar): This was one forest officer who had missed the wood for the trees. He had no clue about developments in his own area of Latehar in Palamau. As his van carrying stolen timber came around the corner, it was waylaid by a group of villagers. They belonged to the local '*van samiti*'* (forest committee). Their raid saw the recovery of timber worth hundreds of thousands of rupees from the officer. He is now facing departmental action.

'The lives of the villagers depend on the forests,' Mohammad Abbas Ansari, a *van samiti* member, tells me. 'We will fight to stop their destruction.' Palamau once enjoyed great forest wealth. But large scale illegal felling and timber smuggling have devastated that resource. By the mid-'80s, Palamau's poor saw the forests they so badly needed vanishing. So they began doing something about it.

Close to ninety *van samitis* have sprung up across the district. 'Of these perhaps fifteen are very effective,' says S.K. Singh, the young and popular divisional forest officer (DFO) based in Latehar. Singh's own role is quite dynamic. He is also a realist. He feels that 'the rest of the groups need more experience, but most are very enthusiastic'.

Enthusiastic seems the right word. The *van samiti* of a single village, Jhabhar, has overseen the planting of more than 60,000 trees. That's pretty good going for this village of less than 1,200 people in the Balumath block. And it has contributed to Jhabar's relative prosperity. Earnings from these efforts have funded a community hall, a water tank and the expansion of the school building.

Jhabar seems to have set a trend. Nearly twenty-five *samitis* have come up in Latehar, Chandwa and Balumath blocks, too. And the *van samitis* of Palamau don't stop at just getting people to grow trees. They are also fighting illegal felling and timber smuggling. Springing up from within the villages, they show some signs of developing into a popular movement. But they will not be so easy to sustain.

Palamau is notorious as a drought-prone district that has faced famine

---

* Also called *van suraksha samiti* or forest protection committee.

twice in twenty-five years. We know much less about its environmental crisis. The destruction of the forests is shattering lives, particularly those of very poor tribes like the Birhors, Asurs, and Kurwas. For them, the jungle is the great provider. Adivasis often depend on minor forest produce for up to 25 per cent of their food. With some tribes, this dependence goes beyond 50 per cent.

During the last century, Palamau had nearly 90 per cent forest cover. Early this century, that fell to 70 per cent. Today, officially, it is around 40 per cent. Off record, senior officials concede that forest cover may be just 25 per cent. Drought has closely followed deforestation.

'The forests were always the shock absorber,' says Santosh Matthew, Palamau's deputy commissioner. 'The loss of forests means the loss of the sponge effect that keeps the streams and rivers alive.'

With this region having perhaps the finest concentration of *sal* (tree yielding valuable timber) trees anywhere, timber smuggling is big business. 'Good timber fetches Rs.700-Rs.800 per cubic foot,' says DFO S.K. Singh who is battling that trade. 'An average tree can produce up to 20 cubic feet of timber, a good tree up to 40 cubic feet.'

This means that 'if you fell just four good trees and smuggle out the timber, you can make over Rs.120,000 on that deal alone. And the smugglers have strong networks.'

Besides, says political activist Narendra Chaubey, there's another line of profit. 'The substance from the Khairi tree here goes into making pan masala. It sells at Rs.300 per kilogram. So you can imagine the pressure.'

The pressure is intensive and the networks extensive. In Balumath, the ultra-left Maoist Communist Centre (MCC) extracts money from smugglers. The day I arrived in Balumath, the MCC killed the *mukhiya* (headman) of a small village. A timber smuggler himself, he had apparently grudged raising their cut when revenues went up.

In tribal areas, *mahajans* (trader-moneylenders) force adivasis in their grip to cut trees. Unable to repay their debts, the tribals have to cut and smuggle out timber for their creditors. When caught, they take the rap.

While the poor face harassment, organised smugglers have less to fear. As one forest officer in Balumath tells me: 'We can confiscate the timber, the smuggler's vehicle, and prosecute him. The cases drag on. In theory, they can be jailed for six years, but usually remain inside for less than a year.'

Some years ago, Jhabar's villagers set up a youth group, the Jagruk Naujavan Sabha (Society of Conscious Youth). It took up the issues of migrant labour, primary education, development and environment. By 1985, this group had graduated into a politically conscious outfit. In 1989, spurred by the realisation that the great forests around them were disappearing, it formed Palamau's first *van samiti*. With S.K. Singh's arrival in 1990, says Narendra Chaubey, 'things really picked up. He encouraged and aided the *samitis*.'

For Singh, it is quite simple: 'The villagers are the last hope. How much of raiding villages and alienating people can one do? Even policing works better if the people are with you. We tried showing them that afforestation is profitable.'

Jhabar's villagers have found it so. 'An individual can earn Rs.1,500 a year by planting trees,' says Kailash Singh of the *van samiti*. 'We get 30-40 paise per tree, plus help with seeds, plants or even, occasionally, a little fertiliser.'

The *samiti* tries to be humane. 'When a villager builds a house,' says Kailash Singh, 'we examine the matter and say, okay, he needs so much wood. After all, our building material is wood. And the ranger allots the wood going by the *samiti*'s estimate.'

So while Jhabar profits from the sale of produce, there is less danger of deforestation here. The *samiti* ensures that copsing and felling are controlled and phased. Fines levied on illegal felling raised Rs.2,500 last year. Yet their effort has had its problems. For one thing, a large number of the trees planted are eucalyptus.

'This was the craze in the early days,' explains Gobind Singh of Jhalim village. 'We did not know then what a monster this eucalyptus is. It drinks water from all around, hurting the other trees. The trees born of our own soil – *khari*, *sal*, *seesham*, *akasi*, *gumhar* and many others – are better.'

That knowledge is growing, though slowly. The early craze for eucalyptus was not accidental. Nor did people seek it only because it grew faster. For years, a strong industrial lobby with influence in the forest department plugged it consciously. Eucalyptus goes into roofing materials, is used as a prop in mining activities and has other industrial functions. But S.K. Singh claims the craze is now dying.

'Palamau's advantage,' says Singh, 'is that its forests are naturally regenerating. But they should be protected, allowed to grow.' In the year before Singh arrived, not a single hectare had come under afforestation. Last year, the forest department covered 400 hectares in its drive, apart from woods revived by the *van samitis*. Using different varieties they grew around 2,500 plants or trees per acre, at a cost of Rs.3 per tree. They could cover more, but funds are shrinking.

The enemy is not just timber smuggling. Deforestation in Palamau has pushed a perverse process. Contrary to common belief, Palamau gets excellent rainfall in most years. However, relentless felling has killed not only large forests but also the streams and rivers. And with so many people needing those forests for survival, the distance between drought and famine in Palamau is much less than in most other places. As Narendra Chaubey puts it: 'The poor here are also confronting serious causes of drought and famine. The great thing is that they have begun to fight to save their forests, and thereby themselves.'

Whose forest is it, anyway?

Nuapada (Orissa): The assistant conservator of forests (ACF) was pleading with the villagers of Kendupatti, who were preventing his men from laying a finger on the surrounding trees: 'We're here to help the trees. We're only going to prune and cut a few branches so that the trees grow straighter and stronger.'

Picharu Sangh of the Jagrut Shramik Sanghatan, among those guarding the trees, asked the ACF: 'If we cut off your hands, will you grow straighter and stronger?'

The battle over the Kendupatti woods had reached a peak.

When the people of Kendupatti in Khariar block decided in the mid-'80s to revive the dying forests around them, they unknowingly invited one of the most curious of possession disputes. By 1992, the experiment was a huge success. They had nurtured forest across 140 acres of land, with maybe half a million trees on it.

It was, says Picharu, too much of a success. 'The department came and claimed the forest. Others too started acting as if they owned this place. Actually, if not for our villagers, not a single tree would have grown here. The forest department, seeing how good our forest was, simply appointed a guard to "look after it". What were they looking after when there was just barren land here?'

At the heart of the dispute is not so much a fight over credit for the achievement but a more sordid consideration – the sheer commercial value of the trees. 'Basically these people want to sell the trees,' says Mohan Baug. 'That's all these forest department people do anyway – sell the timber they are supposed to protect.' The forest department admits that if the trees and forest exist at all, it is due to the efforts of the villagers. Their point is that it is on land belonging to the government and not to the village. Hence the assigning of 'watchers' to keep an eye on the Kendupatti woods.

There seems little doubt, though, that the department's concern rose with the commercial value of the trees. There are different varieties of trees here, including teak that can fetch up to Rs.250 per cubic foot. The villagers are in no position to ensure they get actual market prices for their trees, concedes Eashwar Podh. However, they would still be, he points out, in possession of

313

thousands of teak trees that could fetch a minimum of Rs.150 a piece anywhere.

'There are about seventy teak trees to the acre,' claims Podh. And at that rate, those trees alone would be worth close to Rs.40 million. At market value, the figure would be astronomical, running into hundreds of millions of rupees. In any case, even on a very conservative basis – that the trees apart from teak will fetch no more than Rs.75 each – the villagers still have a forest worth many millions of rupees.

'But we didn't grow this forest to make money,' says Mohan Baug. 'We felt the need to plant trees, improve the area. We may use one tenth of the trees in selected stretches for house construction, for personal use by the villagers. Or sell some to create a village fund for a proper school building, other amenities – and even to help preserve the forest itself. But we won't allow destruction of this forest. How can we? We laboured so much to grow it.'

Even as the fight with the forest department intensified, other predators sneaked in. The *sarpanch* of a nearby village began to encroach on the forest, widening the theatre of battle. The *sarpanch*, says the villagers, entered into some sort of collusion with a few forest guards and 'watchers'. A conflict followed. And one of the department's 'watchers' experienced the quality of the forest's timber when caught felling trees. The villagers flogged him with a stout branch.

Charges were traded, and cases were filed against the villagers. Surprisingly, the police took a positive attitude when the Kendupatti villagers marched down to the station and gave their side of the story. The police persuaded the other side to compromise and had some of the charges dropped. The problem, though, remained.

Subsequently, a person appointed by the forest department was caught by the villagers after he cut down a few branches. He responded by charging the villagers with the crime he had committed. The range officer found his charges to be false. But the main dispute still persists.

So who owns this forest? The villagers who grew it? Or the government on whose land it stands? Or the forest department, whose duty it is to look after such resources? Seems complicated. Except that the dispute arose simply because the villagers created something beautiful and valuable and turned a barren land into a forest. They could, in fact, end up being penalised for doing something the government and its forest department should have done, but never did.

In the eyes of the villagers, the issue is fairly straightforward: 'If the forest department wants to take over this forest,' says Mohan Baug, 'all men, women

The villagers of Kendupatti stand in the forest they have grown through their own efforts. The trees alone are worth crores of rupees. The villagers now have to guard the forest against predators – such as the Forest Department.

and children here will resist. We will readily go to jail.' The Jagrut Shramik Sanghatan (Organisation of Conscious Labourers), a local organisation which persuaded them to grow trees in the first place, is ready for battle.

Kendupatti is learning that while failure might be an orphan, success has no shortage of proud parents, fighting for possession of a priceless child.

315

Who says money doesn't grow on trees?

Nuapada (Orissa): Ratu Naik is a little drunk, and a little unhappy, too. But, he informs me, 'I am better off than I was ten years ago. I have nearly a hundred trees and this season, I will sell quite a few of them. Believe me, the *bamur** is a good tree.'

Naik, a small landowner in Konabira village of Komna block, is a practitioner of 'ridge-farming'. Which means he grows trees along the ridges of the plots of land owned by him and his family members. Not just any trees. His specific choice is the *bamur* (also called *babul*) tree. 'This could be Kalahandi's miracle tree,' says Jagdish Pradhan of the Paschim Orissa Krishi-jeevi Sangha (The Western Orissa Farmers Association).

He could be right. Estimates show that ridge cultivation of *bamur* trees could add up to Rs.6,000 to the income of small and marginal farmers each year. That is a great sum in the Kalahandi region. *Bamur* has several other uses, too.

'Its leaf is good for manure,' says Ratu Naik. 'When it falls on the field, it improves the paddy yield. Its wood can be used in making bullock-carts, agricultural implements, door frames and other household items.' Naik won't cut down all his trees at one go. He practises planned felling. Between ten and twenty trees will go down this season.

With the assistance of the Banabashi Sangha and the Orissa Tree Growers Association, Naik made Rs.5,000 in his last sale – without altering the balance in the number of trees substantially. 'It's hard to make Rs.5,000, with thrice that effort, from agriculture,' he says. Naik used to purchase good quality seeds that made his subsequent harvest outstanding.

'For years,' he says, 'I had to hire bullocks to cultivate my land, borrow money to buy seed. But not now.' He has purchased his own cart and bullocks and can afford the seed.

Unlike disastrous official experiments with the now notorious *subabul* tree in this region, the *bamur* is seen as a local species. 'It grows very well and swiftly in our soil,' says Sunadhar Barasagadhia, an expert at the Project Sambhav in Nuapada. 'And its leaves and fruit provide fodder for the cattle. So it becomes a money-saver.'

---

* *Bamur – acacia nilotica*, a hardwood tree.

The tree has another interesting feature, points out Jagdish Pradhan. 'It does not create dense shade, so it does not greatly block sunlight from the crop grown beneath it. Maintaining an optimal distance of five to seven feet between each tree would ensure this. Indeed, its leaves serve as green manure for the crop below. Moreover, the branches begin at an appropriate height, so you can store your straw there, out of the reach of cattle and also to dry out after the rains, if it gets wet.'

Little stretches of the Kalahandi region are dotted with *bamur* trees holding the farmers' straw. In some villages of Nuapada, farmers now seem to be growing these trees quite systematically.

So how come the farmers here took to *bamur*? How did they resist the craze for, say, eucalyptus? Duryodhan Sabar of Bargwon village says: 'After massive deforestation in our areas, we had to think of *bamur*. It is only during the last six to ten years that ridge-farming of *bamur* has occurred to us as a strategy.'

The value of that strategy was driven home by the growing scarcity of timber. Earlier, the *bamur* would grow naturally and farmers only had to tend it. Now, most *bamur* trees coming up are the result of conscious efforts. The idea of planting them as a cash crop is catching on. The tree can also be grown along tank bunds and in common lands. It needs neither manure nor watering and stands up pretty well under drought conditions.

Growing the tree costs next to nothing. But what are the economics of the operation thereafter? The total cultivable area of the undivided old Kalahandi is around 500,000 hectares. Of that, 300,000 hectares constitute paddy and other crop area. The average landholding in the region is around half a hectare or less. So even by planting *bamur* only along the ridges of the plot, farmers can get around 250 trees per hectare.

At present less than 10 per cent of farmers have gotten into the act. 'If 70 per cent of them were to adopt this practice,' says Pradhan, 'then 2.1 lakh hectares would be utilised. We would have around 52.5 million *bamur* trees at 250 per hectare. These would be cut in rotation. Each year, the farmers would cut one-seventh of the trees and plant an equal number. So there would be 7.5 million saleable trees annually. The demand for them is very good.'

Each tree produces five quintals of wood and there is a minimum market rate of Rs.100 per quintal. That gives a base value of Rs.500 for trees that are around six years old. 'This promises an earning of Rs.3.75 billion a year to the growers,' points out Pradhan. 'Most of them, remember, are small farmers with minor holdings. Extend this experiment to Orissa as a whole, say, by multiplying the figure by ten times. There would be an earning of close to Rs.4 billion.'

That could be more than all the money invested by the Orissa government in coming years in the sixteen sugar factories and other projects it hopes to set up across the state. The Orissa Tree Growers Association calculates it could dramatically add to the incomes of the small farmers. Together with a sister organisation, the Banabashi Sangha, it has set about creating a self-regulating marketing mechanism for them. Previously, all those functions were in the hands of traders and moneylenders.

Marketing has not been an easy ride. As late as 1992, traders were buying up *bamur* at Rs.25 a quintal or less. Transportation wasn't easy either. The following year, the Banabashi Sangha and the Jagrut Shramik Sanghatan started organising the farmers. A year later, they had broken the Rs.100 a quintal barrier. As their marketing skills improve, that rate is going up. A mature tree, one that is around fifteen years old and can provide around fifteen quintals of wood, can today fetch Rs.2,000.

Perhaps the most interesting aspect of this idea is that it evolved from the farmers' own experience. Jagdish Pradhan stresses this despite his own pioneering role in bringing back the *bambur* tree in a significant way. The practice existed earlier but somehow died out decades ago, he says. However, NGOs such as the Banabashi Sangha and Jagrut Shramik Sanghatan, did play a major role in selling the idea to farmers in the early '90s. That these bodies had purely local roots probably helped.

There's more to the *bamur* tree than the cash it fetches on sale, however. As one farmer told me: 'Don't just calculate what money it makes on the market. Calculate what it saves each one of us by way of expenses. The nitrous roots fertilise the soil, the branches protect our straw. This is the farmer's tree.'

Postscript

When I returned to Kalahandi region a year later, the process had grown stronger. A telegram had come from a traders' body giving in to the farmers' demand for a better price. The main problem the farmers face now is that posed by the forest department. Growers taking their trees to market are often stopped by officials who accuse them of stealing timber from the forest. Some of the officials simply demand a commission. However, the farmers' bodies seem to be sorting out the problem.

To market for greens, back with elephant

Matringa, Surguja (Madhya Pradesh): 'We didn't know anything about it. We were told to become members of the panchayat* and we did. We didn't ask to be elected. But we were.' Jugmania and Guruvari are both Majhwar tribals. They have become *panchas* (members of the panchayat) in Madhya Pradesh's first-ever serious panchayat polls. Certainly the first after the constitutional amendment.

Both now represent wards reserved for women in Matringa village. And both were elected unopposed. Matringa shot to notoriety after seven children died from a lethal combination of measles and dysentery between February and April 1994. The panchayat polls, spread over ten days from May 25, present a picture of splendid confusion. Especially so in Surguja, which has 2,793 panchayats.

So how did Jugmania and Guruvari enter the fray? 'When we went to the bazaar one day, the *patwari* [keeper of village records] and *patel* [chief of a village] stopped us, made us put our thumb impression on the forms and told us we were elected. We protested. But the *patwari* said the prestige of our village would be wounded if we didn't do as we were told.'

'*Sabzi laane ke liye gaya bazaar, haathi lekhe aaye*, [they went to the market to buy vegetables and returned with an elephant]' laughs a neighbour. Didn't the *patwari* tell them about why it was important to have women in the panchayats? 'No,' says Guruvari. 'He told us: "You just do what we tell you to." And later, our husbands also told us to do whatever the *patwari* wanted.'

The *patwari*'s concern is not entirely about the prestige of the village. Senior officers suspended both *patel* and *patwari* last month after the measles-dysentery deaths. Neither had made any effort at all to alert the authorities or otherwise help the victims. The *patwari* sees, in the election of the two women, a way of retaining his hold over the panchayat. Immediately, he might be right. In the long run, he could be making a mistake.

Now that they're in, Jugmania and Guruvari are not terribly unhappy. Both agree that women ought to be in the panchayat. Yet they feel afraid of

---

* Panchayat – earlier, simply village council. Now often comprises more than one village. To be elected by direct voting.

319

'speaking in front of everyone'. They come from families of very poor farmers. Neither knows the name of the panchayat or which wards they were elected from. But they're willing to learn.

Later, I was to see a similarly odd situation in Jhabua district. There, Gendhubai heads an all-women's panchayat at Rama village in Rama block. They have had a female *sarpanch* (head of a panchayat) for some time now. Curiously, though only 65 per cent of seats were reserved for women, it has become an all-female panchayat. And every member has come in unopposed.

While this has been beneficial, the male generosity involved is a little suspect. As one of them told me: 'If two-thirds were going to be female, how could we men sit in a minority in front of the women? It isn't right. So we thought: better to have only women on it. After all, their work is to sign the papers when they have to sign.'

This could prove to be a miscalculation over time. The process is having an impact on the women's consciousness. They speak of the need for a female doctor, for more jobs. They want to improve the school. Yet in the present framework, male dominance continues. Most of the elected women are too intimidated to speak up and assert themselves.

Back in Surguja, one official says: 'You're going to have this for a while – the men manipulating the women. Still, the very entry of women could change things over the years.' The picture is varied. Some voluntary bodies are training villagers for participation in panchayats. The NGO Ekta Parishad (Unity Council), for instance, has taken a lead in this. In Lakhanpur, Chandana Padwal is an exceptional candidate. She is the only woman candidate in this or many other blocks with a postgraduate degree (in sociology). She aims to be a *sarpanch*. She is articulate and credible. Her victory would threaten male hegemony in that area.

There is, though, no candidate for *sarpanch* in Matringa. Several wards in that panchayat are uncontested. No parties have done any direct canvassing. (Unless you count one pro-BJP candidate who is promising his village a temple.) And a very low level of consciousness prevails. Still, there are positive signs, too.

Most of the men in Matringa, Jajgi, Udaipur and Lakhanpur agree that women ought to be in the panchayat. In Matringa, Ghasiaram, who lost a three-year-old son in the measles-dysentery outbreak says: 'They certainly can't do worse than the men. Apart from the women, how do the old and new panchayats differ? People are dying just the same.'

'At least the basis of some useful structures is being laid,' says a senior official from Bhopal. 'The sheer presence of a third of women will make its impact felt over time. True, we are going to see a lot of manipulation. But let's hope democratic movements emerge alongside, raising consciousness. It could make for a great combination.' Such movements, however, are some way off from emerging in Surguja and much of rural Madhya Pradesh.

Where the candidates are serious, so are the issues. These range from handpumps for the villages, to roads and payment for working on those roads. In Matringa, a road of sorts came up simply because of the mandatory ministerial visit after the deaths. But locals who worked to build that road are yet to be paid. In Jajgir in Udaipur and elsewhere, delayed payment for *tendu patta* collection is a burning issue.

There are 30,294 *gram* (village) panchayats, 459 *janpad* (block) panchayats and 45 *zilla* (district) panchayats in Madhya Pradesh. Each *gram* panchayat has at least ten members, rising to twenty where the village's population exceeds 1,000. Apart from 33 per cent reservation for women, 25 per cent of the seats are reserved for scheduled caste (SC) and scheduled tribe (ST) candidates where they are less than 50 per cent of the population in a block. Where their population is over 50 per cent, the reservation moves up to 33 per cent. There are more reservations for women within the wards reserved for SC and ST candidates.

The creation of 'women-only' wards has confused the district's dull election officers. They began telling women candidates that they could only contest these seats. So an exasperated Collector had to explain to them that they could not bar women from other wards. As one woman candidate points out: 'If we can't contest in general wards, there are no general wards. All would be reserved wards!'

This, of course, does not mean there has been massive participation. In a huge Surajpur centre, just one person had filed a nomination for the post of *sarpanch* on the first day of the poll process. And there are seventy-nine *sarpanch* posts in the centre. In Surajpur block, not a single ward member's nomination, male or female, had been filed during the first two days.

The officer-in-charge, Satyanarayan Nema says: 'At the moment, political cliques are forming in the villages. In the final days, they will get someone literate to fill in the forms properly so they won't be rejected.' When I last heard, some forms had come in, but nowhere on the scale expected by Nema.

'There is no problem of rigging here,' joked one of the officers at the Surajpur centre. 'Anyone can get elected who wants to.' The security deposit for women, SC and ST candidates for the *sarpanch*'s post is Rs.50. For those in the general category it is Rs.200.

The politically more conscious are sceptical about a system that makes the local MLA and bank officials ex-officio members of the *zilla* panchayats as it does the Lok Sabha and Rajya Sabha* MPs. 'This bring in all the un-elected vested interests,' asserts one political activist. 'They will undermine the panchayats. How will elected members stand up to the MP if he comes? How many will defy the bank manager who controls their loans?'

His point is irrefutable. With no organised political movements and a poor level of consciousness in this district, such problems could prove greater over here. Yet, there could be some surprises. Some change seems inherent in the very process and the kind of people it will draw in. We might be seeing a fight back in embryo. As Jugmania and Guruvari now say of their elections: 'Isn't it the woman who keeps the *hisaab* [the accounts] at home?' The *patwari* and *patel* may yet rue the day they had these two elected.

---

* Lok Sabha – Lower House (People's Assembly) of the central Indian Parliament. Rajya Sabha – Upper House (Council of States) in the central Parliament.

Where there is a wheel

Pudukkottai (Tamil Nadu): Cycling as a social movement? Sounds far-fetched. Perhaps. But not all that far – not to tens of thousands of neo-literate rural women in Pudukkottai district. People find ways, sometimes curious ones, of hitting out at their backwardness, of expressing defiance, of hammering at the fetters that hold them.

In this, one of India's poorest districts, cycling seems the chosen medium for rural women. During the past eighteen months, over 100,000 rural women, most of them neo-literates, have taken to bicycling as a symbol of independence, freedom and mobility. If we exclude girls below ten years of age, it would mean that over one-fourth of all rural women here have learnt cycling. And over 70,000 of these women have taken part in public 'exhibition-cum-contests' to proudly display their new skills. And still the 'training camps' and desire to learn continue.

In the heart of rural Pudukkottai, young Muslim women from highly conservative backgrounds zip along the roads on their bicycles. Some seem to have abandoned the veil for the wheel. Jameela Bibi, a young Muslim girl who has taken to cycling, told me: 'It's my right. We can go anywhere. Now I don't have to wait for a bus. I know people made dirty remarks when I started cycling, but I paid no attention.'

Fatima is a secondary school teacher, so addicted to cycling that she hires a bicycle for half an hour each evening (she cannot yet afford to buy one – each costs over Rs.1,200). She said: 'There is freedom in cycling. We are not dependent on anyone now. I can never give this up.' Jameela, Fatima and their friend Avakanni, all in their early twenties, have trained scores of other young women from their community in the art of cycling.

Cycling has swept across this district. Women agricultural workers, quarry labourers and village health nurses are among its fans. Joining the rush are *balwadi* and *anganwadi* workers, gem-cutters and school teachers. And *gramsevikas** and midday meal workers are not far behind. The vast majority are those who have just become literate. The district's vigorous literacy drive, led

---

* *Balwadi* – largely a pre-school care centre, something like a kindergarten. In some states works for not much more than two hours a day. *Anganwadi* – centre for children under six

by the *Arivoli Iyakkam* (Light of Knowledge Movement) has been quick to tap this energy. Every one of the neo-literate, 'neo-cyclist' women I spoke to saw a direct link between cycling and her personal independence.

'The main thing,' says N. Kannammal, *Arivoli* central co-ordinator and one of the pioneers of the cycling movement, 'was the confidence it gave women. Very importantly, it reduced their dependence on men. Now we often see a woman doing a four-kilometre stretch on her cycle to collect water, sometimes *with* her children. Even carting provisions from other places can be done on their own. But, believe me, women had to put up with vicious attacks on their character when this began. So many made filthy remarks. But *Arivoli* gave cycling social sanction. So women took to it.'

Early among them, Kannammal herself. Though a science graduate, she had never mustered the 'courage to cycle' earlier.

Visiting an *Arivoli* 'cycling training camp' is an unusual experience. In Kilakuruchi village all the prospective learners had turned out in their Sunday best. You can't help being struck by the sheer passion of the cycling movement. They *had to know*. Cycling offered a way out of enforced routines, around male-imposed barriers. The neo-cyclists even sing songs produced by *Arivoli* to encourage bicycling. One of these has lines like: 'O sister come learn cycling, move with the wheel of time . . .'

Very large members of those trained have come back to help new learners. They work free of charge for *Arivoli* as (oddly-named) 'master trainers'. There is not only a desire to learn but a widespread perception among them that *all women ought to learn cycling*. In turn, their experience has enriched the literacy movement. The neo-cyclists are bound even more passionately than before to *Arivoli*.

The whole phenomenon was the brainchild of the popular former district collector, Sheela Rani Chunkath. Her idea in 1991 was to train female activists so that literacy would reach women in the interior. She also included *mobility* as a part of the literacy drive. This flowed from the fact that lack of mobility among women played a big role in undermining their confidence. Chunkath pushed the banks to give loans for the women to buy cycles. She also got each block to accept specific duties in promoting the drive. As the top official in the district, she gave it great personal attention.

First the activists learned cycling. Then neo-literates wanted to learn. *Every* woman wanted to learn. Not surprisingly, this led to a shortage of 'ladies'

---

years of age for nutritional and health care and pre-school education. *Gramsevika* – village worker reporting to the rural development bureaucracy.

Visiting an Arivoli 'cycling training camp' was an unusual experience. All the prospective learners had turned out in their Sunday best. In Pudukkottai, the bicycle is a metaphor for freedom.

cycles. Never mind. 'Gents' cycles would do just as nicely, thank you. Some women preferred the latter as these have an additional bar from the seat to the handle. You can seat a child on that. And to this day, thousands of women here ride 'gents' cycles. Thousands of others dream of the day they will be able to afford any bicycle at all.

After International Women's Day in 1992, this district can never be the same. Flags on the handle bars, bells ringing, over 1,500 female cyclists took

Pudukkottai by storm. Their all-women's cycle rally stunned the town's inhabitants with its massive showing.

What did the males think? One who had to approve was S. Kannakarajan, owner of Ram Cycles. This single dealer saw a rise of over 350 per cent in the sale of 'ladies' cycles in one year. That figure is probably an underestimate for two reasons. One, a lot of women, unable to wait for 'ladies' cycles, went in for men's bikes. Two, Kannakarajan shared his information with me with great caution. For all he knew, I was an undercover agent of the sales tax department.

In any case, not all males were hostile. Some were even encouraging. Muthubhaskaran, a male *Arivoli* activist, for instance. He wrote the famous cycling song that has become their anthem.

When, in the blazing heat of Kudimianmalai's stone quarries, you run into Manormani, twenty-two, training others, you know it's all worth it. A quarry worker and *Arivoli* volunteer herself, she thinks it vital that her co-workers learn cycling. 'Our areas are a little cut off,' she told me. 'Those who know cycling, they can be mobile.' In a single week in 1992 more than 70,000 women displayed their cycling skills at the public 'exhibition-cum-contests' run by *Arivoli*. An impressed UNICEF sanctioned fifty mopeds for *Arivoli* women activists.

Cycling has had very definite economic implications. It boosts income. Some of the women here sell agricultural or other produce within a group of villages. For them, the bicycle cuts down on the time wasted in waiting for buses. This is crucial in poorly connected routes. Secondly, it gives you much more time to focus on selling your produce. Thirdly, it enlarges the area you can hope to cover. Lastly, it can increase your leisure time, too, should you choose.

Small producers who used to wait for buses were often dependent on fathers, brothers, husbands or sons even to reach the bus stop. They could cover only a limited number of villages to sell their produce. Some walked. Those who cannot afford bicycles still do. These women had to rush back early to tend to the children and perform other chores like fetching water. Those who have bicycles now combine these different tasks with nonchalance. Which means you can, even along some remote road, see a young mother, child on the bar, produce on the carrier. She could be carrying two, perhaps even three, pots of water hung across the back, and cycling towards work or home.

However, it would be very wrong to emphasise the economic aspect over all else. The sense of self-respect it brings is vital. 'Of course it's not economic,' said Fatima, giving me a look that made me feel rather stupid. 'What money do I make from cycling? I lose money. I can't afford a bicycle. Yet I hire one every evening just to feel that goodness, that independence.' Never before reaching Pudukkottai had I seen this humble vehicle in that light – the bicycle as a metaphor for freedom.

'It is difficult for people to see how big this is for rural women,' says Kannammal. 'It's a Himalayan achievement, like flying an aeroplane, for them. People may laugh. Only the women know how important it is.'

I suppose the norms of standard journalism demand at this point some 'balancing' quotes from men opposed to the cycling movement. Frankly, who the heck cares? There's a hundred thousand neo-literate women cycling out there and that's the story.

Those men opposed to it can go take a walk – because when it comes to cycling, they aren't in the same league as the women.

Postscript

When I returned to Pudukkottai in April 1995, the craze was still on. But a large number of women are unable to afford bicycles – each now costs around Rs.1,400. And a new generation is coming up that was too young to gain from the first round. Nevertheless, Pudukkottai remains unique among Indian districts for the stunning proportion of women who have taken to cycling. And the enthusiasm for gaining the skill among the rest.

11

*Poverty,
Development
and the
Press*

Development is the strategy of evasion. When you can't give people land reform, give them hybrid cows. When you can't send the children to school, try non-formal education. When you can't provide basic health to people, talk of health insurance. Can't give them jobs? Not to worry. Just redefine the words 'employment opportunities'. Don't want to do away with using children as a form of slave labour? Never mind. Talk of 'improving the conditions of child labour'. It sounds good. You can even make money out of it.

This has been true of development, Indian style, for over four decades now. Central to its philosophy is the idea that we can somehow avoid the big moves, the painful ones, the reforms that Indian society really needs. So the closest you come to land reform, as in the first story of this book, is when you give people an acre of land to grow fodder for their cattle. Not food for themselves.

Is there some way we can improve people's lives without getting into annoying things like land reform? There isn't, but there are powerful people who'd like us to believe there is.

The same illusion runs through what we call our 'globalisation'. It has the Indian elite excited. 'We must globalise. There is no choice. Everybody else is doing it. Look at Singapore, Malaysia, Indonesia, Taiwan, South Korea.' (Currently, that ardour is somewhat dampened with some of the 'miracles' coming apart at the seams.)

Of course, 'everyone' who is doing it did a lot of other things. All those countries – if you must take authoritarian states as a model – went through land reform. They gave their people literacy and education. Also, some standards of health, shelter, nutrition. Point this out – and the Indian elite discover our 'cultural uniqueness'. The same is true of child labour. Dozens of other societies got rid of it. But 'India is different'. So India's uniqueness does not stand in the way of globalisation. It stands in the way of land reform, education, health. It does not prevent external agencies making policies for India on a wide range of subjects. It does stand in the way of doing away with child labour.

The Indian development experience reeks of this sort of hypocrisy across its four and a half decades. Ignore the big issues long enough and you can finally dismiss them as 'outdated'. Nobody will really bother.

People, however, do bother. The issues of land, forest and water resources remain fundamental to real development. The poor are acutely aware of this. After all, 85 per cent of the Indian poor are either landless agricultural labourers or small and marginal farmers. They know where it hurts. Real development would mean more than just letting them know the plans of the elite. It would mean their involvement in the decisions for *all* development, especially their own.

Let's say we hold a seminar on medical issues. To this we invite not a single doctor, nurse, patient or medical expert. A lot of people would consider that odd. And rightly so. The many symposia and conferences where land reform gets trashed are likewise odd. They never have a single landless labourer to state his or her case. To the elite that is perfectly natural. Isn't India unique, after all?

There isn't a single migrant worker amongst millions who would not tell you how crucial the land issue is. But what do they know, anyway? They didn't go to the right schools and are not part of the Old Boy network. Land reform has taken place within our own country. The bulk of it in just four states. If it could take place in Jammu and Kashmir – apart from the familiar examples of Kerala, West Bengal and Tripura – it is surely possible elsewhere in the nation?

Take the country as a whole and you get a different picture. Just a little over one per cent of total cultivable area has been redistributed. That is, of 455 million acres, only 4.5 million have been distributed among the poor. The eighth plan says about 2.6 million acres 'are still to be distributed'. Even if this is done, that would still come to about two per cent of total cultivable land in India. There are other ways of going about it. But let's not hear those old stories again, shall we?

A profoundly undemocratic streak runs through India's development process. Exclusion doesn't end at the symposia. As the reports in this book show, peasants are excluded from land issues in real life, too. Villagers are increasingly robbed of control over water and other community resources. Tribes are being more and more cut off from the forests. Elite vision, meanwhile, holds the poor and their experiences in contempt.

Real development would involve the transformation of the human state to a higher level of being and living. Almost all versions of development accept that. However, such a transformation must have the participation and consent of those affected by it. *Their* involvement in the decision-making process. And the intrusion on their environment, culture, livelihood and tradition by that process should be minimal.

But that sounds too much like work. So you can have a play staged and enacted with all the main actors sitting in the audience – if they are around at all. If reality smells, rewrite the script. Take the current champions of 'change'. Those shouting loudest about change among the elite are the very people who ran this country for over forty years. If it is in a mess, they had much to do with it.

The most amusing side to what passes for a debate on the economy is not so much the change as the amazing continuity of so many elements. Sure, June 1991 represents a major leap in some ways. But it was not one in a more progressive direction. In that month, under a Congress government led by P.V. Narasimha Rao India began to practise what have been called the new economic policies or 'economic reforms'. World Bank–IMF style structural adjustment programmes were introduced and the government increasingly abdicated its responsibilities in the social sector. Elite consumption was encouraged even as the living standards of the poor further declined.

Then Prime Minister P.V. Narasimha Rao and his finance minister Dr Manmohan Singh were quintessential representatives of the old order they wanted to 'change'. They were party to, even authors of, some of the policies of the past that are now in disgrace. Oddly, the 'adversarial' media saw no irony in this.

If 'change' is to come, those who seek to author it must have credibility. And that, a credibility of record. Not one invented by a media chorus that has no link at all to what hundreds of millions of Indians are thinking. This growing disconnect of the 'mass' media from mass reality is getting worse.

The unfinished agenda

The rituals, of course, are always observed. Editorials on the economy end, after much celebration of policy, on a mandatory note of 'concern' for the poor. Most discussions in elite fora on the economy go the same way. The intellectuals, the economists, the bureaucrats, policymakers all agree on one thing. Something must be done about poverty. Everyone agrees that 'not enough is being done'.

Many speak with passion to insist that 'both' things must go together. That is, poverty reduction on the one hand, and economic reforms (or what the elite see as reforms) and growth on the other. So, in theory, there is always this two-part agenda. It makes all participants in the debate feel good. Progress is being made. The reforms are fine. But 'something must be done about poverty'.

Poverty, education, health . . . these make up 'the unfinished agenda'. The discussion ended, the participants go back to what they're really working on. That is, part two of the agenda. Because part one is a sham. But it makes you feel good, doesn't it?

One example of the Narasimha Rao government's commitment to fighting poverty came in March 1995. That month, it announced the formation of several new departments in key ministries to tackle poverty on a war footing. This was on the front pages of most newspapers on March 9. The official notification made curious reading but the press missed out on it.

The first responsibility listed in it for the new department of food was: 'Participation in international conferences and other bodies concerning food . . .' The second? 'Entering into treaties and agreements with foreign countries . . .' Those priorities tell us so much, it seems pointless to repeat the rest.

The poor in India today exceed the entire population of the country in 1947. Yet, the government celebrates the swift decline of poverty. A good part of the media have joined them in this. Never mind that at the Copenhagen World Summit for Social Development we said 39.9 per cent of the population were below the poverty line. That was to make some money from donors. Look at it now, just 19 per cent!

If we were to define a sleeping bag as a house, India would move swiftly towards ending her housing shortage. A shortage of nearly thirty-one million units. Accept this definition, and you could go in for mass production of sleeping bags. We could then have passionate debates about the drastic reduction in the magnitude of the housing problem. The cover stories could run headlines: 'Is it for real?' And straps: 'Sounds too good to be true, but it is.'

The government could boast that it had not only stepped up production of sleeping bags but had piled up an all-time record surplus of them. Say, thirty-seven million. Conservatives could argue that we were doing so well, the time had come to export sleeping bags, at 'world prices'. The bleeding hearts could moan that sleeping bags had not reached the poorest. Investigative muckrakers could scrutinise the contracts given to manufacturers. Were the bags overpriced? Were they of good quality?

That ends the housing shortage. There's only one problem. Those without houses at the start of the programme will still be without houses at the end of it. (True, some of them will have sleeping bags, probably at world prices.)

If all this sounds insane, that's only because it is. Yet what passes for a debate on poverty in this country is not very different. There's a point beyond which the numbers game – based on present definitions – gets as insane as the sleeping-bag argument.

An understanding of poverty anchored in the calorie norm serves us about as well. But these basics are seldom questioned by the non-poor. (See Appendix 1 for a note on the official poverty line and how it is arrived at.)

One of the newspaper stories on a 'decline' in poverty appeared several days before the Planning Commission 'unveiled' its new figures in January 1996*. It said poverty had 'dropped sharply to the lowest levels ever'. That only around 19 per cent of the population were below the poverty line. It sourced this finding to 'highly-placed government officials'.

There you have a flavour of the poverty debate. The 'sharp' drop in poverty is something to be revealed by 'highly-placed officials'. Such modesty, too. It's like Einstein not wanting to be credited publicly with the Theory of Relativity. Not yet, anyway. Is poverty a state secret? One that can only be revealed by highly placed official sources?

Interestingly, the most conventional of methods still show that while rural poverty declined in the 1980s, it rose steeply in just the first eighteen months of the 'reforms' alone. The Commission's own mid-term appraisal (MTA) of the reforms makes interesting reading.

But let's leave sleeping bags lie.

It is crucial to understand this about the landless agricultural workers and marginal farmers who make up 85 per cent of India's poor: they are net purchasers of foodgrain. Hikes in grain prices hit them very badly. Inflation is strongly linked to food prices. So its impact on these sections is always worse.

For instance, urban middle-class professionals spend much less of their incomes on food than, say, industrial workers. Both spend less on food than do landless labourers and small farmers. So when food prices go up, those spending more on it are hit harder. Industrial workers suffer, but agricultural labourers have it worst.

Millions are eating less. How does that constitute a reform? The availability of pulses and cereal per person in this country has declined. Inflation has crushed agricultural labour. Their real wages have declined. But there's a 37 million ton surplus of foodgrain of which we can all be proud. The sleeping bag syndrome at its best.

---

* This fraudulent 'decline' was later rejected by no less a person than the deputy chairperson of the Planning Commission. Soon after taking over that post, Prof. Madhu Dandavate directed the Commission to drop the 19 per cent estimate and return to the more sober figure of 39.9 per cent of the population below the poverty line.

The collapse of the PDS

The public distribution system (PDS)* is in a state of advanced decay. Pointing to a slight rise in offtake in a few months of 1995 makes a poor joke. Over a four-year period, grain purchased through the PDS fell drastically. Why? The government raised issue prices by around 85 per cent in that time. This is unprecedented in the country's post-Independence history. So offtake from the PDS declined six million tons. This, in part, allows us to boast of our gigantic buffer stock.

Between March and June 1995, nineteen children belonging to poor tribal families in Dhule, Maharashtra, died of starvation. Not far from where the deaths occurred, were godowns stocked to the roof with foodgrain. The families of the victims just could not access or afford that grain.

In 1992 Prime Minister Rao put in place the scheme called the Revamped Public Distribution System (RPDS). This was to be part of a 'strictly targeted regime'. The PDS was wasteful. But this government would set that right. It chose 1,778 very backward blocks in the country for the RPDS. It would 'target' the poor on a special basis.

It did. It was precisely in the targeted blocks that starvation deaths occurred in the past five years. In Thane, Dhule and Amravati districts (all in the rich state of Maharashtra). In Surguja district of Madhya Pradesh. In other RPDS blocks elsewhere.

In practice, RPDS simply meant selling grain in these blocks at around 50 paise (not even 1p) less per kilogram than elsewhere. Since prices in even the regular PDS were hovering around Rs.8 a kg, this did not help. In Surguja in 1994, the then district collector confirmed that people were getting employment for only 130 to 145 days a year. How were they to afford these prices?

The upward revision of grain prices was never matched by rises in daily minimum wages. The current minimum wage in such zones varies from Rs.20-Rs.22. In practice, poorly organised labourers don't get much more than Rs.15 to Rs.16 per day.

In 1995, the man who had been the main expert on poverty in the Prime Minister's office, K.R. Venugopal, wrote in anguish that: 'the PDS and RPDS have become irrelevant'.

---

* Public Distribution System – a government scheme that seeks to provide basic rations and essential items of daily use to the public at controlled prices through outlets like ration stores and fair price shops. The idea is to stabilise general living standards, particularly those of the poor, insulating them against rising prices. Items like wheat, rice, sugar, edible oil, kerosene, soft coke and controlled cloth are among those sold on the PDS.

The trauma of the rural poor has left the elite unmoved. Some even talk of exporting the grain at 'world prices'. (The vast majority of Indian agriculturists are *net buyers* of grain.) Within the country, food prices have shot up. Who talks of 'world prices' for the labour of the Indian peasants or workers? So Indians face world prices, but will not get world-class incomes. In short, globalisation of prices, Indianisation of incomes.

A midday meal scheme that works out to spending around 0.57 paise per meal per child. A housing programme that is a disaster. An approach to public health that has seen a huge resurgence of malaria, among other diseases. A 'massive' rural development budget of a little over Rs.70 billion – that works out to roughly the subsidy on two major fertilisers (used mostly in ninety-five not-so-poor districts). That has been this government's response to the 'unfinished agenda'.

Again, many attitudes on view in this period go back some years. Among these, the attempt by governments to abdicate their duties towards citizens. The dilution of people's rights did not begin with Narasimha Rao. (He can claim credit, though, for hastening the process.) Whether on child labour or in the field of education, the actions of successive Indian governments violate the Constitution.

The forms and channels of abdication are many. One, in recent times, has been most favoured. That is: leave it to the NGOs. Non-governmental organisations are supposed to be able to take care of gigantic problems affecting hundreds of millions of people. Problems that elected governments, with the full force of state machinery behind them, apparently can't handle.

Passing the buck

The best among NGO activists see through this. Some of them are quite clear that many major issues have to be handled and resolved by the state. They do see that the state is just trying to pass the buck to them. A lot of others, however, seem to revel in the new era. Their growing links with the state render them anything but non-governmental. Yet despite many scandals, particular types of NGOs remain the sacred cows of the press, its blind spot. (Often, these are NGOs with links to the corporate sector.)

The way the press covers development issues does not help. There have been, broadly, two tracks in what many call 'development journalism'. The 'government' or 'official' mode and the 'non-governmental organisation (NGO) or alternative journalism' mode. Both have largely failed. The first, already discredited, requires little argument. (Though there are critical elements in this framework, too, which are not to be dismissed offhand.)

It is about what governments are doing, which is important. (Some of the things governments do defy imagination.) For example, there are 2,000 water wells sunk in one drought-prone area. The critical element of this mode would be: Were those wells enough? Did they come too late? Should there have been another sort of well?

But yes, the NGO or alternative mode of development journalism has also failed. Worse, its virtuous halo has deflected critical comment. Somehow, there is often a willing suspension of disbelief when journalists begin to interact with NGOs.

Development theology holds that NGOs stand outside the establishment. They present a credible alternative to it. The majority of NGOs are, alas, deeply integrated with the establishment, with government and with the agenda of their funding bodies.

A little reality therapy is in order: The Indian government wants a 'partnership' with NGOs. In this, it sees an opportunity to discard its commitments towards 921 million citizens on fundamentals like health, education, housing. These are best left to NGOs, while the state tinkers around with a few trifling issues, like how to double the wealth of the richest five per cent.

The World Bank is no less enthusiastic. Its bulletin of September 22, 1994 says: 'NGO Involvement in Bank Projects Grows Rapidly'. It notes approvingly that 'involvement by non-governmental organisations jumped from 30 per cent to 50 per cent of Bank projects'. And we all know what a saintly NGO the Bank is.

International funding agencies are using NGOs to dump fertilisers, harmful contraceptives and obsolete technologies. Even for corporate market research. NGOs are sometimes created for this purpose. There are groups in this country that have tried to push 'drip irrigation' in districts that have abundant rainfall. They hawked a technique used for the deserts of Israel (in regions not lacking in rain) because some corporation had something to sell. Besides, in India many NGOs are contractors for government schemes.

They also provide white-collar employment. Nepal, next door, has over 10,000 NGOs – one for every 2,000 inhabitants. Compare that with how many teachers, doctors or nurses it has per 2,000 citizens. Funds flowing in through its 150 foreign NGOs account for 12 per cent of Nepal's GNP. Whose agenda do these funds push? In India, it is hard to even work out a credible figure, but the fund flows are much larger in dollar terms.

Some government officials have relatives running NGOs. Quite a few launch an NGO or begin to head one the moment they retire. This makes a good sinecure. NGOs in India need certificates under the Foreign Contributions Regulation Act (FCRA) before they can receive foreign funds. It is much easier to get such a certificate if you are a government official yourself. Some start the process during their last years in office. At that point, the NGO is nominally headed by someone else. After retirement, they head it themselves – complete with certificate. Former officials, especially senior ones, have one more advantage. They know the inside funding track and priorities of government. So they can and do design their projects and proposals accordingly. And they have all the right contacts. This means they do well. The same way that retired army brass make good arms salesmen.

In Uttar Pradesh, numerous NGOs focusing exclusively on population issues were born overnight in a few districts. They materialised soon after a 1992 USAID deal brought US $325 million solely for population control in just ten districts of that state. In urban India, quite a few NGOs have sprung up around AIDS, partly because that's where the money is.

In Kandhmal district of Orissa, a tribal group has declared war on fifteen NGOs, including some well-known ones, for racketeering. It has given them six months to leave the district altogether. It has also published in the newspapers a list of activists from several groups who it says have corrupt and criminal backgrounds. No one has so far challenged the list.

The Council for Advancement of Peoples Action and Rural Technology (CAPART) is a government-established organisation that generously funds NGOs. In 1995-96, it blacklisted over 350 of them for corruption running to crores of rupees. CAPART officials say this is only the beginning. True, this is not a one-way problem and some of the NGOs have much to say that is unflattering about how CAPART itself functions. Nor is the blacklist an edict carved in stone. It can hardly be used to tar all NGOs. What is undeniable, however, is the extent to which corruption is now entrenched in the NGO sector. Since the CAPART incident, other government bodies have blacklisted nearly 3,500 NGOs, often on the advice of auditors. Corruption was one of the reasons.

Dutch agencies initiated legal proceedings in January 1998 against an Indian NGO they accuse of embezzling Rs.500 million. But that's a rare case. Mostly, problems of this sort don't enter the courts.

Some of the NGOs that have been held up for years as 'models' of development on the international scene have in fact seriously damaged the interests of people where they work. Their public relations techniques, however, are effective. They belong after all to the same classes the media most interacts with. Their leading activists are from the same strata as so many journalists. Their global networking so effective, that funds from donors continue to pour in to the same bodies despite recurring scandals. Sometimes because the donors are so gullible. Sometimes because the donor has a hidden agenda and this kind of NGO suits their purpose.

But the obsession with viewing development through the NGO prism persists. Of course, a few NGOs have done great work. And clubbing all sorts of widely varying bodies under the category 'NGO' causes its own problems. The good ones get tarred with the doings of the bad. But the romanticisation of this sector has got ridiculous.

A British NGO in India has commissioned a multi-episode TV programme on 'change makers' (read activists on its projects). This will cost a bomb. The activists, not the villagers, will be its heroes. In short, a contemporary version of the heathen savage approach. The people are not change makers, NGO activists are. As the missionaries once were.

Development is a money-spinning industry. So much so that it merits, twenty-six times a year, a United Nations journal called *Development Business*. This is a 'Fortnightly guide to consulting, contracting and supply opportunities around the world'. The development industry has co-opted many NGOs, and much of development journalism.

Quite a few 'development journalists' (often among the more sensitive and decent elements in the profession) unquestioningly accept the role of NGO spokespersons. All the critical faculties they exercise when reporting politics or business get lobotomised on this front. Lack of scepticism makes for bad journalism and wearisome copy.

NGOs can and do excellent work when filling gaps. They can and do outstanding work within modest objectives. They cannot be a substitute for the state. They cannot fulfil its responsibilities. The worst of governments in this country has to face the public after five years. The worst of NGOs is only accountable to its funding agency – which might well support, even spur on dubious activities that do not benefit the poor.

True, many actions of some NGOs have proved most valuable. I have tried to record a few in this book. Yet, however supportive one is of such actions, far greater changes, beyond their reach, are also required. All the NGO projects across the country together will not achieve the lasting effects a major land reform will in a single state. Again, the best NGOs and their activists know this. They are quite embarrassed by governmental attempts to co-opt their sector while abandoning the state's own responsibilities.

As for government projects: a number of disparate, often contradictory, fire-fighting measures pass for development. Even where criticised, the notion that these amount to development at all is not often questioned. Mostly, these function without popular consultation, leave alone participation. So a high rate of failure gets built in. That can happen to the best of schemes.

You can have both: pressure on the state to perform its duties towards citizens, and good NGO activity. But that calls for a sense of proportion. About development. About people's entitlements. About the *real reforms* this country needs. Reforms to do with land, water and forest resources. With education, health, nutrition and employment.

Signalling the weaknesses

What does it call for in the press? In covering development, it calls for placing people and their needs at the centre of the stories. Not any intermediaries, however saintly.

It calls for better coverage of the rural political process. Of political action and class conflict, not politicking. Quite a few good journalists hold back from this territory. They fear, perhaps justifiably, being branded as 'political' (read leftist). Yet, evading reality helps no one. A society that does not know itself cannot cope. And development itself has a political core.

It also calls for facing the truth about the living standards of Indians.

After more than four decades of 'development', these facts remain: One out of every three persons in the world lacking safe and adequate drinking water is an Indian. Nearly one in every two illiterates in the world is a citizen of this country. Nearly one of every three children outside schools in the planet is an Indian.

The largest number of absolute poor live in this country. So do the largest number of those with inadequate housing. Indians have among the lowest per capita consumption of textiles in the world. There are more job seekers registered at the employment exchanges of India than there are jobless in all the twenty-four nations of the OECD put together. At the same time, this nation has over forty-four million child labourers, the largest contingent in the world. India's dismal position in the UNDP's Human Development Index has not improved in the last five years. It has, if anything, fallen.

Every third leprosy patient in the globe is an Indian. So is every fourth being in the planet dying of water-borne or water-related diseases. Over three fourths of all the tuberculosis cases that exist at any time world-wide are in this country. No nation has more people suffering from blindness. Tens of millions of Indians suffer from malnutrition.

341

Decades ago, an attorney in the United States commenting on the dismal role of the American press in a miscarriage of justice, said they failed 'to signal the weakness in society'. That remains a fine definition of the minimum duty of a decent press: to signal the weaknesses in society. It is a duty the Indian press increasingly fails to perform.

More stories on the rights and entitlements of the poor could help. The press can and does make a difference when it functions. Governments do react and respond to the press in this country. The Indian press has been very strong in some respects. For instance, in its coverage of events it could compare with the best in the world. Even in the '80s, the stories on Kalahandi could force two prime ministers to visit the place.

But it has proved increasingly inept at covering processes. Especially the development process. The more elitist it gets, the less it will be able to do this. Even its coverage of events will suffer. Most big publications now cover a wide array of beats and issues. Far more than the basic politics, sports and commerce divisions of a decade ago. You can have several people covering aspects of business in the same publication. Newspapers also find space for fashion, design and society/glamour columns. Even eating out columns.

Fair enough. Surely a little more space can be found for social sector issues – if you want to? Compare the space given to the death of Rajan Pillai, a businessman, in jail to that given to the deaths of the children in Dhule. The biggest journals in this country gave far more space to cricketer Imran Khan's wedding than to the starvation deaths. How many newspapers have reporters covering the issues of rural poverty full-time? (I do not mean analysts – though they are important. I mean reporters.) In most publications, the correspondent covering education also often has several other beats to attend to. The same is true of those covering other social sector beats. How will justice ever be done to the 'unfinished agenda'?

The Indian press has very strong traditions on this score. Those who led the freedom struggle understood its importance and most nationalist leaders doubled up as journalists at some point. The journalists of the '20s, '30s and '40s may have been very ill-equipped. Some would call them pamphleteers. Yet from within a very narrow press, they reflected much wider social concerns.

As early as in 1893, Reuters assigned a correspondent, S.H.S. Merewether, to cover the famine-hit districts of this country. Apart from his reports, this resulted in a book, *A Tour through the Famine Districts of India*. In it, he wrote that his assignment came about after a request Her Majesty's Government had made of Reuters. The Raj, among other things, wanted to counter the riffraff of the nationalist press. The Reuters man stood up for the Raj. Denouncing the Indian press for its 'sedition', he wrote that 'a censorship of the native press would not only be expedient, but seems an absolute necessity'.

It seems extraordinary that so minuscule a press should have had such an impact. Over a hundred years later, a much larger press has failed to do the same. Issues crucial to hundreds of millions of Indians demand its attention. But it has not put the government on the mat.

Yet, even now, the press can do much more. Even allowing for the limits a growing process of corporation places on its character. It has very many journalists of high calibre and many who would like to signal those weaknesses in society. It is in some ways more well-equipped than ever to do the things it wants to. The question is, will it do the things it has to?

Changing choices

Meanwhile, the elite continue to kid themselves about how 'change' can be brought about. The turmoil in East Asia has rendered some of those who clamour for the emulation of those 'miracles' less vociferous. But there is no willingness at all to change the terms of the development debate. Changing the ownership and control of basic resources like land, water and forests is not on the agenda. The further withdrawal of the state from the social sector is.

Yet even as the elite refuse to budge, the rest of the country is changing and changing rapidly. The India of 1998 is a more federal nation than ever before since Independence in 1947. In different parts of the country, people are asserting themselves, against great odds, in different ways. In some cases, those may not be the healthiest of ways. But all of them represent this reality: the ruled are no longer willing to be ruled in the old way.

In region after region of the country, battles over the control of vital resources and for democratisation of society, are heating up. Battles for human rights and against inhuman bondage, against poverty and for justice, continue to intensify. Feudal relations and the institution of unfree labour in agriculture are being vigorously challenged.

The choice before the elite is no longer whether they can 'allow' or 'prevent' the changes in the offing. The choice before them is whether those changes will occur with their consent or outside it.

Acknowledgements

I was awarded a *Times of India* Fellowship for the year 1992 (work beginning in mid-1993). This publication is the result of work carried out in that capacity between May 1, 1993 and June 15, 1995 (plus a few later trips to update some details), with financial support from the Fellowships Council lasting a full year till April 30, 1994. I gratefully acknowledge the support of the *Times of India* Group.

Interacting with the *Times* Fellowship Council was a positive experience. The Council remained wholly supportive throughout the project. My sincere thanks to all its members. Chairman Ashok Jain spoke to me more than once during the project, expressing his support for the work underway. That was reassuring and important feedback.

Honorary Secretary of the Council, K. Balakrishnan, played an extraordinary role. He made it possible for me to focus all my energy on the field work and writing. He and Narayanee Mantoo were a great help. Their efficiency made up for my laziness with paperwork. A trained economist, Balakrishnan also made valuable inputs and suggestions between my trips to the different states – one of the reasons I always went via Delhi.

I was lucky in having the support of all the editors I worked with. Dileep Padgaonkar and Darryl D'Monte gave me complete freedom while making helpful suggestions. Many, many thanks to them. Most of my reports were published when the two of them were at *The Times*. Dileep was ever encouraging. Darryl probably holds some sort of record for phone calls received from really far out places. His suggestions resulted in some of the most important stories from Kalahandi. Later, with Dina Vakil, I found the same freedom.

A million thanks to Susan Ram for the work she did on this edition. As a result of her efforts, many things in the book are now much tighter than they ever were before.

One editor who believed this project could be pulled off even before it began was N. Ram of *Frontline*. I owe him a great deal.

Friends who made invaluable inputs at all levels included Venkatesh Athreya, N.D. Jayaprakash, Anil K. Chaudhary, K. Nagaraj and Sitaram Yechury.

344

Sanjay Kapoor, Surender, Kamal and others in Blitz's Delhi Bureau helped in many ways. Thanks to Jaya Mehta for her assistance.

Thanks also to innumerable other journalists in many publications across the country who gave me their unstinting and unselfish assistance.

I owe much to P.V. Ramaniah Raja and the trustees of the Raja-Lakshmi Foundation for their handsome support at a crucial juncture. The award they gave this work made affordable two other parts of the project: a visual archive of people at work and an oral archive of hundreds of interviews. I also thank Jayesh Shah of Humanscape, and the juries of the Humanscape Fellowship, The Statesman Rural Reporting Award, and the PUCL Human Rights Journalism prize for their support. No one bore the troubles, disruption and expenses the project brought – and they were many – more patiently than my wife, Sonya Gill. If I could continue the work long after the official fellowship period, it was because of her. From Chennai, miracle man P. Mohan Rao helped spur me on at all times.

Tamil Nadu: G. Ramakrishna, the *Arivoli Iyakkam*, K. Suresh. Volunteers of the Tamil Nadu Science Forum.

Pudukkottai: N. Kannamal, one of the finest activists I have ever met. Special thanks to Prabhakaran, Sivaramakrishnan, Raj Kumar, Vivekanandan, Manikatai, G. Shekhar and the Quarry Women Workers Association. Also, then collector Anuradha Khati-Rajivan.

Ramnad: My friend Kasinathadurai. Rajendran, Karunanidhi and Muralikrishnan and other activists of the *Arivoli*. Gynavasalam of the All India Kisan Sabha. K. Rajan, K. Sudhir, T. Paneerselvam. L. Krishnan who was then collector.

Bihar: Nothing would have happened without my oldest friend S.P. Tiwari. Many thanks to the ever helpful Uttam Sen Gupta and other colleagues at the *Times of India*, Patna. Also, to Ujwal Singh. K. Suresh Singh in Delhi was a mine of information. Many thanks to Arvind Das in Delhi.

Godda: Manjul Kumar Das, Ram Swarup, Inderjeet Tiwari, Motilal, Suman Dharadhiyar, S. Murmu and the villagers of Dorio.

Palamau: Bachan Singh and family, who put up so kindly with some ridiculous schedules and my abrupt disappearances. My friend Narendra Chaubey who made it possible for me to meet and stay with communities like the Birhors and Parhaiyas. Chaubey took me to places and on trips I had not thought possible. Pascal Minj, F. Petras, Bishwamber Dubey, Dalip Kumar and S.K. Singh. Shatrughan and Arjun of the Chottanagpur Samaj Vikas Sansthan. My friend, the late Baidyanath Singh. Dilbassiya Devi of Latehar and the many families of Balumath and Netrahat who put me up. The then deputy commissioner, Santosh Matthew, was not only helpful but also frank and honest in discussing the problems of his district.

Orissa: My former *Blitz* colleague Surya Das functioned like a human dynamo. I have still not figured out how he handled the logistics of it, but he managed to reach me with films and have my rolls collected in really remote places. My old friend Balaji Pandey's inputs and knowledge were invaluable. He and the staff of the Institute of Social and Economic Development, especially Hrushikesh, helped in an astonishing number of ways. Special thanks to Santosh Das and Janardhan Pati. Walter Fernandes in Delhi for the tons of information on displacement issues.

Malkangiri and Koraput: Surendra Khemendu was a great help and perfect interpreter. Thanks also to Ajit Kumar Das, B. Majhi, Kamraj Kawasi, R.K. Patro, T.S. Sabar. Raghunath Majhi and K.K. Mohanty in Bhubaneswar. Malkangiri collector G.K. Dhal.

Nuapada and Kalahandi: Meeting Jagdish Pradhan was one of the high points of the project. How much he added to my knowledge and perspective! What I learned from him helped right through the rest of the project. No one knows the Kalahandi region better. Special thanks to ex-MLA Kapil Narain Tiwari in Khariar. My friend S.K. Pattnaik gave me a great deal of his time and knowledge. Ghanshyam Bithria, Bishwamber Joshi and A.V. Swamy.

Madhya Pradesh: Special thanks to Raju Azad of the MPVS who dropped all his work to take me to Surguja. Also to Shailendra Shaily. A big debt to R. Gopalkrishnan, perhaps the most unusual bureaucrat I have met. Talking to him helped shape up a number of ideas. Again, the old *Blitz* network came in handy – many thanks to Manoj Mathur. Also, Vinod Raina and Anita Rampal.

Surguja: Mehdi Lal Yadav who tramped all over that huge district with me. Jitender Singh Sodhi, Arjun Das, Nanka Ram, Ashok Kumar Das. Special thanks to advocates H.N. Shrivastava, Mohan Kumar Giri and S. Verma. Also to Nesar Naaz, K.S. Yadav and Dalip Kumar.

Jhabua: I was really lucky to meet Amita Baviskar. A scholar and expert on the area, she was also interpreter for some crucial interviews. I would have missed many vital nuances of displacement-related issues but for her inputs. The amazing Meerza Ismail Beg, painter and retired teacher who assisted me so greatly – and Purshottan Tiwari of Indore. The ever helpful Hemant Jain who produced all the data I needed. Jagannath Bharati, Sunderlal Jain and M. Valia. And Ashok Mandoloi who gave me so much of his time. Special thanks to Luaria and his family for putting me up, and for all their help in Jalsindhi.

Many thanks to Jayshree, Amit, Chittaroopa Palit and other activists of the Khedut Mazdoor Chetana Sangath.

Mumbai: A large number of people helped right through, especially ex-students. Special thanks to Dionne Bunsha and Priyanka Kakodkar for all their assistance – and the many readings they gave each story – while I was writing the book. The indefatigable Dionne saved me an enormous amount of running around. The help that Priyanka and Dionne gave me did not stop with the first, Indian edition of this book. It finds reflection in all subsequent efforts. Thanks also to Saloni Meghani and Aparna Talaulicar. A very big thanks to Sheetal Mehta who, while still in India, helped so much. Many thanks, too, to Rajesh Vora and Naresh Fernandes.

Smruti Koppikar's help was immeasurable. From day one, she helped co-ordinate many things that I could not handle from where I was. Films, tapes and other material I needed at short notice reached me wherever I was. She was a great help in data collection, and later in editing, and also in organising a few thousand negatives and several hundred photographs. Her ideas were always useful and her inputs those of a *de facto* editor.

Bharati Sadasivam, while still in India, was a great help. Many thanks to Chitra Sirur for all her assistance and encouragement. I never had to worry much about the statistical side of things. That was invariably taken care of, as always, by my old friend Anoop Babani. Sanjay Shah of Standard Photo Supply and the Fort Copying Centre was a great help at all times.

One group of people and one individual had an unspoken presence in all this throughout: my former colleagues at *Blitz*, Mumbai. And my old employer, R.K. Karanjia, an editor who took as much pride in any achievements of his juniors as in his own. Never mind that we parted ways in early 1993. Every one of the awards this project won had first to be displayed on his desk. What a human being!

Appendix 1
The official poverty line

In January 1979, a 'Task Force' drew up a methodology for estimating the incidence of poverty that has been used by India's Planning Commission ever since. That was the 'Task Force on Projections of Minimum Needs and Effective Consumption Demand'.

The Task Force defined the poverty line as the per capita expenditure level at which the average calorie intake was 2,435 calories for a person in the rural areas and 2,095 calories for urban areas. It took into account norms recommended by the Nutrition Expert Group of 1968. Using these, it estimated the average daily per capita requirements of people in rural and urban areas based on age, sex and occupational structures of the population. For convenience, it rounded off the calorie norms to 2,400 calories per person per day for rural areas and 2,100 per day in urban areas.

The Planning Commission uses surveys conducted by the government's National Sample Survey Organisation (NSSO) every five years on the consumption patterns of over 500,000 households across India. From these, that expenditure group is selected whose spending on food affords a rural person 2,400 calories a day and an urban person 2,100 calories a day. So the per capita expenditure of this group becomes the 'line'. All groups whose spending is below this are below the poverty line.

Currently the 'line' is defined for urban India as consumption worth Rs.264 per person a month at 1993-94 prices. In rural areas, it is Rs.229 per person a month at 1993-94 prices. In the consumption basket of the rural poor at this poverty line, food items get a weightage of around 70 per cent. (NSS 48th Round.)

For those wanting that translated into English: Let's say you are an Indian belonging to a rural household of five members. If your total monthly consumption is less than Rs.1,145 (£17.89) a month (individual = Rs.229 or £3.57), then you are below the poverty line. Being slightly above that in no way solves the problem of your poverty. But it satisfies official criteria – and places you above the line.

In 1989, an Expert Group was set up by the Planning Commission to study this methodology. In 1993, it submitted a report with several suggestions. (Those wanting more details can look at the 'Report of the Expert Group on

Estimation of Proportion and Number of Poor', Perspective Planning Division, Planning Commission, Government of India, New Delhi, June 1993.)

If the modified methods suggested by the Expert Group had been adopted, the number of people below the line would have shot up. For instance, there was a huge gap in the number of poor as estimated by the old methods and those used by the Expert Group. For 1987-88, the Group's figure of those below the poverty line was 312 million, against the 237 million arrived at by the old methods. But the Planning Commission in Prime Minister Narasimha Rao's time simply threw out the recommendations of the Group. Poverty fell massively, till it affected just over 19 per cent of the population. It was only when the United Front government came to power that this particular piece of dishonesty ended. New deputy chairperson of the Planning Commission, Madhu Dandavate dumped what were little more than deliberate miscalculations. As of January 1997, the percentage of people below the poverty line was back to 39.9 per cent.

It does stand to the credit of Dandavate that he threw out the falsified figure. But the experience of the Narasimha Rao period shows that the movement of huge numbers of people above or below the 'line' can often bear little relation to ground reality. It can happen simply owing to changes in methods of calculation.

The Expert Group recognised the 'continued necessity and utility of poverty estimation'. But it drew attention to several limitations of the existing approach. Some of the observations made by the Group were and remain valid. Among them:

- 'The poverty line provides the conceptual rationalisation for looking at the poor as a "category" to be taken care of through targeted ameliorative programmes, ignoring structural inequalities and other factors which generate, sustain, and reproduce poverty.'
- It does not 'take into account items of social consumption such as basic education and health, drinking water supply, sanitation, environmental standards, etc., in terms of normative requirements or effective access'.
- 'The poverty line, quantified as a number, is reductionist. It does not capture important aspects of poverty – ill health, low educational attainments, geographical isolation, ineffective access to law, powerlessness in civil society, caste and/or gender based disadvantages.'
- The head-count ratio based on the poverty line 'does not capture the severity of poverty in terms of the poverty deficit (total shortfall from the poverty line) or additionally the distribution of consumption expenditure among the poor'.

- 'In a country of India's size and diversity, a poverty line based on aggregation at an all-India level ignores state-specific variations in consumption patterns and/or prices.'
- 'The notion of "absolute poverty" is inadequate because "relative poverty" is also an equally important aspect of poverty and is, in fact, a determinant of absolute poverty at a given level of national income. More generally, the concepts of inequality and poverty, although distinct, need to be constantly viewed together as closely associated concepts.'

The first attempt at defining a poverty line in India came in 1962. A Working Group of eminent economists and social thinkers tried to draw up one after taking into account the recommendations of the Nutrition Advisory Committee of the Indian Council of Medical Research (ICMR, 1958) on a balanced diet. The Working Group included such highly respected figures as Prof. D.R. Gadgil, Dr Ashok Mehta, Dr V.K.R.V. Rao, Shriman Narayan, Anna Saheb Sahasrabudhe, B.N. Ganguli, Dr P.S. Lokanathan, Pitambar Pant and M.R. Masani.

Why did such fine, upright people exclude things like expenditure on health and education from the 'national minimum' they set up? Because they were sincere, idealistic people who believed the State had certain duties to fulfil. They believed, for instance, that the State was bound by the Constitution and other commitments to provide its citizens with both health and education.

The cruel joke is that three and a half decades later, the State has provided none of these. Nor has it delivered on many similar obligations. Yet we hold on to the calorie norm and private consumer expenditure as if it covers everything that is important. But we remain silent on the obligations of the state towards its citizens.

Appendix 2
The districts: a few indicators

There is a degree of overlap in the indicators of some of these districts. This was unavoidable. Koraput, Kalahandi and Ramnad, for instance, were all divided into two or more districts in the last few years. Even Palamau was divided to make Garwha a new district. Godda emerged from the division of the old Santhal Paraganas.

The new districts do not as yet have their own gazetteers and basic published data on some aspects is also lacking. So data between the old and new districts tend to overlap. But 'Kalahandi' here refers to the old, undivided unit, *including* Nuapada which is presently an independent district. Koraput refers to the old, undivided Koraput, including Malkangiri – now a separate district.

Secondly, for the same reasons the base year for some indicators tends to vary. While most indicators are pegged on 1991, this is not strictly the case throughout. For instance, per capita foodgrain production in the undivided Kalahandi is for 1989-90. Therefore, the Orissa and India figures also vary. In the case of Malkangiri and Nuapada, per capita foodgrain production figures are newer and are for 1993-94.

Besides, census data district-wise has been slow in coming on some aspects. The literacy figures reflect this in a couple of instances. At the bottom in each set, I have tagged on the period during which I lived in that particular district. (That is, the period I spent there for the specific purpose of the project. Subsequently, I have visited some of these districts more than once but have not included these details.) Having seen how a bit of this data is put together at the district level, I cannot but view a few of the indicators with some trepidation. Still, such as they are, here they are.

District: Godda
State: Bihar
Area: 2,100 sq. km
Forests: 239.34 sq. km
Net Sown Area: 966.09 sq. km
Net irrigated area: 108.97 sq. km

351

Population: 861,180
Males: 448,070
Females 413,110
Female literary: 18 per cent (Bihar 22.89 per cent, India 39.29 per cent)
Male literary: 48.56 per cent (Bihar 52.49 per cent, India 64.13 per cent)
Per capita foodgrain production: 105 kg (Bihar 118, India 173)
District HQ not linked by rail
I stayed in this district during September-October, 1993

District: Jhabua

State: Madhya Pradesh
Area: 6,782 sq. km
Forests: 1133.18 sq. km
Net Sown Area: NA
Net irrigated area: 84.59 sq. km
Population: 1,130,400
Males: 571,760
Females: 558,640
Female literacy: 8.79 per cent (Madhya Pradesh 28.85 per cent, India 39.29 per cent)
Male literacy: 20.15 per cent (Madhya Pradesh 58.42 per cent, India 64.13 per cent)
Per capita foodgrain production: 148 kg (Madhya Pradesh 208 kg, India 173 kg)
District HQ not linked by rail
I stayed in this district during May-June 1994.

District: Kalahandi

State: Orissa
Area: 11,772 sq. km
Forests: 4,770 sq. km
Net Sown Area: 5,890 sq. km
Net irrigated area: 620 sq. km
Population: 1,600,390
Males: 800,060
Females: 800,330
Female literacy: 14.56 per cent (Orissa 34.68 per cent, India 39.29 per cent)

Male literary: 45.54 per cent (Orissa 63.09 per cent, India 64.13 per cent)

Per capita foodgrain production: 331.86 kg (Orissa 253.03 kg, India 203.13 kg)

(Base year for foodgrain production in old Kalahandi is different from others. Therefore, Orissa and India figures, too, are different. This figure is for 1989-90)

Period of travel here obviously overlaps with Nuapada, which was my major focus in the area.

District: Koraput
State: Orissa
Area: 26,961 sq. km
Forests: 12,300 sq. km
Net Sown Area: 7,690 sq. km
Net irrigated area: 890 sq. km
Population: 3,012,550
Males: 1,510,520
Females: 1,502,030
Female literacy: 13.09 per cent (Orissa 34.68 per cent, India 39.29 per cent)

Male literacy: 32.15 per cent (Orissa 63.09 per cent, India 64.13 per cent)

Per capita foodgrain production: 193 kg (Orissa 162 kg, India 173 kg)
Period of stay: overlaps with Malkangiri, my main focus in the area.

District: Malkangiri
State: Orissa
Area: 6,115.3 sq. km
Forests: 1,553
Net Sown Area: 1,500 sq. km
Net irrigated area: NA
Population: 422,000
Males: 213,000
Females: 209.000
Female literacy: 11.69 per cent (Orissa 34.68 per cent, India 39.29 per cent)

353

Male literacy: 28.22 per cent (Orissa 63.09 per cent, India 64.13 per cent)
Per capita foodgrain production: 268 kg (Orissa 201 kg, India 205)
District HQ not linked by rail
Stayed here during December 1993-January 1994. Visited nearby Rayagada region in June 1995.

District: Nuapada

State: Orissa
Area: 3,407.5 sq. km
Forests: 1,803 sq. km
Net Sown Area: 1,480 sq. km
Net irrigated area: NA
Population: 469,000
Males: 234,000
Females: 235,000
Female literacy: 12.78 per cent (Orissa 34.68 per cent, India 39.29 per cent)
Male literacy: 42.31 per cent (Orissa 63.09 per cent, India 64.13 per cent)
Per capita foodgrain production: 235 kg (Orissa 201 kg, India 205)
District HQ not linked by rail
Stayed here during February-March 1994. Returned to the district last in May-June 1995.

District: Palamau

State: Bihar
Area: 12,749 sq. km
Forests: 5,559 sq. km
Net Sown Area: 2254.31 sq. km
Net irrigated area: 480.76 sq. km
Population: 2,451,190
Males: 1,269,810
Females: 1,181,380
Female literacy: 16.15 per cent (Bihar 22.89 per cent, India 39.29 per cent)
Male literacy: 44.80 per cent (Bihar 52.49 per cent, India 64.13 per cent)

Per capita foodgrain production: 61 kg (Bihar 118 kg, India 173 kg)
Stayed in the district during October-November 1993. Revisited it briefly
in early May 1994.

District: Pudukkottai

State: Tamil Nadu
Area: 4,651 sq. km
Forests: 237 sq. km
Net Sown Area: 1987.40 sq. km
Net irrigated area: 1024.13 sq. km
Population: 1,327,150
Males: 661,780
Females: 665,370
Female literacy: 43.62 per cent (Tamil Nadu 51.33 per cent, India 39.29
per cent)
Male literacy: 71.78 per cent (Tamil Nadu 73.75 per cent, India 64.13 per
cent)
Per capita foodgrain production: 184 kg (Tamil Nadu 124 kg, India 173
kg)
(Note: Literacy figures for the district date to the period before the literacy
movement here took off. Once the movement had taken root, Pudukkottai
was declared the first district outside of Kerala to have achieved 100 per
cent literacy. I keep the old figures for contrast. The movement achieved
its 100 per cent goal within three years)
Stayed here during May 1993. Revisited the district in April 1995.

District: Ramnathapuram (Ramnad)

State: Tamil Nadu
Area: 4,232 sq. km
Forests: 45 sq. km
Net Sown Area: 2060.18 sq. km
Net irrigated area: 627.41 sq. km
Population: 1,144,040
Males: 568,670
Females: 575,370
Female literacy: 48.70 per cent (Tamil Nadu 51.33 per cent, India 39.29
per cent)

Male literacy: 74.76 per cent (Tamil Nadu 73.75 per cent, India 64.13 per cent)
Per capita foodgrain production: 111 kg (Tamil Nadu 124, India 173)
Stayed here during June 1994.

District: Surguja

State: Madhya Pradesh
Area: 23,000 sq. km
Forests: 10,830 sq. km
Net Sown Area: 5,933.43 sq. km
Net irrigated area: 204.16 sq. km
Population: 2,082,630
Males: 1,064,630
Females: 1,018,000
Female literacy: 17.40 per cent (Madhya Pradesh 28.85 per cent, India 39.29 per cent)
Male literacy: 42.13 per cent (Madhya Pradesh 58.42 per cent, India 64.23 per cent)
District HQ not linked by rail
Stayed here most of April and early May 1994.

Sources:

Census data
Profiles of Districts, November 1993, Centre for Monitoring Indian Economy (CMIE), Mumbai
State Statistical Handbooks
District Statistical Offices data
Other state government and official publications

Glossary

Indian language words and terms used frequently in this book

The meanings given to the words below are within the context of their use in this book. Some of the lower level government posts and institutions mentioned here might carry different functions even within the different states covered in the reports.

Almost all the words that appear in italics in the book are listed here, except those that occur just the once in a story. In such cases, the meaning in English is indicated right away in brackets or in a small footnote at the bottom of the relevant page. In many cases, even those words are listed and explained here. Especially if they happen to recur in different stories. Also detailed here are a number of words and terms that do not appear in italics in the book but which are specific to India. Sometimes, a small footnote accompanies their first appearance in the book – with a more detailed explanation in the glossary here (e.g., **adivasi** and **dalit**).

Adivasi: First dweller or original inhabitant. Tribal peoples. In some countries, adivasis would be referred to as indigenous peoples. The words 'adivasi' and 'tribal' have been used interchangeably throughout this book. Legally referred to as 'scheduled tribes' (ST). Members of scheduled tribes are entitled by law to certain benefits such as reservations or quotas in government jobs or seats in educational institutions. A few seats in the central Parliament and the state legislatures are also reserved for these groups. The aim is to help redress the imbalance caused by centuries of exploitation, enforced poverty and deprivation such communities have suffered. British colonialism had a devastating effect on these forest-dependent peoples, appropriating their forests and reducing them to penury. Also by using merchant-moneylender-revenue farmer networks to penetrate their areas. Their complex, often more egalitarian, social and property-relations systems were disrupted. Tribal groups lost huge tracts of land to conquest, via debt and through other mechanisms. Presently, people from the more than 400 scheduled tribes account for 8.08 per cent of the Indian population, nearly 76 million citizens.

Anganwadi: A centre under the Integrated Child Development Services (ICDS) scheme for children under six years of age. Entrusted with nutritional care, pre-school education, and health and, in theory, maternal care as well.

Arrack: A distilled country liquor. Very popular in the countryside in some states, like in Tamil Nadu. The arrack lobby wields substantial clout in Tamil Nadu politics.

Balwadi: Largely, a pre-school day care centre. Some functions vary from state to state. In some states works for not much more than two hours a day.

Bamur: A very versatile tree (*acacia nilotica*) of great value to farmers. Also called *Babul.*

Banabashi Sangha: Forest Dwellers Association. An NGO active in the Kalahandi region of western Orissa.

Bania: Person belonging to a moneylending and trading caste.

Beedis: Rough, country-style cigarettes. See also **Tendu** in this glossary.

Benami: A transaction where a major party, often a buyer or owner, remains anonymous. For instance, land owned by one person but held under the name of another, or under fictitious names, would be a *benami* holding.

Block: For development purposes, districts in India are divided into blocks. The block is thus the unit of development in India. The main officer presiding over development here is the Block Development Officer (BDO).

Block Development Officer: BDO. See **Block**, above.

Chowkidar: In general use, watchman. But used in this book in the sense of a formal government post. Please see Village *Chowkidar* or *Kotwar* in this glossary.

Circle: A Circle is mostly a unit of revenue, sometimes coinciding in area with a block. In some states, could be a unit of development below a block, with some revenue functions.

Circle Karamchari: Post of worker attached to a Circle. May do the ground level recording of land details in his Circle during a survey of land in the state or district. In Bihar, equivalent to *patwari.*

Collector: The district collector is the seniormost administrator of a district in India. Indian states are divided into districts. There are more than 625 districts in the country. The collector is from the elite Indian Administrative Service (IAS). See also **deputy commissioner**.

Crore: Ten million.

Dalit: The term dalit simply means oppressed or ground down. Communities formerly considered 'untouchable' under the caste system increasingly describe themselves thus. Mahatma Gandhi called them 'harijans' (God's people). But many have discarded this term, preferring 'dalit' which indicates their opposition to the dehumanising caste system – and the existence of an oppressor. Legally, they are termed 'scheduled castes' (SC) and there are nearly 450 of such castes. Those listed as scheduled castes are entitled by law to certain benefits such as reservations or quotas in government jobs or seats in educational institutions. A few seats in the central Parliament and the state legislatures are also reserved for these groups. The aim is to help redress the imbalance caused by millennia of exploitation, enforced poverty and deprivation such communities have suffered. Presently, people from the scheduled castes account for 16.48 per cent of the Indian population, or nearly 155 million citizens.

Deputy commissioner: Head of the administration in a district. Also called the collector or district magistrate in some parts of the country.

Dissari: Hereditary practitioners of traditional medicine in the Koraput-Malkangiri region of Orissa state. Theirs is a system which combines the use of herbs, roots and similar produce with medico-religious practices.

Falia: Hamlet within a village, mainly in tribal villages. Could be clan-based.

Gram Sabha: Sub-sect of a panchayat and coinciding in area with a revenue village. The smallest unit of electoral democracy. (See also panchayat.)

Gramsevika: Woman village worker reporting to the rural development bureaucracy. *Gramsevak* (male).

Haat: Rural market or bazaar.

Harijan: Please see **dalit** in this glossary.

Havaldar: Sergeant. But in common parlance used to refer to any police constable.

Jaggery: Coarse brown sugar made from palm sap.

Jagir: A hereditary assignment of land.

Jagrut Shramik Sanghatan: Organisation of Conscious Labourers. A non-governmental organisation very active in the Kalahandi area of Orissa state.

Jan Sangarsh Samiti: People's struggle committee.

Jatha: Procession. Often used to refer to long marches or journeys undertaken by organised groups to press a cause.

Jawan: Young man, especially a private soldier in the Indian Army. In this book, refers to soldiers.

Karamchari: Worker. See Circle *Karamchari* in this glossary for the sense it is used in this book.

Khata: An individual's account in village land records.

Kotwar: Please see Village *Chowkidar* or *Kotwar* in this glossary.

Kutcha: Imperfect, crude, unripe. As in a *kutcha* (mud-walled) house. Or *kutcha* (unmetalled) road.

Lakdi: Firewood, timber, wood, stick.

Lakh: One hundred thousand.

Mahajan: Moneylender, trader, merchant or broker.

Mahua, mahua wine: An Indian tree species. The yellow flowers from these trees, *Madhuca Indica* and *Longifolia*, are distilled to produce an intoxicating liquor. *Mahua* wine is very popular in many parts of the Indian countryside.

Mandi: Wholesale market.

Manu Smriti: One of the most promiment of the *smritis*. Please see *smritis* in this glossary. **Manu** 'The Law Giver' is believed to have authorised this *smriti*. But there is no real evidence that this was the work of a single author, or even that such an individual called Manu existed.

Mela: Fair.

Mukhiya: Village headman. In Bihar, *Mukhiya* would head the panchayat. (Also see *sarpanch* and panchayat.)

Narmada Bachao Andolan: The Save Narmada Movement. This organisation fights for the interests of people affected by the massive displacement of villages by a chain of dams being built on the Narmada river in central India. The NBA is led by Medha Patkar.

NGO: Non-governmental, usually voluntary, organisation.

OBCs: Other Backward Classes. Mainly peasant castes, above the SC/ST groups in the traditional caste hierarchy, but below groups such as the Brahmins, Kshatriyas and Vaishyas. The hundreds of castes in this group are said to account for over 50 per cent of the population or nearly 500 million Indians. Though having generally better educational and living standards relative to the SC/ST groups, large numbers among them also suffer poverty and deprivation.

Padayatra: A walk or journey on foot. Undertaken as part of a mission, to make a point, further a cause or crusade, as a demonstration.

Panchayat: Earlier, simply village council. Now often comprises more than one village. Elected by direct voting.

Panchayat Bhavan: Panchayat office.

Patel: Chief of a village. The post was born of custom and is hereditary, but was sanctified by government. In the new panchayati raj (governance or rule of panchayats) dispensation, the *patel* will lose much of his power.

Patidar: Landowning caste.

Patta: Title deed.

Patwari: Keeper of village records. Paid by government. Called a Village Officer (VO) in the South.

Public Distribution System: PDS – a government scheme that seeks to provide basic rations and essential items of daily use to the public at controlled prices through outlets like ration shops and fair price shops. The idea is to stabilise general living standards, particularly those of the poor, and to insulate them against rising prices. Items sold through PDS outlets include wheat, rice, sugar, edible oil, soft coke, kerosene oil and controlled cloth.

Puranas: A compendium of legends, mythologies, beliefs and rituals. The major *puranas* were mainly produced between the first and twelfth centuries AD.

Reserved forests: In forests declared 'reserved', state control is total. The rights of traditional dwellers and others there cease to exist or are transferred elsewhere or are, in exceptional cases, allowed very limited exercise.

Rupee: The Indian rupee is valued at approximately Rs.64 for one pound sterling.

Sal: Species of tree (*shorea robusta*) yielding valuable timber.

Samanwita: Means 'integrated programme'. In this book refers specifically to a government-run poverty alleviation programme in western Orissa between 1978-82.

Sardar: In the sense used in this book – recruiter or contractor of labour. Also means chief or leader. And **sardarji** is a common form of address to a Sikh.

Sarpanch: Head of a panchayat. In Bihar, the *Mukhiya* would head the panchayat. The *sarpanch* would, however, have quasi-judicial powers in an area coinciding with that of the panchayat.

Smritis: Brahmanical norms of social obligation. There were many *smritis*, composed mostly between 200 BC and AD 1000. The best known of these is the *Manu Smriti*.

Subabul: Species of tree (*leucanaena leucophala*).

Sudras: The lowest of the four broad divisions of the caste system. They were required by that system to serve the three groups above them. (Brahmins, Kshatriyas and Vaishyas – the priestly, warrior and trader/other castes).

Tehsil/Taluka: Unit of a district for revenue administration. Normally, a taluka is coterminous with a block in geographical terms, but not always strictly so.

Tehsildar: First original authority on revenue matters within a tehsil.

Also keeper of land records in his area. The first person a villager approaches on revenue matters.

Tendu, Tendu patta: Leaf from which ***beedis*** (rough country-style cigarettes) are made.

Tharagar: Commission agent. Term commonly used in rural Tamil Nadu. Often, the ***tharagar*** is also a moneylender, a landowner and a merchant.

Thekedar: Contractor.

Toddy: Fermented liquor derived from certain palms.

Van Samiti/Van Suraksha Samiti: Forest protection committee.

Village *Chowkidar* or *Kotwar*: (Spelt *kotwal* in some states.) Paid a small sum in cash or given a little land, or both, this functionary maintains the register of births and deaths in a village. He reports the arrival of new or 'suspicious' characters in the village to the police thane. He is paid by the revenue department but reports to the police. He could be described as the lowest unit of the police in India. Perhaps the lowest link in the apparatus of state.

Zamindari* region:** A region characterised by feudal relations in agriculture and dominated by ***zamindars or feudal landlords. Holdovers of such relations, including unfree labour in agriculture, still exist in several parts of the country despite the formal abolition of ***zamindari*** in free India nearly fifty years ago.

Commonly used abbreviations

BDO: Block Development Officer
CAG: Comptroller & Auditor General
C.O.: Circle Officer
DPAP: Drought Prone Areas Programme
IRDP: Integrated Rural Development Programme
NGO: Non-Governmental Organisation
PDS: Public Distribution System
PHC: Primary Health Centre
RPDS: Revamped Public Distribution System

References

The system of references in this book is slightly unusual, but easy to follow. The idea was to avoid burdening the reader with too many footnotes and endnotes. The only footnotes in the book are those explaining an Indian language term or usage. The actual reports from the districts, in any case, did not need either. All sources for those reports can be found within the text. And anyway, district data is almost invariably governmental – few alternative sources exist. So the question of sourcing or referencing statistical material arose only for the essays preceding some sections of the book.

To make it simple, the reference note is preceded by a telegraphic summary, usually within brackets, of the point or quote being referred to from the concerned essay. For instance, you want to know the source of the figures on respiratory attacks, pneumonia and diarrhoeal episodes that you saw in the essay on health. The reference to that will be found here under the section on health. And it will be preceded by, in brackets – (diarrhoeal attacks, respiratory failure and pneumonia). The notes are divided in line with the sections of this book. Not all sections needed them, though.

SECTION: The Trickle Up & Down Theory
(Or Health for the Millions)

(Annual deaths and figures relating to tuberculosis): Figures from National Tuberculosis Institute.

(Diarrhoeal death figures): *A Profile of Common Diseases in India*, Future, Vol. 13. Winter 1984-85, p. 43.

(Diarrhoeal attacks, respiratory failure and pneumonia): from *Combined Surveys of ARI, Diarrhoea and EPI*, National Institute of Communicable Diseases, New Delhi, 1988.

(USAID: $325 million for population control): Saroj Panchauri, *Population & Planning*, In Seminar, Vol. No. 410. October 1993, New Delhi, p. 17.

(Spending on nutrition as percentage of GNP): K. Seetha Prabhu & S. Chatterjee, *Social Sector Expenditures and Human Development*, Reserve Bank of India, Bombay, 1993, p. 13.

(Health spending as percentage of GDP, India and other countries): *Investing in Health*, World Development Report, World Bank. Washington, 1993. Table A-9, pp. 210-211.

(Indian health spending as share of Five-Year Plans): Successive Five-Year Plan documents, Govt. of India.

(Numbers of registered doctors and nurses): *Health Information of India*, Govt. of India. Central Board of Health Information, New Delhi, 1992, p. 11. Later figure from Prime Minister P.V. Narasimha Rao's speech, Sept. 14, 1995.

(Gujarat & Maharashtra investment figures): Prakash Karat, *The Wages of Liberalisation*, Frontline, November 18, Chennai 1994, p. 120.

(Kerala IMR and other figures): V.K. Ramachandran, *Kerala's Development Achievements: An Overview*, Paper at Indira Gandhi Institute of Development Research, Bombay, 1995, Tables 7 & 10. To appear as chapter in Sen & Dreze, *Indian Development, Selected Regional Perspectives*, OUP, Oxford & Delhi, 1996.

(IMR, Life expectancy figures for Gujarat & Maharashtra): *Health Information of India*, Govt. of India. Central Board of Health Information, New Delhi, 1992.

(PHCs handle only nine out of every 100 patients in rural areas): K. Seetha Prabhu & S. Chatterjee, op cit., p. 10.

SECTION: This is the Way We Go to School
(Getting educated in rural India)

(Quote on 'efficiency' of our school system): Anita Rampal, *Education For All, Rhetoric & Reality, The Madhya Pradesh Human Development Report 1995*. MPHDR Project office, Bhopal 1995, p. 30.

(Data on enrolment, facilities, infrastructure, distances): Fifth All India Educational Survey, Selected Statistics. National Council for Educational Research & Training (NCERT), New Delhi, 1989.

(Education spending as percentage of plan outlays): Plan figures based on successive Five-Year Plan documents.

(Spending comparisons – Tanzania, Kenya, Malaysia): Myron Weiner, *The Child and State in India*. OUP, New Delhi, 1992, p. 14.

(40 per cent of drop-outs cite economic reasons): Estimates from Tilak & Varghese, 1992 and CMIE, 1992, cited in K. Seetha Prabhu & S. Chatterjee, *Social Sector Expenditures and Human Development*, Reserve Bank of India, Bombay, 1993, p. 10.

(Female literacy in 123 districts): Anil Sadgopal, unpublished background paper on Education, New Delhi, 1995, p. 72.

(Actual gap between SC/ST literacy levels and others): Ibid.

(Reference to *Smriti* laws): Prabhavati Sinha, *Smriti Political and Legal System, A Socio-Economic Study*. PPH, New Delhi, 1982, pp. 75-76.

(Drop-out rates for SC/ST students & comparisons): Sheel C. Nuna, chapter on *Education & Social Development*, in book, *Indian Society Today*. Ed. Muchkund Dubey. Har-Anand publishers, New Delhi, 1995, pp. 60-61.

(Sen & Dreze on literacy rates in India compared with other nations): Quoted in *The Pioneer*, New Delhi, Aug. 19, 1995, p. 12. Also see: Amartya Sen and Jean Dreze, *India: Economic Development & Social Opportunity*, OUP, 1995, New Delhi.

(Non-Formal Education figures, MP & India): Anita Rampal, opcit., p. 33.

(60 per cent of government expenses on schools going to private institutions and extent of subsidies): K. Seetha Prabhu & S. Chatterjee, *Social Sector Expenditures and Human Development*, Reserve Bank of India, Bombay, 1993, p. 11.

(John K. Galbraith on illiteracy and poverty): Quoted A.K. Shiva Kumar,

India's Development & the Well-Being of Children, in book, *Indian Society Today*, opcit., p. 290.

SECTION: And the Meek Shall Inherit the Earth
(Until a project comes along)

Estimates of displacement in India are from:

Walter Fernandes, *Power and Powerlessness: Development Projects and Displacement of Tribals*, Social Action No. 41 July-September, New Delhi, 1991, pp. 243-270.

Walter Fernandes & S. Anthony Raj, *Development, Displacement and Rehabilitation in the Tribal Areas of Orissa*, Indian Social Institute, New Delhi, 1993, pp. 1-36.

Vijay Paranjpye, *Evaluating the Tehri Dam: An Extended Cost-Benefit Proposal*, Indian National Trust for Art & Cultural Heritage, New Delhi, 1988.

L.K. Mahapatra, *The Rehabilitation of Tribals Affected by Major Dams and Other Projects in Orissa*, in Aloysius P. Fernandez (Ed.), Workshop on Rehabilitation of Persons Displaced by Development Projects, Bangalore: Institute for Social & Economic Change and MYRADA, 1990, pp. 85-99.

L.K. Mahapatra, *Tribal Development in India, Myth & Reality*, Vikas, New Delhi, 1994.

Balaji Pandey, *Development Induced Displacement: An Agenda for the Social Summit*, paper issued by the Institute for Socio-Economic Development, Bhubaneswar, 1995.

Jaganath Pathy, *Development Syndrome and Dispossession of the Defenceless.* Paper at Institute for Socio-Economic Development, Seminar on Development Projects and Rehabilitation of Displaced Persons, Bhubaneswar, 1994, pp. 8-10.

Report of the Commissioner for Scheduled Castes and Scheduled Tribes, 29th Report. (1987-89) Govt. of India, New Delhi.

Official position on rehabilitation and norms thereof are from:

(Nearly 75 per cent 'awaiting' rehabilitation): *National Policy for Rehabilitation of Persons Displaced as a Consequence of Acquisition of Land*, Ministry of Rural

366

Development (third draft), Govt. of India, New Delhi. Main references and quotes from pp. 1-16.

Draft Recommendations of the Committee of Ministers for Laying Down Norms for Land Acquisition and Rehabilitation, Govt. of India, New Delhi, 1982.

Office Memorandum on Land Acquisition and Rehabilitation of Displaced Persons Due to Major Projects, Ministry of Industry, Dept. of Public Enterprises, Bureau of Public Enterprises, New Delhi, 1986.

Figures on global displacement and quotes from Cernea are from:
Michael M. Cernea, *Understanding and Preventing Impoverishment from Displacement (Reflections on the State of Knowledge)*. Keynote opening address, International Conference on Development-Induced Displacement & Impoverishment, University of Oxford, 1995, pp. 10-15.

Michael M. Cernea, *Putting People First*, World Bank Publication, OUP, USA, 1991.

Michael M. Cernea, *Internal Refugees and Development-Caused Population Displacement*, World Bank Discussion Paper No. 345, Boston. Harvard Institute for International Development, Harvard University, 1991.

SECTION: Lenders, Losers, Crooks & Credit (Usury, debt & the rural Indian)

(Household debt figures): *All-India Debt & Investment Survey*, 1981-82, Govt. of India.

(Misuse of IRDP funds): *Report of the Comptroller & Auditor General*, Govt. of India, New Delhi, 1985, pp. 14-18.

(One hundred towns accounting for 65 per cent of all credit): R.P. Gurpur, *Banking Blues*, Seminar, No. 395, New Delhi, July 1992, pp. 39-43.

(IRDP – failure of insurance claims): V.K. Ramachandran, *Wage Labour & Unfreedom in Agriculture, An Indian Case Study*, Clarendon Press, Oxford, 1990, p. 246.

(Debt of small farmers and big businessmen): Extracted from Parliament debate and ministerial reply to question in Lok Sabha, figures valid to March 1994. Also, quoted in *The Week*, Feb. 16, 1995, Cochin, p. 33.

(Manu, the Law Giver, on debt – quote): George Buhlerg, *The Law of Manu, Sacred Books of the East*, Ed. Max Mueller, Vol. 25. Motilal Banarasidass, Delhi & Varanasi, 1984, pp. 253-262 and p. 382.

SECTION: Everybody Loves a Good Drought
(Water problems, real & rigged)

(Maharashtra expenditure of Rs.1,170 crores): Computed from official data, including budget figures and emergency expenditures of Revenue, Forest, Finance departments. Irrigated area figures from government pre-budget survey.

(Rs.4,557 crore for Orissa drought): From Prime Minister's speech launching the project in Koraput, August 1995. Figure quoted again in the *Times of India*, March 16, 1996, p. 8.

Figures on DPAP blocks are official and from the concerned departments dealing with them in the respective states for which numbers are given.

Rainfall figures are from collectorates and district statistical offices. Long-term rainfall data from district gazetteers.

(Kalahandi 20 year rainfall analysis): Jagdish Pradhan, *Drought in Kalahandi, The Real Story*, Economic & Political Weekly, Bombay, May 29, 1993, pp. 1084-88.

For a discussion of rainfall, sugarcane and crop problems in Maharashtra, see: D.N. Dhanagre, *1992 Drought in Maharashtra, Misplaced Priorities, Mismanagement of Water Resources*, Economic & Political Weekly, Bombay, July 4, 1992, pp. 1421-1425. Also H.M. Deserda, *Is only Nature to Blame for this Drought?* the *Independent*, Bombay, May 9, 1992, p. 4.

SECTION: Poverty, Development & the Press

(Land distribution figures . . . 2.6 million acres still to be distributed): Eighth Five-Year Plan document.

(New priorities for food department . . . 'participation in international conferences'): *Official notification*, Doc. No. CD.-163/95, Rashtrapati Bhavan, New Delhi, March 8, 1995, p. 6.

(Expert Group figure of 39 per cent below poverty line): *Report of The Expert Group on Estimation of Proportion and Number of Poor*, Perspective Planning Division, Planning Commission, Government of India, New Delhi, June 1993.

(Drop in per capita availability of grain): *Economic Survey*, Govt. of India, New Delhi, 1995. And analysis of Eighth Plan Mid-term Appraisal (MTA). Figure up to 1994 also quoted in *Indian Express*, Bombay, Aug. 21, 1995.

(Irrelevance of PDS & RPDS – quote): K.R. Venugopal, *Poor Strategies: Rising foodstocks, but no nutrition security*, Frontline, Madras, July 28, 1995, p. 98.

(World Bank on NGO involvement in Bank projects): *World Bank News*, Vol. XIII, No. 35, Paris, Sept. 22, 1994, p. 5.

(Nepal NGO-citizens ratio and funding figures): Chandrani Ghosh, *Slipping into an aid trap*, Business Standard, Calcutta, March 22, 1995, p. 12.

(Tribal organisations declare war on NGOs): Two groups, Kandhmal Vikash Parishad and Anchalika Vikash Samity, issued a declaration to the effect, jointly in late 1994 and again in early 1995. The latter version was titled: *Promotion of sexual exploitation, anti-social action and corruption in the name of a common action programme in Kandhmal.*

(Quote from Reuters correspondent's book): S.H.S. Merewether, *A Tour Through the Famine Districts of India*, A.D. Innes & Co., Bedford St. London, 1898, p. 11.

District-wise index of stories

Note: Quite a few stories did not confine themselves to the administrative boundaries that make districts. Some spilt over into villages of adjacent regions. This was particularly true where the district concerned had only recently emerged from the carving up of another. (For instance, Nuapada from Kalahandi). Also, in some cases, tracking migrants meant that the occasional report had to be filed from a district in another state (as in the case of Odiya migrants working in Andhra Pradesh). Thus, in the index, stories from Nuapada, Kalahandi of Orissa and Vizianagaram of Andhra Pradesh figure in the same list.

Ramnad, Kamrajar (Tamil Nadu)

Surguja (Madhya Pradesh)